A Hidden Agendas

A Hidden Agendas

Lora Leigh

St. Martin's Paperbacks

This is a work of fiction. All of the characters, organizations, and events portrayed in this novel are either products of the author's imagination or are used fictitiously.

HIDDEN AGENDAS

Copyright © 2007 by Lora Leigh.
Excerpt from *Killer Secrets* copyright © 2007 by Lora Leigh.

Cover photo © Shirley Green

ISBN: 0-312-93993-0
EAN: 978-0-312-93993-9

Printed in the United States of America

St. Martin's Paperbacks edition / July 2007

St. Martin's Paperbacks are published by St. Martin's Press, 175 Fifth Avenue, New York, NY 10010.

10 9 8 7 6 5 4 3 2 1

For all our men and women in the Armed Forces.
We can only imagine the danger and the darkness you live
with, but we know the freedoms you protect for us.
And we thank you.
We think of you.

Hidden Agendas

Prologue

DIEGO FUENTES STARED INTO THE vast panorama of cliffs and ocean outside his borrowed home, and reflected on destiny. The destiny of a man and what he builds through his life, and how his legacy would be carried on. The destiny of a man born to power, but whose greatness is often diminished by those he loves.

The destiny of a man determined to protect and nurture the last resource that would guide his empire into the future.

At his side lay the report smuggled from the United States offices of Homeland Security. The detailed pages of reports on the men he sought. Their strengths and weaknesses, code names and locations. Their operational status and the fact that each man was part of the highly organized strike that had killed his youngest son and whore of a wife eighteen months previously.

The information on his oldest son was there as well. A strong, proud man, and one who had been involved in that same operation.

There were threads and ties, loyalties and friendships, among the five men. Five now. There had once been six. And each of them was another link in the chain that led to his son.

He couldn't kill them, not and achieve his aims. As much as he wanted to kill all but one of them, his hands were bound.

This game must be very carefully played; the sacrifice of his nephew and uncle in the operation against the DEA several months before had been regrettable, but they had known the risks and they had failed. Failure was not acceptable. Now, he must decide which pawn to move in the delicate battle waging between himself and the son he had slowly been courting for many months now.

His fingers tapped against the arm of the leather chair as he stared into the distant skyline with narrowed eyes.

Along with the reports had come the information on the U.S. senators heading a committee to oversee the enforcement of America's drug laws and to advise on certain operations being carried out.

One such operation was Deep Sweep, a multiagency task force set up to draw out the spy Diego had planted within their midst.

A smile tipped his lips. He was no fool, despite the appearance of it that he had given lately. He saw the pawns, accepted the sacrifices, and allowed the illusion of his own humility for one end. To test the boy who would eventually inherit all Diego had built.

Now, another move must be made.

He turned, spreading his arms on the desk to encompass the files and reports laid out before him. Across the desk, his father's old advisor, Saul, waited patiently, his lined expression filled with sadness at the news that had come in that Santiago and Manuelo had been arrested and were now being held in an American prison to await trial.

"You have provided for my nephew and uncles comfort?" He asked Saul then.

Saul nodded patiently. "The money was passed to the proper hands as of this morning. All their needs will be taken care of."

Diego nodded as he leaned back in his chair and regarded Saul quizzically. "And our spy, Mr. White? What have you learned?"

Saul sighed heavily. "As I have warned you, my friend,

this man, he is greedy and growing powerful, as is evidenced by his new association with the European terrorist Sorrell, who wishes to make use of your cartel. Together, they will move against you when they believe the time is right. They have evidently not decided that time has yet come."

Diego nodded. This he knew as well. He had seen it coming in the past years, and in the carefully worded information he had been given by his spy. Power meant everything to some men. To this man especially. And he believed his association with the terrorist cell of Sorrell would bring him that great power.

Diego would show him the error of his ways. Eventually.

"Are his reports accurate?" Diego asked.

"They are accurate, but he neglects to mention important key factors regarding each one. He is holding information back, saving it for his own ends, or for a time when it can bring him rewards."

"Such as information on this man?" Diego picked up a file and tossed it to Saul.

The picture on the front of the manila folder was harsh. Either from the low light or from something within the man himself. Savage features, piercing emerald eyes, and a brooding, dangerous expression. This was a man others were always wary of.

"Kell Krieger. He is the grandson of a very prominent Louisiana family. What your friend neglected to mention is that Mr. Krieger has crossed our path once before in New Orleans, nearly fifteen years ago. We made an example of his wife in retaliation for his work with a New Orleans detective there. He killed two of our best men, bare-handed."

"Interesting that our friend did not mention this," Diego mused.

Diego did indeed remember the incident, though he hadn't remembered the name. Disowned for marrying his pregnant girlfriend, a woman born on the streets with nothing to her name but the clothes on her back. Krieger had fallen in love with her at the tender age of seventeen. He had married before he turned eighteen. Six months later, he had left New Orleans and joined the Navy, a widower.

To support his young wife Kell had worked at a local diner in New Orleans, an establishment that two high-ranking suppliers within Diego's cartel had frequented. Krieger had been spying on the cartel members for a local police investigator. It had resulted in their arrest during a particularly important drug deal.

They had warned the young man, Diego thought with regret. They had warned him not to testify against the suppliers, but he had not heeded that warning. His wife and child had paid the price. Though Diego had been unaware at the time of the wife's pregnancy. Perhaps he would have stayed his hand had he known. Allowed the wife to live rather than giving the order for her death. But that was so long ago, and during a time when Diego believed that power only came with blood.

Ah, the mistakes he had made as a youth. The blood he had shed that in time would have been better served had he allowed mercy. Such mistakes made a man, but even more, they reminded a man, as age began to creep up on him, of his own mortality.

"What of this one?" Seeing threads and connections, Diego tossed another file toward Saul.

"Senator Richard Stanton and his daughter, Emily. The senator is former Navy, a SEAL. Fairly public knowledge. What your spy did not tell you is that he was instrumental in the planning and attack on your South American estate that resulted in your wife's and your son Roberto's deaths. Of course, we did abduct his daughter along with the other girls that were brought there. His daughter, Emily, is a teacher at an Atlanta school. Another piece of information not imparted is that she enjoys a rather eccentric hobby. She writes books of romance, though she has not yet published any of her writings. Her research efforts I have included in my attached report."

The girl did enjoy some unique ways of research, Diego

thought with a hidden smile. She was as wild as the winds and yet as innocent as newly fallen snow. The innocence he hadn't expected, but her doctor's records confirmed it.

"You are, as always, thorough." Diego tapped his fingers against the desk. "I believe it is time to show our friendly spy that his efforts to defeat me will not succeed. I have a particular little game in mind for this one."

"In what way?" Saul asked, leaning forward now with interest.

"He has requested that we take care of a certain problem for him," Diego mused. "This Senator Stanton worries him, and he wishes him taken care of as well as his daughter. It seems he fears the girl will remember something of her stay here, especially those events which pertain to the other two girls who were kidnapped with her. Tell him we will do this. Then, send a message to Judas and inform him that this action will take place and that the SEAL team Durango is the only force that I now fear. After all, two of its members have already defeated me. Perhaps I worry, late into the night, that these men are too powerful for me to defeat." His lips twisted at the thought.

"Judas will question the information," Saul warned him. "He is not so easy to fool, Diego."

Diego shook his head. "When you impart this information, tell him also that we have uncovered a rumor that the missing SEAL he seeks is being held by the same man that the senator seeks and there is the chance we can negotiate his release. Tell him, then, that all things come with a price, and he must decide if this is a price he can pay."

"Do you want the boy when you must blackmail him into your arms, Diego?" Saul asked gently.

Diego's fist slammed onto the wooden desk. "I will take my son however I can get him!" he snarled. Then, with a force of will he regained control, his jaw tightening with the effort it cost him. "I will not have to blackmail him. He is a man of his word and he is loyal. I have pulled back each time I have encountered his men. I give him things he needs to save those he loves. I have shown him my loyalty, now he must show me his. Tell him this. This woman is in danger." He pointed to the file. "She is in danger because of her father's investigations into the identity of the government spy. A spy who also knows the location of his missing SEAL brother. This team will be assigned to her protection. I know this. And I will then have the final key to the chains that will tie my son to me. The man we hold is no longer of use to us without the drug we were using on him to perfect. With the scientist's death, financial gain will no longer be an option. But his safety will be of importance to the boy."

Saul stared at him for long moments before realization began to dawn. "He will have to compromise himself in the eyes of his people to save his friend. He will no longer have their trust."

Diego nodded slowly. "That one called Macey, he works diligently to uncover Judas's identity. Discovering this informant is very important to him. We will give Macey the final key to uncovering Judas if he does not come to us willingly before then."

Saul inclined his head in approval. Disconcertingly, Diego felt a rush of pride at the old man's response. This was as close to his father as he could ever come, and the approval was nearly a benediction to him.

"I will begin this plan." Saul rose to his feet slowly, his age hampering movements that had once been smooth and powerful. "You will have your son soon, my friend."

Diego nodded in agreement, but in his heart he feared nothing with his boy would ever be easy. His son had been raised with hatred for the father he had never known. His son had feared him as a child, and the mother who bore him had been terrified for his life because of Carmelita's vindictiveness.

A child he hadn't known of until the bitch's death. The teams of assassins sent out to track him down and kill him, the constant threat of death or kidnapping, had resulted in a child who had known only a blood lust for vengeance.

Defeating the blood lust had been the hardest battle. It had taken nearly two years of careful maneuvering before his son had accepted the truth. And now, now, Diego was so close to drawing him in, to gaining the loyalty of a man known among his peers as one who could always be trusted. He was a man of his word, and of his weapon. He was the man to lead the Fuentes cartel into the future.

But first, one more small game. It would take one more finely tuned move to draw him in. This woman, Emily Stanton, would have the option of only two protectors. Diego knew which one it would be, for Judas would never give his heart to such a tender thing until Diego's death or imprisonment.

That left Krieger. He had learned much about this SEAL team over the past eighteen months. Two were married, and fiercely devoted to their wives. They were also the senior officers of the team. The protection of the girl would go to one of lesser rank while the superiors guarded the senator and this Macey worked the computers for information.

They each had their roles, separate but working together in every operation they undertook. Disciplined and in control, they were powerful warriors. And when his son accepted his rightful place, then he would bring this discipline and control to the men beneath him.

Diego smiled. A cartel of men trained with the same degree of precision as a Navy SEAL by a man dedicated to the cartel's future, and the Fuentes power would only increase tenfold.

And this was his dream. To one day lie safely in his bed, taken from this earth because age could not be denied, and knowing that his legacy, the legacy of his father and grandfather, would thrive through Fuentes blood. A dream he could now see coming to fruition.

One

IN THE MIDDLE AGES EMILY Stanton would have been tied to a stake and set aflame for witchcraft. Or bound in chains and stuck in a dark little hole where she couldn't drive sane men crazy, Kell Krieger thought with a grin as he kept a careful distance between himself and Emily's Trailblazer as they traversed Atlanta's increasingly heavy traffic flow.

Were it the Middle Ages, he would have rescued her from a dark hole or the stake, outfitted her in leather, given her a sword and followed her into battle. Because sure as hell, any man who saw her coming at him would have been struck dumb long enough for a strong warrior to lop his head from his shoulders.

But it wasn't the Middle Ages, and Atlanta's traffic wasn't really a war zone, it just resembled one sometimes. Like now, just before rush hour, when those fighting to escape the maddening traffic jams were driving like kamikaze students with no fear of death.

Emily certainly had no fear. But then again, he couldn't remember a time when she had known fear. Even when she should have, the time she was bound and shoved into a dirty shack on the Fuentes compound and glared at her captors with hatred.

What she had on the freeway was experience. Someone

had taught her aggressive driving techniques that would have done a SEAL proud. Hell, she had lost the tail he was certain she hadn't known she had, miles back.

Research. He was betting she had taken some kind of lessons on the pretext of research for the books that were never published and stories that were still only half finished.

And he had to grin at the thought of that. She was driving her father crazy with the so-called research, and over the years she had given Kell no end of amusement as he listened to the senator rant and rave about her exploits on the rare occasions Kell had managed to meet with him over the years.

But now, the danger she was in had him and the senator sweating, especially after her kidnapping by Fuentes nearly two years ago.

She wasn't safe. And the way she wrapped her bodyguards around her slender fingers, they would be of no help to her when Fuentes decided to take her again, as the information suggested he would. She wasn't safe, but she thought she could protect herself. She was just smart enough to be dangerous to herself, and too gentle to ever be a danger to the evil stalking her.

They thought she was safe. God help him, he had believed Fuentes would adhere to the rules of the game and leave her be after her rescue from the first kidnapping. And perhaps he would have, if the spy codenamed Mr. White hadn't grown increasingly worried about her father's efforts to track him down.

Now, here was Emily, fighting to find a life despite her father's overprotection and the shadow of danger. For seven years she had lived with one bodyguard after another, had endured her father's overprotective love, and had tried to balance her needs against his fears.

From the look of things, she had grown tired of the battle, though.

Today, she wore the disguise she had been using for the past week before heading from her condo on the outskirts of Atlanta to the strip joint on the other side of the large town.

The long brown wig and makeup adjustment would only fool someone who didn't really know her. Kell would have recognized her in a second, no matter what her disguise.

His conversation that morning with her father when he gave his oral report had been telling, though. The bodyguard Dyson was ready to break, if the report he sent in the night before was any indication.

Chet Dyson had warned the senator that the situation wasn't working out and his daughter was becoming too confrontational for him to effectively protect her, especially considering that the senator refused to allow Dyson to tell her of the renewed threat. Dyson was getting nervous. It was time to pull him out.

Damn, she was good in this traffic. She flipped in front of an eighteen-wheeler with plenty of room to spare but with a move that nearly caught him off guard and kept him from advancing with her.

Horns blared and he was sure there were men cursing her from one lane to the next. Men got nervous when a woman drove like that. It made them unpredictable. Few men could handle a woman that aggressive and unpredictable.

Kell loved it. The challenge fired his blood and had a smile of anticipation curving his lips. Never had he met a woman whom he found exciting outside the bed. But this one, she would keep a man on his toes well beyond the age where it should be possible. And he had known that since the night she celebrated her eighteenth birthday and turned his little world upside down with a smile.

She was a woman who enjoyed life. It sparkled in her eyes and showed in her smile. She was a woman guaran-damn-teed to drive him insane and he wasn't even officially her bodyguard yet. He was just the dumb shit ordered to follow her and her present bodyguard around until gears were put into motion and Durango Team could be rounded up from their various locations. God help him when he had to stay in her home under the cover his commander had informed him he would be using.

Because he had lusted after Miss Emily Stanton for seven years. The only thing that had saved her was the fact that he was rarely around her. Living in her home, sleeping under the same roof with her, pretending to be her lover was going to break him and he knew it. Soon, he would have her in his bed; the only battle would be keeping her out of his heart.

As he fought to keep up with her in the traffic, Kell found himself cursing along with all the other men in vehicles around them. If he hadn't been trying to follow her, he would have acknowledged her cunning and daring. But he was trying to follow her, and she was making it damned hard to do so.

It happened every time he trailed her anywhere. He cussed her for hours. Swore he was going to tie her up and stuff her in a closet. That he would find a nice little uninhabited island to stick her on where she couldn't endanger herself or others.

It made a man glad he had a will, even if he didn't have an heir.

Who knew an SUV could move like that? He was on his Harley and he couldn't gain the momentum she had on an interstate packed with four lanes of prerush-hour traffic.

He was reciting every curse he had learned, in Arabic, in a Middle Eastern prison three years ago. Then he tried the Russian versions that he had learned in a cold little jail in some back mountain province he didn't want to even think about.

But he made it, with only inches to spare between the back tire of his precious Harley and a four-by-four pickup as wide as a barn.

But he was back in place on her ass, and snarling as she zipped and whipped through the inner-city traffic.

Because it was obvious her bodyguard couldn't do a damned thing with her. He wasn't even smart enough to call in backup to contain her. As though backup could do anything with a slippery little fox, he thought with a spurt of amusement.

Keeping a careful distance between his Harley and her SUV, he flattened his lips once again and promised himself that the minute he took over her security he was locking her in a room with no escape routes and throwing away the damned key.

Then his lips quirked in amusement. Hell no, he wouldn't lock her up. The first thing he was going to do was see how damned fast he could get all that restless fire and passion between the sheets.

He had waited long enough for her. She was older now, mature. She could go to bed with him and not be destroyed when it was time for him to walk away.

As she pulled into the back lot of a strip club, he amended the previous idea. He wasn't locking her in a room. A room was too good for the hell she was getting ready to put him through when he pulled her out of Timbo's. He was locking her in chains and finding a hole deep enough to contain the little witch. Because sure as hell, if he dragged her out of this place, he was going to end up pissed off, bruised, bloody, and maybe with a few bones broken. And for that, he was going to demand a bit of satisfaction.

No, not just a bit. A lot. And likely more than either of them needed. Definitely more than he should be thinking. Because he kept imagining her, not in a hole, but in a bed, her arms stretched over her head, her legs spread, open and inviting. And that lush little body panting for him.

Damn, a hard-on sure as hell wasn't what he needed right now.

He pulled the Harley into an alley alongside the back parking lot, concealing it behind the trees that struggled to live amid the rot and decay that surrounded them, and watched as Emily and her bodyguard moved from the vehicle.

He was going to end up in a fight before this was over with.

Not that Kell cared to fight. Hell, he loved to fight. But he didn't think the senator would appreciate the fact that his little girl had been to a strip club, not with the danger facing her now. And the senator wasn't going to be happy either.

Kell wondered about Emily's present bodyguard and his obvious lack of sanity.

Chet Dyson was a former marine, tough, supposedly fearless, but that was fear Kell saw on his face. Desperation. He was looking around for an escape route, not an attacker, even as he argued with his charge.

Kell shook his head. He had heard the other man arguing with her as they left, demanding her keys, threatening to call her father, cursing. But the dumb ass had parked it right in the passenger seat anyway and let Emily have her head.

They disappeared in the back door of the strip club and Kell sighed wearily. He was going to have to go in there and find out what the hell she was up to. That was something he had hoped to put off, because knowing the research habits he had uncovered so far, he had a feeling it could be control destroying. It was his luck she was researching the criminal underbelly of Atlanta, a move guaranteed to get her pretty little head shot off her shoulders.

Shaking his head, he started the Harley and pulled around to the front lot where he parked it beneath the eagle eye of Timbo's doorman. Kell snorted at the title. Tiny was no one's idea of a doorman. He was seven feet of hulking muscle and an expression that made a grizzly look nice. Narrow black eyes watched him silently as he swung off the Harley and powerful black arms crossed over his wide chest.

"What kind of trouble are you stirring up here, Krieger?" Tiny asked suspiciously as he neared the door.

"Nothing too messy, Tiny." Kell grinned. "Let me in for a drink. My pigeon just walked in the back door and I need to keep an eye on her."

Amusement flickered in Tiny's eyes. "That little thing Cherry's giving dancing lessons to?" If Kell wasn't mistaken an edge of affection crept into the big man's voice. That was scary. Predictable, but scary nonetheless. She had a way of drawing people to her, of making them care whether they wanted to or not.

He sure as hell hadn't wanted to. But from the moment he

had met her fifteen years before, only weeks after the death of his young wife and their unborn child, he had found himself looking into her too perceptive gaze and knowing that if he wasn't careful, she would make him care.

"Yeah," Kell drawled, narrowing his eyes. "Why?"

"She's doing a lap dance this afternoon. For me."

Every bone and muscle in Kell's body tightened as rage flickered across his senses.

"She's doing what?"

Tiny grinned down at him. "She's been taking lessons from Cherry this week. Today's test day. She's doing her moves and Timbo said she could do them for me."

Like hell. As Kell stared back he moved his hand to his wallet, pulled it free, and knew he was in deep shit when Tiny glanced at it with satisfaction.

"Now how did I know you wouldn't like that?" The other man's voice filled with smug satisfaction. "Boy, you got the look of a man getting ready to drown. Maybe I should save you from yourself."

"How much?"

"I like you, Krieger." He shook his head. "But she's damned pretty."

Kell pulled a hundred free.

"And I know what Cherry's been teaching her." Tiny's grin got wider.

Kell pulled free the second hundred.

"And she's just the prettiest little piece of candy."

Kell pulled the knife from his boot in a move so fast Tiny barely had time to blink before the edge was pressing against his throat.

He swallowed tightly. "But she ain't that sweet." He reached out and took the two hundreds from Kell's other hand with a tentative movement. "Better you than me. That woman's trouble."

Kell's lips thinned as he lowered the knife and slid it back into the sheath at the side of his boot.

"Don't let anyone else in," he ordered.

"I wasn't supposed to let you in," Tiny grunted.

Kell sliced a hard, killing look back at him.

"But, hey man, I know you and that knife." He grinned. "I'll keep the place clear. Those were the orders anyway. Better hurry, though, show starts soon. It's guaranteed to be a killer."

No shit. Kell was beginning to guess that if Emily Stanton was involved, then no matter what it was, it had the potential to kill.

Her father, a former SEAL, had made a grave tactical error in giving her a taste of excitement as a child before jerking it away from her and trying to marry her off to men determined to control her.

Kell had watched from afar for years, never interfering, despite his disagreement with the senator. He had watched the steady stream of men sent in to guard that delectable body with aspirations of marriage. Those aspirations never lasted long. A few weeks to a few months. They slinked out of her life with their tails between their legs.

Until two years ago. When she had put her foot down for the first time and refused another male presence in her home. Three months later, Fuentes had taken her. And she had only become more determined since then to learn how to protect herself.

This wasn't a woman who accepted limits, unless they were her own. She made her own rules. And Kell understood that. He respected that. Even if he was determined that before it was over, she would shape those rules to suit not just her needs, but his as well.

He had found a vixen. Taming her wasn't on the agenda, but touching her, tasting her was, and that would take careful planning. Because vixens didn't give in easily.

There would be nothing easy about Emily. But that was okay, because there was nothing easy about him either.

Two

EMILY MADE CERTAIN THE LONG, dark brown wig was firmly in place, the strands of hair hiding the fact that it was indeed a wig. Her makeup exaggerated the arch of her brows and the tilt of her eyes, and the slouchy clothes were nothing like the cool, comfortably loose clothes she normally wore.

Not that she thought Cherry the stripper was fooled. She knew Emily was in disguise. But she didn't know who Emily was and that was all that mattered. When a senator's daughter went for extreme research, she did have to at least attempt a measure of decorum. Especially when said senator's daughter had managed to totally screw up once before and get herself kidnapped.

Her father still hadn't let her live that one down, and he wasn't likely to forget it for a while. She wasn't likely to forget it either, her nightmares assured her of that. That didn't mean she intended to bury her head in her father's cocoon-wrapped hideout and forget about living.

If she did that, then Fuentes and the monster that haunted her nightmares would have won. She wasn't about to allow that to happen.

"So, which outfit?" The stripper Emily had hired to teach

her the dance moves indicated a row of gaudy, sparkling material to choose from.

Emily glanced at the row of clothes on the racks as the dancer waved toward them negligently. Cherry Layne was tall, at least five eight without her high heels, and skinny to boot. Damn, Emily hated skinny women.

Long red-gold curls cascaded to Cherry's slim shoulders and framed a kittenish face that held a smile more often than not.

"How about the schoolgirl outfit?" Cherry indicated the little plaid skirt and white top she had hung on the rack. "Men just go wild for this one."

"Eww, Cherry. That's just wrong." She couldn't go there. She was a teacher, for pity's sake. At least, she would be a teacher again after summer break. That was close enough.

Cherry's grin was wicked. "Sweet girl, you don't know the fantasies you're missing out on."

Emily shuddered and shook her head with a grimace. "Not me. No, thank you."

The stripper only laughed and fingered through the outfits again.

"Cheerleader?"

"Ugh." Emily grimaced. "Keep going."

"There's not a lot here that will fit you." Cherry frowned as Emily cast her a mocking glare.

"You don't have to rub it in." She sighed.

"Sweetie, you got curves," Cherry said. "I'd love curves, but some of these outfits just trash a solid body."

She held up a pair of thongs and wispy bra as an example. "Not exactly curvy material." She laughed.

"Not exactly my material either." Emily shook her head. "Let's keep it simple."

Very simple. She didn't want to flash every inch of skin, just see how sexy it felt to do the dance. Kira swore it would awaken hormones she didn't know she had. Cherry promised it would make her feel hot and desirable.

"Hmm. How about this one? It would go perfect with your figure as well as your personality. Nice and sweet on the outside and all slut on the inside."

"Slut?" Emily lifted her brows, not knowing if she should be offended or amused.

She had never been considered slut material in her entire life. Prude. Ice queen. Frigid. But never slut. Maybe she should just take it as a compliment, she thought, amused.

"On the inside, sweetie." Cherry's eyes sparkled with mirth. "Men love the public good girl and the private whore. Haven't you figured that out?"

No. She hadn't. But she admitted, her education was lacking.

"Interesting," she murmured, wondering if she had managed to hide the fact that she didn't have a clue what the stripper was talking about.

"Now, some of the highbrow types like to pretend they don't want it." Cherry shrugged. "Men like that come here. They have their little madonnas they married, and they have their hot little tarts on the side. But some men, men who know how to treat a woman, now, they understand it."

And she was supposed to find one of those where?

"Here, try it on." Cherry handed her the outfit.

It wasn't exactly a costume; rather it looked more like a simple business skirt and white cotton blouse. But it would work.

"Did you get the sexy undies I told you to pick up?" Cherry asked as she laid the skirt and blouse on the chair beside Emily.

"Wearing them now." Emily grinned at the thought of the sexy, lacy underwear she was wearing. "Are you sure this is going to work?"

"Perfectly." Cherry waved a manicured hand negligently at Emily's question. The owner was supposed to arrange for one of the bouncers to be available for her lap dance. "Timbo doesn't cheat his customers. He'll have someone out there and you'll knock them dead."

What was the point in going to the trouble to learn the exotic dance steps and, specifically, the lap dance if she couldn't try it out on someone? The research she needed was specific. And if she didn't find a way to convince her agent that her characters could and would get nasty, then her writing career was over before it ever even truly began.

"Get hot!" Cicily had told her. *"Get nasty. Show the editors that your women know how to be women and your men know how to love them, or you're not going to sell."*

She rolled her eyes at the thought of it as she dressed in the short skirt and blouse. Get hot. Get nasty. She needed to get sex before she dried up and turned into an old prune.

Her bad-boy heroes weren't bad enough and the women they loved were cardboard characters. Perhaps she was the problem. The cardboard writer. How did one write hot when one never had a man desirable enough to get hot over?

Biting her lip, she stared back at the woman in the makeup mirror. Herself. She could do this. Her friend Kira said dancing for a man would make her feel hot. That tempting him, seducing him, was a major turn-on. Unfortunately, so far, it had just been work.

"Ready?" Cherry tilted her head to the side, her long red hair falling over her shoulder, as she gave Emily an encouraging look.

As ready as she would ever be after nearly a week of instruction by the drill sergeant Cherry had turned out to be.

"Ready." Yes. She could do this.

Emily slid her feet into the ridiculously high black heels Cherry had placed on the floor in front of her then pressed her hand to her stomach before following the other woman from the dressing room.

"I'll be watching you," Cherry assured her. "And remember, the guy Timbo got to practice the lap dance is not allowed to touch you. I'll be watching and so will David. If he tries, he's hamburger meat. Okay?"

David was the ridiculously large bouncer who adored

Cherry. They were the oddest couple, but Emily had to admit, they seemed to match.

She paused at the side of the dance stage as Cherry moved across it, her long legs eating the short distance until she stepped into the sound cubicle. Seconds later, the music began.

Emily sauntered onto the stage, moving in time to the music, hips swaying, counting beats to movements, wondering where the pumping adrenaline was that Cherry talked about. The need to feel sexy. The need to . . .

Oh. My. God.

She stopped in the center of the stage.

There came the blood. It rushed to her head, raced through her system, and sent her senses into overload. She had seen the men that came to the establishment over the past two months, several of them, and none of them looked like this.

This was male chocolate. A smorgasbord of it. It was bad boy extreme and wicked temptation. Leaning back in a chair, muscular arms crossed over a broad chest, a dark gray T-shirt tucked into jeans that were covered with snug leather chaps. Dark glasses covered his eyes, and his expression was frankly sensual.

Black hair fell just a little long over his collar, shaggy and windblown, and framed a face that had her mouth at first drying, then watering with the need to taste those starkly male lips. To taste, to touch. He was tall, hard, muscular, and bad.

If the dictionary had a description of a bad boy, it would be this man. This was lust incarnate. It was pure erotic heat and sexual hunger.

He was a panty creamer.

She had met a few of those over the years. As far as looks went, they could do exactly what he was doing to her now. Making her cream. But she had never gotten close to one. Well, except one. But just within a few feet. She had definitely never gotten as close as a lap dance was going to require.

She trembled as she stared at him, her lips parting as she fought to draw in air, her limbs shaking with sudden nerves. She was insane to do this now, today. When she was weak. When she was restless. When her awareness of losing time, losing the opportunity to have the ultimate adventure, was so clear in her mind. When her own independence felt at risk. At a time when her hormones were spiking.

They did that sometimes. They were doing that now.

They were reminding her that intimacy be damned, she needed to be touched. She needed to be held. She needed more than a one-night stand, though.

Then those beautiful eatable lips kicked up in a mocking grin. A cynical dare that had her eyes narrowing and her senses balancing. She heard the music then, the sexual beat, the erotic undertones, and the sensual, sexual core of her soul awoke to it.

She imagined the only bad boy she had fantasized about for years as she let the bad boy watching her spark the memory of the first.

Kell. Tall. Broad. Bad. She remembered him. Eyes as green as emeralds. His unsmiling countenance, his air of wicked knowledge. The way he made her wet with just a look.

Just like the bad boy across the room was making her wet. Making her feel. Assuring her she was alive.

Emily began to move. Gripping the dancing pole, she stared back at the arrogance in this man's expression, the mocking curve of lips that she remembered, though she knew they weren't the same. The full contours she wanted to nibble, and she set out to seduce—a memory—

THAT WAS NOT A KINDERGARTEN schoolteacher. This wasn't the eighteen-year-old he had danced with or the young woman he had stayed carefully out of sight from over the years. But it was definitely Emily Stanton.

When she walked out on the stage, the breath had punched

from his chest with a force that left him dazed. She was
dressed like a teacher. The slim black skirt and white blouse
buttoned modestly. Heels made her taller, but made her legs
sexier. Legs that could wrap around a man and hold him in
place as she arched to him. Legs that had his back aching to
feel them tightening there.

As she stood there, poised like a frightened doe, his lips
kicked up in a mocking grin. The innocence was a damned
good effect. Almost good enough to believe.

The narrowing of her eyes surprised him, but her movements shocked him. With seductive skill, her arm lifted, her
hand gripping the metal pole beside her, and her body began
to sway to the music.

Beneath his jeans, his cock was throbbing with joy as she
began to move against the phallic symbol she gripped. Leaning her back against it, her features flushed, her eyes gleaming with sensual awareness, one hand lifted to the first
button of her blouse.

His mouth went dry at the hint of cleavage. Breasts a man
could get lost in. Fill his hands with. His hands itched with
the need to be filled.

The hard techno beat of the music throbbed with sex. It
pulsed and pounded around them, swayed with her body and
stroked over his nerve endings. For God's sake, he was almost panting.

She was supposed to be a prim and proper little social
miss. The daughter of a United States senator. A kindergarten teacher.

She was a provocative little hellion who knew how to get
nasty. She was making him crazy.

He shifted in his seat, trying to make room for the hard
ridge of his cock as it swelled to fill the confines of his jeans
and demanded more room. If it could howl, it would have
brought the building down with the sound of its hunger.

His teeth clenched as he forced himself to sit still, to appear relaxed. He was anything but relaxed.

The second button came free and his mouth watered. Her

fingers played with the third, and just when he thought he would see the tantalizing flesh beneath she turned her back to him, leaned against the pole and undulated. From her ankles to her shoulders she moved against the pole and his abdomen tightened.

Shit. He was going to come in his jeans.

She turned, and the button was free. Beneath, he glimpsed the sinfully red lace of a bra.

Take it off, sweet darlin'. Come on, give us just a taste.

She played with the next button, released it as she braced her legs apart, and let her hand slide past the edges of the shirt as she gripped the bar behind her and arched her back for him.

Oh mercy, just a bit more, eh?

The last button slipped free, but the little tease turned again, shimmied around the pole, and sweat popped out on his forehead as her fingers went to the button at the side of the skirt.

He forced himself to leave the dark glasses on. Not to lean forward. Not to open his pants and show her just how appreciative he was as she began to unwrap every birthday and Christmas present he could have ever lusted for.

This was his greatest fantasy. Innocent, proper, eyes gleaming back at him with certain hunger, face flushed with damp desire, and he'd bet her pussy was wet. He'd bet his last dollar on it. Her nipples were sure as hell hard.

"Have mercy . . ." he breathed as the skirt fell slowly down her curvy thighs, leaving her dressed in French-cut lace and a bra that was more thought than actual covering.

And her nipples were hard. Spike hard. They made his tongue ache to lick them; his mouth watered at the thought of sucking them.

She leaned into the pole again, her arms reaching, her legs braced apart, her rear rubbing against metal while something just as hard pounded in his jeans. Oh yeah, she could rub against him anytime.

Then she was moving again, a sensuous slide of flesh, a

roll of her hips, her hands moving over her head as she swayed and came slowly down the steps that led to the raised stage.

Toward him.

Drawing closer.

The opened blouse slid over her shoulders, caressing flesh he longed to touch, touching her, easing over her arms until it dropped, forgotten behind her.

His arms tightened over his chest as he fought the urge to jump up, throw her over his shoulder, and rush her the hell out of there.

"Touch her, dude, and I'll make you hurt."

Behind his shoulder the monster bouncer David murmured threateningly. Kell's lips parted in amusement though his eyes never strayed from the bounty coming toward him.

Lap dance.

Timbo had been firm when he realized Kell was taking Tiny's place. He had to play the part or he was out of there. The girl had paid to learn to dance, and evidently, she had paid quite a bit.

He was her audience. And being her audience was worth paying for. Men would line up in droves for this. They would pack the house, tear onto the stage and demand a touch. Just one soft touch against that damp silk she called skin.

As she came closer he saw the pure lust lighting her eyes and had to grit his teeth to sit still. Fuck, hard nipples, and sweet mercy, that little shadow at the junction of her thighs had to be dampness. Her sweet pussy was creaming and his mouth wasn't even there to taste it.

He licked his lips.

Her eyes flickered to his lips, held there, and the dance became a gliding temptation, a slow, aching swing of hips, of full breasts, of rosy flesh.

She turned her back on him, pulling a chair gracefully in front of her as she bent, filling his vision with the most delectable little ass he had ever laid his eyes on.

The red lace of her thong separated the cheeks of her ass,

curved and luscious, as her thighs clenched, her hips rotated, and her ass flexed before him.

He fisted his hands, more uncertain of his control than he had ever been. He watched her move as she turned, his gaze lifting to her face, seeing the sultry promise and erotic innocence that battled in her fierce blue eyes.

He sat back in his chair, forcing control over his muscles when he wanted nothing more than to touch, taste, devour.

Especially when she came closer, when those soft legs straddled his knees, and the soft, sweet scent of peaches and cream assaulted his senses. And beneath it . . . Ahhh God, he was man enough to know the scent beneath it. The heady heat of arousal, of a woman's need wetting the lace covering an obviously bare pussy. There wasn't a single soft curl to be glimpsed under those panties.

Her breasts were at his face, hard nipples pressing against fragile red lace. A rivulet of moisture eased over the lightly tanned mounds not covered by the lace, caught on the material, disappeared.

Her thighs scraped against his jeans, then she lifted, came to her full height, which wasn't that tall to begin with, and the scent of arousal nearly had him coming in his jeans.

He could smell her. He could almost taste her. He was dying for her.

As the music began to reach its crescendo she gripped the back of the chair she had placed at his side, a slender leg lifted high, a black heel moving to brace on the back of his chair, and the soft flesh of her pussy was so close he could have tasted it. Could have licked over fine soft lace and silk beneath. And he would have tasted her. Would have tasted the essence of her hunger on the damp material of her panties.

Instead, he breathed out roughly, his breath aimed at the tempting, almost hidden folds.

And only by sheer will did he hold back his release, because she lost hers. He watched her thighs tighten, heard her exclamation, and before his wondering eyes, the dampness on those panties darkened.

His eyes jerked to hers.

She came? Emily came?

Her leg jerked back as she stumbled, her face paling, eyes growing wide as her lips parted in shock.

She came?

Then she turned and, before he could move, she kicked off the high heels and ran.

"Shit." He came out of his chair, meaning to go after her. His cock ached like an open wound and only God knew what would happen if he got his hands on her.

Instead, hamlike paws settled on his shoulders, likely with no more intent than to push him back into his chair. Before he could think, Kell gripped a wrist, twisted and jerked the deadly blade he carried at the side of his boot.

"Back off, dude," Kell rasped, the knife's edge resting on the bulging vein at his neck. "Don't make me cut you."

"Chill." The bouncer's eyes widened. "I can't let you have her, man."

Kell's eyes narrowed.

"She's a friend of my Cherry's. I can't let you have her."

Steely determination filled the dark eyes staring back at him. The bear of a man would clearly die for the woman who had most likely already escaped through the back door.

"Who is she?" Did they know who she was?

"She didn't say, I didn't ask." The thick neck lifted as though to escape the feel of steel against his jugular. "She paid Timbo but my girl said to watch after her. I do what my girl says."

The sound of a gun's hammer clicking had him turning enough to see the slender form of the girl Timbo called Cherry, holding a wicked .45 from enough distance that she could fire before he could disable her.

"Back off, asshole," she snarled. "You hurt him and I empty this gun in your hide."

Fuck.

He lowered the knife, his gaze connecting with the giant's

and expecting no less than a fist for his efforts. Instead, a smile tugged at heavy lips.

"Timbo says you know Reno and Clint," he grunted. "I shouldn't have grabbed you. But the girl wanted to go."

Kell turned his head slowly back to the woman. The gun was steady; the hammer stayed pulled back, the snap in her eyes assuring him she wasn't as trusting.

"The girl is gone." He inclined his head slowly. "If you don't mind . . ." He waved his hand at the woman.

"Let him go, Cherry angel," David said and sighed. "Reno and Clint know him. And Timbo's right scared of him. I don't think he can catch her now anyway."

The gun lowered. Reluctantly.

"Do you know her?" he asked the girl then.

"She didn't offer a name, I didn't ask," the woman snapped.

"What was she doing here?"

She shrugged as though answering him didn't matter. "She called it research. She paid to learn to dance and I taught her. Money talks, and I don't question it."

Money didn't buy loyalty, and it was clear that the stripper felt loyal to the dynamite who had just escaped him.

"She was never here," he said softly. "You never saw her. You never taught her shit. And if Timbo even acts like he's thinking of remembering her presence, tell him I'll kill him."

Her eyes widened.

Sheathing the knife, he stalked to the exit and left the strip joint with a slam of his hand against the door. The sound of tires screaming from the back lot assured him Miss Emily Stanton and her inept, useless, dead-man-walking bodyguard were definitely escaping. But that was okay, because he knew exactly where to find her.

Three

OH. MY. GOD.

What had she done?

That had never happened. Ever. As slight as her climax had been, hell, she could do better on her own. Maybe. But despite the strength of the orgasm, she still had orgasmed from nothing but a breath of air.

"What the hell happened back there?" Her bodyguard, Dyson, was suspicious. Of course, why wouldn't he be? She had run out of the back of the club in nothing but a long coat and her undies and dived into the Trailblazer like the hounds of hell were after her ass.

They may as well have been. The minute Dyson had jumped into the passenger seat she had been out of there in a scream of tires and a jerk of the back end of the Trailblazer that would have done a high-speed car chase proud.

She'd lost her mind.

That was exactly what had happened. She'd lost her mind. For one impossibly long second, she had been certifiably insane.

"I knew better than this." Dyson was snarling again, his brown eyes furious. "Were you attacked?"

Only by her own lust.

Emily lifted a shaking hand to her flushed cheek as she

breathed in roughly and fought to keep her foot from lying too heavy on the gas. She wanted to be home. Now. But she didn't need a ticket. God, if she were pulled over she would likely be arrested.

"I wasn't attacked."

"Then why are you running like a scared chicken with nothing over your underwear but a frickin' long coat? I've been with you for four weeks and I've never seen you run."

He was too familiar. Two months in her house seemed to be the lucky time limit for her bodyguards. This one was getting more frustrated by the day.

"I'm not running."

Of course she was running. Like hell. Like an endangered dinosaur fighting for survival.

She could still feel her body flaming, the heat moving from her thighs, up her abdomen to her breasts and her face, even as she listened to Dyson bitching and moaning. She felt as though she were on fire, as though nerve endings she had never known she possessed were suddenly coming to full-fledged life.

She had orgasmed.

Shamefully. Without warning. Without control. She had orgasmed in a stranger's face.

And what a face it had been. The closer she had moved to him, the more starkly sensual it had become. That was a man who made a woman want to get down and dirty. Made her want to show the hidden slut hiding inside.

She almost cringed at the thought. Okay, so for the right man, maybe Cherry was right, she could get down and nasty.

For that man.

Oh man . . . He had been so righteously hot and hard. His abs had rippled beneath his snug T-shirt. His jaw had flexed as she straddled his lap. His expression had gone slack in amazement when he realized what she had done.

Oh God. She had come right there, right in front of his face.

She fanned her own face.

Of course, he hadn't appeared in the least offended. He had looked . . . hungry. Very hungry. Very stark. Very eatably male. Undeniably male. Getting-ready-to-grab-her-and-do-her male.

He was a one-night stand waiting to happen, because that was not a "happily forever after" type of stud.

She breathed out roughly. It had to have been his resemblance to Kell, that was all there was to it. She hadn't seen him in years. Her father had sworn he had been part of the group that had rescued her from the Fuentes compound nearly two years before, but she hadn't seen him. All she had seen were the black masks that covered her rescuers' faces.

She hadn't recognized Kell in any of them.

But this man, she could have imagined Kell's hard jawline. His sharp blade of a nose. Kell's nose hadn't been broken that she remembered, but this stranger's had been.

There was a scar on the stranger's neck; Kell hadn't had one. That she remembered. God, it had been so long since she had seen him. Years. Years since she had even thought about him.

Until now.

She shivered.

She should have been shuddering in revulsion. What kind of man went to a strip joint to get his jollies anyway? Only the lowest sort. The sort that couldn't get a woman any other way perhaps?

But that man could easily get a woman. Hell, he could have almost had her.

She barely held back her moan of mortification, aware that Dyson was already watching her with an edge of violence in his expression.

And here she had taken such pride in the fact that unlike her friends, she was *not* ruled by her hormones. She did *not* come unglued by pesky desires. She controlled her needs, not the other way around.

Well, she had sure as hell come unglued today.

And those pesky desires? They were torturing her,

wetting her expensive French lace panties and causing her clit to throb and beg for more. Just one more hard breath. Just one more of those pulsing, heat-radiating little climaxes that only made her hungrier.

She pressed her thighs together, wincing at the incredible sensitivity of her swollen clit. Right where he had breathed on her. Where his breath had touched her. It might as well have been his fingers, the results had been so devastating.

He was bad to the bone. She had seen it in what little of his expression had been visible. His eyes had been hidden by the dark glasses, but his lips . . . She licked her own lips. Those lips had been expressive. Full of sensual hunger, but with a restrained, taut appearance that suggested utter control over himself and his environment. His muscles had been tense, his body restrained. Like a panther coiled and ready to spring.

She could have sworn she heard him growl at one point.

Oh God, this is so not good. So not good, she thought as she pulled at the long jacket she had literally stolen from the dressing room. She would have to mail it back to Cherry. But she couldn't have taken the time to find her clothes. To actually dress. He had jumped for her, started to chase her. There had just been no time.

She cranked up the air conditioner further, hoping to alleviate some of the heat burning inside her body, and pushed back the regret tearing through her even as she ignored Dyson's further mutterings.

The ultimate bad boy. The man of her sexual fantasies, and she had no choice but to run from him.

This was a wake-up call. A warning, she decided. Fate was telling her to watch herself because she was beginning to step into dangerous territory. That wannabe slut that tried to run rampant inside her needed to be reined in before she messed up beyond any possible chance of repair.

Because God help her if she actually went to bed with a man like that. Her heart was the least of what could be broken.

Breathing in deeply, she had to forcibly remind herself that she was safe. Her suddenly traitorous hormones might be going crazy, but there was no way the bad boy with sizzling breath was ever going to find her.

Cherry didn't know her real name. Neither did the owner of the club. She was confident there wasn't a chance in hell she was ever going to meet him again.

She ignored her hormones' howl of regret. They could just chill out and forget it. She could dream of bad boys. She could write about them. Well, try to write about them anyway. But in real life . . . Well, a person had to realize reality started somewhere. Right?

She wiped the sweat off her brow as she turned to look at Dyson. He was pulling his cell phone from the clip on his belt.

"What are you doing?"

"Calling your father." For the first time since he had moved into her home his expression was almost interesting. It was stamped with male arrogance and command. A little bit too late, but it was there.

"Why?"

"Because he needs to have a talk with you. I've had enough of this—" He froze when the Trailblazer swerved with a jerk, then righted itself, his narrowed gaze piercing into her.

"Nothing happened," she stated calmly. "I got spooked. That's all."

"Spooked taking dancing lessons?" he snapped.

"No, spooked giving a lap dance," she stated calmly.

The silence that filled the Trailblazer then was scary. She risked another glance at him. He was staring back at her with a cold, assessing gaze.

"There was no one there but the club owner, that dancer, and two bouncers," he said with obviously forced control. "I checked."

"Well, he must have come in after you checked." She swallowed tightly.

He inhaled harshly. "And you didn't let me know?"

"Umm, I didn't know until I was dancing."

He turned his head to the back window, watched, turned back, and stared at her with harsh contempt. She nearly flinched under the look before jerking her eyes back to the road.

"Why do you have a bodyguard, Ms. Stanton?" he finally asked.

"Well, because Daddy stresses after that last kidnapping?" she asked with false innocence, restraining her own disgusted wince at the words that slipped sarcastically from her lips.

Okay, so she had been kidnapped once because of his work against that damned drug cartel. But he had told her, as long as she kept the bodyguards, it wouldn't happen again. That she would be safe.

"Did it occur to you that you could be in danger?"

"I'm sure I would be if I didn't have a big tough marine watching over me," she said, trying to placate him.

"Don't give me your bullshit," he ground out. "This is going in my report. Go ahead and wreck the damned truck, see if I care. The injuries would be nothing compared to what your father will do when he finds out how I've let you run over me. I'd be ashamed of myself if I weren't fairly certain he's going to kill me."

He sounded disgusted with himself and with her.

Emily winced. "I won't tell if you won't tell."

"Forget it."

"I promise to be good. No more strip clubs. I swear."

His expression didn't waver. "Not on your life. Not on my life. Sorry, kid, your gig is up."

Okay, so maybe he wasn't the wuss she thought he was after all.

Her hands tightened on the steering wheel as she realized she was going to have to endure another of her father's lectures. How she had to be careful to stay safe. He was a senator. He had made enemies.

Yes, he was a senator, and she was hellaciously proud of everything he did and had done. He had raised her alone since she was five, since her mother's death, and he had taught her to be careful. But he had also taught her about adventure. How to shoot, how to hunt. How to be strong and how to look for strength.

Until she turned eighteen. Suddenly, he wanted her in dresses and makeup and married and with babies. He didn't understand that core of adventure he had placed in her soul that now had no place to go.

She had given up the idea of joining the armed services the day he paled when she mentioned it. His hands had actually shaken as he pushed them through his short hair and stared back at her in horror.

She didn't want her dad that scared for her. She didn't want him worrying. So she had tried to settle down, tried to ignore the need for adventure.

She went to college and looked for a husband.

She graduated and found a job at a very exclusive private school, and began to hope just for a lover. Hell, a broken heart would be bearable if she could find a man worth letting her heart get broken over. And she appreciated the candidates he sent her in the form of bodyguards. She really did. But she was sick of them. And unfortunately the only time she had refused to have one, was the time she was actually kidnapped. Go figure.

"Emily, your father isn't playing games with you," Dyson said long moments later, his voice serious, full of warning. "He doesn't make you accept having a bodyguard just for the hell of it."

She blinked back the sudden, burning warmth behind her eyes.

"I'm his daughter. His only child. He worries."

"Have you considered that he worries for good reason? You were kidnapped once already. Do you understand the effort it took to rescue you and the other girls?"

She tightened her hands on the steering wheel before flashing him an angry look. "Have you considered that I try not to get in trouble? That I try to be nice and prim and proper and all the things he wants in a daughter? That I try to stay safe?" She laughed mockingly. "Forget it, Dyson. You wouldn't understand."

"You're not a man, Emily. You've got balls, I admit, but you're never going to make him see you as anything other than his little girl." Maybe he understood more than she gave him credit for.

"I'd settle for that," she whispered. "It beats being the brood mare he keeps hoping I'll become for some dimwit male with less sense than morals. And it doesn't even matter anymore. Tell him whatever you want to. I don't give a damn. But don't think you're hurting me when you do. Because I promise you, unless you're a sperm donor for the grandkids he wants, then he'll just replace you like he does everyone else."

Just as he always had. Even when she was a child. As soon as she started getting used to a housekeeper or nanny, they were replaced. As soon as she found someone she could talk to, they were gone. She had stopped trying to care years ago. She wasn't going to care now.

Strangely, Dyson didn't say anything more. She noticed he kept looking behind them, kept playing with his cell phone, but he stayed silent. And so did she. She had stopped explaining herself years ago. And until her father gave her a better reason than he had given her over the years for making certain she didn't have a life, then she was going to have just that. A life.

As soon as she stopped shaking. As soon as she stopped remembering a bad boy in leather who there wasn't a chance in hell could stand up to her father. Eatable lips, a hard body, and the breath of lust vibrating on her clit.

Hell, forgetting that one just might take a while.

T HE SENATOR'S PRIVATE PLANE LANDED and taxied into its hangar at Atlanta's airport as Durango Team moved from the limo awaiting him and waited patiently while the senator disembarked.

The unscheduled trip from D.C. had come as a surprise as the final team members returned to the naval base and prepared for the operation with the senator. The information that Diego Fuentes was targeting him and his daughter once again had come as a surprise to them all, considering the fact that Fuentes usually played by a different set of rules. Best him in one of his games and he walked away. He didn't retaliate and normally he didn't strike again. Unless, apparently, one got away with memories that she shouldn't have, as Fuentes suspected the senator's daughter had done. Add that to the senator's investigation into the government mole known only as Mr. White, and it placed Emily and the senator in Fuentes's sights once again. Durango Team had been after Diego Fuentes for over three years, ever since his name had been connected with the elusive Sorrell, the terrorist arms dealer they had come up against in the Middle East.

As the senator stepped from the plane, Kell watched him carefully. The senator had taken him under his wing nearly fifteen years ago. He had helped train him. Helped Kell to achieve the goals he had set for himself. This was the man whose daughter was a demon on Atlanta's highways and danced like a fucking wet dream. He couldn't see anything of her wild impulsiveness in Richard Stanton's closed expression and gray eyes, but he knew it was there. As a younger man, the senator had been just as wild, but with a steel core of control that only a Navy SEAL possesses.

Stanton was barely six feet, but still a powerful man at the age of fifty-five. His deep voice and commanding presence managed to get things done in the capital. He was serving his first term, and making a name for himself there just as he had in the SEALs. He was a man to depend on, but he wasn't a man to cross.

"Kell, it's good to see you again, son." The senator returned his salute quickly before directing his gaze to the rest of the team.

"Chavez. Men. Thank you for meeting me here. If you'll get in with me, then my assistant will drive."

He nodded to the interior of the limo.

Minutes later, the five men of Durango Team were in the limo, waiting silently as the senator removed a bottle of water from the tiny refrigerator and took a long drink before pinning Kell with an accusatory stare.

"That girl is going to make me crazy," he muttered as he capped the water and turned his gaze instead on Reno. "Do you know what she was doing?"

Reno's gaze shifted to Kell. "Yes, sir. Lieutenant Krieger was following her this afternoon and reported her whereabouts. It seemed her bodyguard is a little overwhelmed by her."

"A little overwhelmed?" Senator Stanton asked rudely. "Chet Dyson, remember him?"

"Yes, sir," Reno answered severely, but Kell caught the gleam of amusement in his eyes.

They had all read Dyson's record. He was one of the toughest marines the corps had had at one time. He still would have been if his kneecap hadn't been blown to hell and back by a sniper in Baghdad.

"He quit." The senator scowled.

Kell wasn't in the least surprised.

"Excuse me, sir?" Reno stared back at him in surprise.

"Dyson called an hour ago from his cell phone and gave me twenty-four hours to find a replacement. He called her a danger to herself and every sane man in existence." His jaw worked furiously. "I had hopes for that boy. He would have made a damned fine son-in-law."

Once again, the senator pinned him with a gaze that screamed in accusation.

Kell arched his brow in question. He was aware of the others watching the senator with hidden shock. Kell watched him with silent amusement. Hell, everyone who knew Emily knew that her father carefully selected her bodyguards. He wanted a son-in-law, and he was determined to be the one to choose him.

The senator was trying to direct his daughter's life the

same way he had directed his SEAL team when he was still
in the Navy. Someone needed to remind him that he was no
longer an active SEAL but a senator, and his daughter
wouldn't have any problems finding her own man.

Hell, no. All she had to do was put in half the effort of
that dance she had given Kell and they would be lined up on
her doorstep.

FTER HIS SEAL CAREER HAD ended, courtesy of a mission
that went to hell and nearly killed him and the team he led,
Captain Stanton had returned home and entered politics.
With the backing of a personal fortune, courtesy of his parents
and his wife's inheritance, he had moved quickly up the political ladder and begun providing his daughter with a steady sup-
ply of bodyguards from the day she turned eighteen.

Potential sons-in-law.

It was no damned wonder his daughter was a wild child
looking for escape.

"She was involved in a relationship with Dyson?" Reno
asked.

"No!" the senator snapped. "The girl is too damned picky
to even go that far." He sighed then. "That's beside the point.
He faxed me the reports she had convinced him to hold back
while we were on the phone." He ran his hand over his
face. "God help that child, she's going to get herself killed.
Fuentes's man won't have to lift a hand to hurt her, she's
going to do it on her own."

She wasn't that bad, Kell thought silently. He had been
watching her for days. She was impulsive, intelligent. And
haunted. He had seen her face when she thought no one was
watching, in the middle of the night when she sought sanctu-
ary in the little courtyard outside her condo. She had looked
lonely. Lost.

"She's going to be a problem?" Reno asked. "Lieutenant
Krieger's cover depends on her cooperation. Without it,

he's no more than another bodyguard they have only to wait out."

"She goes through bodyguards like water," Stanton griped. "Two months max and she has them wrapped around her little finger. They would die for her, but the problem with that is that they start getting enmeshed in her little fiascoes and adventures. The girl hasn't realized yet that she needs to settle down."

"Sir, the question remains, will she cooperate?" Reno asked again.

"One thing about Emily Paige is the fact that she has the heart of an adventurer," he growled. "She'll go along with it and try to twist your man into so many knots he won't know if he's coming or going. For a girl who refuses to find a husband or a lover, she sure has a way of making tough men melt in a puddle at her little feet." He glared at Kell.

Kell refused to flinch. He respected the senator, he was damned wary of the power the man held, but he had never agreed with him where Emily was concerned, and he hadn't hesitated to inform him of that fact several times.

"You think you're tough enough to handle her, don't you, Kell?" The senator's smile was understanding, if disdainful. "You're sitting there telling yourself you're tough enough. You're hard enough and you're cold enough. I give you a week before you're panting after her like every other male I put in her vicinity. And like all the others, she'll wave with a smile when you walk out the door."

No, he was smart enough. That was the difference.

Kell allowed the corner of his lips to quirk at the senator's words.

The senator shook his head pityingly in reply. "I'm going to do you a favor, son, simply because I hate to see a good man go down too fast and because I like you. Do whatever it takes to keep her safe. I don't care if you have to lock her in her own damned closet, because God help you if you let anything happen to my daughter. Do you understand me?"

"No interference," Kell said then, ignoring his commander's warning look. "If she calls crying, you don't pull back. If she gets pissed because she doesn't like my rules, you don't change them."

Stanton's gray eyes narrowed at the challenge in Kell's voice. He stared back for long moments, his expression thoughtful.

"No rough stuff," he finally stated. "I won't have her mistreated."

"You know better than that, Richard. She won't be mistreated." He was a lot of things but Kell didn't hurt women.

Stanton watched him a moment longer before nodding slowly. "Agreed. You have control."

Something Stanton had never given any of her bodyguards. Kell restrained his feeling of triumph but he had to admit to a twinge of wariness at the satisfaction that filled the senator's gaze.

Stanton sat back in his seat then, turned to Reno, and began discussing the protective detail Reno would be leading. Not that it appeared Reno was going to have much control over it. The senator had definite ideas on how to run the show, but he was willing to listen to Reno's suggestions. As the limo made its way through Atlanta toward Emily Stanton's condo, the plans were argued into a viable operation.

Laying the groundwork to catch Fuentes's spy within the committee the senator chaired would be handled by Reno, Clint, and Macey, while Kell and Ian had the responsibility of protecting his daughter.

"Emily has various functions, charity and political, that she attends throughout the year; a couple are scheduled during the next few weeks," he informed Kell. "She can't miss those. No matter what. They're too important. And Emily isn't to know that Ian is involved in this. She's to know nothing more than that he's her new neighbor."

"Why?" Kell asked. "Knowing the full extent of the danger could help her in determining how far to push her own safety."

Stanton's eyes flashed with rebuke.

"Emily's different," the senator snapped. "A writer. A dreamer. She'll never understand how much her life is in danger so there's no sense in trying to explain it, and it could endanger Ian's cover if she pulls one of her tricks and tries to slip away from you. Let's not give her more to worry about than we need to. You just keep her out of the strip clubs and off strange men's laps, if you don't mind."

Kell omitted the fact that the lap dance had been for him. But as he listened to the finalization of the plans, he began to draw his own conclusions about the senator and Emily's relationship. He was betting money the coming meeting wasn't going to go smoothly.

Emily had a strong dislike of control, and Senator Stanton, formerly Captain Richard Stanton of the Navy SEALs, was all about control. It was there in the thin line of his mouth, the frosty hue of his gaze.

And he wanted his daughter controlled. No matter what it took. No matter how much fire burned inside her at the action. No matter how little of the woman she was would remain. As far as the senator was concerned, nothing mattered but restraining the life inside her. A fire Kell intended to stoke in far different ways than Miss Emily Paige Stanton could ever imagine. Ways her father would likely kill him over.

Four

A COLD SHOWER DIDN'T HELP. Pacing the floor didn't help. Changing from the sexy underwear to her normal loose cotton pants and overly large T-shirt didn't help. And listening to Chet Dyson pack, and watching him load his car, sure as hell hadn't helped.

Because she couldn't forget one man, a breath of air, and a fear unlike anything she had ever known in her life.

She was more aroused than she could ever remember being. All she could remember was the feel of warm breath between her thighs a millisecond before pleasure pierced her clit and sent vibrations of ecstasy racing through her body.

The Pudgy Prude, as one of her boyfriends once dubbed her, wasn't entirely without sexual desire. She masturbated, she thought fiercely. She knew how to get off, she knew how to want to be touched, how to imagine being touched, she knew how to touch herself. She just hadn't particularly cared if any of the men she actually knew got close enough to touch her. But she had always been smart enough to maintain a distance between herself and the type of man that she knew would completely run her over.

Men like her father. Strong, determined, dominant men who enforced their control, supposedly for a woman's own good. Daughter or wife. For their own peace of mind, such men made certain that the women they loved were smothered beyond hope.

The exact type of man that turned her on the most. Especially the type whose glance assured a woman that he had the soul of a bad boy. A man who could turn the bedroom into an adventure. Men like Kell Krieger and the stranger in the strip joint.

Why was she thinking about Krieger now? It had been so many years since she had seen him that she wondered if she would even recognize him now. She knew her father met with him fairly often and still counted him as a friend. But Kell was the one man her father had never suggested as one of her bodyguards.

Of course, Kell hadn't been like other men. She had no doubt in her mind he might be more adventurous to a woman than her father deemed necessary.

Unfortunately, Emily craved adventure. And not just in the bedroom. But outside of it. She craved a challenge and she hungered to live. If a man couldn't provide both, then what good was he?

The men her father sent as potential candidates, aka bodyguards, had never really tempted her. They whined too much. They were too scared of her father to even suggest a little fun, and all they wanted to do was call and ask his permission for the least little bit of adventure.

She rolled her eyes at the thought of it. Sometimes, she wondered if what she craved even existed. A man who was strong inside and out. A man who knew the world wasn't fair, and knew he had to take responsibility for his part in it. A man who knew there was more to sex than simply the act and that there was more to a woman than breasts and thighs and what lay beyond. A man who accepted the fact that a woman might need adventure as well.

That was what she craved. A man she could trust enough not just to give in to her desires with, but to accept her need to live. A man who, even if he wasn't there forever, was at least there long enough to care about fulfilling not just the physical desires, but the adventurous ones as well.

Until now, whenever she thought of the perfect lover, Kell's face had always filled her imagination when she fantasized. Now, a stranger had taken his place.

She was definitely fantasizing now. Much to her own dissatisfaction, because masturbation hadn't helped. She had tried that the moment she was naked. Despite the orgasm that had rippled through her at the club, her body was still simmering with need when she returned home. Unfamiliar, desperate need.

She knew how to hurt for sex now; unfortunately, Emily knew she was doomed to disappointment. There wasn't a chance in hell the object of her lust could be allowed into her life. She doubted he would even want to be.

Men like that did not "do" chubby little schoolteachers with no intentions of entering the darker side of life.

Emily didn't do drugs and had no intentions of trying them. She wasn't a part of the criminal element, as he surely was, and she had no desire to dance on the fringes of it by becoming involved with someone like that. The need for adventure only went so far.

Now, if she could just convince her body of that, because it wasn't listening very well. It was definitely interested, even now, hours later.

She paced her living room, following the path of the thick throw rugs that lay between the overstuffed furniture and heavy walnut coffee table. The evening sun glinted off the hardwood floor, and sent warmth blazing through the room as Atlanta's heat shimmered beyond the patio doors.

Outside, her small courtyard, which was surrounded by a heavy brick wall, looked cool and inviting, but not as peaceful as it had once been. The shade of the ornamental trees and the blooms of summer's splendor couldn't quench the lust that filled her. Finally. She couldn't shake her reaction to today's events, no more than she could shake her arousal.

For as long as she could remember, her ultimate fantasy

image had been the leather-wearing, motorcycle-riding bad boy. That was her weakness. When she was in high school she had watched them from afar, lusted, dreamed of them, but she had known them too well to ever be drawn in by them.

But today, she had almost succumbed.

She twisted her fingers together as she paused at the sliding glass doors that led to the courtyard and frowned at her own blurred image there.

She wasn't really pretty. She was sort of plain and not the type of girl that the bad boys had ever noticed. Which had suited her fine until now. With her shoulder-length auburn hair, plain blue eyes, and less than slender build, she didn't exactly draw men to her. There were too many women much prettier than she, and much more exotic. Women who knew their own sexuality and how to please a man. Women who didn't freak out when a man blew on the sensitive flesh between their thighs.

She had come for a stranger.

When his face had flushed and the heavy lust in his expression had hit her, a second before his breath had rushed over her sex, she had known she had made a horrible mistake. She should have never risked herself that way, her identity, her safety, her father's reputation.

Her own peace of mind.

She dropped her head against the cool glass of the door, her lips tipping into a grimace of regret. It would have been nice. To touch that hard body, to feel his muscles tensing beneath her fingertips, to feel his hands sliding over her.

He had smelled so clean, so masculine. There hadn't been a scent of drunkenness or sloth, just clean male. No heavy aftershave or cologne. Just hard, primal male. The type of male that never gave women like her a second look.

It was the lace underwear, the sexy dance, the overwhelmingly sexual nature of the atmosphere that had surrounded him. He hadn't really been aroused by mousy, pudgy, quiet Emily Stanton. And it was better that way, wasn't it?

The harsh ringing of her cell phone interrupted her thoughts. Turning to the bar that separated the kitchen from the living room, Emily snatched up the phone, checked the caller ID and answered it quickly, knowing what was coming.

"Hi, Daddy." She pushed the thought of bad boys to the back of her mind for the man who had cared for her, cherished her. And fought to restrain her.

"Emily, how are you doing, sweetheart?" Affection filled her father's voice as it came over the line. "Are you busy?"

"Not hardly," she answered, pushing back her regret that she wasn't. Hell, it was Friday, she should have a date at least.

"Can you make time for your old man then?" His voice was too serious; the normal good humor and gentle teasing were absent.

Emily frowned. "Are you going to yell at me?"

She hated it when he succumbed to frustration and actually yelled at her. Not that it happened often, but it had happened enough times for her to dread it.

"No yelling," he promised quietly. "I'm about five minutes from the house. I'm bringing some friends with me. I'll see you then."

Friends. That meant bodyguards and more than the one that normally traveled with him.

Emily breathed in carefully. "Are you okay, Daddy?"

"I'm fine, sweetheart." But her heart clenched at the gentling of his voice. "Just be watching for us. We'll be there soon."

Emily disconnected the phone seconds later, staring down at it with a frown as she bit at her lower lip. Thoughts of bad boys and arousal dissipated as worry began to fill her. Her father was worried, worried enough that he wasn't hiding it from her.

Something was wrong, very wrong.

Five minutes later, barely enough time to change from the slouchy clothes into a pair of white Capris and a dove-gray cotton tank, Emily heard a vehicle pulling into the front drive.

Pushing her feet into comfortable sandals, she moved to the door, checking the peephole quickly before opening it for her father.

"Hi, Daddy." Moving back, she watched as he entered and gave her a quick hug.

He was followed by three tall, hard-bodied men, handsome enough to make a girl pant if she hadn't been distracted by the fierce frown on her father's face.

She glanced over the three quickly before closing the door and moving slowly into the living room behind them.

One of the men moved to her sliding door and whipped the heavy shades closed over it before moving to the windows and closing the plastic-backed curtains over them as well.

"Why is he closing my curtains?" She stared at his back. A very fine back. Broad and heavily muscled beneath the white cotton shirt he wore. The broad back tapered to snug jeans. Jeans that did nothing to hide a luscious butt.

"I'm sorry, baby," her father said softly as she turned to him, seeing the heavy lines in his face, the concern in his light blue eyes.

At fifty-five her father was still a fit, handsome man. He had never remarried after her mother's death nearly twenty years before, though she was aware he had certain "friendships."

"What's wrong?" She kept her attention on him as the other three men began moving through the house. "Look, I know Dyson is pissed. And I know you probably are too. But it was just a little research—"

"Emily, this isn't about the strip club." He shook his head, but she could see the flat line of his mouth, and knew she had disappointed him again.

"It wasn't that big of a deal," she said. "Dyson just gets really intense over things, ya know?"

"Men have a way of doing that." He nodded. "Speeding. Flirting your way out of a ticket while he sat beside you. The strip club, the attempted attack at that dance club a few weeks ago. Sweetheart, I have gray hairs from the report Dyson sent me before I landed."

And why had she ever imagined Dyson wouldn't do it? They all did it when they finally managed to cave to their fear.

"I was safe." She shrugged. "The bodyguards are like ticks. They suck the fun out of everything."

She heard a snort of laughter from one of the men behind her but didn't turn away from her father to glare at whichever one it was.

"Emily. Sit down with me." He took one of her hands and led her to the couch while her heart began to race in terror.

He wasn't angry. He wasn't yelling at her. And that was scary. He had the same expression on his face that he'd had the night he awakened her to tell her that her mother wasn't coming back home. That she would never come home again.

"What's wrong?" She pushed back the instinctive aggression she felt whenever she knew something she didn't like was about to happen. She knew this expression, knew the look in his eyes.

He sat beside her. "Emily," he said. "Fuentes is back, sweetheart, and the information we've received is that he's going to attempt to kidnap you again."

For a moment, darkness nearly overwhelmed her. The scent of rotting vegetation and the stink of unwashed male bodies filled her senses. She had to swallow back the bile and fear, had to force back the overwhelming panic. Shifting memories that weren't quite memories shadowed her mind. Whimpers of pain, betrayal.

As she stared at her father, fighting back that fear, she wondered where the knowledge of betrayal had come from. How did she know they had been betrayed? What had she seen or heard that she couldn't remember once the drugs they had pumped into her had worn off.

"You're certain?" She breathed in deeply, drawing in the fresh scent of vanilla that filled her home.

This was going to be an imposition, no doubt about it. Besides the fact that it was frankly terrifying. She didn't remember much of the kidnapping, but what she did wasn't pleasant.

"We're very certain, Miss Stanton." Tall, black-haired, eyes as gray as thunderclouds, one of the men stepped forward. "The Fuentes cartel is serious about this as well. They seem to think you may have seen or heard something that could threaten them. In addition, your father is determined to catch the Fuentes mole within the government, and Fuentes has to ensure that that doesn't happen."

"Emily, this is Commander Reno Chavez. He's the SEAL in charge of our protection."

"Hello, Mr. Chavez." She gave him a trembling smile. "I hope you're watching over Daddy well. He can be hard to keep up with."

The man's smile was pure sex appeal. "I'm doing my best, ma'am." He nodded. "He's more worried about you now."

"Behind Reno is Lieutenant Commander Clint McIntyre, and coming out of your bedroom," her father cast the third man a disapproving frown, "you should remember Lieutenant Kell Krieger."

Emerald-green eyes, predatory and liquid hot, sliced into her as Emily finally gave the man her full attention. She felt the breath leave her chest as shock slammed through her system. Those eyes. Something about them almost held her mesmerized, sent heat curling through her and had her cringing at the thought that he had been in her bedroom.

Where the red lace underwear was thrown over her bed, the panties carrying the scent of her previous arousal. Mortification flamed beneath her cheeks as she fought to cover her embarrassment.

"Mr. McIntyre. Hello, Kell." She cleared her throat as she fought to swallow past the nerves now rioting through her body.

"Emily. I need you to do me a favor," her father said then,

drawing her attention back to him. "Kell will be staying here with you. He'll be your personal bodyguard until this investigation I've begun is over. I need you to cooperate with him."

"I always cooperate, Daddy," she reminded him with a smile. "But I promise, this time, I'll make an extra effort not to cause him to quit. I'd hate to run a friend off."

Oh hell. Damn. She was in trouble. Kell, in her home? Sleeping beneath her roof? She could already feel the overwhelming heat that had begun building in intensity between her thighs. This was the wrong time for this. This wasn't good.

Her father winced. "There's more to this one, sweetheart. No one can know he's your bodyguard. You just fired your bodyguard because your lover was jealous of him."

Oh. Shit.

Her gaze swung back to her father. He was kidding. He had to be kidding.

But he wasn't. She could see it in his eyes, feel it in the tension emanating from him.

Her eyes swung back to Krieger and she felt the world drop from beneath her. That mocking smile. She had seen it before. Just as she had seen that particular shaggy cut of hair, that hard, muscular body. No sunglasses now. No leather chaps. And he had shaved that rough, day-old growth of beard from his face. But it was him.

Sweet heaven. She had come in his face less than five hours before and now he was going to pretend to be her lover?

He had disguised who he was. He had to have been following her. It was her fantasy lover all along and she had come in his face.

This was so not good. This was the *Twilight Zone*. She could hear the theme music playing in the back of her mind.

"This isn't a very good idea." She tried to fight back her shudder of impending pleasure and doom as she turned back from her father. "Why don't I just move back home for a while?"

That was the perfect solution. He had been wanting her back in the house ever since she moved out anyway. She could just go home. She would have to cancel some activities she had planned, put aside the research she still had to get into for the new book.

One being the live sex show she had been playing with viewing. But she was sure her agent would give her some extra time for this book. Most of it was research anyway. It wasn't like she didn't know what to write. She just didn't know *how* to write it.

But her father was shaking his head slowly. Damn, of course it couldn't be that easy.

"Sweetheart, these people can get to you there as easily as they can here. I'm not even staying at the house. I'm staying in an apartment close to the Capitol instead with my own security detail. This is the only answer."

Oh no. There had to be another answer. There was never only a single way to do anything. Wasn't that what she tried to instill in her students, the ability to try new things in different ways. Of course there was an answer to this, she just had to find it.

"I could move in with you—"

"That's not possible, Emily." Kell's voice was firm, determined. "We need to maintain the impression that the senator knows nothing about this threat for reasons of security. If you come to D.C. and go into hiding, they'll suspect."

She stared back at her nemesis. The bad boy in leather. God, she had to get rid of him. She could already feel her reaction to him blooming once again, heating her body, reminding her of the outrageous dance she had performed for him. Wanton, sexy. Letting the inner slut free hadn't been hard, and she was terribly afraid there was no way to keep it locked up if she had to actually live with him.

"Emily. You can't tell anyone why he's here." Her father sighed heavily, drawing her gaze back to him. "We have to maintain the secrecy of the information. You have to convince everyone he's your lover."

Emily cringed. He had said it again. Her father had said *lover* in regard to her and a man? Especially this man.

Wide-eyed, filled with shock, she stared back at him.

His lips twitched in sudden amusement. "I'm not that old, little girl," he told her. "And I'm smart enough to know you likely know what the words mean too."

Like hell. Geeze, how do you tell your father you're still a twenty-five-year-old virgin? Especially when he was constantly sending big tall muscular agents and bodyguards to protect her and, hopefully, inhabit her bed?

She knew why he never sent female bodyguards. Just as she knew that each man he had sent had been personally vetted and handpicked as son-in-law potential.

Think, Emily. There has to be an answer here. No way could she live with a man she was dying to get her hands on. Especially this man. A man she had already dubbed the baddest of the bad boys. A man she knew she could never have yet had never been able to stop wanting.

"I could go stay with Aunt Betha," she said then. "Only the devil himself would dare mess with her."

Betha Alderman was a Boston lawyer with enough temper to scare even her father.

He was shaking his head. Okay, it wouldn't be nice to involve Betha.

"You're serious about this," she said weakly.

"I'm afraid so, baby," he said. "But don't worry, Kell is a professional. This isn't his first private security job. He's protected presidents and foreign nationals. I'm sure he can keep up with you."

Yeah, but how the hell was she supposed to keep up with him? She turned her gaze back to him, fighting to keep from revealing the fact that she had been up close and personal with him in ways she was certain her father would use to force the poor man to the altar.

How was she supposed to get out of this one, now? She couldn't refuse the protection. Her father would never have planned this if he weren't genuinely convinced she was in danger.

"I understand." It was all she could do to push the words past her lips and to paste a friendly smile on her face as she glanced back at Kell Krieger. "If I remember correctly, he eats a lot though. I'll have to stock up."

Kell smiled. It wasn't a smile for the faint of heart, it was pure male challenge, and that glimmer in those emerald eyes wasn't just amusement, it was heat. Sexual heat. And she was woman enough to shake in her sandals.

"Emily." Her father drew her gaze back to him. "I want you to promise me you'll listen to Kell. No running off on your own for the hell of it. No strip clubs or dance clubs. Promise me you'll let him keep you safe."

She met his gaze straight on, letting him see the suspicion in her eyes that she could feel rising inside her. She didn't know as much about the armed services as she probably should, she admitted, but some things weren't adding up for her.

"Why are Navy SEALs involved in this instead of the Secret Service?" she finally asked as she rose to her feet and walked to the bar that separated the living room from the kitchen, then turned to face him. "I thought SEALs were a strike force."

"We're that as well," Reno answered her. "We have the most experience with the Fuentes cartel, how they strike, and the men they use to strike with. We're working with the Secret Service in D.C. with your father's security, and there will be two Secret Service agents assigned as backup here. But this is an investigative operation as well as protection, hence the cover story."

That made sense. She knew from the few things she had overheard from her father when she was younger that a SEAL team could follow a single investigation for years. It wasn't a common occurrence, but it happened.

"Since when have I ever lied to you, Emily?" Her father

rose from the sofa, a heavy scowl creasing his features as Reno finished his explanation.

"I didn't say you were lying to me, Daddy." She lifted her chin defiantly. "But we both know that you never tell me the whole story or the truth about the danger involved. Nine times out of ten you put those stupid bodyguards in my house based on nothing more than rumors and a hope of keeping me from doing whatever it is you've heard I'm about to do."

She saw the surprise flicker in his gaze then. He thought she was so dimwitted that she had no idea what he was doing.

"You like to get into trouble," he muttered, glancing at the three SEALs with ill-concealed discomfort.

She hated that accusation.

"I don't get into trouble, Daddy." Emily kept her voice smooth, even. She didn't want to fight with him.

"You give lap dances to strange men," he bit out. "What do you call that?"

She flushed in embarrassment. "Fun," she snapped back. "Just think, Daddy, that could have been the son-in-law you've been pushing so hard for."

She clamped her mouth shut the minute the words left her lips. Angry words. Accusations. Dammit, her nerves were just about pushed to their limit and he expected her to keep her mouth shut and just accept his condemnation once again. And he expected her to do it in front of the man assigned to protect her.

She shook her head abruptly, turning her back on him and lifting her hand to forestall the chilling response she knew would cut into her soul.

"You'd have to get off your high horse and give him the time of day first." The words came anyway. They stabbed into her, causing her to flinch in shame because the man she had given that lap dance for was watching, listening.

She inhaled roughly, blinking back her tears, determined that she wasn't going to be hurt this time.

"So." She turned back to him. "How long are you allowing Kell to stay?" She glanced at Kell's thoughtful expression, striving to keep from meeting his gaze. "Two weeks? Four?"

"As long as he can control you," he snapped back.

Her lips thinned. "Then you might as well take him with you when you leave, because no man controls me, Daddy. You should have figured that one out on your own by now."

Five

BY TIME HER FATHER LEFT, Emily was drained. She could feel the suffocating feeling that came with each bodyguard change, and the feeling of helplessness she couldn't seem to shake.

It was worse this time, though, because Kell was more than just a bodyguard. He was a mysterious friend, a part of her life since she was ten years old, and a part of her dreams since she was a teenager. She had been half in love with him for as long as she could remember, and now, she was supposed to pretend he was her lover. That he touched her. That she knew his kiss and the stroke of his hands.

God help her, she couldn't even write the fantasy to that one. She had no conception of how it would feel, but she knew the hunger for it. A hunger that left her shaking when she pulled herself from the dreams of his touch, always so close and yet never actually on her flesh.

She could feel it now. It rippled through her bloodstream and reminded her that Kell was part of the reason why no other man had ever measured up to her idea of the lover she wanted. Because she had wanted Kell. Wanted him with a stubbornness that didn't leave room for other men.

"The rules in this house are simple," she stated as she forced herself to turn and face her too-wanted houseguest.

She might as well start as she intended to finish. "Stay out of my way and I'll stay out of yours."

He stood in front of her patio doors, the lengthening shadows of evening filling the house and gathering around him like a cloak of danger.

He looked dangerous. He was dangerous. More so than she had remembered. She had a feeling that even if she had been inclined to try to run him in circles the way she had the others, it wouldn't be possible.

"Stay out of your way?" He smiled suggestively as his gaze raked over her body. "I don't think that's going to be possible. Bodyguards have a purpose, Emily. They guard the body. And I take my job very seriously."

His gaze settled at her thighs for a long second before lifting to her face with a wicked smile.

"I just bet you do, but I believe I'm safe enough in the house. The security system alone is better than Fort Knox, so we shouldn't have any problems staying out of each other's way. Now should we?"

She was shaking. Shaking and certain that he could read her nervousness in every move she made. She had never been good at hiding her thoughts, and hiding her desires were even harder.

Every time he had looked at her since she became a teenager she had seen the knowledge in his eyes. The certainty that he knew the hungers building in her. Of course, that was why she hadn't seen him in five years. He had been avoiding her. And that was just damned humiliating.

"It doesn't work that way," he stated calmly.

There was no frown. There was no flicker of calculation in his gaze as he tried to decide how to handle her. They all had that moment of indecision, as though they weren't quite certain what to do with a client who didn't really want them there.

"Why doesn't it work that way?" She kept her voice reasonable. "School starts again within another month and I'll be busy working on class plans and so forth, as well as some writing I do. I know how to entertain myself, and I do it quite well. I hope you know how to do the same."

"Some things are better taken care of together though," he pointed out, pacing closer, his emerald eyes snaring hers and holding them against her will. "You made a promise to me earlier, Emily. Do you intend to renege on it?"

"What promise?" She could smell him. She wanted to moan at the scent of hard, impossibly powerful muscles and male sensuality as he began to invade her personal space.

She should retreat. Step away. But she was locked in place, staring up at him, feeling invisible bands of heat wrapping around her body.

"I didn't promise you anything."

"You did." The sensual male croon in his voice had her womb clenching. "When you dampened those panties on your bed because of my breath against your sweet pussy, you made a very firm promise. One I intend to collect on. A taste I intend to take."

Shock held her motionless.

"My panties?" she whispered desperately.

"Red lace." His hand lifted, the backs of his fingers stroking along her collarbone as she trembled before him. "The ones lying on that pristine white bed in there. Still wet and smelling of peaches and cream. Do you know that I'm very partial to peaches and cream, Emily?"

Emily jerked back, nearly stumbling against the wall she backed into as she stared back at Kell in amazed shock. His eyes seemed to brighten while his face became darker, intent, sexually hungry.

She shook her head desperately. "It wasn't supposed to be you," she wheezed. "It was supposed to be a bouncer."

"And I had to pay him well to stand back," he murmured with a smile. "Very well. And I intend to collect on that one as well. Right in there in that big bed of yours, all over you like wild rain. Tell me, sugar, you ever had a man cover you like wild rain?"

Cajun. The soft flavor of a Cajun accent slipped into his

voice and sent a hard shudder down Emily's spine as she shook her head. A jerky movement she didn't seem to have control of.

This wasn't happening. And she wasn't responding. She wasn't hot. She wasn't getting horribly wet between her thighs. And dammit, her nipples were not pressing tight and hard against the shirt she wore.

"Never?" His voice lowered as he moved forward again, caging her in, restraining her. His hard body within a breath's distance of her and the wall at her back.

"Stop!" She meant the word to be forceful. God, she meant to sound as outraged and furious as she knew she should be. "I haven't seen you enough in the past five years to recognize you when you walk into a bar and you think I'm going to just jump into bed with you?"

Her body was more than ready to do just that.

"Stop?" His head lowered, his lips touching her brow.

She was going to choke on her own breath. Pleasure swamped her just that quickly, a weakness that had her knees giving out and tremors suddenly shaking her body.

"Please stop." She closed her eyes as she pressed her hands tight against the wall, using the last amount of strength to keep from touching him. If she touched him, she was going to humiliate herself further. She would moan and arch against him. She would beg him for things that she knew would ultimately destroy her independence.

"Sure, sugar?" His hands whispered down her bare arms. "Are you sure that's what you want? I could make you come again. Instead of a little ripple, I'll make you explode with pleasure. Wouldn't you like that?"

She would love it. She ached for it. She was dying for it.

"No!" In a move she couldn't believe she had made, her hands slammed into his chest, pushing him back as she threw herself from the wall, staring back at him in fury.

He was laughing at her. It was there in his eyes, in the smile on his face. Laughing at her and daring her. Trying to control her.

"You bastard," she choked. "You have no right to molest me in my own home like this."

"Molest you?" He was clearly laughing now. The amusement on his face slid into her gut like a knife, and burned through her mind with the shameful realization that he might be aroused, but nothing like she was. He was playing. Nothing more.

"Stay the hell away from me," she ordered harshly, blinking back her tears. "I don't like your games and I don't appreciate your damned lies. I can do without both."

She turned, intent on racing away from him, on locking herself in her bathroom and trying to wash the shameful embarrassment from her mind.

"Hold up there, sugar?" His hand wrapped around her arm, turning her to him firmly as he frowned back at her. "This is no game. And this sure as hell isn't."

Before she could stop him, he forced her palm to the bulge beneath his jeans, pressed it close, and his gaze flared with brilliance again. "I might enjoy playing with you a little bit, but trust me, I know how damned serious I am about touching you. I will be in that bed with you, the only question is when."

"When hell freezes over."

"Really?" His smile was gentler now, but still filled with humor. "I hear global warming is coming fast, cupcake. You sure it ain't already froze over?"

"I'm quite sure," she snarled back. "Because if it were we sure as hell wouldn't be standing here and your master would have called you back to chip ice. Now let me go!"

He released her, but his amusement had her pushing a strangled scream from between her teeth. She whirled away from him, stalked to her bedroom, and slammed the door with enough force to rattle the frame.

Shaking with rage she stomped to the side of the bed, jerked the phone off its cradle, and dialed her father's cell phone number with jabbing stabs of her finger.

"Emily?" His voice came over the line, concerned, questioning.

"He's fired!" Her voice was shaking. Her heart was racing hard enough to choke her. "Do you understand me? Right now. Get back here and get him, he's gone."

Silence filled the line for long moments.

"Did he hurt you, Emily?" he asked quietly.

She wanted to lie. For the first time in longer than she remembered she wanted to lie to her father.

"He's crazy," she bit out instead. "Certifiable. I will not stay here with him."

"Has he hurt you, Emily?" The demand in her father's voice became stronger, firmer.

"No, he hasn't damned well hurt me," she cried out. "But if you don't come collect your bulldog I swear I'm going to hurt him."

Silence again. She hated the silences.

"Daddy, I've never asked you to do this," she suddenly whispered. "I've always let your boys stay. I've always let them follow me around like the guard dogs they were. I'm asking you this one time, please, get someone else."

She hadn't begged her father for anything in years. She had tried to be independent, tried to be self-sufficient and reasonably responsible.

She heard him sigh wearily. "I can't do that, Em. Your life is more important to me than your wants right now. He stays."

Shock raced through her, increasing the shaking in her body, the fear that began to cloud her mind.

"You can't mean that," she whispered.

"If he hasn't hurt you, if you're not scared of him personally, then yes, I do mean it. Now, I'll ask you one more time, has he hurt you? Are you afraid he's going to hurt you?"

He was going to break her heart. He was going to rip her soul from her body.

"I'm sorry I bothered you." How she managed to control the shaking in her voice, she didn't know. But she did. Pride firmed it, chilled it, and drew her upright as she stared at the wall across from her.

"Emily—"

"Goodbye, Daddy." She hung the phone up softly as she blinked back her tears and realized that she never should have called him to begin with.

"Scared, Emily?"

She swung around and there he was. He had opened the door soundlessly and now leaned lazily against the frame, one ankle crossed over the other, one broad forearm leaning against the doorframe.

"Of you?" she asked with a sneer. "Not hardly, Kell. Not ever. Now if you'll excuse me, I need a shower." She began to move around the bed when she saw the panties, crumpled at the end of the bed rather than lying in the middle where she had tossed them.

She picked them up gingerly, stared at them then turned and tossed them to him coldly. And of course, he caught them, with one hand, with no effort.

"You can have them," she stated harshly. "And enjoy them, because it's the closest you'll ever come to that particular part of my body again."

Turning on her heel, she forced herself to move slowly to the bathroom, to enter it and close the door softly before locking it behind her and swallowing her scream of fury.

Kell Krieger wasn't a man that a woman played with. A little light teasing, harmless kisses, or whispers in the dark. He was a male animal in the truest sense of the word and she suddenly felt helpless, like a prey.

What was it she had wished for earlier? A man she couldn't control? A man who didn't whine but took the reins?

She had to have been insane.

KELL STARED AT THE CLOSED bathroom door and let a frown work across his brow. She was scared. He had seen it in her eyes when she ran from him, had heard it in her voice. But it wasn't the fear of a woman who sensed physical

danger, it was the fear of a woman facing something unknown, something uncertain.

He shook his head, his lips tightening at the memory of
her voice when she had begged the senator to take him off
the assignment. The cry of a child to its father, a plea for
understanding, and evidently the senator hadn't bothered to
heed that cry.

The senator had never heeded her cries though. He had
told her to "buck up," he had encouraged her to dry the tears
and work harder. He was proud of her. Confused by her. But
in the end, he did as he wanted, not as Emily needed.

SHAKING HIS HEAD, HE STEPPED back from her doorway,
closing the door gently behind him as his hands clenched
around the silk and lace panties. He had to fight to keep
from bringing the soft material to his face, to restrain himself from drawing the scent of peaches and cream into his
head. If she thought she was getting them back, she was
wrong. But he would see her in them again. And he promised himself he would pull them off with nothing but his
teeth and devour the silky sweet flesh they covered.

As he moved through the living room the cell phone at his
belt rang demandingly to the tune of AC/DC's "Hells Bells."
Grinning, he pulled it from the holder, checked the number
coming through then flipped it open.

"Good evening, Senator," he answered.

"What the hell is going on?" the other man snarled into
the phone. "You haven't been alone with her an hour and she
called me nearly in tears begging for a replacement. What
the hell did you do to her?"

"We're just getting our ground rules established,
Richard," he assured the senator calmly. "She's a little upset
over it."

"Don't try to pull shit over my eyes, son, I'm not a fool."

"No, you're not," Kell answered firmly. "You're a father
answering to your daughter's anger. If you want me off this

assignment I understand that." Like hell. "But as long as I'm on it, then I'll protect her as I see fit."

"Did you hurt her?"

"Do you really need to ask me that question?"

He could hear the silence in the background, he could practically hear the senator's mind churning.

"Emily is an intelligent, cunning woman. We both know that," Kell said then. "She twists her bodyguards around her little finger as easily as she would a ribbon. She's frighteningly brave, as she proved today at the strip club and in the excursions she's dragged her bodyguards into. I won't be conned, twisted, or convinced to let her endanger herself needlessly. It will take us a few days to establish the ground rules, but once we do, she'll settle in fine."

That was his story and he was sticking to it.

The senator remained silent. Kell followed suit. He checked the patio door locks, then the windows, working his way through the house and into the room he had been assigned.

"She's a good girl," the senator finally said softly. "Her feelings are easily hurt. Don't run roughshod over her, Kell. You could hurt her more than any of the others. She's always been infatuated with you."

And strangely enough, the senator had never pushed that infatuation and he had never pushed Kell toward her.

"I don't run over anyone, Richard. I simply convince them of my way."

Senator Stanton grunted at the comment. "If she calls me again, I'll consider her request. Whatever you're doing, fix it."

"You promised no interference," Kell reminded him.

"That was before the woman who's already halfway in love with you called, nearly in tears, begging for something she's never begged for before. Fix it, Krieger, and do it gently. Or we'll have words. And you don't want that."

He would prefer to avoid them, but he could handle it.

"That's your choice, Richard," he finally answered as

politely as he could. "Just let me know when I need to pack and I can be ready to roll. Until then, please refrain from calling to take me to task over your daughter's anger. It's detrimental to the assignment and creates a tension neither of us needs."

"Lieutenant Krieger, you are testing my patience."

"And you should remember how well I excel at testing everyone's patience," he pointed out. "I guess you'll just have to forgive me for it again."

"You better hope I do," he snapped. "Now fix this. And that's a damned order."

The call disconnected as Kell shook his head on a wry smile. Dealing with the father might turn out to be more trouble than dealing with the daughter.

He laid the lacy panties on the dresser by the door, turned to the duffel bags, and began to unpack. The weapons went close to the bed, with the holstered back-up weapon strapped to the top of his lace-up work boots and the legs of his jeans covering it.

The Glock he normally carried on his belt was tucked into the bedside table, the automatic rifle and extra ammo pushed beneath the bed.

Clothes were hung in the closet and pushed into the dresser. Within minutes he was unpacked and staring around the room with a vague sense of discontent.

What was it about Emily Stanton that had always called to him? From the day he'd realized what a beauty she was growing into and how the fire was barely banked within her, she had made him hard. Hard enough to hurt. Hard enough to scare the hell out of him and keep him running in the opposite direction for the past five years. There was something fresh about her, something wild and untamed. But it was restrained. Driven down and simmering beneath the surface as it fought to survive amid the life her father, loving though he was, was trying to force her into. Emily was never going to give her father what he needed from her. Senator Stanton wanted a pretty little dress-up doll who followed his commands and never thought to question them or her own happiness.

The problem as Kell saw it was that the two of them were too much alike. If Emily had been born a man, she would have made a hell of a Navy SEAL. But she hadn't been born a man. She had been born soft and gentle, easy to break and easy to scar.

He knew exactly how easy it was to break something that soft and delicate. Fuentes had already destroyed one woman in Kell's care. He wasn't going to let the drug lord destroy another.

He felt something twist inside him at the thought of his wife, Tansy, and the son he had never known. Tansy hadn't been wild. She had been gentle, ethereal, as though her body knew she would be on this earth for only a short time.

She had made him laugh. She had made him see himself as something other than the heir to the combined Krieger and Beaulaine fortunes though. She had opened his eyes and taught him how to begin maturing when his family would have continued to convince him he was perfection and that everything in his life had to be the same.

He could barely remember her face now. He hadn't dreamed of her in years, and the burning lance of pain had dimmed over the years. He felt regret. Fury at the evil that had taken her away from him and the knowledge that Emily had the power to hold him with a strength that he now knew Tansy never would have.

He had loved Tansy as a boy. If Emily stole the man's heart, then the risk to his soul could be that much greater.

He would never survive losing her.

She was like the little fox he always compared her to. Inquisitive. Stubborn. Sensual.

She was determined. She might not always know what she wanted, but she was working her way there, and Kell intended to become what she wanted. All those wild impulses, all that heated hunger was going to be his.

A man learned young that he couldn't tame the wind, so

instead, he learned to become part of it, to channel it. That was the key to Emily. Channeling all that frustration and pent-up need for adventure. Like a vixen, like the wind, there was no taming her. But he could enjoy her. And that he definitely intended to do.

Six

YOU DIDN'T TELL ME THAT the elusive Kell Krieger was now your lover, why?"

Emily restrained a sigh as she stared across the small patio table at her best friend, Kira Porter, the next day and gauged the suspicion in her eyes.

Heavy suspicion. She wasn't fooling Kira in the least, and she damned sure couldn't tell her the truth.

She had tiptoed around Kell the night before, watching him warily, trying to get an idea of the best way to handle him. She hadn't come up with anything yet. Of course, it would have helped if she actually knew a bit more about him than she did. She knew he wouldn't hurt her. She knew he could be trusted, depended upon. He was a friend to her father, and in the back of her mind she had always known she could call on him if she needed him.

Though she never had.

"He can hear you, Kira," she pointed out with a frown instead. "Keep your voice down."

The other half of that coin was the fact that he didn't know her as well as he thought he did either. She didn't need to give him any added information.

"Emily, the man just pulled you out of your bed, fixed you coffee, and somehow procured cinnamon rolls before you awoke, all without a single kiss or tussle. He's another body-guard, isn't he, and you're just too ashamed to admit you gave in to your daddy again."

"He's not a bodyguard." Emily kept her voice firm and free of frustration with a struggle. "Really, Kira, you're making too much of this. I don't tell you everything."

"When it comes to men you do." Kira snorted. "I've listened to you rant for hours."

"Only when they fail to please me," Emily pointed out with a smile. "Maybe Kell pleases me."

Emily kept the smug smile on her face as she sat back and savored the coffee Kell had made. It was excellent, damn him. And somehow, he had managed to get fresh cinnamon rolls without leaving the house.

"Yeah. Right." Kira propped her chin on her hand, her gray eyes staring across the table mockingly as her shoulder-length black hair fell forward and gave her face an exotic slant.

Kira was quite simply gorgeous. Perfect facial features, pouty lips, seductively tilted eyes, and perfectly arched brows. She considered herself the ultimate seductress with just enough mocking amusement to assure a person that she didn't take it seriously.

But more than one of Emily's bodyguards had fallen half in love with her, while the others had been panting like wolves after a prime slice of meat.

"Yeah, right." Emily nodded, wishing her friend would drop the subject, and much too aware of Kell sitting in the living room just inside the door, pretending to watch CNN.

"So, he relieved you of that nasty virginity problem you had without so much as a love bite? He should be congratu-lated."

Emily choked on her coffee, nearly spewing it in Kira's amused face as she stared back at her friend in horror. Oh God, she was going to kill Kira. She was going to string her up. She was going to lock her front door and never, ever al-low the other woman in her home again. At least, not until Kell Krieger was gone.

She felt mortification sweep through her, burning beneath her cheeks before spreading over the rest of her face.

There wasn't a chance in hell that Kell hadn't heard that one.

"Maybe I prefer my love bites to be hidden, Ms. Porter." His voice sounded behind them, calm, controlled, displeased. "And I never considered Emily's virginity to be a nasty little problem."

Emily propped her hands on the table, covered her face, and felt like sinking into the cement beneath her.

"I do not need you out here." She gritted her teeth as she forced her hands down and turned her head to glare at him.

The corner of his lips kicked up in a grin, his green eyes sweeping over her as though he owned her body and knew every inch of it better than she did herself.

He leaned casually against the doorframe, staring down at her with mocking arrogance and amusement. "We need to go to the grocery store, sugar," he told her as though she didn't already know that. "Those cinnamon rolls only last so long and then I'm going to need food. Takes energy to keep up with you."

Kira snorted. Emily felt like snarling.

"I'll excuse myself then." Kira straightened from the chair, sleek tanned skin revealed by the low-cut camisole top she wore and snug low-rise white shorts.

She looked like a sex goddess rising from a pedestal and deigning to give mere mortals the briefest glimpse of her perfectly flat stomach.

Emily reminded herself that she hated skinny women. Sitting there, still dressed in the loose sleep shirt and cotton leggings she wore in bed, she felt like a frump.

Her hair was barely brushed, she was makeup free, and she felt like she had wrestled her bed all night long. She'd just wrestled the blankets and her own arousal instead.

"Show up a little later tomorrow morning, Kira," Emily asked as she rose from her own chair, determined to ignore her lack of polish and less than glamorous effect in doing so.

"She might be busy," Kell murmured.

"Uh-huh." Kira's snicker wasn't in the least cruel. It was good-natured, but that didn't detract from the disbelief in it. "It always amazes me how Emily manages to draw her bodyguards into whatever scheme she decides to set up." Her gaze went over Kell. "But I have to admit, she did very well this time."

"Go to hell, Kira." It wasn't the first time she had consigned her friend to those fiery depths.

"They're tired of me there." Kira laughed. "I think I'll head out shopping instead. Uncle Big Bucks sent me a gift card for my birthday and I intend to put it to very good use."

Kira's uncle kept her in gift cards, vehicles, and a round of invitations to the best parties. The other woman was the slightest bit spoiled, but good-natured. The problem with Kira was that she never let Emily get away with even the smallest lie. She seemed to see right through her.

Emily followed her friend through the house and watched as she left, giving her a jaunty wave before she turned slowly to Kell as he closed the patio doors.

"This is so not going to work," she snapped. "People know me, Kell. I don't lie worth shit and Daddy knows it. Now you know it. Revise your little game plan and figure out how to fix it."

"I'm getting a little tired of people telling me to fix their problems," he grunted, his gaze brooding as he stared back at her. "Why didn't you tell me before this that you were a virgin?"

She was going to burn to ash she was blushing so much. Emily glared back at him as she ground her molars in frustration.

"Because it's none of your business?" she questioned him sweetly.

"Everything you do is now my business," he informed her. "Get used to it. Now, let's see what we have to do to convince your very suspicious friend that I'm already making a meal of your delightful little body."

Instant melting.

Oh God, she hated instant melting. But she could feel it, feel the heat that slammed instantly into her womb, burning into her pussy then her clit, swelling them, sending moisture to saturate another pair of panties.

His expression instantly became darker, dangerous, sensual.

"You should have given her details," he said then.

"Details?" Emily backed away from him despite the fact that he hadn't moved. "What kind of details did you want me to give her?"

"Do you know where I would lay the perfect love bite?" he asked softly, moving then, pacing closer to her as she felt her breath slam out of her lungs.

"Where?" The question was breathless, filled with an awareness of the sexual animal suddenly pacing ever closer.

She felt stalked. Her virginity was on the endangered species list and the ultimate hunter was now stalking it relentlessly.

It was too sexy.

It was too dangerous.

He stopped in front of her, staring down at her breasts as they rose and fell harshly, her nipples spike hard and pressing against the thin material of the sleep shirt that asked "Am I awake yet?"

"Should I tell you, or show you?"

Show me. Show me.

"Telling me would work fine." She stepped back again, only to come up against the low arm of the couch and the realization that he had very neatly maneuvered her into it.

"I'd rather show you." His head lowered.

Emily whimpered.

She stared into the dark emerald of his eyes, mesmerized, watching as lust, hot and wicked, filled them and she felt herself sinking beneath a wave of sensual, sexual excitement.

The wave became a fury of pleasure a second later. His

lips touched hers, a sipping kiss that had her hands reaching for him, suddenly desperate for more. She couldn't imagine feeling no more than this whisper of ecstasy.

His lips were perfect for kissing. Like rough velvet stroking over hers a second before his tongue licked over her curves and his teeth nipped at the bottom curve.

"Are you going to open for me?" he asked as his hands settled firmly on her hips. "Or do I have to take it?"

Excitement tore a path of destruction along her senses as she flinched beneath the whiplash of sensual heat.

Emily inhaled roughly. "If you have to ask for it, then you don't need it. Do you?"

Mistake!

No sooner had the words left her lips than her senses were screaming. With a hungry growl he took her kiss. His lips slanted over hers, his tongue whispering past them, licking at them, driving her crazy with the need to touch it as she felt him jerk her against him.

The next instant the world was tilted. She found herself stretched above him, one hand dragging one of her thighs over his as the other tangled in her hair and held her to him.

Oh God. She was straddling him. She could feel his cock between her thighs, rubbing against her as his lips and tongue destroyed her mind.

Her hands were buried in his hair, holding him to her, trying to devour him as pleasure became a force she couldn't fight.

She had always fought before. She knew how to fight sexual desire. She knew how to fight attraction to her bodyguards and her father's potential grandchild donors. But she couldn't fight this.

She felt his hand move from her hip, dragging her nightshirt up her body, but she couldn't stop him. She was too busy trying to hold on to that kiss.

Lips that eased back and forced her to follow. That slanted over hers and dragged a hungry cry from her throat. Lips she couldn't stand the thought of never kissing again.

His kiss was a firestorm, burning away objections and suspicions and leaving her adrift within the most pleasure she could have ever imagined.

She had never known pleasure this good. This hot. This dominating despite the fact that she was on top. Wasn't she supposed to be in control?

"There, sugar," he whispered against her lips as he drew back again, forcing her to open her eyes as she nipped back at his lips in retaliation.

"Don't stop. Please, Kell . . ." Oh hell, she was going to beg.

His lips dipped from hers, his tongue trailing over her jaw, before his cheek scraped against her neck. Emily couldn't stop the shudder of reaction. The rasp of a newly growing beard sent a hard tremor racing through her as pleasure swamped her.

It was so good. So good, she moved her head, turning her neck into his cheek to feel it closer, rougher.

"Like that?" he whispered as his hands moved beneath her shirt, his fingers callused and hot on her back as his teeth suddenly scraped over her neck.

Like it? No, she didn't like it. It was destroying her, stealing her strength and her common sense and leaving her weak beneath his touch.

"Yes," she panted.

"Like this?" He stretched beneath her then, his hips rolling and lifting, grinding the hard ridge of his cock deeper between her thighs as fireworks ricocheted in her mind and exquisite sensation sent her reeling.

Her hands gripped his hair tighter as she fought to hold on to control. Hell, right now, she just wanted to stay conscious as his lips turned into hers again, and his hands moved, lowered and pushed beneath the snug leggings and the lacy band of her panties to cup the cheeks of her rear and squeeze.

She was a goner.

"Oh shit! Boy, was I wrong!"

Kell jackknifed beneath Emily, gripping her and jerking her to his side away from the door as his gaze sliced to the woman standing in the open doorway.

He had expected this. Before joining Emily and Kira on the patio he had contacted Ian and had him watching the front door, just on the off chance that it wasn't Kira who decided to breach the unlocked portal later.

The other woman was staring at them in shock, her gray eyes wide and filled with startled amusement and a hint of mocking acknowledgment.

"God, I didn't lock the door," Emily muttered beside him, fighting to straighten her clothes as Kell rose to his feet.

"Did you forget how to knock, Ms. Porter?" he asked her lazily, noticing the understanding that filled her eyes when she recognized the tone in his voice.

"I never knock unless the door is locked." Kira waved the question away. "Emily always leaves the door unlocked for me."

Kell turned to stare down at Emily.

"I was a bit distracted if you'll recall," she muttered, the blush on her cheeks frighteningly endearing as he gazed at her.

He turned back to Kira. "The doors will be locked for now on," he informed her. "Did you forget something?"

She cocked a hip, propped her hand on it, and watched him coolly. "Nothing in particular. I just wanted to see if Emily wanted to do a little shopping later."

"She'll be with me," he answered for Emily as she rose from the couch behind him.

"He needs to go grocery shopping," Emily snapped as she obviously regained control of herself. "Maybe some other time, Kira."

"Grocery shopping." Kira's gaze raked over him. "Well, honey, one thing about it, I don't think you have to worry about buying beef while you're out. It looks like you have plenty in residence as it is." She fought down her laughter as she waggled her fingers at them then turned and left, closing the door behind her.

Kell moved to the door, locked it carefully, then turned back to Emily.

"Lock the doors from now on," he ordered.

"Of course." She breathed in roughly then, staring around the room for long seconds before coming back to him. "That can't happen again."

"What can't happen again?" he asked her suspiciously.

"On that couch." Her hand fluttered to the furniture. "It can't happen again."

"Fine. We'll go straight to the bed the next time." There wasn't a doubt in his mind now exactly where this was leading.

A frown snapped between her brows.

"I mean it can't happen again at all," she snapped. "Ever."

Not even in his worst nightmare would it never happen again. Kell stared back at her, remembering the heat of her pussy through two layers of clothes, the hunger in her searching lips and how her hips had moved, grinding onto his cock with an inborn sensuality that still had him gritting his teeth in hunger.

"You're fooling yourself, Emily," he said softly. "I didn't take you for a woman who denied the obvious. It's going to happen again. And often. Don't doubt that."

She licked her lips; the pouty curves were swollen from his kiss, but restrained. Tight with the effort it cost her to control the need rising inside her.

"I won't let myself have you, Kell. Don't fool yourself. That." She waved to the couch again. "That was a temporary lapse in judgment. Nothing more."

"Why won't you let yourself, sugar?" he asked her gently, seeing the shadows in her eyes, the sharp pain that seeped into the blue depths.

Her lips twisted cynically. "I already have a father who feels the need to control me, Kell. I don't need a lover doing the same thing. And I sure as hell don't intend to hand my father the son-in-law he's dreamed of by giving him the opportunity to force you into a marriage neither of us wants. So give it up. Find someone to babysit and go out and get your piece before coming back to work. Just like the others did. Don't worry, I won't tell on you. Unlike my bodyguards, I know how to keep my damned mouth shut."

Hell, it was no wonder she hadn't let any of those morons her father hired touch her. Not that he completely blamed the bodyguards, living in the same house with her, knowing she wanted nothing to do with them, that would suck. They would have to find relief somewhere.

"And what did you do, Emily?" he asked her then. "When you needed to be touched? Held?"

"Why, Kell, I just reminded myself of the price." She sneered. "My freedom. Once I put it all in perspective, it was really quite easy. I've lost enough independence since I reached the age where my father could safely marry me off. I'd really rather not lose any more if it's all the same to you."

"And how would you lose that independence with me, Emily?"

Bleak acceptance filled her gaze at that point.

"I'm not on birth control, Kell. I can't take it. The pill, the shot, the IUD, the inserts. I've tried them all. My body rejects them all. That leaves a condom. Condoms break. Babies are made, and once they are, if you don't marry me my father will destroy you. Careerwise, lifewise, personally, and professionally. And I won't marry you. Because I know the type of man you are."

"Do you?"

Her laughter was mocking. "Your wife will stay at home, have your babies, and toe the line while you're gone. You'll play your war games with your buddies, watch ballgames with them when they're home, and screw your wife when you have nothing better to do. Thank you, but no thank you. Being a virgin for life sounds a hell of a lot sweeter than marrying a big, tough, Alpha asshole with more damned testosterone than common sense when it comes to his wife."

Kell listened to her voice rise with each sentence. When she finished, her teeth snapped together, her lips compressed, and she turned her back as her fingers raked furiously through her hair.

"Is that what your father did?"

Her laughter was bitter now. "Mom was leaving him when she was killed. Because he loved her too much, she said. I didn't understand that. Daddy loved us. What was there to hate about that?" She shook her head as Kell felt the helplessness that flowed from her. "After she died, he was devoted to me. He taught me how to fight, how to hunt and track, and he was teaching me to mountain climb. Then I turned eighteen."

"And he decided to marry you off," Kell finished.

She turned back to him. "As you well know. Hell, you've been around long enough to know about the fights we've had over it."

"So why didn't you sleep with one of the boys from college? Hell, I think I would have halfway understood if you picked a married man. Why stay a virgin, Emily?"

Her expression sobered. There was no mockery, no cynicism. "Because it wouldn't be enough," she whispered sadly. "You miss what you've had worse than you miss what you haven't. I don't want to miss more than I already do."

"Why, Emily?" he ground out again. "If you've gone to these extremes to keep your father from winning, despite your love for him, then why give up? Why not live as you want to and tell him to go to hell?"

"Because he didn't tell me to go to hell," she whispered miserably. "I can't hurt my father like that, Kell. I love him too much."

"It seems to me, Emily, that he doesn't care to hurt you or to use that too developed sense of responsibility you have against you," he pointed out. "What you're forgetting, though, is the fact that you have a responsibility to yourself as well. Now, I will end up in a bed with you. I'll protect you as best I can, but if the rubber breaks and you end up pregnant, your father won't have to threaten me to take care of my child or my woman. I'm not a kid anymore. I know how it's done now. I guess it's just up to you to decide if you're going to take what you want, or if you're going to stay daddy's little girl forever."

Seven

H E WAS GOING TO END up falling in love with her.

Kell accepted the truth about the time they were going through the produce department and he caught Emily eyeing the cucumbers just a little too intently before trying to sneak a glance at his thighs.

Comparing size. The little vixen was trying to figure out dimensions by comparing the bulge with the cucumbers.

He covered his grin before choosing two of the cylindrical vegetables and putting them in the cart. Then he chose the rest of the salad fixings before heading for the fruit.

"Any preferences?" he asked as she paused next to him, her face still flushed.

"Watermelon." She eyed one with particular interest.

Kell let his lashes drift over his eyes as he stared at it himself. He knew how to eat watermelon. At least, how he intended to eat it with her. He put it in the cart before moving her to the fresh meat section.

She let him choose, watching the cart warily before they headed to the canned foods and flour and sugar section. By the time he pushed the cart to the check-out stand he could see the worry in her face.

"I can't pay for all this," she finally muttered as he threw a handful of chocolate bars into the cart. "I'm a school-teacher. We don't make big bucks here."

He frowned down at her. "The groceries go on my card and are turned in to the expense account. It'll be handled by your father at the end of the month."

"Boy, are you in for a surprise then." She sighed. "Just give me the bill after you pay for it. I'll get some money out of the ATM. I know I don't have enough cash and I didn't bring the credit card."

She was chewing at her lower lip as she stared at the food. "You eat a lot."

He pushed the cart into the check-out bay and moved ahead as the cashier dropped the back bar and began pulling items toward her across the scanner.

Surely she hadn't been paying for her bodyguards' food?

"Hi, Miss Stanton." The cashier flashed Emily a smile that gleamed with braces. "Are you having a good summer?" She slid a sidelong look at Kell.

"It's quiet, Kimmy," Emily answered. "How's your brother enjoying his vacation?"

"He's doing great. Mom told me to tell you thanks for the tutoring you did after school let out. Mark's doing a lot better in reading now. He should be good to go to the first grade."

Emily nodded with a small smile. "He's a smart kid. He just needed some extra help."

"Well, he's taking to reading, I know that." The girl laughed as she scanned the items quickly while talking. "I took him to the library the other day and loaded him up. Is this your new bodyguard?" She nodded to Kell.

Emily's shoulders slumped with resignation. "No, Kimmy, this is my, umm, friend." She cleared her throat as Kimmy paused with the scanning.

She blinked at Emily, then turned and stared at Kell in amazement. She flushed when he winked slowly and grinned back at her.

"Wow," she breathed out in obvious admiration. "Miss Stanton, that is so righteous. And he's drop dead, ya know? Does he have any brothers?"

"Let's hope not," she muttered, barely loud enough for Kell to hear before forcing a smile and answering the girl with a quick "no."

"Too bad." Kimmy sneaked another look in his direction. "Really and truly drop dead, Miss Stanton."

"Thanks, Kimmy," she said as the final sale rang up.

Kell felt an edge of anger as her face paled just slightly at the cost. Pulling out his billfold, he handed the girl his credit card, but he wanted to hit something instead. It was more than obvious she had been paying for the food her house-guests consumed. And men, being men, especially the men Kell knew Stanton had hired, ate a lot.

"This one pays too." Kimmy looked back at him with new respect. "I'd keep him for a while if I were you, Miss Stanton."

Emily said nothing but as Kimmy handed the receipt toward him she reached for it. Kell beat her, smiling in triumph as he dangled the receipt out of her reach.

"There you go, show her how a real man takes care of her." Kimmy at least seemed to be enjoying it.

"I'm trying, Kimmy." He winked again. "She's stubborn though."

"Yeah, she's pretty tough." Kimmy nodded. "But she's killer cool, man. Don't forget that."

"Kell. Kell Krieger." He reached his hand out to her, watched her blush prettily and accept the handshake.

"Kimberly Aikens," she squeaked. "And you are so drop dead." She sighed with teenage hormones and obvious pleasure.

"So are you," he said, chuckling as the bag boy sliced him a glare and Emily frowned back at him with disapproval. "Goodbye, Kimmy."

"Goodbye," she breathed out wistfully. "And please be sure to come back soon."

He lifted his hand in farewell as Emily shot him another disgruntled glance.

"Stop flirting with the check-out girls," she hissed. "It's disgraceful."

"You won't flirt with me." He grinned. "It's an ego boost."

"You are so wrong," she snapped out. "And I want that receipt."

"Forget it."

"Now."

He paused by the Trailblazer. "It will cost you," he murmured as he pulled her keys from his jeans pocket and smiled down at her in satisfaction. "Are you sure you want to pay?"

"You're fired!" she snapped.

Kell pushed the unlatch button and glanced at the bag boy as he began loading the back. He leaned down, watching her eyes as he let his lips touch her ear.

"Coward," he breathed softly against her ear.

Emily jerked back, staring at him as her teeth ground together in obvious annoyance. She was working her way toward a full-fledged temper tantrum that would beat the hell out of the helplessness he saw in her earlier. She was like a caged bird. The bars were made of love, guilt, and responsibility. She felt responsible for her mother leaving, for her death, and for her father's worry.

There was a woman inside her, filled with strength and life, clawing her way toward freedom with no idea which direction to take.

"I'm not a coward," she choked out.

"Prove it, Emily," he dared her as his head lifted and he moved her back from the Trailblazer enough to allow her to lift herself to the seat. "Prove it to both of us."

He closed the door before she could argue and moved to where the carry-out boy had finished loading the groceries. He was a kid in a man's body, all arms and legs and unfamiliar muscles growing in his lanky body. Hazel eyes glared at Kell in dislike as a surprisingly firm mouth flattened in anger.

"Pouting won't get you what you want," he told the boy, aching at the realization that when he had been this kid's age he had already lost a wife and child. He had already known the horror of being disowned, only to face his parents' offer to reinstate him in the family now that the trash he had married had been taken care of.

"What do you mean?" the youth snapped.

Kell stared down at him, silently showing his strength in the look in his eyes, on his face. The boy's gaze jumped to the side.

"Be a man, son," he growled. "If you don't know how, then learn how. And don't blame your girlfriend for being impressed. I'm a man, not a kid."

The boy glared back, but Kell could see the kid's mind turning, and sometimes that was all it took.

"That's your tip for the day," he informed him. "Because you beat the cart over every speed bump on the way over here. Think about it. Better yet, practice it."

He moved around the Trailblazer then, opened the driver's door, and stepped into the vehicle.

"You didn't check for a bomb," were the first words out of her mouth. "If I'm in danger, then how do you know Fuentes didn't rig the Trailblazer and it's going to blow up the minute you start the engine?"

He laid his arms over the steering wheel and stared back at her in disbelief.

"You watch too much television or read too many books. I haven't decided which yet."

She sniffed disdainfully. "My father was a Navy SEAL. Or did you forget?"

"It would be damned hard to forget that one," he assured her, smiling as he turned the key and the only thing that ignited was the motor.

She stared back at him balefully before turning her head and looking around the parking lot.

"Where's your backup?"

A grin tilted his lips. She was quick as hell, and he liked that about her.

"We have two Secret Service agents following us." He didn't mention Ian. The Secret Service was good, but Kell didn't trust anyone outside his group worth squat.

"Dad always said you should check things for yourself," she stated.

"I didn't see you lying on the ground and checking the undercarriage."

Her shoulders lifted dismissively. "I've had a bit of trouble figuring out exactly how to recognize a problem. But I'm working on it."

His eyes narrowed as he glanced over at her. "You're trying to figure out how to tell if a vehicle has been wired?"

"Seemed like a good hobby." She crossed her arms over her breasts. "I'm all about learning things. Research, you know."

Lust slammed into his gut. Research. He would never hear that word again without remembering her sinuous little body straddling his lap and the sight of her panties dampening in need.

"Yeah, research." He could feel the sweat popping out on his brow now. "We need to do something about that hobby of yours, Emily."

She breathed out deeply. "So I keep hearing, Kell. So I keep hearing."

THE GROCERIES WERE PUT AWAY, and there wasn't a spare inch of space left in her refrigerator or her cabinets by time they finished.

So much for her diet. The extra pounds she had been fighting with since she was a teenager were just doomed to stay in place.

They had stopped for lunch, a nice little Italian place with loads of calories, sinfully rich desserts, and a wine so smooth and delicious she had to force herself not to buy a bottle.

She was going to have a hard enough time paying for the groceries.

Maybe she should let go of her pride in this instance and tell her father to reimburse her for the eating machine she now had living in her house. The good senator owed her that much at least. The problem was, she hated asking him for money. Hated it.

For a while, he had deposited money in her account to take care of the eating needs of his goons, but the last argument they'd had over the amount he was depositing had resulted in him depositing nothing at all. And she had been too stubborn to do anything about it.

Now, she was stuck with the object of every sexual fantasy she had ever known, and she would be damned if she knew what to do with him. She knew what she wanted to do, she wanted to lick every inch of his body. She wanted to drape herself over him and become a part of his damned skin.

And that was just so wrong. Because no man should be that damned sexy, so rough and ready that she was creaming her panties just looking at him.

AFTER THE LAST OF THE groceries were in place Emily moved around the house, staring at the closed curtains, the locked windows, and tried to fight the arousal building inside her.

Hell, she had already come in his face. It wasn't like pretending he was a favorite treat that needed to be licked was going to hurt her good "virgin" standing.

"I can take care of cooking if you don't like to cook."

She turned around quickly, staring across the room at him as he moved from the pantry and the small chest freezer stored back there.

His jeans rode low on his hips, a wide leather belt cinching it. Long muscular legs encased in denim drew her eyes, and the bulge between them made her mouth water before she jerked her gaze up to his amused green eyes.

"I don't mind cooking." She pushed her hands into the pockets of her Capris as she watched him move through the kitchen.

Muscles rippled in his arms and chest, emphasized by the snug fit of the T-shirt and the jeans that had seen one washing too many. They cupped his butt and his crotch like loving hands. The way she wanted to cup them.

She whirled away and stalked toward the patio doors only to turn back when she realized they were locked. She was in danger. She couldn't just stalk outside because she was in a snit.

She closed her eyes as something whispered through her mind. A shadow of a memory, perhaps? A voice she knew she should remember from that time Fuentes had held her in captivity.

"Do you think you can catch him?" she asked. "Fuentes, that is?"

"We'll catch him." Supreme confidence filled his expression and glittered in his cat's eyes as he watched her. "Him and his spy."

"Dad didn't tell me much about the spy."

"Fuentes has a spy, very high up in the government, that's supplying him with information. If we catch the spy, Fuentes will tip his hat in a game well played and leave you and your father alone."

"He will?" she asked suspiciously. "Now, why do I have trouble believing that? That was what he was supposed to have done when you and your team rescued us after the kidnapping."

Of the three of them, Emily had fared the best. One of the girls, the youngest, was still in a near-catatonic state from the drugs she had been given. The other, Senator Bridgeport's daughter, had died within days.

"Extenuating circumstances. Our information suggests that Fuentes's spy demanded this hit." Kell opened the freezer and pulled free the beer he had slid in there earlier. "All we have to do is keep you and your father safe until the rest of the team tracks down the spy, then you'll be okay."

"I don't remember you being there." She rubbed at her forehead, frowning as she tried to delve into the dark space in her mind where those memories lay. "I should have remembered you being there."

He twisted the cap off the beer and tossed it to the trash with a tight flip of his fingers as his lips flattened angrily.

"You were drugged, Emily. Whore's Dust affects the memory. It was designed to do that."

"It makes the victim beg for sex." She tightened her fists in her pockets as she faced him. "Did I beg you for sex, Kell?"

He stared back at her with level, calm eyes.

"Did anyone else see me?" she whispered worriedly. "Did I embarrass you?" Or herself.

His head shook once as a wry smile tugged at his lips. "You didn't embarrass me, Em. And you didn't beg me for sex. Didn't your dad tell you what I had in my report?"

He hadn't.

"He just said that I was brave." She shrugged helplessly. "I've wondered what he meant by that."

"Exactly what he said," Kell told her softly, his gaze softening with approval. "You were very brave. You gathered the other girls together where I told you to, and you trusted me to get you out of there. You let me do my job."

A swell of pride infused her. He wasn't lying to her. She could see it in his eyes. For the first time in two years something inside her loosened, relaxed.

"Thank you." She cleared her throat uneasily then, suddenly uncertain amid the tension thickening in the room. "I couldn't ask Dad—"

He nodded quickly before lifting the beer and taking a slow drink, as though he needed something to distract himself with.

"Richard should have given you my report," he said as he lowered the beer.

She crossed her arms over her breasts, hugging herself against the chill that seemed to invade her at the realization that her father held back much more from her than she had realized.

"I told Dad, when he accepted that position on the oversight committee, that it wasn't going to be safe for either of us."

"What did he say?"

"That he would protect me." Emily rolled her eyes.

"And he's making sure you're protected," he said softly, his expression too intent, his gaze too probing as he brought the beer to his lips again and drank.

It was sexy, watching his lips pull the liquid from the glass bottle, the way his tongue flicked over his lower lip when he was finished.

He hadn't shaved that morning, so his cheeks were still covered with the overnight growth of beard. It gave him a rakish, piratical look that made him seem darker and more dangerous than ever before. Sexier. More primal.

"Oh yes." Her lips twisted mockingly. "He's making certain I'm protected." She crossed her arms over her breasts now. "Tell me, Kell, what are you going to do if you end up in my bed and Daddy finds out? When he pulls you aside and gives you the rules to this little game. You'll marry his daughter, and keep her out of trouble, or your career and all your dreams are shot to hell."

"Won't happen. He just lets you think it will happen."

Her eyes widened in amazement. "I thought you knew my father better than that, Kell? You evidently have no clue how bad he wants me married and knocked up."

"Oh, I can safely say I know your father's plans as well as anyone." He grinned mockingly. "But I know how to be careful, Emily."

"You're just like him." She could see the same arrogance, the same determination stamped on his features that she often saw on her father's. "So certain you're right and that you can have what you want the way you want it. I'm not a prize, Kell, and I'm not a plaything to relieve your boredom."

His smile was blatant male confidence and sexual intent.

"No, you're a habitual virgin who's too frightened to take what you want." He lifted the beer, drank again, and his eyes gleamed with amused certainty.

"Are you insane?"

"I'm horny." He shrugged. "So hard for a taste of that sweetness you were rubbing in my face at that strip club, I can barely walk for it."

"So that makes it okay?"

"That makes it more than okay, sugar. That's going to make it a certainty. Because I might be harder than hell, but right now, I bet you dollars to doughnuts your panties are wet again. Shall we put it to the test?"

He was insane. He was crazy. He was the most impossibly confident man she had ever laid her eyes on. He was totally unlike the bodyguards. He didn't bother to hide his lust and he didn't give a damn what anyone thought of it.

Her gaze raked over his tall, muscular body. She paused at his thighs, seeing the length of his erection beneath his jeans. The impressive bulge was a temptation in and of itself.

"You think you can handle me." She smiled slowly. "I can see it in your face. You think all you have to do is get me addicted to your touch, to touching you, and everything else will be a piece of cake."

His lips quirked in response.

"You are so deluded." She dropped her arms and moved closer, watching his eyes narrow as she brushed against him, stopping a breath from his hard chest as she let one hand drift across his tight abs.

"Am I?"

"You are." Her fingers brushed over his belt before she began to slowly loosen it. "I could become addicted, Kell. So easily." His eyes narrowed as the belt came undone and her fingers tugged at the metal button holding his jeans. "I could do all the things I've researched, hungered for, dreamed about." The second button came undone. "I could go crazy with you in my bed." The third button, the fourth.

His jeans parted beneath her fingers, revealing the snug white briefs he wore and the heavy ridge of flesh beneath.

"Teasing, sugar?" he dared her. His voice. His eyes. They sent out a challenge she couldn't resist.

Carefully she eased the material of his briefs over the hard flesh, catching her breath on a silent moan as the thick, heavy wedge of flesh was revealed. Dark, pulsing with blood and strength, the head engorged, flushed nearly purple with arousal and heat as a creamy drop of semen beaded at the flushed crest.

"I don't tease," she whispered.

She had known what she wanted as she came to him, and she had been certain he wouldn't allow it. That he would steal control, that he would take her as he wanted, not as she wanted.

But he stood still, his body growing more tense by the second.

Emily could feel the hunger rising inside her now, beating at her brain, searing through her bloodstream. Her mouth watered with the need to taste him, to put to action all the research she had done on going down on a man.

"Take your shirt off." She meant to whisper the words, she hadn't meant to make it a command.

But the shirt came off. Slowly. Too slowly. Revealing tighter than tight abs, a rippling chest, and powerful arms.

She had to touch him. She didn't have a choice. Bronzed flesh filled her vision as her hands, pale against his skin, pressed against his stomach and eased upward, scraping over the sprinkling of black hair that bisected it. Feeling the rush of heat from his flesh, the pounding of his heart. The prickle of the small hairs against her palms was electric.

"How long since you've touched a man, Emily?" he asked her then. "Since you've let your senses be captured?"

She shook her head slowly, dazed, mesmerized by the pleasure building in her palms and rushing through her body.

"Too long." She could barely breathe, could barely remember. "So long."

Her fingers curled against his chest as her head lowered. She wanted to taste him. Her tongue touched flesh and he jerked beneath the caress. But he didn't touch her. He didn't hold her. He didn't force her to do what he wanted.

The taste of his flesh exploded through her senses. Dark, male, clean. There was nothing artificial. Just stark earthy male. Slightly salty. A hint of musk. Addictive. So addictive she let her teeth grip the flesh over his breastbone as she licked again.

"I just want to touch," she moaned, shaking now with the power that seemed to whip around her. "Just once. Just this time." She was out of control. Her lips smoothed over his chest, her tongue licked, her teeth scraped, and her senses became drugged, dazed, weakened by the incredible freedom she could feel moving through her. "I've dreamed of touching you, Kell. For so long."

"Touch, sugar." His voice was a breath of sound, a dreamy rasp over her senses that urged, encouraged, that gave her license to do as she needed. As she dreamed. "You can touch me all you want to."

Freedom. It surged through her, arcing through her body and mind until nothing mattered, nothing made sense but the taste of him. The feel of him. The wicked, liberating sense of holding the reins on this powerful sexual beast.

Eight

WHEN A MAN SET OUT to tame a vixen, he didn't grab her. He didn't manhandle her. That was a surefire way to lose a finger. And the vixen. She was cunning, she was wily, and she was as free as the wind. But she loved touching. She was affectionate and playful, tempting and teasing, but she wanted to be caressed and held.

The man who was determined to capture a vixen learned patience early. He learned control. And he learned to let the vixen set the rules. At first.

Kell's fingers tightened on the side of the bar as Emily's hot little tongue licked over his chest. The pleasure was exquisite. Heated little electric shocks raced over his flesh and drew his muscles tight. Staring down at her, he became absorbed in the small glimpses of her expression, the slow, steady immersion of her senses into the freedom of touch he was giving her.

He was out to trap a vixen. To seduce her. To stroke her. To control her. And it seemed he had found the perfect bait. Something she had never had before, a treat particular to the heated woman smoothing her hands over his flesh, her tongue licking, tasting. The illusion of control.

It was going to be torture. The torture of feeling a pleasure so extreme, so liquid hot, it was all he could do to keep his hands to himself, to keep from trapping the vixen in his grip.

But some things were far better for the wait.

"Kiss me, Kell." She lifted her head, staring up at him with sparkling blue eyes, hunger flaming in their depths as his head lowered. "I've dreamed of you kissing me."

"You kiss me," he suggested in a dare. "Show me what you have, sugar."

He let his lips touch hers, and expected hesitancy. He didn't expect her teeth to nip at his lower lip before drawing it between hers, her hot little tongue stroking over it like a lick of fire.

She smiled at the involuntary groan that came from his chest. Slender fingers moved up his arm to his nape, then into his hair. They tangled in the long strands and tugged him to her, her lips settling against his, first in a whisper of need, then with fiery demand.

Her tongue was silken and damp, stroking against his as she lifted against him, her beaded nipples pressing through her bra and shirt and burning into his chest.

He was dying to touch her. His hands itched to touch her. But he kept one on the counter, the other at his side. And he thought of the vixen and his need to hold her.

"Emily." He whispered her name gently as her lips moved from his, then to his neck and to his chest once again. He began to move, easing slowly to the couch.

"Stay. Don't go." Her hand gripped his waist as he continued to ease back.

"Let me sit down, sugar," he crooned, seeing the effect of his voice on her senses. Her expression lost its look of worry, sensuality taking over again as they reached the couch. "Just let me ease back here, and you can have whatever you want."

If he didn't sit down, lie down, find some way to get off his feet, then once her mouth completed its southward path he'd collapse on the floor. Damn her, she was making his knees weak. She was making his cock harder than ever.

She followed as he sat down gingerly then slowly eased back to the pillow at the arm. Her knee was on the cushion beside him, the other between his thighs. Her mouth was blazing a conflagration to his abs as her slender fingers moved past the material of his jeans and briefs and touched the sensitive shaft of his cock.

His hips jerked, arched. Fingers fisted over his head as he gritted his teeth against the need to grab her, to roll her beneath him and tear the clothes from her body.

"Emily." Her name ground from between his teeth.

"Just a minute," she whispered breathlessly. "I know how to do this. I do. I read about it. I know how."

Ah shit. Her voice was lost, so filled with excitement it shook from her lips as her fingers attempted to wrap around his erection.

"Sugar, there's more to this," he ground out.

"I have movies," she assured him. "And books. I know how to do this."

Her research was going to kill him.

Her mouth surrounded the engorged head, her tongue tucked against the ultrasensitive flesh beneath the head, and she began to suck.

"Sweet God, have mercy!" His body jerked as though a whip had been laid to his balls.

Pleasure tore through him. It wasn't insipid, it wasn't a slow burn. It was hard, searing, it tore across his nerve endings as he bared his teeth in painful pleasure and growled in ravening hunger.

And he watched her. Watched the initial hesitation, felt it in the movement of her lips until she found the exact position she was looking for to tear his soul from his body.

Auburn curls fell like flames to caress his thighs as she began to move her mouth over his cock. Taking as much as she could hold, sucking deeply, her tongue flaying too sensitive flesh as her mouth tightened and worked over the thick cock head and sucking it against the roof of her mouth.

Oh God. Her fucking research was going to drive him

insane. What the hell was he thinking? His fingers uncurled, his arms lifted; the only thought in his mind was to grab her hair and to force her mouth to move as he wanted.

Then she moaned. A sound of sheer pleasure, of wild temptation. Kell forced his hands back, tried to breathe through the pleasure and felt the sweat running down his brow.

He was crazy. He hadn't tried to tame a vixen since he was a teenager and he hadn't managed it successfully then. What the hell made him think he could do it now? Especially this particular vixen.

But he would never forget her face, her expression, at this moment, for as long as he lived. Her lashes drifted over her eyes, showing only a glimmer of her dark blue gaze. A flush darkened her cheeks and her cupid's-bow lips were stretched wide over his engorged cock as her slender fingers wrapped around the stalk.

It wasn't his first blow job, but he'd be damned if it wasn't the sexiest one he'd ever had. Her lips moved up and down the throbbing head, her fingers stroked the shaft, her tongue licked and tasted, and he swore she was stealing his soul with the delicate greed of her sucking mouth.

"Ah sugar." He winced at the thickening of the Cajun accent he thought he'd defeated years ago. "Your mouth is perfect. So sweet and hot."

Her passionate little whimper vibrated on his flesh, causing him to stretch, to thrust against her lips. Hell, holding back was killing him. He could feel the need for release tightening his balls and tingling up his spine.

"So greedy," he growled as her tongue licked over the small slit, probed and drew a pulse of semen that slipped past his control. "There you go. Suck me like you mean it, sugar."

His fingers were digging into the couch cushion, his teeth bared in a grimace as he fought the pleasure. Just another minute, he swore. One more minute.

The soft suckling sounds pierced his head as she drew

him deeper into her mouth. Slowly, oh hell, so slowly, drew him to her throat. Paused and released him. Drew him back again, released. Drew and swallowed, the reflex motion tightening and caressing the head of his cock in a move that had him snarling, pulling his hips down, trying to force her to release him.

The pressure eased, but for a second only. It returned as he watched moisture seep from the corner of her eyes at the effort it took to hold him there, to swallow and retreat.

"Emily." He growled her name fiercely, staring down at her in desperation as her lashes lifted and he glimpsed the incredible pleasure that filled them. "Stop, vixen. Enough."

She bore down again as he nearly jackknifed into a sitting position only to have her hand press imperatively against his abs.

"Do you know what's coming?" he snarled, shaking the sweat from his eyes as he glared down at her. "I'll fill your mouth, sugar. Ease up. You don't want that this first time."

A virgin. Sweet Lord, have mercy, a virgin vixen was destroying his control. Stealing it. Her eyes gleamed with satisfaction and her mouth sank on his cock again, took him deep and swallowed.

Kell flung his head back, his hands jerking from the cushions to her hair, tangling in the strands, holding her still, and filled her mouth. He felt the hard, violent ejaculations spurting in hard jets as pleasure, ecstasy, ripped through his body and drew it achingly tight. Every bone and muscle tautened as a harsh groan tore repeatedly from his chest.

It was rapture. It was like nothing he had known. She could give lessons in blow jobs. She could destroy a man with that mouth, and she was destroying him as she consumed every drop of passion pouring from him.

"Come to me," he grated out as she eased up, one last lingering lick of her tongue to his cock as her head began to lift.

His hands were still tangled in her hair as the sight of her rosy lips, damp and gleaming with moisture, seared into his brain.

"Kell." Her voice filled with aching need as he drew her up his body, pulling her to him.

"Come to my mouth, Emily," he ordered roughly. "Come, sugar. Right up here. Let me taste that sweet pussy. Let me show you what you gave me."

She was shaking, shuddering against him, as he drew her to him. She was still wearing her clothes. No way in hell was he giving her time to think as he removed them. As she moved above him, his hands eased her knees onto the cushions and he dragged his body lower. Until his lips were poised beneath her, his fingers gripping the material of the soft cotton Capris on each side of the seam and pulling.

It parted, the sound of rending cloth bringing a gasp from her lips and a warning tension to her body. A tension Kell didn't allow to last for long. As the material parted, his lips were there. His teeth caught the edge of the triangle of silk covering her, pulling it to the side and then catching it with the fingers of one hand.

Then his tongue was free to touch her. Free to slide through the juicy slit, to taste ambrosia, the nectar of the gods, a heated, sweet syrup he knew would be his downfall.

Emily knew she had made a grave mistake. A tactical error, and she couldn't stop. She was lost. The minute she heard the material of her Capris tearing, she knew nothing could stop this. Definitely not her. She couldn't stop anything, she was too lost in that first lick through the folds of her sex and too desperate for more.

Then he kissed her. He covered the lips of her pussy with his lips, and gave her a kiss that nearly destroyed her.

The rasp of his short growth of beard sizzled across her flesh. The slightly rough rasp of his tongue, the flickering flames of sensation that crashed through her womb, drew her body tight.

"Oh God. Kell. Kell." Her head was swimming as his lips placed light, sucking kisses around her clit, over it, then down, drawing the swollen folds of her pussy between his lips and kissing them with heated fervor.

Lightning crashed inside her body, her mind. Brilliant pinpoints of light clashed and exploded behind her closed eyelids as she began to shake.

"Kell—so good. So good."

He licked again, painting the entrance to the tormented channel with heated licks and fiery sensation. Dazed pleasure filled her, the world narrowed itself to nothing but Kell's touch, to his mouth, his tongue. To the incredible sensations racing through her with a speed that had her gasping for breath.

She was racing toward something. Something she had only read about, only dreamed about. Something she had never believed she would experience.

Panting for breath, she tried to move her hips against his tongue, tried to reach the pinnacle of pleasure she could feel waiting for her. But Kell's hands were firm now, demanding. They gripped her hips and held her in place, restraining her above him as he drove her rapidly insane with each kiss, each lick.

One hand clenched in his hair, the other in the back cushion of the couch, as she titled her head back, forcing her eyes open. He chose that moment to press his tongue inside her.

One hard thrust, a rapid lick and another thrust, and Emily was screaming. It was too much. Flames tore through her body as she felt something tear free in her soul. Sensation and emotion wrapped around her, strung her tight, then shot her rapidly through an ecstasy so intense, so violent, that every muscle in her body began to tremble in response.

It was so good. Too good. It brought tears to her eyes as her wailing cries echoed around her. And he didn't stop. He licked and groaned against her flesh, continuing to consume the soft flow of her release as she wilted over him, too weak, too confused by the dazed pleasure, to hold herself up any longer.

"There, sweet sugar," he crooned as he lifted her, supporting her weight as he rose, letting her slide down his chest as his arms wrapped around her.

Emily whimpered as she found herself lying back on the couch, Kell rising between her thighs as he ripped the remainder of her pants from her body.

"I'll buy you more," he promised as he tossed the scraps of material to the floor. "I need to see you. Naked and wild beneath me."

His hands gripped the edge of her shirt, pulling it quickly from her body and sending it the way of the torn Capris as he stared down at her fiercely. His gaze seared her as his large, warm hands settled at her stomach, then smoothed up to the swollen mounds of her lace-covered breasts.

Disposing of her bra took only seconds. A flick of his fingers at the front clasp and he peeled it from the swollen, sensitive mounds with a growl of pleasure.

Callused fingers cupped the curves, weighed them, tormented them as his thumbs rasped over the painfully hard nipples.

Catching her breath was impossible. Emily had never felt such pleasure, had never known such intensity of sensation. It spasmed through her womb, exploded in her bloodstream, and left her helpless beneath the driving ache that invaded her system.

A grimace of hunger creased Kell's expression. His green eyes were dark, emerald fire blazing in the depths as he gazed at her.

"So damned pretty," he snarled.

He pushed his jeans lower on his hips, one hand gripping the shaft of his cock as he began to lower himself to her.

She couldn't protest. She knew she should protest. She knew she should be screaming out at him to stop, to think, but it was so good. So hot and desperate and filled with the sound of "Hells Bells."

They both froze.

Emily's gaze jerked to the cell phone still hanging at the band of his jeans as a curse ripped past his lips.

"Hells Bells" echoed around them again as he jerked it from the holder and flipped it open.

"Senator. How can I help you?"

Emily stared back at Kell with a sense of horror. Her gaze went from the hard stalk of his erection poised only inches from her flesh then snapped back to his gaze. There was mocking amusement there, and wry acceptance.

She began to pull herself back together, sitting up on the couch as she fumbled for the shirt on the floor and then jerked it over her head.

She felt adrift. As though something had torn her from an unconscious tether and now she was fighting to recover her balance. Dragging herself from the couch, she pushed her fingers restlessly through her hair and watched him as he spoke to her father.

His voice was quiet, not so much as hint of his earlier passion shading it, as he rose from the couch, fixed his jeans, and discussed a party she was required to attend the next day.

She had no desire to attend another of the political functions her father had arranged and she especially had no desire to attend the party with Kell.

Not now. Not while her body was flushed and burning with need and he was talking to her father with a steady cool voice as he turned his back on her.

She shot him a glare as he moved across the room, picked his shirt up from the floor, and pulled it back on without a single interruption in his conversation.

He was too tall. Too broad. And his touch was too knowing. As though instinctively he had known her weakness, her need to explore and to touch. To be touched.

Her hands still tingled from that need. Her body burned for it. And she had no idea how to fight it.

She had known sexual desire in the past. Moments when she had considered throwing caution to the winds for a particular touch, but she had always managed to maintain her control and walk away. She hadn't maintained control this time. She hadn't been walking away, she had been gasping, begging for more. If it hadn't been for her father's ill-timed call, then she would be moaning beneath Kell's possession now.

She bit her lip, glancing over at him beneath her lashes as he leaned against the counter and talked, his tone a low, rough rumble as his gaze tracked her every move.

Suddenly, she felt more restrained than ever. The walls were closing in on her, the air became too close, suffocating, filled with the scent of sex and her own regret.

Shaking her head fiercely at the thought, she turned and stalked back to her bedroom, slamming the door behind her in frustration before heading for the shower.

A cold shower.

She had to find her control. Somehow, it had been stripped away from her one slow touch at a time, one erotic discovery after another. And she had no idea how to recapture it. Or how to save her heart.

Because she knew Kell Krieger was stealing it. Stealing her heart and endangering her soul with each kiss, each touch. Letting him go would break her. And keeping him wasn't an option.

Her father dreamed of such a match. And it was her greatest nightmare. A man who could imprison her with his love, with his fears for her. Who would sap all the dreams that filled her and leave her with nothing but regret.

Was that how it had happened with her mother? she wondered as she stepped into the shower. Had her father hemmed her in so tightly that nothing mattered but escape? Had she regretted it when she lay in the hospital dying from the injuries of her crash? Had she known? Had she regretted? Had she thought of the husband and child she was leaving behind and the horror her choice would bring to them?

Emily had sworn years ago that she wouldn't let that happen to her. She wouldn't be weak. She wouldn't marry a man determined to control her. She wouldn't give in to loving a strong man until she could learn how to stand firm against her father's demands.

If a woman couldn't stand up to her father, then how could she have any hope of standing up to a lover or a husband?

And would a woman ever have a chance of standing up against Lieutenant Kell Krieger? She had a feeling he would be the ultimate mountain to climb, as well as the most dangerous. The most challenging. And certainly the most tempting.

She was going to have to be very careful. He was becoming a weakness, and right now, Emily knew she couldn't afford this particular weakness.

Nine

HELL DISCONNECTED THE CALL WITH the senator and stared broodingly at the cell phone in his hand for long seconds. He had to give the man credit. His timing sucked. One more minute and the call would have been ignored for the sheer pleasure he would have found giving Emily her first passionate ride.

Or the sheer insanity of blowing his own head off. It was only after hearing the phone sing out its distinctive song that he had realized he hadn't sheathed his raging hard-on in a condom.

Dumb. Stupid. And here he had assured her that he knew how to protect himself, if not her.

But it was also the most pleasure he swore he had ever known.

He should have been shaking in his boots at the thought of taking a virgin. Especially a virgin whose father was actively seeking a particular brand of husband for her. A virgin who eroded his common sense and self-preservation. The one who had been tempting his dreams for too many years. He should have felt the noose tightening around his neck the minute those hot lips of hers touched his flesh.

But there was something *right* about her touch. Something

that called to him despite his misgivings. And he had a lot of misgivings, her father being one of his chief concerns.

Shaking his head, he flipped the phone open again, hit Reno's speed dial and waited.

"I have five minutes," Reno said quietly. "The senator has a meeting on the Hill and we're escorting him."

"Keeping you busy, is he?" Kell smirked.

"Watch it, Lieutenant, I could have Macey trade places with you and let you play the senator's aide."

Not in this lifetime. "No, thank you, Commander. I'll get right to the point. This party we're attending day after tomorrow. The senator didn't mention Ian. I want him in place. If our mole is government and close enough to the Stantons to be worried about the senator's investigation, then we could be walking into trouble."

Reno was silent for long moments. "You'll be followed by the Secret Service. I've gone over the agents' files, they're good men."

"My gut is rocking here, Reno. I need Ian in place."

He could feel that vague sense of danger moving in. It had begun to build the minute the senator began talking about the political party Emily was required to attend.

"You'll have him." Reno made the decision quickly. "Your dress blues will be waiting when you arrive at the senator's town house tomorrow afternoon. I'll arrange for Ian to have clearance on the flight in. We'll leave one of the Secret Service agents in the condo Ian's using to keep an eye on Miss Stanton's home while you're gone."

Kell nodded at the shift in personnel. "We should arrive in D.C. by late afternoon according to the senator's itinerary."

"Clint will be waiting at the town house with the security layout of the mansion the party's being held at and the route he's laying in for the drive there."

"Will you and Macey be in position?"

"Only as long as the senator is at the party," Reno answered. "On another note, watch your ass. The senator is a little too pleased by something going on out there. If you're playing tango with the senator's daughter then he could make a very bad enemy when things go sour."

"Any idea what he suspects?"

"None, but he got a phone call last night and the man's smile was positively smug. When he finished, he pulled up your file and spent quite a few hours going through it. So watch your six, my friend."

There could be few things worse than a former SEAL plotting another SEAL's downfall by way of a wedding band. What concerned Kell was who would have called to assure the senator it was happening. Only one person had seen them together, seen them touching, and his investigation into her background had revealed nothing but a spoiled, bored little rich girl. Evidently the little rich girl was more than she allowed others to see.

"I'll keep my eyes open—"

"And your jeans zipped," Reno reminded him. "I know damned good and well what was going on after you saw that strip she did."

"It was a lap dance." Kell grimaced at the satisfaction in his own voice.

Reno snorted. "Make sure I get an invitation to the wedding. This would almost be worth watching."

"In your dreams," Kell growled. "I'm out of here now."

"Watch your six, my friend," Reno reminded him again. "I'll be waiting when you show up in D.C."

Kell disconnected the phone, his gaze lifting as Emily stepped out of the bedroom. Her hair was still damp, her face still free of makeup, and rather than another pair of Capris, she was wearing jeans, a T-shirt tucked into the low band, and a wide belt cinched tightly around her hips.

Her expression was mutinous, her body language assuring him he had offended her in the worst possible way. He was good at reading that particular message, he was just never real good at figuring out how he had managed to effect it.

"Father should cancel that party," she announced as she stalked to the fridge and pulled out a bottle of water. "It's a waste of time. An excuse for a bunch of highbrows to get dressed up and stand around drinking someone else's champagne."

"A thank-you for the political contributions and advice for the election that put your father in office," Kell finished for her. "You're his hostess. You've done the parties up until now, no one else can fill your place at this point."

She didn't need him to tell her that. Emily could feel the frustration raging through her body, the irritability that stemmed from the unquenched desires racing through her, the fear of the step she had nearly taken.

"Has he arranged my flight into D.C.?" she finally asked. "I hope he told you, because he certainly didn't tell me."

There was a big broad set of shoulders in the house, so her father didn't bother to apprise her of any of the plans. Typical. Infuriating.

"We'll leave in the morning for the naval base. We'll be catching a Navy helicopter bound for Annapolis. Your father's car will pick us up there, and drive us into the capital to his town house."

"Then to the Dunmore Mansion the night of the party," she finished for him. "I know how it works."

The Dunmores were political allies of her father's, and very influential within his political circle.

"Then you know you can't get out of it." He shrugged, his gaze moving over her again, pausing at her breasts, her thighs. "Why did you get dressed?"

Emily froze. She hadn't expected him to be nearly so blunt regarding her lack of complete sanity earlier.

"Because I thought it best to accept my near escape while I had the chance."

His eyes darkened with amusement as his lips quirked. Powerful arms crossed over his chest as he watched her intently, refusing to let her ignore the lust that filled his expression.

" 'Near escape.' That's an interesting way of putting it."

"You weren't even wearing a condom," she ground out.

"I wasn't wearing one when I had my cock buried to your throat either," he reminded her. "That didn't stop you."

His response only fanned the flames of the anger brimming inside her. He was working her. Controlling her. She could feel it, just as she always felt her father doing it.

"That won't get me pregnant either. What are you trying to do, Kell? Get into Daddy's good graces by knocking me up and giving him the son-in-law he wants? Have you decided the Stanton money and power might be enough incentive?"

"I don't need your daddy's money, sweet pea," he said with a smirk. The self-satisfied smile shouldn't have made her heart race faster and it sure as hell shouldn't make her remember what his kiss felt like. "And knocking you up isn't exactly my game plan. Getting you hot and wet and full of me is all that matters at this point."

She nearly gaped at him. Blinked.

"You dog!"

His eyes gleamed back at her, filled with laughter and lust as he lazily scratched his cheek.

"I'm not a dog," he assured her. "I promise, not just any woman will do, Emily Paige. I've decided I'm gonna get in your pants before this mission is over. And I'm going to make damned sure I get in there hard enough and deep enough that you never forget I was there."

Emily gasped. "You're crazy."

"It's not the first time I've heard that accusation," he assured her, his expression supremely confident.

She had to fight to keep from curling her fingers into a fist. To keep her foot on the floor instead of slamming it into his shin.

"You are a pain in the ass!" she snapped.

"Not yet." He winked. "But give me time, sugar, and I'll get there. But while you're thinking about it, see if you can't get your little bag packed for our trip tomorrow. And remember to pack light, those Navy helicopters we're hitching a ride on don't always have a lot of spare room."

She was right, Kell admitted as he watched her expression turn from shock to amazement, he was insane. He should be running from this woman as hard and as fast as possible. Instead, he was standing here, staring down at her, watching the flames of anger simmer in her blue eyes as the temper he had been waiting for began to rise to the surface.

That red hair was hiding a hellion and he knew it. He shouldn't be encouraging her—hellions could be dangerous—but damn if he wasn't anticipating the fireworks.

"Do you know what I really, really hate about SEALs?" She suddenly snarled, eyes narrowing, a little quiver of anger working over her body.

Kell arched a brow mockingly. "We're always right?"

"You are always so damned egotistical. You think you're so right. So in control. You *think* the whole freakin' world revolves around you, don't you, Kell?"

"This one does," he amended. He made certain of it. "It's called training, sweet pea."

He didn't expect the flash of hurt in her eyes when he said that.

"Yes, it's called training," she bit out. "It's called being free, Kell. It's called being given control."

"You want control, Emily?" He shook his head. "I don't think it's something you want. Because if you wanted it, you would have taken it years ago. Let me clue you in on SEALs, baby. We know how to read strength, but we also know how to read weakness. If your daddy controls you, then it's only because it's what you wanted. You want control? Then show him who the boss is. Be a woman who can back down a SEAL, sugar, and he'll give you the respect you're looking for."

Emily stared back at him in shock. He had no idea what went on with her and her father.

"You do not understand—"

"I don't have to understand, only you do." He shook his

head firmly. "You're woman enough to stand up to any SEAL. Just because it's not what your daddy wants doesn't mean you can't have it."

She was ready to scream. She was ready to throw something at him. Where in God's name had her father found the one man guaranteed to make her want to kill?

"I never imagined it did," she snapped, a flush working from her neck and over her face, the dark pink color rising to her hairline and making an interesting contrast to her auburn hair, creating a fiery image as her eyes glittered a furious blue. He had never seen anything so gorgeous in his whole damned life.

"So, we going to make use of that bed or make use of the stove? I could be getting hungry."

His gaze assured her that the hunger could go either way. Impossibly, she felt the anger sparking the desire as lust beat a hard-driving rhythm in her womb and anger surged through her head.

"We're going to make use of your gun," she choked out furiously. "One nice, neat little hole in the middle of your empty forehead."

Kell sighed. "Let's wait till after dinner. I'd hate to die on an empty stomach."

"You think you know so much!" She had to fight to keep from screaming, to hold back the inner rage driving forward. "You think you have all the fucking answers, don't you, Kell?"

"No, Emily, I don't," he answered forcefully, hating the pain he saw in her gaze now. "I don't have all the answers. I only have what I see and what I learned from those dipshit bodyguards you've had in the past. Do you know what I see?"

She flinched. "I don't care what you see."

"I see a woman who loves too fiercely. One who is too aware of others' pain and others' heartache, and who doesn't demand the same respect from those she loves. I see a woman who has remained a virgin, a virgin, Emily. An incredibly passionate woman dying to touch and be touched, and she's doing without it so she won't have to hurt her father. So she won't have to explain to him that whoever she marries and whenever she marries is her own damned business, and not his."

There was no censure in his tone; if there had been, she could have fought him. She could have railed back in turn.

"You're wrong," she whispered. "I've remained a virgin not because I didn't want to fight him. Because I didn't want others to pay for my fight with him. If you don't believe me, give Charlie Benson a call. I have his number if you need it. He was an Annapolis graduate and my first boyfriend after I turned eighteen. When Daddy caught him sneaking out of my bedroom and I refused to marry him, Daddy destroyed a damned bright naval career. Daddy destroyed a man for my decision, Kell. And I won't forget that. Maybe it's something you should remember."

There was no escape from here. She couldn't stalk outside, she wasn't about to spend the rest of the summer in her bedroom. That left facing him, fighting him.

But despite the humiliation she could still feel at remembering Charlie's fate, Emily realized she enjoyed sparring with Kell. He didn't raise his voice, he didn't yell, he became forceful. And that forcefulness challenged something inside her, brought it to the fore and demanded that she challenge him in return.

"Benson was sneaking in to your bedroom, Emily." Kell laughed. "You were barely days past your eighteenth birthday and he was already in his twenties. He deserved what he got."

"Daddy had him kicked out of Annapolis."

"He was messing with an officer's daughter; he knew the risks."

"See?" she yelled back. "You're just like Dad. Charlie was young. He was being romantic."

"He was being horny." He crossed his arms over his chest arrogantly. "He was all dick and no brain. You deserved better."

"And I guess you have a brain hiding in that head of yours?" she mocked in angry response.

"I'm not a kid," he assured her, his green eyes filled with his own self-confidence. "The fact that I knew what to do when I got my head buried between your thighs should have assured you of that."

"This is not about sex." She pushed her fingers through her hair, gripped it and wondered if pulling the strands would pull the frustration out of her.

She was ready to scream. He was impossible.

"No, it's about a hell of a lot more than sex. It's about us, Emily, and your precious daddy has no dog in this race. You can tell him to keep his nose out of it or I will."

"You wouldn't!"

"He won't catch me slipping out of your bedroom window. He pulls his normal stunts and he'll catch me in your bed. You can deal with it before that happens, or after. Your choice. I'm an officer, sugar, and he's not in the Navy any longer. He can't touch me."

"You are not getting in my bed!" she yelled. She couldn't help it. He was outrageous. Demented.

"Sugar, one kiss." He held up one finger. "Give me one kiss to prove otherwise. I'll have you flat on your back and penetrated before you know it's happened. Test that one out for size. Better yet." His expression shifted, became hungry, sexual. "Try me on for size."

Oh, my God! She lost her breath. She was certain she'd lost her womb too, because the miniexplosions that detonated inside it couldn't have been good. And then there was the melting sensation in her vagina, the liquid heat and contracting pleasure that had her catching her breath.

"Not on your life. Sorry, Kell, but I crossed SEALs off my list years ago. I'll just keeping looking if it's all the same to you."

She turned to stalk back to her last refuge, her only refuge, her bedroom.

And she almost made it. She was at the door when he

caught her, pulling her around and pressing her against the wall as she stared up at him in surprise

Surprise, because his expression wasn't playful anymore. It wasn't filled with amusement *and* lust. It was pure lust. It was heavy-lidded, wicked, dark, and sensual lust.

"Struck them off your list did you, chère?" The Cajun accent was heavy now, flavored with sex and rich with hunger. "Then you best be putting this SEAL right at the top of the candidates, 'cause I promise you, my little vixen, this SEAL is gonna get that pretty cherry you been saving. And he's going to relish every taste, every cry, every thrust. You can bank on it, eh."

Emily stared back at him in shock. This wasn't the cool, self-possessed, overly confident Kell Krieger she had come to know, though some was still there.

This was a wild man. This was a man who knew every flavor of sex and it showed in his expression, in the brilliant depths of his eyes. It echoed through her body, burning her with the memory of his lips on her pussy, his tongue thrusting and licking inside her.

She tried to breathe evenly. Tried to push back the response that surged inside her, as instinctive as breathing, as old as lust itself.

Her wrists were gripped in his hands, pressed against the wall, restraining her with the strength of the muscular arms behind them. His hips pressed into hers, his cock thick and hard beneath his jeans, his intent clear, just as he stated. He intended to have her.

"Not on a bet." She almost winced at the breathless quality of her voice. It was smoky, sensual. A beckoning dare.

"We'll see about that." The accent dissipated, smoothing from his voice as the devil-may-care smile returned. "That, darlin', we'll just have to see about."

Ten

H E WAS LOSING HIMSELF TO her, Kell could feel it. He forced back the lust, the hunger that had no place in the mission he was on. He put distance between himself and the fiery woman who stole reason from his mind.

He was the one who retreated to his room, packing carefully for the trip to D.C. the next day. One small pack carried his weapons, extra ammo, and a change of casual clothes. Inside the pack, cushioned at the bottom in a waterproof bag, was an ID and credit cards in an alternate identity and enough cash to get him through most situations he might find himself in. Tucked in with it was a small case of tools that would get him into any locked door and several security systems.

He was prepared.

He packed the other weapons, his rifle, two backup revolvers, ammunition, and a dagger back into the larger duffel to store at Ian's condo until their return.

There were more weapons stashed around Atlanta and outlying areas. Two safe houses, a bus stop safe. He was a man who'd learned the hard way to prepare for anything.

And for that reason alone he should have known better than to think he could walk into Emily's life with nothing but lust. She was trouble with a capital T, and she was worming her way into his heart. Just as he had always sensed she would do. Hell, he had steered clear of her for the last five years for a reason, hadn't he?

Or had he?

He hadn't exactly stayed away. He had slipped in and out of her periphery, checking out her bodyguards, checking on her when he was in town. When he learned of her kidnapping he had just come off another assignment with a nasty little gunshot wound and more days without sleep than a man should be able to endure.

The minute he got the word, he had his pack in his hands and had talked his way onto a flight heading out to the carrier where Reno and his men were briefing for the rescue.

He had arrived just in time to join the team, pulling strings with the senator and Reno to get in position to protect Emily and the girls while the battle raged around the compound.

And by God, he had protected her. Even drugged, out of her head with arousal from the date rape drug pumped into her, she had fought. She had held the other two girls in the far corner of the shack, low to the ground, and watched him with hunger and hope.

And it was the memory of her eyes when she realized who he was that tormented him. Hope and hunger. The way she whispered his name. The way she fought to stay on her feet and to do whatever it took to aid in her rescue.

He couldn't stop it. He wanted to stop it. He wanted to close her out of his head and his heart, eradicate the lust and need and return to being the man he had been before that night. Before he gazed into wild blue eyes and saw a need that echoed in his own soul. Before then, staying away from her hadn't been hard. After that, he had found himself unable to stay away.

She was a woman dying to be free. Like a bird in a very pretty cage. One made of guilt-enforced bars and locked with the knowledge of a youthful indiscretion. That, and a father's determination to see his daughter married to a man able to defend her.

Stanton might have gone about things the wrong way, and Kell had no doubt that was true, but he could see the senator's love for his daughter. Just as he saw Emily's love for her father.

It had been there fifteen years before when Richard had first brought him home for dinner. Only weeks after Tansy's death. Richard Stanton and the detective Kell had worked for had been school friends and Navy buddies until the detective opted for civilian duty. One call and the then-Commander Stanton had come straight to Louisiana and picked up his charge.

That love between father and daughter had only grown.

What he also saw was the fact that Emily's love for her father was so tainted with the past and her awareness of his pain in regards to her, that she drew back rather than fighting for what she wanted. And Richard took complete advantage of that.

That would have to stop. When he finally got his ring on Emily's finger, it would be because she wanted it there, not because her father guilted her into it.

He froze at that thought. Hell, he was screwed for sure now and he knew it. He was going to marry the damned little vixen. He wasn't a man prone to flights of fancy. Once it came to him, he went with it. Just as he knew that for once in his life he would be giving his grandparents what they dreamed of. A granddaughter-in-law that they approved of. And for years he had found the thought of that unacceptable.

He paced through the bedroom, into the small bathroom, and stared into the mirror at the man he had become. It was something he had avoided for years, staring himself in the eye. Because each time he had, he saw his own failure to protect those who had depended on him so long ago.

He had seen his own self-hatred. His fury. The useless blame he had placed on his parents' and grandparents' heads.

At one time, he had wondered if he could ever forgive them. If he could ever think of the family he had lost with something other than wrenching pain.

Tansy had been seven months pregnant when she had died. Their son had died in her womb. And Kell's parents, his grandparents, hadn't even come to their funeral. He had stood beside the coffin with the detective he had worked for and raged, virtually alone.

He had cried. On his knees, the last of his youth had drained out of him with the bitter tears he had shed.

He stared at himself now, and saw the man he had become. Reno swore he had never been sane. Kell took chances other men didn't dare, even SEALs. And he saw the world differently in too many ways to be comfortable for others.

He was no longer the boy who had lost a dream. He was a man now. The emotion building inside him where Emily was concerned was a man's love for a woman. A man who had finally accepted that no man or woman was completely safe and that too many took their safety for granted. Emily would be the woman who could stand by his side and aid in her own protection.

He was man enough to know he couldn't continue with the loneliness that fed into his soul. He needed a home, love, a woman he could depend upon, one strong enough to understand the dangers she would always face.

And Emily was that woman.

He couldn't have imagined wanting more than an affair a week ago.

But now, he wanted that and so much more.

Eleven

SHE COULD FALL IN LOVE with Kell Krieger.

Emily admitted it when she woke up to coffee and cinnamon rolls before the sun had risen the next morning. She was madder than hell at him, her sleep had been restless, her thoughts filled with their argument from the night before, but one thing had become firmly implanted in her mind.

Kell was worming his way into her heart. And he shouldn't be. She should be as wary of him as she had been of every other man her father had sent her. She knew he was a SEAL. She knew he was dominating, in control, and had the type of personality that would make her bite her nails at any given time.

But he had been her fantasy for so long.

That, and he didn't try to restrain her.

Not that she had actually tried to do anything that he could protest. Yet. But he hadn't given the restlessness a chance to take hold of her either. He challenged her, confronted her, and he made her think.

He made her think about herself, her life, and a relationship between her and her father that she admitted was rapidly deteriorating.

He made her realize it was just as much her fault as it was her father's.

The only question remaining now was, Could she survive without murdering the man in his sleep over time? The only way to answer that was to actually get in a bed with him.

The thought of that had the blood pumping through her body as she showered then drank that first cup of coffee of the day with him. And she realized she was comfortable.

"We're meeting the Navy helicopter in a few hours." He checked the watch on his wrist as he wrote something in the small notebook he carried.

He was left-handed, she realized. That shouldn't have been sexy.

"And we're flying to Annapolis before going to D.C." She nodded.

"I want you to give me an extra change of clothes. Jeans, T-shirt, and a long-sleeved shirt as well as underthings. I want them packed in my emergency pack in case anything goes wrong."

She stared at him in surprise as he continued to make notations.

"Why?"

His head lifted, his green eyes intent. Not cool, but focused.

"I just told you, in case anything goes wrong."

"Are you expecting anything to go wrong?" She didn't feel fear. His gaze didn't allow for it.

"I always expect something to go wrong," he told her before returning to the notepad. "It's called preparation."

"It's just a party. What could go wrong?"

"Snipers. Assassins in hiding or posing as friends. A million things could go wrong, Emily. The key to surviving it is in being prepared for it."

"Daddy said security was flush around the mansion," she pointed out. "How could they get past James Dunmore's guards? They're good men."

His head lifted again; this time his gaze was piercing.

"Do you know all those men personally? Well enough to

know to the bottom of your soul that they won't blink or take a bribe?"

"No," she answered slowly.

"Then you don't trust your security to them. You trust it to me."

"And when you're gone?" she asked mockingly. All her bodyguards left at some point.

"Then you use the example I'm giving you and the training you'll receive from me." His head was lowered, missing her look of surprise. "Always be prepared, Emily. Always question others' arrangements for your safety and always, *always,* trust your instincts." His head lifted again, his gaze probing, before he lowered it and made another note.

"Why are you willing to tell me this?"

She watched his lips quirk though his eyes didn't lift again.

"Consider it my small contribution to your research."

Her eyes narrowed at the answer.

"That's not good enough."

"It's going to have to be." He rose to his feet, snapped the notebook closed, then hauled her from the chair before she could do more than gasp.

She didn't have time to struggle, even if she wanted to, before his arm latched around her hips, jerked her up against his erection, and his lips stole the kiss he so obviously wanted.

She melted. Why fight it? She had accepted the night before that she was going to end up in his bed. She was panting to get in his bed, dying for more of the pleasure she had only found in his arms.

She was in his arms now. Hers twined around his neck, her fingers threading into his hair as he did the same with one hand in hers before tugging her head back farther.

Whimpers left her throat as colorful bursts of sensation exploded behind her closed eyelids. The arm around her hips lifted her closer as he bent his knees enough to notch the hard ridge of his erection between her thighs. And she was lost from there.

His lips slanted over hers and her lips parted further for him. Her tongue stroked against his aggressively, not content to allow him to set the pace of this first acceptance, this preliminary introduction to the decision she had made late in the night.

He wasn't tameable. He would probably end up walking away long before she was ready to consider letting him go. But for as long as she could hold him, he would be hers.

"Jesus, you taste good," he growled as he nipped at her lips before pulling back to stare down at her.

"You taste better." She licked her tongue over the lower curve of his lips, watching as his eyes flared and lust filled them.

"You would pick this morning to go all sweet and soft in my arms," he griped, before releasing her with a sigh. "Grab your things, I'll put our dishes in the sink. We have to head out of here."

"We should take the Harley," she suggested.

There could be advantages, she thought suddenly, to letting him into her bed. Her life could get more exciting.

"Not on your life." He disabused her of that idea quickly. "We'll take the Bronco. It's secure."

"Can't outmaneuver the bad guys on your bike then? I understand."

"No, I can't outmaneuver bullets when I don't know which direction they could come from," he informed her. "The Harley is for times when it's safe enough to forgo protection. You're not there yet."

Emily paused and stared back at him in surprise.

"I'm not going to argue with you, Emily. I always have a reason for saying no. Realize that now. Because the day could come when I won't have time for explanations." A grin tugged at his lips as she watched him closely.

"I'll try to do that." She finally nodded as she wondered

who the hell Kell Krieger was, and why he was so different from the bodyguards her father usually managed to acquire.

"Do more than try. Find enough control to make it happen. I have to be able to trust you when things go from sugar to shit, darlin'. Let's make an effort to ensure I have that trust if that time comes."

She watched him closely then. Seeing more than the man she wanted to sleep with, seeing more than the hired muscle her father had brought in to protect her. She saw a man. She saw shadows in his eyes and realized how often she had caught the flash of hidden demons lurking beneath the surface.

What had made him a man strong enough to realize that she didn't want to be patted on the head and put on a shelf?

"I'll do that," she finally answered. "I'll make the effort."

He nodded abruptly. "That's all I ask. Now grab your gear and let's get on the road. The pilot flying us into Annapolis has his own schedule that he can't deviate from. So we need to accommodate him."

She was already moving, heading to the bedroom for the large overnight bag she had packed with a change of clothing. While she was there she grabbed the other change of clothes he had requested before pulling her purse from the dresser and heading back into the living room.

He was waiting for her. He took the change of clothes, stuffed them into a plastic bag then secured it with waterproof tape before shoving it into the black pack he carried along with a regular-sized duffel bag.

"Your neighbor, Ian Richards, is riding in with us," he announced as he led the way to the door.

"My neighbor Ian?" She stopped and stared at him in confusion. "The blond in the back condo? The one who likes to flash his hard abs at Kira? Let me guess. He's your partner?"

"That's the one." His voice rasped with a hint of male displeasure. "You're not supposed to notice my partner's hard abs."

"They were hard to miss."

His eyes darkened, his brows lowering, as he deactivated the alarm and unlocked the door. He looked . . . jealous. Emily felt a surge of excitement at the prospect. She hadn't anticipated that.

"So, was your partner Daddy's idea too? And was it Daddy's idea not to tell me he was there?"

"He's additional protection, nothing more." He shrugged.

Emily sighed. "At least he's nice looking. If I have to have trained escorts it helps if they're good eye candy."

"Eye candy, huh?" he muttered as he motioned her out. "I'll have to smash his face a little and fix that."

Emily looked at the face in question, attached to the hard body dressed in jeans and a cotton shirt, and turned to smirk back at Kell.

"Shame on you," she said, pitching her voice low enough that only he could hear. "I promise I won't molest him. You don't get the same promise."

"Vixen," he accused her roughly as he reset the alarm and closed the door as he stepped out. Locking it quickly, he turned back to her, let his hot gaze rake over her. "I might have to spank you for being so insolent."

She grinned as she tucked the handle of her overnight bag over her shoulder and winked back at him suggestively.

"Spankings only make me worse."

"That's what I was hoping." He grinned smugly. "That just makes it a hell of a lot more pleasurable to give it, sweetheart. Didn't you know that?"

"Pervert." She laughed, feeling something lighten inside her as she headed for the Bronco where the other SEAL waited.

"Wench."

This was going to be fun.

But hours later, she wondered if it would be nearly as much fun as the flight from Atlanta to Annapolis had been. She had ridden in a Black Hawk. Not just *any* Black Hawk, but the newest model, which her father had informed her was supposed to be radically more efficient and militarily progressive.

She was still flying when they landed and the pilot gave her the thumbs-up.

"Ma'am, thank you for providing support." He flashed her a bright smile as she sat in the copilot's seat, and she had to keep herself from bouncing. "I'll give you back to Lieutenant Krieger now."

The door beside her opened, and Kell stared up at her with that almost hidden smile of his, his expression rueful as he gripped her waist and lifted her to the tarmac.

"Did you see me?" She squealed, bouncing, certain she was still flying as her hands gripped his shoulders and she laughed with a vibrance she hadn't felt in years. "That is so incredibly cool, Kell. He even answered all my questions about the instruments and everything. Can you believe he let me sit there?"

She hugged him. She couldn't help it. But his arms returned the embrace, strong, powerful arms that surrounded her with warmth and approval.

"I saw, little fly girl," he said, laughing back. "Come on, the limo is waiting and Lieutenant Greary has places to go."

He saluted the pilot before closing the copilot's door and maneuvered her so that he and Ian seemed to surround her clear to the limo.

Ian moved into the front with the chauffer as Kell opened the back door and helped her in, staring around the Navy yard with narrowed eyes.

Getting into the limo, he closed the door, raised the partition between the driver and the back, and watched Emily with a hunger that immediately had her breath tightening in her chest.

She was exhilarated from the flight but the look in Kell's eyes drove that excitement from her and replaced it with a sudden, overwhelming hunger nearly impossible to resist.

"We have approximately forty-five minutes before I have to explain to your father what you were doing in the cockpit of the Navy's newest baby instead of the transport he ordered," he growled. "I want payment before I take the ass-chewing that's coming."

As he spoke, he moved close to her, crowding her, forcing her to lie back on the leather seat as he came over her like a hungry predator determined to devour a meal.

And he was in a devouring mood. A hungry mood. His lips didn't catch her lips first as she expected though. Instead, his teeth raked over her neck as he parted her thighs and pressed the thick bulge of his cock between them.

Her hips jerked as pleasure swamped her. Determined to keep her unruly hunger under control—after all, her father was waiting for her at the town house—her fingers dug into his hard biceps and she turned her head to the side.

But the pleasure only grew. His lips, teeth, and tongue built a fire that began to whip through her bloodstream. Rough velvet and heated sharp tingles resulted from the stinging kisses, until she was desperate to feel it at her lips. To consume him. To taste him.

"Oh God, Kell, I can't stand that," she whimpered as he locked his fingers in her hair and held her in place, his lips trailing from her neck to her collarbone as the fingers of his other hand tugged at the loose neckline of her summer top.

The light weave of the stretchy threads gave easily, revealing one swollen mound, and the lace of her sexy half bra.

"God, I love your breasts," he rasped as his lips followed his fingers.

Emily would have shrieked with the incredible pleasure of his tongue swiping over her nipple if she'd had the breath. Instead, she gasped, going completely still beneath him to make sense of the incredible sensations whipping through her.

His tongue ringed her nipple slowly before licking over it. That made her hot. Incredibly hot. Then, his lips surrounded the peak, drew it into his mouth, and began to suck.

Her hips jerked from the powerful punch of pleasure that sang from her nipple to her womb. Her pussy drove into the hard ridge of his cock, then she paused to writhe. Not that she could help writhing. The pressure on her clit was incredible, almost enough. If she could just move into the right position, if she could just find the right rhythm—

"Here you go, sweetheart." His hand clamped on her hip, and as his lips returned to her nipple, his hips began to move.

It was incredible. It was a shock of driving heat each time he thrust against her, but it was never enough. Her clit became a hard, swollen knot of sensation. Her nipples began to burn and she couldn't touch him enough.

Tugging at the shirt he wore, she struggled to reach bare skin, then gave up and jerked at the neckline instead, dragging it aside so her lips could move to his neck. Once there, she proved what an apt pupil she could be.

She ate at his flesh, nibbled, and drew her tongue over the tough flesh throbbing with life before she let her teeth rake over the pounding vein. The caresses were instinctive. Because the firm, heated draw of his mouth on her nipple was too good, too good to think. She could only feel. And burn.

"Kell. It's so good," she moaned against his neck as he drew the material of her blouse back into place before revealing her other breast.

"Damned good," he muttered against the flushed mound. "So good I should be shot for starting this here."

Her head tipped back on a cry as his teeth raked over her nipple and his hands drew her shirt up, pushing the material past both breasts as he stared down at her with wicked, knowing eyes.

"Tell me what you want," he groaned.

Her lips parted on a gasp. "What?"

"Where do you want my mouth? Tell me, Emily."

"Tell you? I want your mouth everywhere, Kell," she cried out fiercely. "I don't care where you put it. Just put it someplace."

She couldn't get enough of his wild kisses, his caresses, or his cock rubbing between her thighs, his goal hampered by the jeans they both wore.

"Tell me where, Emily," he commanded then, his voice darker with passion now. "Tell me what you want."

What she wanted. Her tongue touched her lips as she tried to drag in enough air. She couldn't seem to get enough oxygen to her brain. Just enough to clear the fog of hunger.

"I want you to take me," she whispered.

His eyes flared as a grimace twisted his features.

"Not in a fucking limo," he groaned. "Hell, I need more time than I have for that."

His head dropped between her breasts, his lips moving between them, his tongue caressing her with little laps that had her holding his head to her, needing more.

"Kell?" She felt the loosening of her jeans, his fingers parting the material.

"I have to feel you." His fingers slid inside. "Just for a minute."

Callused flesh rasped over her, slid beneath the band of her panties, and before she could prepare herself, touched the naked folds of her pussy.

"God, I love your pretty naked pussy." He nipped delicately at the side of her breast as she arched and cried out his name again.

His fingers slid through the heavily saturated flesh, sliding erotically around her clit as she arched and cried out breathlessly.

The shock of pleasure stole what breath remained in her lungs. Then his fingers slid lower, found the entrance to the desperately aching flesh below as his thumb found her clit again, and rocketing sensations began to explode along her nerve endings.

She could only hang on for the ride. His lips moved past her breasts, licking and kissing her stomach, her abdomen, then moving to the parted material of her jeans as his hand drove her insane.

She wanted to touch him, but she couldn't pull her senses together enough to figure out how. She needed to scream, but she couldn't drag enough air into her lungs.

All she could do was writhe beneath the fingers gently probing, pressing against the entrance and sending a shock of heat and pleasure exploding through her system.

When they slid inside, stretching her, filling the entrance, her womb spasmed with an impending orgasm.

"Kell." She twisted beneath him desperately. "Oh God. More."

"More," he muttered against the flesh above her mound. "God yes, more. The scent of your pussy is making me crazy, Emily."

He was jerking, tugging at her jeans, his thumb sliding from her clit only to be replaced by his suckling mouth and licking tongue.

Emily's fingers locked in Kell's hair. Her hips arched and as she felt his tongue moving slowly, too damned slowly, around her clit, she began to beg.

"I need to come, Kell."

He lapped at her clit with a slow, long lick.

"Oh God. More. Harder."

His lips puckered and he kissed it gently, almost pushing her over the edge.

"Please don't tease—please."

He licked around it, causing it to tighten further, to throb in need. The blood was racing through her veins now, perspiration slickening her body as she writhed beneath him. She was dying for more, reaching, pressing against his mouth as her hands tightened in his hair to drag him closer.

She wanted to be rid of the jeans. She wanted to be naked in his arms and covered by his weight. Instead, the denim material around her thighs held her in place as his mouth tormented her. Tortured her. As his fingers stroked, stretched the opening, and had her lifting, trying to force them deeper.

She needed them deeper. Agonizing hunger resonated from the depths of her pussy, tightening the muscles, spasming through them with a force that had her flying higher, faster, than she had in the Black Hawk.

"Kell, please," she tried to scream his name. "Please. I'm dying—I need—more."

The wail that left her throat was one of exquisite agony. Pleasure too sharp, too fierce to be endured. Yet she endured it. Ecstasy ruptured through her, piercing her bloodstream and burning through her body with a force that tightened her body and left her shuddering in the aftermath.

Twelve

ONCE HE GOT HIS DICK inside her, he was going to kill them both before he managed to satisfy the hunger clawing at his balls.

Kell fixed her clothes quickly, drew her into a sitting position, and breathed out a shaky breath as he moved into the opposite seat and stared back at her.

At least the panel between the driver and the seats was soundproof. Damn, that cry that had come from her had nearly had him coming in his jeans. Long, drawn out, aching with pleasure and need combined.

Looking through the windows, he quickly estimated how much time was left before they arrived at the house then ran his fingers through his hair, attempting to restore some kind of order to it as Emily pulled a comb from her purse and quickly straightened hers.

"Want me to do yours?" She flashed him a saucy grin as she held the comb out.

"Go for it." He loved daring her.

The smile that curled her lips had his thighs tightening and his fingers digging into the seat beneath him as she moved across the short distance and straddled his legs before sitting on his lap.

"Brave girl," he growled playfully. "It's all I can do not to tear those jeans off you and show you just how tenuous my control is right now."

"Hmm." She drew the teeth of the comb through his hair, using her free hand to smooth over the strands as she worked. "Just imagine the surprise Daddy's butler would get when he opened the door for us."

Kell grimaced. He knew that butler. Seaman Rogers had been with the senator's SEAL team at the time the senator had been wounded. Several years later Rogers had been taken captive. Before his team could rescue him both legs had been broken, several ribs cracked, and the fingers of one hand nearly pulverized.

Once he healed and took a discharge, Stanton had hired him. The other man had been with the senator ever since. Nearly twelve years now. His wife kept the town house ready for occupancy and both of them adored the senator and his daughter.

"There, you're all nice and tidy. If it weren't for that hickey on your neck, Daddy would never know I'd been molesting you in the limo."

His gaze caught hers. There was a hint of fear in her eyes.

"I didn't mean to do it," she whispered as she moved back to her own seat and rubbed her hands nervously on her jean-clad thighs. "Maybe he won't notice."

"Probably not." Bullshit. Kell knew that was the first thing her father would notice. "But that's not as much a problem as the one on your neck. And I did mean to put it there."

Her hand flew to her neck then she dug into her purse, pulled her mirror free, and stared at it in shock.

It wasn't blatantly obvious. It was small, the slightest marring of her creamy flesh from the bite of his teeth. It would be gone within hours. But they didn't have hours.

"We're dead." She swallowed tightly. "This is bad, Kell. Very bad."

"Yep, we've broken several laws," he agreed mockingly. "Look at it this way, at least he can't tell I had my mouth buried in your pussy."

"Stop trying to shock me." She snapped the mirror closed and shoved it back into her purse. "What is your deal? Why are you so insistent that he know we have anything between us? This is insane."

"Why would I want to hide it?" He crossed his arms over his chest and stared back at her thoughtfully.

Her head dropped back against the seat as she stared at the upholstered ceiling.

"We are so screwed. He's going to demand you marry me, I'll refuse, and he'll have you demoted to ship's barnacle remover or something."

His lips twitched. "I hardly think so. He's a senator, not an admiral."

Her head lifted slowly. "You forget, my godfather is an admiral, Kell," she whispered in horror. "And he'll be at the town house."

"Admiral Holloran." He nodded. "Don't worry, he likes my brash sense of humor."

YOU SHOULD REALLY BE MORE worried about this."

"I'm not worried, Emily." Because he had every intention of marrying her, just as soon as she came around to the fact that it was going to happen.

A man didn't force a woman like Emily, he gently led her. Like the vixen she was, she'd dig her heels in and stubbornly refuse to breathe if someone were to try to make her do it.

There was no doubt that he and the senator, and most likely the admiral, would be having a hell of a conversation later though.

"I'm not marrying you!" she snapped. "I don't know you. I don't even know if I like you."

"But you'll go to bed with me?" He arched his brow mockingly.

The question had her pausing. "Well, I like you fine when you're kissing me rather than playing games with me. Don't think you have me fooled, Kell. Whatever your agenda is, I'll figure it out. I always do."

He had no doubt she wouldn't.

"No agenda, sweet pea." He smiled back at her, not bothering to hide the fact that he was amused by the predicament she found herself in.

Hell, she should have gotten her father in hand years ago. She had the ability to do it. And if she didn't learn how now, then Kell was going to have to. Then he would have to soothe her ruffled feelings as well as the senator's. And it would be a hell of a lot harder for him to soothe a senator's ruffled feelings than it would be for her.

It was barely eleven in the morning when the limo pulled up in front of the town house. Ian and the driver were out first, flanking the door as Kell opened it and stepped out.

"We have a clear," Ian murmured, touching the earwig communicator he wore.

Kell nodded then gripped Emily's arm and helped her from the limo before moving behind her and following her up the steps to the senator's brownstone town house.

The door opened immediately and Rogers's tall, imposing form slid into view. He shielded Emily's side as she whisked into the house, entering the large foyer and staring around with a sense of regret.

She had left here five years ago and moved to Atlanta to get away from the stifling atmosphere of her father's overprotectiveness. Now, she was returning, and the smothering feeling that had driven her out was coming back with a vengeance.

"Emily." Her father stepped from the study at the far end of the foyer, a smile creasing his face as he moved toward her. Behind him, Commodore Samuel Tiberian Holloran stepped into view, bringing a smile to Emily's face.

Uncle Sam. He wasn't really her uncle, but he was her godfather, her father's best friend, and once an ally she could depend upon.

Behind her, Kell and Ian came to attention, only relaxing

marginally when her father and the admiral returned their salutes.

"Hello, Daddy. I thought you weren't staying here?" She stared around the foyer.

When her father wasn't in semipermanent residence, then Fay didn't come in from the little house they lived in behind the town house. But there she was, her white apron brilliant against the dark blue slacks and matching blouse she wore.

"I'm not, Emily," he assured her. "But I thought you might need Fay's assistance while you're here."

He gripped her shoulders firmly, planted a kiss on her brow then drew back with a frown, his gaze going to her neck before looking behind her.

"Say a word and I'll walk out," she informed him quietly, barely keeping her voice from shaking. "You start a fight in front of Uncle Sam and I'll never forgive you."

He gazed back down at her, his eyes narrowing as his lips tightened in anger.

She could feel the mark burning on her neck. It was a declaration. Even as she had checked it in the limo she had known what Kell intended it to be. A declaration of ownership. A male brand of possession.

"I mean it, Daddy." She stared right back, feeling the dread that began to rise inside her. "I won't have it."

"Emily Paige, girl, you're as pretty as a picture." The admiral stopped beside her father, giving them both a stern look before he pulled Emily into his arms for a quick hug.

"And you're as handsome as always, Uncle Sam." She tried to smile back.

He cut quite a dashing figure for a man who had just celebrated his fifty-fifth birthday. He was trim, his hazel eyes as sharp as ever, though his dark brown hair was now completely gray.

"Of course I'm as handsome as always, unlike your old man here." He jerked his thumb over his shoulder at her father. "I'm only getting better with age."

Emily's lips twitched before flattening at the look in her father's eyes.

"Has my dress arrived?" She turned to Fay to ask the question.

"Everything arrived yesterday, Miss Emily," she answered, her gaze taking in the look on her father's face as well. "I put everything in your bedroom, and Lieutenant Krieger's dress blues arrived as well. They're in the room beside yours."

Emily nodded sharply. "I need to call Wilma Dunmore and make certain everything is running smoothly. I'll have to thank her for taking care of this for me."

"Go ahead and do that, baby," her father said, his voice tight. "I'll talk to Krieger about the information we've gotten so far."

She just bet that was what he wanted to talk to him about.

"Don't cause me to leave, Daddy." She didn't bother to disguise the warning in her voice. "I don't want to let you down this weekend, but I would."

"Emily." Kell stepped behind her, his hands settling on her shoulders in a move that she considered highly unwise. And to make matters worse he kissed the top of her head gently.

The commodore's brows lifted to his hairline as he glanced back at her father.

"For a smart man, you're starting to make me believe you have very little sense of self-preservation, Kell," she snapped, stepping away from him. "If you'll excuse me, I have things to take care of. If you want to be stupid, you can do it all on your own."

Pulling away from him, she took her overnight bag and purse from the chauffer before heading to the stairs.

"Daddy." She paused at the first step and stared back at him intently. "Do you love me?"

A frown darkened his brow. "Don't pull that on me, Emily. It's beneath you."

"Do you love me, Daddy?"

"You know I do." He glowered back at her.

"Then you won't make any threats or demands, will you?"

His frown darkened. "I never make threats."

"No demands or ultimatums, or the next time you try to put a bodyguard in my home, I'll call the police. Are we clear?"

His jaw flexed in frustration. "We're clear."

"Good." She nodded sharply, praying that the shaking in her knees couldn't be seen. "I'll take care of the party then. We'll talk again before I leave."

She heard his irritated grunt as she moved unhurriedly up the stairs. Reaching the landing, she stared back down at him for long seconds before walking to her bedroom, entering and closing the door behind her.

There, she breathed out roughly and pressed her hand tightly to her stomach. She was starting to think she might have been better off staying at home after all.

H ELL RESTRAINED HIS SMILE AS the senator turned a dark look on him. The admiral's lips were twitching, if he wasn't mistaken, and his hazel eyes were alight with mirth.

"Lieutenant Krieger, consider yourself at home in this house." The admiral nodded to Kell's "at ease" stance.

"This is my home, Sam," the senator growled. "You don't have that authority."

"I outrank you," the admiral reminded him in amusement.

"My home!" the senator pushed out between clenched teeth.

Sam Holloran shook his head with a smirk. "Look at it this way." He indicated Kell's neck. "She can give better than she gets. Stop acting like a momma bear with a cub, Richard. She's a woman, not a teenybopper."

Richard's face flushed as he glared back at Kell.

"I intend to marry her, Richard." Kell kept his voice carefully low, but no less firm. It wouldn't do for Emily to hear him.

Both men stared back at him in surprise now.

"You do?" the senator asked with wary hope. "Does she know that?"

"No. She doesn't. And I'd prefer she didn't know until the time's right."

There was no sense in keeping her father's pride inflamed by holding back the information from him. She was still his daughter, and Kell could imagine how he would have felt if a man had dared to so blatantly touch his daughter without the benefit of an engagement or wedding band. Hell, come to think of it, Kell barely managed to restrain his wince. It would be hard to see such a mark on his daughter's neck if she were married. If he had a daughter.

The senator and admiral exchanged concerned looks.

"Into my office." Richard Stanton turned on his heel and led the way to the open office doors. "If we're going to discuss this, then I'll be damned if I want her to hear it. I didn't like that look in her eye." He muttered the last sentence with an edge of confusion. "That girl has never talked to me like that."

"She's growing up, Richard." The admiral's gaze was approving as he gave Kell a small nod.

"She's learning bad habits," the senator snapped back, before leveling a piercing look at Kell. "And I have a feeling it's your fault."

"I don't doubt it a bit, Senator," Kell agreed with no small amount of pride.

Hell yes, it was his fault. He didn't want a woman too scared of her own shadow to survive while he was on a mission. Nor did he want a woman who couldn't add a measure of common sense and precaution to her own defense.

Emily would always have resources to fall back on, but he wanted to be certain she could get to those friends if trouble arose and he was out of the country.

It wouldn't be easy, working the senator to a place where he understood that his daughter was never going to allow them to wrap her in cotton batting and place her on a shelf.

He wanted her to be strong. He needed her to be strong. For his own sanity.

He stood silently now as Emily's father closed the office doors carefully behind them, then turned to stare at Kell with narrow-eyed intent as the admiral walked to the wet bar on the other side of the room.

"You think you can make her marry you?" Stanton asked in disbelief.

"I won't have to make her, Richard."

The senator shook his head. "You obviously don't know Emily well enough. I told you, you should have spent more time here at the house with us."

Kell considered, for the briefest second, pulling his punches with the other man. But it was obvious the senator had no intentions of doing the same.

"No, Richard, it's obvious you don't know your daughter," he said instead. "She's not a timid little girl. If you don't loosen the reins she'll get herself killed trying to have her freedom and satisfy you as well. Give her what she needs and she'll settle down. She'll think about her safety rather than making certain you don't catch her having a little fun."

"A little fun?" The senator growled ominously. "You mean, the kind of fun that found her in a strip club, giving some strange man a lap dance?"

"I don't consider myself that strange," he said as he crossed his arms over his chest and let his comment sink in.

It didn't take long.

"You were there?" Anger vibrated in the tone.

"I was getting the lap dance. And she was damned cautious for a woman who'd paid a nice little chunk of change out of a bank account that was also riding damned low from feeding your goons. She was careful. And the men who got their little bonus for keeping the area clear while she was in there made damned certain she wasn't touched. She watches her back."

"It was a lap dance," the senator snarled.

"It was her business," Kell reminded him. "Not yours.

And I would think about this while you're getting ready to see just how many pieces of my ass you can chew while we're in here. I'm not Charlie Benson. And you don't have the power to strip my rank or my position on my team. So don't bother trying to find leverage there. When it comes to political clout, I won't mind a bit pulling in what's owed to me to protect Emily. From your enemies, or from you."

He couldn't blame the senator for the look of amazement that swiftly crossed his face before he could hide it. Richard knew exactly what kind of clout Kell could pull if he wanted to. Just as he knew Kell had never threatened to use that clout once in the fifteen years they had known each other. "Richard, you found one you can't intimidate," the admiral drawled from the bar where he was nursing a glass of whiskey. "Leave the boy alone. We have other, more important matters to discuss."

Kell stared back at the admiral, seeing the flash of anger that glittered momentarily in his hazel eyes.

"Has something happened?" Kell's gaze sliced to the senator before returning to the admiral.

"Our Fuentes contact sent another message. The order to kidnap Emily has gone out, but they sent an assassin rather than a kidnapper. He left the Fuentes base last night, heading here to D.C. We need to capture that assassin, Lieutenant Krieger."

The implication of that statement nearly staggered Kell. He stared at the admiral, then turned to Stanton as his body tightened in fury.

They were endangering Emily by allowing this party to go forward and that just pissed him off.

"I wasn't informed of this."

He should have been told the moment they heard. Protection for Emily should have been increased. Hell, she should be placed in a undisclosed safe house until this was over.

"That was my fault, Lieutenant." The admiral's voice hardened. "We can't allow the Fuentes mole to know we're receiving this information. We have to carry on as is. You and

Ian will protect her, along with the security we're putting in place at the Dunmore mansion. There was no need to relay this information before you arrived and upset Emily further."

Upset Emily further? Kell stared at the two men, and felt like shaking both of them furiously. Forget the fact that they were both superior officers; they were holding back pertinent information that could endanger her life.

"Sir, might I remind you that I am in charge of her security," he gritted out. "This was information I should have had."

"And you have it now." Richard sighed. "The time delay wouldn't have mattered one way or the other."

"The party should have been canceled. It should be canceled now."

"And if we cancel we won't have a hope in hell of catching the kidnapper and/or assassin Fuentes is sending after my daughter," Richard stated, fear flashing in his eyes then. "That's my only child, Krieger. She's my life. Do you think I like this any more than you do?"

"I don't know, Senator, perhaps you thrive on the elements of danger. One thing is for damned sure. She needs to be out of D.C. now. She has no business being here."

"And then she runs for the rest of her life?" Richard yelled back, the anger brewing inside him showing for the first time. "We have a time and place now. If we change our movements, Fuentes will change his. If we can catch the assassin then we have the chance of gaining the information we need on that damned spy that bargained with Fuentes for this hit. It's our only chance."

"So you keep me in the dark about the additional threat, and on top of that, you draw her straight into an assassin's bullet?" Kell heard his own voice rising, felt the anger brewing inside him with a force he had never had to deal with before. "Are you forgetting, Senator, that her protection depends on my knowing even the tiniest hint of danger coming her way?"

"You have the information," Stanton snarled in reply. "You

have it in plenty of time for Durango Team to protect her. I do not take unnecessary risks with my daughter, Lieutenant."

"That's exactly what you're doing, Richard," Kell stated harshly. "Taking unnecessary risks. By not telling me the extent of the threat involved once she reached D.C. She will not be attending that party. Period."

"Says who?"

Kell swung around to face Emily as she stepped into the office.

"Your voices carried." She lifted her chin and her eyes glittered with defiance as she stepped into the room.

Her auburn hair gleamed beneath the overhead lights and her blue eyes glittered with challenge as she looked first at her father, then Kell.

"Emily, this doesn't involve you, sweetheart." Her father cleared his voice, giving her a smile normally reserved for an infant.

"Really?" Her brow arched, but the tone of voice had Kell wincing. He knew women. He knew that little drawl wasn't a safe sound.

"Kell and I will take care of this, honey."

"I don't think so." She turned her gaze to Kell. "Is this one of those times when I'm supposed to follow you without question?"

Her expression and her tone assured him that it better not be.

"I could hope." But he doubted it.

"Keep hoping," she suggested sarcastically before turning to her father. "And you can stop patronizing me anytime now. This isn't one of your attempts to acquire a son-in-law. If I'm really in danger then you can tell me what the hell is going on. Because I won't cooperate another second without it."

Thirteen

EMILY WALKED AWAY FROM THE meeting with her father, Kell, and the admiral with a sense of unreality. For years she had done her best to maintain her relationship with her father in a way that would ease his mind.

She had pushed back her own needs, tried to confine them, continually telling herself that eventually, one day soon, he would see her as an adult rather than a child. That he would realize that the training he had given her as a teenager gave her an edge against his fears. That the self-defense training she had kept up had only sharpened those earlier skills.

She had let him have the illusion of protecting her while she hid her own needs and tried to still the hunger for them with the brief escapades that drove her bodyguards insane.

She had made a mistake. She saw that as she listened to her father and the man she called Uncle Sam explain what had been going on without her knowledge.

The extent of the threat from Fuentes, the danger she was in now that she was in D.C.

And he hadn't intended to tell her. As she listened, asking questions here and there, and watched each man's expression, she felt a sense of grief well up inside her.

This was how little her father knew or understood her. He

had wanted to *protect* her. He didn't want to worry her. He would have preferred she went into this blind and trusted the team brought in for security to make certain she wasn't harmed.

She glanced at Kell, watching as he sat lazily in the chair he had taken, his green eyes never leaving her face. As though he were analyzing something, taking everything in to go over later.

He sat with his elbow on the arm of the chair, his finger brushing over his bottom lip thoughtfully. It was sensual, distracting. And she had a feeling it was deliberate.

"Kell will get all the particulars of the party tonight from his commanding officer," her father finished, his gaze probing as he watched her.

"Then he better intend to include me in the meeting," she informed him.

"Emily, this isn't necessary, honey. I'll take care of everything." That soothing "daddy" tone was back. She wasn't playing the game this time.

"I'm sure you will take care of everything." She nodded as she rose to her feet and glanced back at the admiral and Kell as they rose as well. "But I'll help you a little bit this time." She smiled tightly. "Please inform Commander Chavez that I'm to be apprised of what's going on, and when it's going on. Until then, I need to let Fay know if you will be in for dinner with the rest of us."

His gaze narrowed on her. "I'm not one of your students, Emily Paige," he informed her broodingly as he rose from his seat as well. "Don't talk to me like one."

"Neither am I, Dad," she said with careful composure. "And I'm tired of being treated like a child anyway. It stops here. And it stops now."

She watched his eyes darken, watched the pain that filled them a second before he turned from her. It pierced her heart. For a moment, she was five again, seeing that look in his eyes seconds before he had to tell her her mother was gone, and his tears followed.

"We can discuss that later," he said roughly, clearing his throat before he turned to Kell again. "I'll be returning to the hotel in about an hour. Chavez, McIntyre, and Macey should be completing the security measures they are putting in place out back and through the rest of the house soon. They'll be leaving with me, but I know your commander wanted to talk to you before he left."

Kell nodded sharply, his gaze leaving her for only the second that was required.

"When you attend that meeting, you'll make certain I'm with you of course," she said with brittle politeness.

"No. I won't. I'll make certain you receive all the information you need though."

Emily felt the anger surging closer to the surface now, frustration and impotent fury combining as she drew in a deep, hard breath.

"That isn't acceptable."

"It will have to be." His gaze was penetrating, watchful. "The commander won't have time for your questions, but you can ask me once I relay the information to you. There's no reason for you to be there and it will only cut into what little time I'll have to get my information."

She pressed her lips together tightly. He had already proved his willingness to allow her to know what was going on. He wouldn't hide the information from her.

Breathing out harshly, she nodded in reply before turning to her father. "Before I head home, we're going to talk."

"I don't like that tone, Emily.

"Then I'm sorry, Dad. But right now, it's the best I can do. And we will talk. We'll talk or you can take your bodyguards and shove them clear to Timbuktu for all I care. Because there won't be a single one leaving with me otherwise. I do know how to hire my own protection."

"Does that include Lieutenant Krieger?" His voice was smooth, but she detected the edge of mockery in it, the knowledge that her relationship with Kell went far beyond that of other bodyguards.

Kell's lips twitched as his eyes gleamed back at her. She had a feeling he'd be right behind her no matter what she decided.

"Kell is another case entirely," she assured her father as she turned back to him. "But I don't think you want to push that subject. Now, if you'll excuse me, I have things to do."

She nodded to her father, turned, and forced herself to walk sedately to the door. She wanted to scream. She wanted to rage at him. She wanted to rage at herself.

It was her own fault it had come to this, and she knew it. She should have fought him sooner. She should have stood her ground years ago and made him face the fact that she couldn't tolerate the control he wanted to place on her. That she needed adventure. She needed excitement. She needed to live, despite his fears.

And why did she have a feeling Kell wasn't going to be as easygoing about this whole "working with her" thing as he pretended to be? She had heard his tone of voice when he demanded the party be canceled. It was rough, deep, filled with arrogant demand.

That lazy attitude hadn't fooled her.

He was like a panther, watching, stalking, waiting. When he struck, it would be with devastating results.

She had already made up her mind that she wasn't running. As she spoke to her father, listened to the reluctantly given information, she had begun making her own plans. Her own decisions. It would begin today. At the moment she stood outside the office and listened to her father's and Kell's raised voices, she had decided she was no longer allowing others to make decisions for her.

She was an adult, and she had been making decisions for herself for years. She could do it. She knew how. And she would let both men know, in no uncertain terms, that she would begin exercising her right to do just that.

More than hour later, Emily disconnected the call she had made to Wilma Dunmore. The other woman hadn't seemed in the least put off by the fact that Emily was asking about the security around the mansion for the party. The number of security guards, the areas most heavily guarded, and the security weaknesses. Of course, Wilma Dunmore never took anything for granted. She was one of the few women Emily knew who could have run the country with little or no help.

Sitting down at her desk she made a quick sketch of the Dunmore mansion, drawing on her memories of it from the visits she had made there since she was a child, and added in the security details Wilma had given her.

As she worked, she saw several points that she outlined to discuss with the hostess later that evening. As she finished the last notes, the bedroom door opened and Kell stepped inside.

She could feel the anger pulsing from him in waves.

"I want you out of here." His voice was dark, dangerous, as he closed the door behind him with a snap. "You don't need to go to this party. You don't fucking need to wave yourself at that assassin like a fresh piece of meat in front of a hungry dog."

Emily leaned back in her chair as she stared at him, watching as he stalked toward her, his body tense as he scowled down at her furiously.

His gaze was predatory, his expression fierce. Before, she might have hesitated to argue with him. She knew this expression. The alpha-male look that said things were going to go his way or else.

In this case, it would be "or else." Because she wasn't backing down.

"What better way to draw him out?" she asked logically. At least, she hoped it was logical. "I can't run forever, Kell, you know that as well as I do."

"Running forever isn't an option, just until we catch the bastard that put Fuentes onto you." He plowed his fingers roughly through his hair. "Emily, be reasonable about this. There's no way to ensure, beyond a shadow of a doubt, that you won't be hurt. I can't do that." She saw the grimace that twisted his expression. "I can't let you be hurt."

"Why? I'm just a job, Kell. When it's over, you'll walk away to the next job, and then to the next job. You do your best—"

"Is that all you think this is?"

Before Emily could do more than gasp she found herself jerked from the desk chair. Kell's hands were wrapped around her upper arms firmly, holding her upright as he glowered down at her.

"What else is it then?" Emily cried back, feeling her heart suddenly racing in her chest, a sensitivity clashing through her body that hadn't been there before.

She could feel the force of his will whipping around her. It was in the fierce brightening of his eyes, the hint of Cajun accent in his tone, and the heavy sensuality that suddenly shaped his lips.

"Why don't I show you what else it is, sugar." His lips pulled back, revealing the line of his clenched teeth and the snarl of determination in his lips a second before his head lowered, those lips shaped themselves to hers, and his teeth parted to allow his tongue to plunge ruthlessly into her mouth.

Hard, desperate. There was no denying, no escaping, the hunger that suddenly ignited inside her.

This was a punch of emotion-fueled need, hunger, a driving quest to sate the greedy sensuality that rose between them each time their gazes met.

It had been building since that first look from across the garishly lit stage where she had stripped for him. That first look, his gaze even behind the dark glasses locking with hers and opening a part of her soul she hadn't known existed.

Nothing had mattered but his touch, since that day. The stroke of his tongue against hers as he took the right to fuel her lusts and to sate them. The feel of his arms suddenly surrounding her, his fingers burrowing into her hair as hers slid into the cool, silky strands of his as well.

She needed this. She was starved for it. The buildup was

destroying her senses, her control. The pleasure was sensory overload. How could one woman bear the tingles of erotic electricity racing through her veins and prickling over her nerve endings? It made her want to scream. Made her want to rub against every inch of him and feel more of it. Like a cat. Like a sex kitten, eager for more.

"Damn you! You steal my mind," he growled, jerking his lips from hers only to move along her jaw to the delicate shell of her ear, then the sensitive nape of her neck.

"Let me steal it more," she whimpered, pulling at his shirt, desperate to bare his flesh. "You're not teasing me again, Kell. Not this time. You have to finish this."

She was desperate to feel him over her, inside her. As her head turned, her lips seeking his, she couldn't stop the mewling little cry of need that fell from her lips.

But it got results. It got his hands gripping the hem of her shirt to pull it over her breasts before he tore free of her kiss to jerk it over her head.

His shirt went next, courtesy of her hands gripping the edges and pulling, jerking, tearing the buttons free and leaving the material hanging on his broad chest.

"Fierce little vixen, eh?" It was a statement. The tone was an erotic thrill of desire that pierced her womb.

"Very fierce." She panted, moving back as her fingers went to the snap of her jeans and she toed her sneakers from her feet. "Get naked, Kell. Now."

Naked came quickly. He sat at the edge of the bed, watching as she released her jeans and began pushing them over her legs.

His boots were untied and jerked from his feet in seconds.

As her jeans passed the lace of her panties he was pushing his over his hips, disposing of them and his underwear and socks in one fell swoop.

Before her own jeans passed her ankles he was lifting her to him, bearing her to the bed and fighting her for the supremacy of being on top as their lips came together once again.

Short little cries fell from Emily's lips as he used his larger, stronger body to hold her in place, sprawling between her thighs, his hands anchoring her wrists to the mattress as his lips ravished hers.

This wasn't the previous, slow, determined seduction that Kell had employed each time he touched her. As though each touch had to be controlled, each kiss calculated.

There was nothing calculated here. This was pure male hunger.

"You'll do as I say." He suddenly tore his lips from hers, his voice ragged, determined. "Promise me, Emily. You'll follow me. Swear it to me."

Her head thrashed on the bed.

"I can't lose you. Not you, Em," he groaned then. "I can't live through it again. Sweet baby. Don't you leave me."

Before she could question him, before she could do more than glimpse the pain burning in his eyes and feel it echoing in her heart, his lips were moving along her collarbone, then to the mounds of her breasts rising above the lace of her bra.

"Sweet ecstasy framed by silken lace," he groaned as he leaned back to stare down at her, his gaze going to the hard points of her nipples beneath the lace. "Have I mentioned, darlin', how much I love those pretty breasts, those sweet little nipples?"

"Kell—" She protested the pain raging in his expression.

"I look at you, and I see peace. A slice of heaven." He released her wrists, his fingers moving between her breasts to the clip that held the lace cups secure.

His face was filled with hunger, and not just sexual. She could feel it. See it. A need that transcended sex and moved into the soul.

As the cups of her bra slid free of her flesh, his lashes drifted lower, the green of his eyes glittered behind thick black lashes.

"I need to love you," he whispered then. "Soft candle-light. No danger. No worry. Just me and you."

"You can have that—now." Her breathing hitched as the

backs of his fingers smoothed over one tight nipple. "I don't need candles, Kell. I just need you."

"I know why your father needs to protect you." He bent to her again, his lips feathering above her nipple. "You touch everyone, Emily. You touch a father's heart. A stranger's loyalty, and the soul I never knew I had. You touch it, and you remind us of all the innocence we've lost in the world."

Emily shook her head. "I'm not innocence, Kell. I'm just a woman."

"Sweet innocence," he said, denying her words. "So pure and bright. Like a living flame." His head lifted, his gaze piercing hers with a sense of desperation she couldn't describe. "Keep me warm, just like this, always."

She had to touch him. Her hands lifted to his face, her thumbs moving over his lips as her fingers framed his cheeks. The feel of the rough, day-old growth of beard that had reappeared since he had shaved early that morning prickled her palms. His lips moved against her thumbs, kissing them, his tongue stroking over them.

"I'm here," she whispered.

"Always be here, Emily."

"For as long as you'll let me."

She would be with him forever, if he stayed. If he loved. As she loved.

She loved him. She had known it was coming. She had felt it building, but had tried to convince herself she could hold back.

There was no holding it back. It already had her by the heart and was moving slowly, irrevocably, into her soul.

The pain eased slowly from his eyes to be replaced by a fierce, untamed emotion. Untamed and unquenchable. She could see it, clear to his soul, as her breath caught.

"You're mine," he told her then, his voice strong, rough. "Mine, Emily."

His hips moved between her thighs, the heavy length of his erection pressing against the thin panel of lace that covered her pussy.

"Yours," she gasped. She had no argument with that. She would always belong to him. She would always need him, ache for him.

She had dreamed of him for years. A bad boy. Mocking. Rough. Strong and determined. Kell was that and more.

A thin, low cry came from her lips as his head descended once again, his lips covering a sensitive nipple and drawing it into his mouth as his hand moved to the elastic band of her panties.

As she arched, pushing her nipple deeper into the heated grip his lips had on it, she felt the band tear. The lace disintegrated beneath the tug he gave it. The other side was treated to the same determined effort, leaving her panties in shreds around her, but the heated length of his cock now slid against the slick folds of her pussy.

"Kell. Oh God. I don't know if I can stand it." The act of having her clothes torn from her body was nearly more than she could bear.

She was ready to come now. Just as she had been the day he had ripped the seam of the Capris to bury his lips between her thighs.

He was wicked and unpredictable. Sensual and sexual. He was heating her to the point that she could feel the flames whipping through her body and searing her nerve endings.

"Ahh, that's more like it," he drawled, his hips shifting, dragging his erection over the folds it was pressed against.

Emily moaned at the feeling of the hard, throbbing flesh against her clit, caressing it, stroking across it.

"God! The feel of you." His head lifted from her breast, his eyes darkening as he shifted, drawing back to sit on his knees and stare down at her with raging need.

The need raged inside Emily as well. She had no idea how to control it, how to do anything but reach for him.

Her hands slid from his chest to his hard abs, her nails scraping against his flesh as she watched the muscles beneath it flex and ripple.

Lower, his cock pressed between her thighs, rising above

her mound, the hard flesh glistening with her juices as a creamy bead of precum welled at the tip of the wide crest.

"Why are you waiting?" she asked breathlessly.

He was breathing harshly, his hands gripping her thighs, his fingers clenching and unclenching restlessly in her flesh.

"Condom." The word was pushed between clenched teeth. "I didn't bring a condom in with me."

"At all?" Her lips parted in distress.

"In my room." He breathed in slowly, carefully. "I left them in my bag. In my room. Your butler put my bag in my room."

Condoms. God, she hated the thought of a condom, the thought of anything between his flesh and hers. But the thought of the consequences had her moving, searching.

She ignored his frustrated growl as she moved back, forcing his flesh from hers as she turned to her side and reached for the drawer at her bedside table.

Her hand fumbled as she felt his palm pat the cheek of her rear heavily. The little slap had her jerking, had stars exploding before her eyes before she could reach inside the drawer, scrambling for the little foil packs she had thrown in there on her last visit home. A girl needed to be prepared.

There. She gripped one, only to collapse against the bed as she felt his lips on her rear, where his hand had landed, smoothing over her skin as his tongue licked a fiery damp blaze across the flesh.

She lay on her side, one leg bent, the other stretched out on the mattress. His hand caressed up that leg, his fingers moving higher, to her thigh, then to the rich center of her body.

"The sweetest pussy in the world," he whispered hoarsely as his fingers skimmed over the swollen flesh and his body shifted. "Give me that fucking condom, Emily, or we're going to make more than a little love here."

Her womb clenched at the sound of his voice. It was tighter, his accent thicker, and his cock was nudging at her as he lifted her thigh to allow the hardened flesh to part the wet folds of her pussy.

Shaking, she dug her head into the pillow at the feel of his cock pressing against her and forced her hand back, holding the foil pack out to him.

"I'm going to spank you for having condoms on hand. Remind me to do that." He took it quickly, there was the sound of the packet ripping, and seconds later, she felt him moving, his erection retreating.

"I wanted to be a Girl Scout," she moaned. "Always prepared."

"That's Boy Scouts," he growled, pressing her thighs as she lay on her side.

"Like this." He smoothed his hand down her flank. "I'm going to take you like this, Emily. You'll feel me deeper, thicker. Like flames pleasuring you."

He lifted her thigh, holding it against his own until he came down to her, covering her, his cock sliding against her as she felt his breath against her ear.

"Feel me, sugar," he whispered at her ear as he began to press forward. "Feel me take you. All the way to your soul, Emily. Feel me take you."

The fingers of one large hand laced themselves with her smaller one as she felt the penetration begin. She hadn't expected it to be easy. She had expected pain. She hadn't expected a lot of pleasure the first time.

But it was there. The heavy stretching sensation, a burning, pulling pleasure that stole her breath as he worked the crest of his erection in and out, opening her slowly.

She could feel his cock throbbing. The head was so thick, so heavy inside her, stretching the tender tissue as explosions of color ruptured behind her closed lashes.

She tried to move beneath him, to press closer. She wanted it done. She wanted to be full of him, possessed by him.

"Easy, little one," he whispered roughly at her ear. "Slow and easy."

Slow and easy? He wanted this slow and easy?

"You'll kill me waiting," she cried out breathlessly. "You've teased me to death, Kell. I can't take more."

She tightened her muscles on him, heard his ragged groan, and moaned in rising ecstasy.

She tightened again, trying to draw him deeper, to force him into taking her. Waiting wasn't what she wanted.

Fourteen

KELL COULD FEEL THE SWEAT beading on his forehead, dampening his hair and shoulders and doing little to cool the fire raging in his body.

God, she was hot. Her pussy was melting around him, heating him, drawing him deeper inside, and searing his mind. He had never known this much pleasure with another woman. He had never felt the blinding heat that consumed him, the loss of control that had him shaking with the need to plunge forcibly into her.

She was so tight. The obstruction of her innocence was a slapping reminder that he could hurt her so easily.

But she was wild beneath him. Despite the position he had her in, on her side, as he braced himself above her, his cock penetrating her from behind as he bent her leg closer into her flexing stomach.

"Kell." Her arm twined around his as he braced himself on the mattress beside her. "Please. Take me now."

He was fighting to breathe, feeling her pussy like a snug, velvet fist around the sensitive head of his dick.

"So slick and wet." He bent his head until it rested at her shoulder, his tongue lapping at the sweat-dampened flesh as he retreated once again.

"If you don't fuck me I'm going to shoot you with your own gun," she cried out harshly.

The words. Sweet mercy. The word "fuck" coming out of her mouth was more than he could bear. His hips bunched, his knees digging into the mattress as his teeth clamped over her shoulder, and he drove home.

Emily screamed. His name. Screamed for mercy and from the sheer electric rapture that drove up her spine and exploded in her head.

There was pain, but it blended with the pleasure, drawing her on a rack of such blinding sensation that she couldn't make sense of it.

It went beyond pleasure. It went beyond anything she could have expected. The delicate muscles of her pussy clenched and rippled around him, stretched tight, exposing hidden nerve endings that rioted with the feel of his cock throbbing against them.

Kell's teeth were still locked in her shoulder, another erotic sensation as his harsh breathing sounded behind her. He was holding himself still, frozen; the only motion from his body was the flexing of his abdomen at her hip, the throb of his cock buried inside her, and his harsh breathing.

He was huge inside her. Heavy. Hot. She shifted beneath him, trying to move, to add to the sensations rippling through her body. She was so close to orgasm that it was almost agonizing to wait.

"Stay still, chère," he groaned then, the sound ripping from his throat. "Let yourself ease around me."

Ease around him? He was huge inside her. A thick heavy weight penetrating tender tissue, each throb of the heated stalk a latent caress that only made her wilder.

His hips jerked against her, dragging a startled cry from her lips as explosions of light shattered in her head. Oh God, she could become addicted to this. To this pleasure. To the sensations bordering on pain, but so exquisitely intense that her body began to riot for more. Every nerve ending, every cell, every cry from her lips as she began to writhe beneath him was a demand, an imploring, as the hunger inside her began to grow to a frantic level.

"Sweet. Chère. Hold on." He buried his head against her neck, his larger body restraining hers. "I'm too close, bebe." His accent began to thicken, deepen.

"Now," she whimpered. "Oh God, Kell. Now. Please. I need it. I need you."

She tightened on him again, an abstract memory of something she had once read coming to the fore. She fought for the control to caress him as she had never caressed another man, and the results were staggering.

A harsh male groan tore from his throat as he began to move. His cock drew back then pushed forward in a long, slow thrust that dragged a wail from her lips.

She could feel every inch of him burrowing inside her. The thick crest parted hungry tissue. Heavy veins throbbed with heat and hunger. And as he slid to the hilt once again, his control seemed to shatter.

Emily fought to make sense of the sensations, but she found it was all she could do to make sense of breathing as he began to move.

He began to tear her mind from her body. His hand gripped her thigh, lifted it, exposing more of her as he began to thrust inside her. Plunging deep and hard, he began to move his hips in rhythm, with a power that stole any ability to think.

Her fingers dug into the mattress as he held her restrained beneath him. She should have fought the control, but the rising sensations building, burning, inside her were too intense. She could do nothing but feel. And the feelings were so intense, so shattering. His cock shafted inside her, almost bruising in its girth, searing in its pleasure.

Reality was a thing of the past. Danger was nonexistent. There was only this. Only the speeding sensations ripping through her nerve endings, the feel of his erection stretching her, filling her. Then the blinding, soul-shattering orgasm that ripped through her with the force of a cataclysmic event.

AH, SWEET HEAVEN. SHE WAS so tight; her pussy clenched around his cock with a strength that stole his breath as her climax washed over her. Kell surged in deep and strong, paused, waiting, flexing inside her as he relished the heat and pleasure of her pussy flexing around him.

Holding back his own release was agonizing. He clenched his teeth, blinked back the sweat from his eyes, and forced himself to wait.

Just once more. He wanted to feel the tightening, rippling heat of her as she exploded around him just one more time.

As the grip eased, marginally, he began to move again. Her breathing was broken, his name a breathless litany on her lips that seemed to soothe something ragged inside him.

"I feel like I'm fucking a dream," he groaned at her ear. "So snug and tight. So much pleasure, chère. So much pleasure, I'll crave it. I'll dream of it should I ever have to leave your bed."

A thin wail left her lips as he began thrusting inside her again. Hard and deep. His hips setting up a powerful rhythm that he knew neither of them could deny for long.

He gripped her hip, holding her to the bed as he began to move harder, faster. His cock shuttling inside the sweetest, hottest pussy he could have ever imagined. Pleasure was like a fire burning inside him now, each stroke pushing the flames higher. The clench of her sweet flesh around him, the driving heat, her cries.

He felt it rising inside her. Her body began to tense as his hand slid between her thighs from the front, his fingers finding her swollen little clit and stroking, massaging, as his thrusts increased.

When she came, there was no stopping his own release. He swore she dragged his soul from his body, through the hard, jetting pulses of his semen into the condom.

He snarled at the reminder that he wasn't filling her. That

he wasn't shooting everything he had so deep inside her that she would never forgot, never know a moment that she didn't remember it.

That she didn't know she belonged to him. That she wasn't aware of his possession, his mark upon her.

His head dropped to her shoulder, his teeth gripping the muscle there, his mouth drawing on her, laying the only seal of ownership he had left.

She was his. He would die for her. He would die without her.

As he collapsed beside her, his breathing harsh, his own groan startled him as he eased his condom-sheathed cock from inside her.

Small, rippling little tremors shook her as he eased his arms around her and pulled her close to his chest. He would make her get up in a minute, drag them both to that monstrously big bathtub he had glimpsed in her bathroom.

She would be tender, sore, if he didn't take care of her. It was her first time, she deserved to be spoiled, eased. To be cherished.

Twenty-five years old, and she was still innocent. It didn't matter what reasons she gave for her innocence; he knew better. She had waited. Waited until the pleasure was too extreme to deny, until she found a man who could match her. One she could be wild with. One who she knew would allow her a measure of the freedom she searched for so desperately.

Once this was over, he would take her to a special practice range, where Durango Team trained in the summer. And he would teach her how to protect herself, how to watch his back, how to watch her own. How to keep herself safe until he could reach her if something happened while he was out of the country.

He would take her to the safe houses, teach her how to prepare herself in case she had to run. He would train her, ensure her safety as he fought to ensure his own. And he would pray.

Because God help him, he couldn't lose her. He had

waited. For too many years he had endured the loneliness that filled his soul until he found the woman who could ease the bleak shadows that filled it.

He was a man without a home, without a family. A man who had once known a warm hearth and a family's love and then experienced a betrayal that had nearly destroyed his soul.

All those years ago, he had hidden Tansy and their unborn child for fear of what was coming. He had taken her to the hunting shack in the Bayou that his family had owned and he had left her there until he could find the detective he worked with and could secure a safer location.

He had left her alone, and only one person had known where she was. The person who had caught him slipping into the home he had once known to steal the key to the old boat that he needed to get to the shack.

His mother had stared at him with such hatred, with fury. But he had never for a moment believed she would betray him. That she would tell his enemies where they could find Tansy and her unborn grandchild.

His mother had betrayed him. And he had never forgiven her. Just as he had never forgiven the rest of his family for turning their backs on him.

He had lived with it endlessly. Daily. Until Emily.

Until her laughter, her sense of adventure, and her need for freedom touched his heart. Until her loyalty, her willingness to forgo that need, touched his soul.

She was a woman worth fighting for and a woman worth living for.

She was the dream he never believed could become reality.

Fifteen

THERE WAS SOMETHING MUCH TOO natural about waking up in Kell's arms, Emily thought the next morning. He had wrapped around her like a human blanket, arms and legs encasing her, his chest a solid warmth at her back.

The blankets were on the floor, pushed there sometime during the night as she flowed over him, taking him again, crying out with the pleasure and the explosive releases that tore through her.

Yes, she thought with a smirk as she stared drowsily at the wall across from her. Releases. Not just two or three, but climactic pulses that seemed to merge, one into the other, until she had no breath left to cry out with the shattering ecstasy.

After that first time, he had immersed them in her large tub, the steamy water encasing them in liquid warmth as he just kissed her. Just held her.

There had been no demands, just his arms around her and a sense of belonging that she had refused to delve too deeply into.

"You scare me when you do that." His sleep-roughened voice grumbled behind her.

"Do what?" She smiled. She couldn't help it. There was something too sexy about his scratchy morning voice.

"Think." His hand smoothed up the outside of her leg to her hip as his erection began to prod at her rear. "When you think, things get dangerous."

"Baloney." She turned, smiling up at him as that lazy quirk tugged at his kiss- and sleep-swollen lips. "I'm never dangerous."

"You were thinking the night before you took that wimp Dyson to the strip club that first day," he pointed out. "I thought he was going to have a coronary as he chased you in the back door."

"You were there?" Her eyes narrowed on him.

"And the day you took him to the canine instruction academy. Emily, how the hell did you manage to convince him to dress in those pads and let those dogs attack him?"

Her lips twitched. "I was the one who was going to do it. But that made him come apart at the seams. So I told him if he did it, he could give me an accurate account and I would settle for that."

He shook his head. "You're a bad girl."

"Does that mean you'll spank me later?" She curled closer to his chest. "You could spank me now, just to teach me a lesson, you know."

Green eyes darkened, became brighter, sexier before an edge of regret filled his gaze and he glanced at the clock on her bedside stand.

"I've been waiting for you to wake up for two hours now. I have a meeting with the other team members when they arrive in about half an hour. With your father." But he considered her suggestion for a few seconds, before shaking his head and loosening his hold on her. "Come on, vixen. I'll spank you later."

"What were you doing while I was asleep?" She lay back on the bed, admiring the lean, muscular perfection that filled her gaze. Erection and all, he was a sight to behold.

Her gaze caressed over his buttocks as he pulled his jeans over them, not bothering to snap them as he tugged the zipper up.

"I was holding you." His look was frankly possessive. "Watching you sleep."

And he wasn't in the least ashamed of it. What had Kira told her once? That men never cuddled. Once they had finished, they were finished.

The bitterness in her friend's voice when she made the comment had clenched at Emily's heart. Because she wanted the tenderness Kell had given her. She hadn't known how much she needed it until he had given it.

The way he held her and bathed her. The fact that he had watched her sleep, that he had just held her.

"I like being held," she whispered as she stared up at him. "I liked it very much."

The quirk of a smile suddenly curled his lips and lit his eyes. He leaned across the bed, bracing his weight on his arms as his head lowered, his overnight growth of beard caressing her cheek before his lips settled against hers gently.

"Get up, sugar," he drawled, gripping her arms and drawing her up with him. "You have a full day ahead of you and I have things to do to keep that pretty little butt of yours safe so I can spank it later."

She wiggled said butt at him, shrieking as he made to slap at it before pulling back at the last second.

"Shower with me?" she suggested, casting a suggestive look over her shoulder as she moved to the bathroom.

He shook his head, drawing in a deep breath before grimacing in denial.

"Not a chance. Reno will skin me alive if I'm late for this meeting. Get your shower and I'll come back for you when I'm done. I want to go down to breakfast with you."

She paused. "You don't think I'm safe here? In Dad's house?"

"I feel better knowing you're safe," he stated firmly. "Let's get through this, Emily. We'll iron out rules later. Deal?"

"The rules are adding up fast, Krieger," she informed him warningly. "I'm making a list, you know."

"I'm sure you are, sweet." He chuckled. "I have no doubt. Now shower. I'll be back here in twenty minutes."

"Make it forty."

"Try thirty. I'm hungry. Someone used me hard last night and I need to restore my energy."

"Yeah, someone might end up using you hard again tonight," she suggested, her heart racing at the look of remembered pleasure in his expression.

He winked wickedly, picked up his boots and then left her bedroom. Before closing the door he turned the lock on the doorknob then pulled it firmly behind him.

She got the idea. Don't open it for anyone but him.

A smile tugged at her lips as she went into the bathroom and adjusted the water for her shower. They would have to talk soon, she knew that. There were secrets Kell was holding back, she could see them in his eyes sometimes, she heard them in his voice. Whatever those secrets were, they were filled with pain.

As she stepped into the shower she thought again how little she knew about him. She didn't know his past, barely knew his present, but he was becoming more important to her than people she had known her entire life.

She was falling in love with him. Hell, she was in love with him, and that part was scary. He owned a part of her, she admitted. A part of her she would never reclaim if he walked away from her.

Breathing in deeply, she promised herself she would savor every moment she had with him. She didn't want to miss this for the world. This euphoria. The sense of someone knowing her and her body as well, if not better than, she did. The feeling that for the first time in her life, someone understood. Not so much understood her, but understood the need to live.

She needed to live. And she wanted to do it in Kell's arms. But if he left her, if he walked away from her when this was over, then he had still given her a gift she knew no one else had given her. He had looked beyond the daddy's girl, and seen the woman beneath.

An hour later, after breakfast with Emily, before turning her over to her father's and the admiral's care, Kell entered the small room set aside as a meeting place inside the mansion for Reno and his team.

"Hey, lover boy. Reno tells me there's wedding invitations hitting the mail soon." Clint McIntyre, Reno's second in command, snickered as Kell walked in and closed the door behind him.

"In a few weeks or so. I'd like to get Fuentes out of the picture first," Kell answered.

It was worth it to see their expressions. Reno, Clint, and Maccy stared back at him in shock. Ian, as always, was harder to read, but he looked more thoughtful than surprised.

"Hell, another good SEAL bites the dust." Macey sighed. "What's with you yahoos? Are you contagious or something?" He looked from Reno to Clint to Kell.

"Could be, Macey. Better not get too close or you'll be looking for your significant other next," Ian's dark, rough voice commented broodingly.

Macey snorted before turning back to the screen of his laptop. "Enough of that crap. Gather round, boys. As of oh four hundred, Judas made contact again. For one of Diego's bastard skanks, he sure gets around on the Internet."

"Not a nice way to talk about our contact, Macey," Ian pointed out with an edge of amusement.

"Son of a bitch," Macey growled. "I'd like to cut his balls off for not being a little more forthcoming."

Kell moved around the table, staring over Macey's shoulder at the e-mail that had come to the secured account Macey used.

Assassin and/or abductor moving in. Location, D.C. Terms are as follows. Senator and/or daughter. Contact sent to senator to resign has been ignored. Fuentes contact requires action. Beware. Once

in D.C., contact will be informing tool of foolproof method of cap-
turing or killing daughter. Kidnapping is highest possibility at this
point to use as leverage. Watch your six while hobnobbing because
others are watching it as well.

Kell narrowed his eyes. There was something about that e-mail.

"Sound familiar?" Macey asked them all, staring up at them.

"Watch your six," Kell murmured. "Military term. Not unusual."

"There's something too familiar about this." Macey shook his head as he went back to the screen. "I've been trying to track this SOB for years now. It's damned strange. I can't get a handle on him no matter how hard I try."

"His information has always been factual," Ian pointed out.

"Too damned factual. He knows too fucking much," Macey growled. "The fact that he found this e-mail address to contact me at is the most worrisome."

The e-mail address had been set up years before as an SOS account. They were a team, no matter what. If one of them was in trouble, then the others would come running.

"You'll find him, Macey. Give it time," Ian said with no small amount of amusement. "My question is why the contact or spy changed his demand that Fuentes murder the girl to kidnapping her instead."

"Kidnapping will give him leverage, just as the e-mail suggests. If he kills her, he has no leverage. Nothing to bargain with."

"Why does he want to bargain?" Kell asked then. "The original idea was to first make the senator pay for his interference by killing his daughter, then to kill Stanton. Why change in midstream?"

"Good ole Diego, I'd guess," Macey bit out sarcastically. "That bastard delights in kidnapping, torture, and breaking men's souls. Not to mention women's. He wants to play."

"Another of his games." Kell's jaw tightened in anger.

"Our main objective is keeping the senator and his daughter alive," Reno said then. "Secondary objectives are catching Diego and/or his spy. I want that fucking spy. Bad. The son of a bitch has been betraying agents right and left in the past year. We lost two Homeland Security agents in California at the first of the year. One in D.C. and three more across the nation. Added to that are four agents outside the U.S."

"He's obviously someone in a position of trust within the government," Clint stated. "Someone with access to our Defense Department and missions around the globe. He could be an elected official, or a private contractor."

"He could be anyone," Kell snarled.

"But he'll be someone at this party tonight." Macey grinned. "This line, 'watch your six while hobnobbing because others are watching it as well.' We're partying tonight, my friends. Right?"

Kell stared at the electronic wizard with narrowed eyes. Macey should have been a linebacker for the Dallas Cowboys. He was tall, wide, and mean. Instead, his long, broad fingers moved over the keyboard of the laptop with the grace and ease of much smaller fingers.

"Here's our guest list." He pulled up the file the senator had supplied days before. "I have these names running through several programs at the moment. It will take time, but there's a chance we could get a hit and a direction to go in."

"Before the party?" Kell asked.

Macey grimaced. "Not hardly."

Kell turned to Reno. "Give me Ian to back me up with Emily."

Reno nodded slowly, though his gaze was piercing.

"Kell, is this getting too personal? Don't risk her life because you have too much on the line here."

Kell stared back at Reno coldly, feeling the hard edge of determination rising inside him.

"She's mine," he stated clearly. "Would anyone else protect Raven for you? Or Morganna for Clint?"

Raven, his wife, was also Clint's sister. A black-haired little minx who drove her husband crazy more often than not. But she still wasn't the handful of dynamite that Reno's sister and Clint's fiancée, Morganna, had turned out to be.

Both men grimaced at the question.

"Ian, keep an eye on his ass." Reno sighed.

"I have it, Commander." Ian leaned back against the wall, watching them all intently, his brown eyes somber, his brow lowered broodingly.

"The senator is arriving at the Dunmores' later than his daughter," Reno announced then. "He has a meeting on Capitol Hill before he can leave. That means you'll be shy of backup other than the two Secret Service agents who will be assigned outside the mansion grounds. I'll contact you as we head toward the Dunmore mansion. You're still undercover. We've not changed the mission parameters on this. Not that I think you'll have a problem with that."

Kell let a grin tug at his lips as the others snickered. As his gaze met Ian's, though, he noticed the somber acknowledgment in the other man's gaze. There were few men who knew the full details of his past. Ian was one of those men.

The other man nodded slowly. A promise. A vow to help Kell protect what meant the most to him.

"The limo is taking Emily, Kell, and Ian to the party. We'll be in the senator's secured SUV when we arrive. Let's keep this short and tight, men, and see if we can ID our spy and make this mission short, sweet, and without complications." Reno's gaze swept the room. "Any questions?"

They shook their heads in reply.

"Good. We'll be heading out with the senator within the hour. I believe he currently has his daughter corralled in the office discussing her recent strip-joint venture and the chances of it happening again. Are we taking bets on who wins this one?"

Clint, Reno, Macey, and Ian put their money on the senator. A former SEAL. A man who had kept his daughter in line, one way or the other, for twenty-five years.

When all eyes turned to Kell he pulled his wallet from his jeans pocket, extracted the required twenty and handed it over to Macey. "My money's on the lady," he drawled. "You don't tame a vixen, you just travel in her wake."

EMILY STARED AROUND HER FATHER'S office. The pictures of her mother that sat in a place of honor on the mantel. The painting he had commissioned, just after Emily's birth, of her and her mother hung across from his desk.

She looked like her mother, Emily thought. The same vibrant auburn hair, blue eyes, and inquisitive features. She had never paid much attention to it over the years. Her own looks rarely concerned her much. But as she stared at the portrait and waited for her father, she saw it now.

Her mother had been more delicate. Fine boned, slender, and graceful. Her hair was longer, hanging nearly to her waist, where Emily kept hers cut to her shoulders.

Her mother had loved parties. Emily preferred adventure. She wanted to go mountain climbing, skydiving, and playing war games in the mountains.

Her mother had lived for fashion. And Emily preferred jeans to silk, but she understood the need for the silk.

She hadn't known her mother long enough, she thought. She hadn't had a chance to hear her laughter often enough; she could barely remember the songs her father said her mother sang to her each night before bedtime.

"She loved you with all her heart," her father said behind her as he came into the office. "She used to say you had the best parts of both of us. I've always agreed with her."

"Weakness?" she asked as she turned to face him. "I hadn't heard either of you were very weak, Dad."

"Is that how you see it? The need to be careful? My need to protect you? That you're weak to allow me to protect you?"

"To foist your candidates for a son-in-law on me? To tie me up with so many strings of guilt and love that half the time I didn't know what living was?" she countered.

He grimaced at her questions.

"I made you a list of the cost of groceries, utilities, and boarding for your little boys during the past seven years." She nodded to the paper he held in his hand. "I realize it's pretty extensive and may require a few weeks to sort through, but the final amount is really rather low for the trouble I was forced to put up with. I'd appreciate being reimbursed."

"Take it out of the interest that's acquired on the account your mother and I set up for you," he suggested.

"Sorry, Dad, that money's being saved for a reason. It's the nest egg I'm saving for any children I might one day have myself. Just cut me a check when you have time and send it to me."

His eyes glittered with irritation then. "Why now? You've never said anything before."

"Because you always deposited far more than I required. I don't want more than you owe me, Dad. That's what you've never understood. I want your respect. Your trust. Not your charity."

"So you thought you'd earn my trust by traipsing through strip joints, bars, and dark alleys after that nonsensical research you harp about? I have yet to see a book, Emily Paige. All I do is hear about it."

She breathed in carefully. She wasn't going to argue with him. "Dad, cut the crap, and while you're at it, just go ahead and cut my check so I can deposit it when I return home."

A frown furrowed his wide forehead. "What crap?"

"The crap where you deliberately start a fight, I get upset and storm out of the office. You know, the crap where you ensure you win whatever fight we're engaged in." She crossed her arms over her breasts and stared back at him in determination. "It's not happening this time."

"Because you're sleeping with Krieger? Tell me, are you at least going to marry him?" he snarled.

Her brow lifted. "Marriage hasn't been discussed. Why are you so upset? Isn't that the reason you keep sending your top picks to play bodyguard? Hoping one of them will end up in my bed?"

"With a wedding ring would have been nice," he growled. "I should have known when he demanded to be added to your rescue team what the hell was going on. At least tell me he's wearing a condom? The last thing I need is to see you knocked up and dead like the last girl he fell in love with."

Knocked up and dead!

Emily stared back at her father for long, frozen moments, feeling something chill in her soul.

"What are you talking about?"

"He didn't tell you about his first wife and child?" he asked her then, something undefined flashing in his eyes, something almost akin to regret.

"I never knew—" she whispered past numb lips.

"Then ask him about it," he snapped. "And make sure you know what you're doing—"

"Don't you dare lecture me about him." Emily felt her hand raise, her finger pointing back at her father imperiously, as rage began to seethe inside her. "You've been sending men to my bed for years. I finally decided to accept one of them, and you have to try to destroy it?"

"Potential husbands, girl," he snapped back. "They knew better than to step within so much as a foot of your bed without an engagement ring. I didn't send Krieger to you as a potential husband, he was protection. He came with the team."

"And he's the one I chose, instead of you handpicking him?" She sneered. "For God's sake, where the hell do you get your nerve?"

"The same place he got his." His chin lifted proudly. "The Navy."

Emily snorted rudely at that. "For some reason, I don't think so. Cut my damned check now. You've dropped your little bomb and you can head to your precious Capitol Hill and make whatever trouble you decide to make today. But your interference with my life is finished. Do you understand me?"

"Like hell." His voice lowered. "Tell me, Emily, do you think he's going to give you free rein? That he's going to let you have all this freedom you crave? He lost his wife and child when he was working as a snitch with the police in New Orleans. He wasn't even eighteen. Do you think he doesn't remember every moment of it? Every fucking detail of their deaths? You think I try to wrap you up in cotton and protect you? Just wait until he gets his ring on your finger and a baby by you. He'll never give you a moment's peace."

In the past, the dangerous lowering of his voice had always indicated that the last measure of his patience had been exhausted. Emily had always walked lightly in response to it, not really understanding what that dangerous undertone meant, but not wanting to find out either.

Now, she really didn't give a damn.

"Do you understand me?" she screamed back then, feeling the tears edge into her eyes, the pain blooming in her chest as she ignored the revelations about her lover's past. "Write the fucking check. And so help me God, you send another man to my home and I'll have him arrested."

He was the one staring back in shock then.

"Emily—" He stepped toward her, his gaze becoming wary. "This is getting out of hand." He rubbed his hand over his face, his expression twisting with indecision then.

"I've never asked you for anything," she said then, forcing the words past her lips, feeling the pain claw at her stomach.

Kell had been married before? He had lost a wife and a child and she hadn't even known. She hadn't wanted to know. She had deliberately kept her distance from him, holding him back even as she tempted the passion that was so much a part of him.

"You've never asked me for anything," he agreed. "And maybe that's been the problem. You don't seem to need me at all."

"Oh, I needed you," she bit out. "When I tried to tell you I didn't want to stop mountain climbing. That I wanted to train in the mountains again. When I tried to tell you I wanted to join the Navy. I needed you, Dad. You just refused to hear any of it."

"It was too dangerous." He shook his head with a sharp jerk. "You weren't a child anymore. You wouldn't see there were limits. You were always pushing for more, going higher."

"Trying to live. Trying to be something other than daddy's little girl?" she asked mockingly. "Forgive me, *Father,* maybe I should have just bowed to your wishes, married the first jerk you brought home and had all those grandbabies you wanted. Maybe I should have found a way to screw my life up worse than I did when I tried to compromise with you instead."

He pushed his fingers through his hair, a grimace contorting his features as he tried to figure out how to deal with her.

"Don't bother looking for an edge on this one, Senator Stanton," she told him roughly. "I'll tell you what. You keep your damned money. When this deal with Fuentes is over, we'll call it even. And I'll make damned certain I live my life then, and you can live yours."

"You don't mean that." He caught her arm as she turned away from him to stalk to the door. "Emily. You wouldn't just walk away from me like that."

She stared at the portrait of her and her mother. Across from his desk, where he could see it. Where he could remember.

"Unlike you, Father, I don't need to control everything and everyone in my life," she said as she turned slowly back to him. "And I don't want to ever face living solely in the past. I'm not your little girl anymore. I'm your adult child. Your daughter. If you could accept that, maybe you could get a life yourself."

She pulled her arm from his grip, turned her back on the pain that flared in his eyes, and stalked to the doors. As she pulled one open she stared back at him.

"Don't interfere with my life again. You won't like the consequences."

She stalked out, coming face-to-face with five hardened

SEALs, whose expressions—except for one—were blank, watchful. The exception was a dark emerald green, rife with shadows and dark pain, as he watched her closely.

"I have things to do before the party tonight," she said sharply. "I'll meet you down here at precisely five o'clock. See if you can't at least give me the time I need to get ready before we have to have our little blow-up, hmm? Because, honest to God, if I have to deal with another stubborn, intractable SEAL for one more minute, I might shoot one of you with your own gun."

With that, she brushed past the five men, refusing to look back, refusing to let the tears that filled her eyes fall.

It was her own fault if she had gone to bed with a man she didn't know. Her own fault if she had allowed her father to have the ammunition he needed to strike back at her.

Her father hated losing a fight with her. He always had. It was one of the reasons she rarely let a confrontation evolve between them, because she was always the one who came away from it hurt.

Sixteen

AT PRECISELY FIVE O'CLOCK, KELL was waiting in the foyer, wearing his dress blues, and watching the stairs with a sense of unreality as Emily descended them.

She was a living flame. Incandescent, radiant. The long emerald gown should have been modest. On her, it was a statement of sensuality. Fragile silk cupped her full breasts before slender straps moved over her shoulders.

The high waist only hinted at her shapely body, but made it seem all the more desirable. Silk smoothed over her stomach and hips, then dropped in a fall of shimmering color to her feet, which were shod in matching heels that added at least three inches to her height.

A shimmering wrap trailed over one shoulder, flowing to the floor behind her as she moved down the stairs as regally as a queen.

Her auburn hair was upswept. Emeralds twinkled in the banked flames and artfully arranged curls, and her makeup gave her face an even more an exotic cast.

He could feel his cock thickening beneath his slacks. His heart raced in his chest.

She was the most beautiful creature alive.

Her blue eyes were shielded by her lashes, refusing to let him glimpse the emotions he knew must be raging inside her.

He had heard the argument from outside the office doors. He had heard the information her father had given her about his past. Information that even his commander hadn't been fully aware of.

She knew so little, yet it was enough to send a prickle of dread down his spine. She knew just enough to demand more later.

Hell, how had this happened so quickly? It seemed from one moment to the next his life had changed. He had gone from existing to living.

The senator had been wrong on one count though. Emily would have her freedom. Kell couldn't afford to try to hide her; to restrain her, in that direction lay madness. To begin with, she would never accept such a life with the man she loved. She would never love a man who tried to enforce it. For another, Kell would never be able to function knowing that his wife, possibly his children, would have no means of protection.

"Wilma Dunmore has done an excellent job putting this party together," she commented as she stepped into the marble foyer. "I'll need to spend a few minutes going over the details with her when we arrive, meeting with the caterers and so forth." She checked her purse as she spoke. "I'd appreciate it if you wouldn't make the same mistake my father's past bodyguards made and glower at everyone. It makes them uncomfortable."

"Yes, ma'am. No glowering." He nodded, restraining his smile.

She was ready for battle. He could see it in her, but even if he had been blind as a bat he would have felt it. It poured off her in waves.

The vixen was finding her claws and God help any man who tempted her to unsheathe them anytime soon.

"Why are you carrying that pack?" Her gaze went to the strap that dangled from his hand.

"Preparation's everything, sugar." He shrugged.

"Preparation. That reminds me." She opened her slender

evening purse again and pulled free a folded piece of paper.
"I was talking to Wilma last night about the security she has
in place for the party. I marked a few weak areas here."

He accepted the paper slowly.

"What sort of weak areas?"

"I intend to discuss them with Wilma before the guests
begin arriving," she stated. "But I didn't pinpoint the areas
until I was looking at this earlier. There are several entrances
and exits onto the grounds through a series of what were
once deep gullies. James Dunmore's father, Winchester, had
cement tiles installed in them and had them covered over
when I was a child. I used to play in them with the Dunmores' children when I visited there."

Kell stared at the sketched diagram she had put together.
It was surprisingly well put together. It showed the mansion,
the entrances and exits from the main house, and the location of the gullies.

"And these tunnels go into the house?" He frowned back
at her.

"They lead to iron grates above the ground. They're easily large enough for a man to access. I wanted to check with
her about security around them. At one time, there were
locked gates at the entrances to the tunnels, but several of
them run to a streambed several miles from the house. They
could have forgotten about them. They never seemed too
concerned with them in the past because the grates were always bolted. But if someone knew what he was doing—"

"They could get through the iron grates and into the party."
Kell nodded slowly. "Don't mention this to Mrs. Dunmore.
Let me contact Reno from the limo and see how he wants to
handle this. If Fuentes has a foolproof plan to get to you tonight, this could be part of it."

Emily nodded. Kell had sent Ian into the study where she
had gone to finish her calls earlier, to give her the information they'd gotten from the earlier e-mail.

She needed to trust him. Sending Ian to her rather than
going himself had been a calculated risk.

"Those tunnels would be a perfect entry point. They're wide enough for a man your size to shimmy through, and the iron grates covering the openings are slightly wider. Winchester Dunmore never considered them a threat to the grounds though, and James and Wilma weren't living there at the time. They could have just been forgotten."

"Let's go then." He extended his arm to her, staring down her at with a sense of possessiveness and pride. Damn, she was slick. The tiled gullies weren't on the security schematics that the team had been given of the estate, which meant they had either been forgotten as she suggested or simply not mentioned for darker reasons.

"I won't be able to stay in one place or keep you informed of every move I have to make."

"I'm sure I can keep up with you, Emily." He didn't smile, he had a feeling she was hanging on to that redhead temper by an inch and he didn't want to unleash it before this damned party. The last thing he needed was to allow her to go into this with her emotions more severely tested than they were already.

"We're coming out." He spoke into the transmitter at the collar of his uniform, testing the reception and the earwig connected with Ian's.

"All clear," Ian responded. "Proceed to the limo."

The butler gave them a concerned glance as he opened the door cautiously.

"Be careful, Miss Emily," he said softly as they neared him.

"I'm very well protected, Denny," she promised the other man as they moved toward the door. "We'll see you tonight."

Kell kept his gaze moving on the area outside, aware that Ian was doing the same until they had Emily safely ensconced in the limo. Ian closed the door behind Kell then moved to the front seat of the limo with the Secret Service agent assigned as chauffer.

Kell hit the button that slid the back window closed as he stared across the seat at Emily. Once they were enfolded in the intimate confines of the darkened area, he pulled his pack forward.

"I have a weapon I want you to wear." He pulled the Velcroed holster and leg strap from inside the pack as Emily began to lift the skirt of her dress.

Silk and taffeta whispered over her legs as his gaze was drawn to them. Black stockings encased her legs, each delectable inch revealed until the skirt edged over a slender leather strap that held a Beretta Bobcat snugly against her inner thigh.

His cock jerked and became so engorged he had to grit his teeth to hold back the growl that wanted to rumble in his chest. Like an animal. Wild with the need to mate.

The sight of that gun, its walnut grip gleaming in the light of the interior, held so intimately against her flesh, was like a punch to his gut. It should have flashed a warning to his overexcited brain; instead, all he could see were black silk stockings, pale silky flesh, and a woman's confidence in herself.

"Do you like it?" She ran her fingers over the weapon caressingly, the pale peach nailtips scraping lightly over the thin leather holster.

"Too much." He had to clear his throat to speak.

"Then you should really like this." The skirt dipped over the gun, rose above her other thigh, and he had to clench his fists to keep from touching her. Strapped to the opposite thigh, just a shade higher than the gun, was a small knife, carefully sheathed but definitely there, the hilt rounded and pointing to territory Kell hadn't explored nearly enough the night before.

He hadn't even known she was wearing the weapons. The location of the strapped holsters allowed her to move freely while not giving any of the telltale signs that she was loaded and damned dangerous.

"Does your father know about those?" He had to force himself to breathe against through the lust whipping through his veins.

Thankfully, the skirt and taffeta underskirt flipped back over her legs quickly, shimmering and pooling at her feet with a whisper of sound.

"What do you think?" Her look was derisive.

Kell pursed his lips and breathed out roughly. "Damned good thing. One stroke tonight is enough."

He could feel the sweat popping out on his forehead, the eager, greedy throb of his dick, and wondered how the hell he was going to make it through that party without finding a dark corner to fuck her in.

That was the best protection, he thought savagely. Cover her body with his own and keep her penetrated. She kept him so damned tense and hard that bullets would bounce off his body like fucking Superman.

By time they reached the Dunmore mansion, he was in control again. Not that Emily helped much. She watched him intently during the drive, her gaze shadowed by her lashes, her expression thoughtful.

They would have to talk soon, he knew, and he would have to explain Tansy to her. It wasn't that he didn't want to explain his past, so much as the fact that his own actions still shamed him.

He hadn't protected his wife and child. Why would Emily believe he could protect her?

As the limo pulled up to the curving cement steps of the mansion and stopped, Kell pushed back lust, pain, and the growing possessiveness he felt toward Emily. He stepped from the limo, looking around carefully before handing her out.

The driveway was still clear, the party, scheduled for several hours later, hadn't yet begun.

"MILY." WILMA DUNMORE MOVED GRACEFULLY from the open double doors, her lined face creasing into a smile of affection as he escorted Emily up to her. "And who are your young men this time?" Her brown eyes twinkled with interest as she stared at Kell and Ian then glanced back to Emily.

"Wilma, may I present my escort for the evening, Lieutenant Kell Krieger. And behind him, my bodyguard for the evening, Lieutenant Ian Richards."

Wilma grimaced at the word "bodyguard."

"Is your father still foisting those bodyguards on you?" She rolled her eyes at the thought. "He isn't getting any better with age, is he?"

"No, Wilma, he is not." Her smile was tight. "But we endure what we must."

Wilma laughed at that. At sixty-eight, she had learned long before that men will do whatever it took to have their way, Emily thought. Her own husband was a dominating force within the international banking business, and paranoid enough that Wilma had bodyguards more often than not.

"Come in. Come in. I'll get you some refreshments and we can go over the plans for the evening. I've kept everything simple, as you asked. I can't tell you how pleased I was that you asked for my help on this, my dear. I do so love throwing these parties."

And that was why Emily had turned to her for help. Wilma loved the whole process, whereas Emily had learned to tolerate it.

She glanced at Kell as they followed the spritely older lady through the house. He wasn't acting like a bodyguard. Ian was taking care of that for him. He was acting interested, just bored enough to prove he was a man, but infinitely polite as Wilma drew them into the ballroom where the guests would be escorted.

The Dunmore ballroom was huge. Chandeliers dripping with crystal hung from the high ceiling. It was large enough to hold hundreds of guests, and even more with the doors to the gardens thrown open as they were now.

The band was positioned just outside the open glass doors at one end of the ballroom. The cool evening air wafted through the cavernous room as it seemed to echo with the anticipation that put a bounce in Wilma's step.

The older woman had already dressed in her party finery. The lace and silk swished as she walked, her still slender figure exuding grace and pride.

Wilma familiarized Emily with the setup with precise details. As they were going over the last of the plans, guests began to arrive and the band started setting up.

Kell's expression hadn't changed, but Emily felt the watchful tension grow in him as the ballroom began to fill up, the caterers and waiters began moving into place. By eight o'clock the party was in full swing.

Silk suits, officer's uniforms, and a variety of ball gowns milled about the room. Champagne was flowing freely and the large marble patio was beginning to fill up with couples moving in time to the music.

Her father still hadn't arrived, and Emily was beginning to feel the effects of smiling at people she either didn't know, or knew too well to like.

That was one of the reasons she hated these events. She knew the backstabbers and the hangers-on and they drove her insane.

As her gaze swept over the crowd from one of the small gatherings she stood at, Emily felt a real smile begin to shape her lips as she watched a familiar form enter the ballroom.

"What is she doing here?" Kell leaned forward to ask curiously.

"Her uncle is Jason Maclane, the head of a multinational legal firm. She attends some of the parties at his request, gathers gossip, and relays it back. In exchange, he keeps her in the style she likes to be accustommed to," Emily answered. "Kira is nothing if not practical when it comes to acquiring her bling."

"Emily. Baby. This party is bursting at its seams." Kira smiled as she kissed her cheek gracefully then drew back. "And that bruiser behind you looks as good as ever."

The bruiser in question was watching Kira thoughtfully, his deep green eyes intent and considering.

Dressed in a figure-hugging black sheath that fell to the floor and displayed a provocative amount of breast, Kira looked fantastic. Her black hair flowed down her back in rich curls and gleamed with a raven's-wing sheen Emily had always envied, and her gray eyes sparkled with laughter.

"The bruiser thanks you," Kell commented wryly as his hand cupped Emily's hip and drew her back against him.

He had been doing that all evening. Little touches. Soft looks. Heated looks. And more than once, purely hot, sexy looks. But he always remained circumspect in how he touched her or held her against him.

"I see our brooding neighbor Ian Richards is here as well." Kira scanned the ballroom, her gaze moving quickly to where Ian stood against the far wall. "That man was not meant to be a wallflower, Emily. In no way, shape, or form."

Emily winced. She knew that tone. Kira was interested.

"He just has the darkest, brooding sensuality." Kira sighed, turning back to Emily with a secretive little smile. "Don't you think so?"

He looked damned dangerous. Like a man she wouldn't have approached for a million bucks.

"She thinks he's ugly as a mud stick," Kell drawled in amusement. "She doesn't see any man other than me."

His tone was teasing but Emily felt a small start of surprise. He sounded like a "real" lover. Like a man who intended to stick around for a while. A man who was invested in a relationship. Like a man whose heart belonged to her rather than a woman and a child he had lost years before.

"You're cute, but not that cute," Kira informed him with a flirtatious wrinkle of her nose. "Now, if you two will excuse me, I'm going to grab a glass of champagne and see if I can convince that tough hard, body to join me on the dance floor."

"Better find the whiskey if you're going to tempt him into anything." Kell chuckled. "Ian doesn't do champagne very often."

Kira waggled her brows, then with a little wave of her fingers she headed across the ballroom.

"Tell me, does she have a chance?" Emily asked thoughtfully as she glanced at Ian. He was watching Kira, his brows lowered, his expression forbidding.

"At what? Sex or love?" Kell asked thoughtfully. "Sex, yes. Love, I sincerely doubt it."

"I doubt she's looking for love." Emily sighed as she turned back to him. "What are you looking for, Kell?"

She wished she could take back her words. Wished she could erase the need to know.

His lips tilted in a lazy grin as his eyes gleamed with a hidden knowledge, an unvoiced emotion. "What I have in my arms, Em. What else?"

What else indeed.

She opened her lips to speak, knowing that the words would betray her own hurt, her own longing.

"Emily. Sweetheart?"

The male voice had her turning in Kell's arms, her gaze widening at the sight of the man standing before her.

He was taller than she remembered. Definitely better built and more mature.

"Charlie." She laughed in delight, feeling his arms wrap around her in a quick brief hug before she pulled back and felt Kell's hand tightening warningly at her hip.

"Charlie, this is Kell Krieger, a friend of mine. Kell, this is Charlie Benson."

Kell didn't look pleased.

Tall, with closely cropped brown hair and laughing brown eyes, Charlie had definitely matured. The silk evening suit he wore stretched across his lean, wiry shoulders, and though he hadn't exactly filled out, he had definitely hardened.

"It's good to see you, Emily," Charlie said softly, his lips still holding his smile despite the glower Kell directed at him. "I was hoping you would be here."

"Your name wasn't on the guest list." She shook her head in surprise. "How did you get in?"

"Dad pulled a few strings at the last minute so I could surprise you." He pushed his hands into his slacks and stared back at her in approval. "You're looking good. Damned good."

Emily could feel Kell tensing behind her.

"Kell, Charlie and his father work in data processing and intelligence at the Pentagon."

"It's good to meet you, Benson," Kell answered, extending his palm toward Charlie.

Charlie took it warily, wincing only slightly before Kell released him. His look when he glanced back at Emily was wry. "Navy SEAL, huh? Did your dad finally talk you into one of his candidates?"

"Not hardly, Charlie." She kept her smile light, but she could feel Kell growing tenser by the second. "Dad just wishes I would become so cooperative. Kell was my choice."

"She's a gift, Krieger, I hope you realize that," Charlie said then, his tone warning. "If you don't, there are those of us waiting to snag her on the rebound."

Emily could feel the blush covering her face then.

"She has to rebound first," Kell growled. "If you'll excuse us now, she's promised me this dance."

Emily hid her smile as Kell led her away, though she did look back long enough to wave back at Charlie. His expression was faintly regretful, with a gleam of longing in his eyes that pricked at her conscience.

She had kept up with him over the years, but this was the first time she had run into him at a party.

"Your taste in men is lousy," Kell remarked as he pulled her into his arms once they reached the patio.

Emily restrained another smile. "I picked you."

"Only under duress," he grunted. "I thought Wilma Dunmore stated earlier that there were no surprise guests?"

"There are always surprise guests." Emily moved against him, her head resting on his chest as he led her around the dance floor.

His arms were warm and strong around her, creating an

impression of security, of peace. She hadn't had that before, had never known how calming it could be.

"We need to leave soon," he whispered against her ear then. "I don't want to stay too long and give anyone a chance to catch either of us off guard."

She felt his erection against her hip, the heat of his body swaying with hers, and let her fingers caress his chest where her hand lay over his heart.

"We can't leave yet. I have to stay at least another hour or so."

She was aware of him watching the room as they danced, she could feel it in the tension in his body, in the way his head moved against hers.

"Something doesn't feel right," he warned her. "Dunmore's wife seemed damned sincere about the fact that there were no surprise guests."

"And I told you, there are always surprise guests. Someone can't make it, they give their invitation to a friend. Someone crashes, slips in, and drinks the free alcohol and eats the snacks from the buffet while pretending to be part of the crowd. It's normal."

But it didn't feel normal. Kell could feel the fine hairs at his nape lifting in response to the closely developed instincts that had saved his ass until now. If Charlie Benson had managed to slip in, who else had?

His gaze roved over the dance floor as he maneuvered Emily until he could see into the ballroom once again. Benson was standing at the double French doors watching with a hint of longing. He lifted his champagne glass to Kell with an air of resignation then turned to the blonde standing several feet away from him.

Ian and Kira were standing just outside the patio doors, watching as he and Emily moved along the dance area. In Kira's gaze he saw something harder, something more calculating, than he believed she wanted him to see. There was more to her, he could sense it.

"I love dancing with you, but until your mind is actually

on the fact that you're dancing with me, I'd prefer to find someplace to sit down for a few moments."

He drew back and stared into her soft blue eyes. God, he wished they were anywhere but here. Anywhere but under the eyes of so many strangers and in possible danger. Someplace where he could hold her, touch her, still the unrest he could see moving through her expression.

She had questions and she wouldn't wait much longer to ask them. He'd prefer to wait a hell of a lot longer before he had to answer them.

He escorted her to the buffet bar. There, they filled two delicate china plates, accepted a glass of wine each, and returned to the patio and the small wrought-iron tables and chairs that surrounded the dance area.

He wasn't hungry. And he didn't need the wine. What he needed was an explanation for the vague sense of warning that kept prodding him.

His gaze swept over the area again, coming back time and again to Emily, as guests stopped to speak, laugh, and draw her into the gossip that seemed to be the spice of political life. There were enough people surrounding her now that he didn't have to worry about an assassin's bullet.

As his gaze moved back to the couples dancing on the patio, he froze.

He hadn't seen them in fifteen years, but he would recognize them anywhere. They were older, aged, their faces lined with grief and weariness, their eyes filled with sadness as they watched him.

Son of a bitch. He didn't need this. Not here. Not now.

"Emily." He rose to his feet and extended his hand to her as she stared back at him in surprise. The guests surrounding her parted immediately as she straightened from her chair and came to him.

No questions asked. She moved to him.

"We need to leave now," he said softly. "Right now."

She nodded swiftly, lifted her purse from the table and turned back to him.

But it was too late. Dammit, it was too damned late.

"Kell." Aaron Beaulaine stopped in front of him, his weathered expression filled with determination and hope as he straightened his stooped shoulders and his arm curved around his petite wife, Patricia.

"Excuse me, sir," he answered coolly. "We were just leaving."

"Kell. It's been fifteen years," Patricia Beaulaine whispered softly. "Can't we have fifteen minutes?"

He could feel Emily's confused gaze as she stared at him and the older couple.

"I'm sorry," he answered again. "But we need to be going."

He tugged at Emily's hand and she tugged back. Stilling, he clenched his jaw and whipped his gaze to her, feeling the anger beginning to rise inside him now.

"Hello." She extended her hand to Aaron. "I'm Emily Stanton."

"Richard Stanton's little girl." Aaron's smile was tremulous. "It's very good to meet you, Miss Stanton. I'm Aaron Beaulaine and this is my wife, Patricia."

The Cajun accent was diluted, but still there. Unlike Kell, Aaron had never been able to completely drown out the low, accented drawl he had been raised with.

Emily looked from Kell's closed expression, then to the older couple once again.

"Kell. It's been so long." Patricia reached out to him then, her green eyes, not as dark as his, not as bright, shimmering with a damp sheen as her fragile hand shook.

She was so much tinier than she had been last time he had seen her. So much more frail.

"Has it been long enough?" he asked her then. "Would it be long enough for you?"

He hated this. For fifteen years he had avoided anything that would bring him in contact with them, that would allow for such a scene.

"A time comes in a man's life when he must make hard

decisions," Aaron said then, his voice gruff. "When he must see the mistakes of his past. Just 'cause we are older, doesn't mean we don't make mistakes."

Mistakes. That was how they saw it. How they had seen his marriage to Tansy. How they had seen the child he had created with her.

"And a time comes when a man has to admit that no amount of regret can ever change certain mistakes or their results." He kept his voice cool, as unemotional as his expression. "This is neither the place nor the time, Mr. Beaulaine. We'll have to speak later."

Mamère whimpered. Before Kell could catch himself his hand reached for her, but he quickly jerked it back, an inner fury lashing inside him at the instinctive response.

"Kell, we'll be gone soon." Patricia kept her voice low, her awareness of those around them evident. "I beg of you, allow us to make amends."

He shook his head. "Amends were never needed." Some things couldn't be fixed.

With that, he dropped Emily's hand, gripped her upper arm, and moved her away from the couple, leading her back into the house and heading for the front door.

She wasn't speaking. He had glimpsed her face though, seen the suspicion in her eyes and the anger.

Damn her, did she think he liked turning his back on them? They were old. So old that the knowledge of their limited time on this earth struck him with startling strength each time he thought of them.

And each time he thought of seeing them again, reaching out to them, he remembered the child that had died with its mother. The child he had never held, never known, and yet had loved with all his heart.

As they said their goodbyes to the Dunmores and Emily made some excuse about a headache and gave her effusive thanks to Wilma for hostessing the party, Kell watched as Ian moved to the limo that had pulled up to the bottom of the steps that led to the circular driveway.

His neck was still itching. He stared around the well-lit grounds, his eyes narrowed on the shadows that ringed the woods around them.

As he moved Emily down the steps, he saw it. The small red bead that began to dance over her chest from the sights of an assassin's rifle.

He jerked her to the side as part of the cement column behind them shattered, and Ian jumped into action. He rushed up the steps from the open limo door, placed himself in front of Emily as Kell gripped her waist and they all but threw her into the limo. Kell jumped in beside her.

Within seconds, the vehicle was moving away from the house as Ian barked his report to Reno into the secured cell phone he carried.

Emily stared across the distance at Kell, her eyes wide, her face pale.

"I saw it," she whispered, the horror in her voice clenching at his soul. "Fuentes has decided to kill me? I thought he wanted to kidnap me?"

"If his assassin wanted you dead he wouldn't have used a fucking laser sight," he snarled, his hands clenching as he fought to keep from jerking her to him, from devouring her just to be certain she was truly still there with him. "The son of a bitch is playing games again and laughing his ass off as we scramble around trying to figure out what the hell is going on. Once I figure it out, I'm going to watch that bastard bleed."

Seventeen

Emily escaped to her bedroom the moment Kell announced that the house was clear and safe. Her father was downstairs with the rest of the SEAL team, planning, trying to figure out what the Fuentes cartel was doing and what their next move would be.

All Emily could see was the small pinpoint of light that had jumped from her chest to Kell's. The knowledge that the laser sight was aiming for him, not for her, and the startling realization that life would never be the same without him.

She wouldn't be the same without him.

She loved him.

He was secretive. Mysterious. Sexy and manipulative and she knew it. He had been manipulating her since the day he had come into her life. But the manipulation was designed to spur her to fight for what she wanted. Not to restrain those needs.

He probed and he pushed, and every time he touched her she went up in flames.

At the moment she was furious with him. And she hurt for him. She had seen the pain in his eyes when his grandparents had approached him at the party.

Oh yes, she knew the Beaulaines, and she knew a part of their history. The only grandchild they had was disowned years ago, before the death of his wife. Once the wife had died, they had tried to mend the break, to bring him back into the family. But the boy they had thrown away had become a man, and the man had refused to acknowledge them.

It wasn't a secret in the political and social sphere she moved within. The Beaulaines were heavy contributors to her father's political fund. And come to think of it, so were their good friends Douglas and Mena Krieger.

Emily froze in the center of her bedroom. Why hadn't she pieced it together? Of course, she had met the Kriegers only once and Douglas didn't resemble Kell in any way. Kell looked like his maternal grandfather, the piercing gaze, the shape of the lips.

They had disowned him because he wed his pregnant girlfriend, a young black girl who had come from the streets, with no family, no home, and most important, no fortune to back her up.

She sat down on the bed with a weary sigh.

She had seen his eyes when he turned away from the couple. They were haunted, so bleak and filled with aching despair that she hadn't been able to protest his rudeness.

He loved them. He loved his grandparents, and he ached for them, but whatever had happened all those years ago had driven a wedge between them forever.

Was that why he pushed her to declare her independence from her father? To stand up to him rather than attempting to compromise between her wants and his? Because he knew the inherent danger, the pain that could result when she finally decided enough was enough?

She stared down at her hands, realizing they were shaking with the shattering realizations pouring through her.

The past week had been filled with so many tumultuous emotions that she hadn't had a chance to question him about his past. She had seen the man he was though. Strong. Determined. He walked the path he had set for himself years ago, and he walked it alone. Out of choice. Better to know he had no one to depend on than to depend on them and to lose something so precious as the woman he loved and the child they had created.

What had happened?

She crossed her arms over her breasts, her fingers clenching into her upper arms as she gripped them tightly, and rose to her feet to pace the bedroom once again.

What had caused him to forever deny himself the family he loved for so long?

And what of his parents? She knew they were dead. Lisa and Sturgill Krieger had died when she was a child. A car accident, she believed. If rumor was to be believed it had happened just after their son had disappeared from Louisiana.

He hadn't done as they had wanted him to. He hadn't turned his back on the girl they considered beneath him and he hadn't walked the line that generations before him had walked. The line that led to more power, more riches, to marrying within the social set of which they were a part.

"Oh Kell," she whispered. "What did they do to you?"

"They killed her."

She swung around, her eyes widening as she realized how silently he had opened her bedroom door.

"What?"

He closed the door behind him, his fingers moving to the buttons of his dress uniform, releasing them to strip it from his broad shoulders and toss it to the foot of the bed.

"Her name was Tansy," he said conversationally, his tone bland, in direct contrast with the pain that filled his green eyes. "She was carrying our son. Tansy let me pick out his name. I wanted to name him Aaron Douglas Krieger, after my grandfathers."

He paused, staring down at the jacket reflectively before giving his head a quick jerk and staring back at her for long, silent moments.

"You know who the Beaulaines are?" he asked then.

"Your grandparents," she whispered, her arms lowering, her hands clenching the skirt of the evening dress she still wore.

He nodded slowly. "My mother's parents. Aaron and

Patricia Beaulaine of the Louisiana Beaulaines. New Orleans to be exact. Did you know Hurricane Katrina destroyed their estate?"

She nodded. She didn't know what to say, what questions to ask.

"They loved that fucking mansion. The lands surrounding it. The history they claimed as their own and the power they had built through the generations. They were the Beaulaines. And because of a freak of nature, they had no son to carry it on, only a daughter. Until they had me. And they were certain I would carry on the tradition. Kellian Beaulaine Krieger." A grimace twisted his lips. "The last great hope of the Louisiana Beaulaines married street trash and tried to forever taint the impeccable bloodlines they had established."

God, the pain in his eyes. His expression was bland, clear, no tears marred his gaze, no grimace of rage creased his face. But his eyes were alive with it.

"How did Tansy die?"

He ran his hand roughly over his stubbled jaw.

"They threw me out. I was seventeen, no money, no job, I'd graduated high school that year but I was still dumb as the road. I took a job in a New Orleans coffeehouse and café that was frequented by my parents' friends." His lips twisted mockingly. "My parents called me a disgrace. I would laugh at night at the expressions on their friends' faces when they realized I was working there. And the pity in their eyes when they tipped me. I knew they were talking. I knew my parents were paying." His expression twisted then, the pain a hard grimace on his face as he turned away from her.

"The café was used by people other than my parents' friends. It was the early days of Diego Fuentes's reign in the cartel. His suppliers were there. They were braggarts and they didn't bother to hide what they were doing. I would pick up the information during the day and sell it to the police detective who approached me one night after work."

"And they found out."

"They found out." He nodded. "They had a hit on a local judge. They were going after him that night. I called my friend, they caught them in the act, and I had to testify."

His hands pushed through his hair. "I had to testify."

He shook his head roughly before turning back to her.

"Did you testify?"

"They threatened Tansy. I got a message at work, that if I didn't retract my statement, they would make her pay. I left work and went to the Beaulaine mansion. The keys to an old boat were there. I needed that boat to hide Tansy. We had a hunting cabin in the bayou. No one knew where it was except the family. No one knew about it."

She could feel it coming. She could feel the pain, the horror building inside her.

"They found her?"

He nodded bleakly. "My mother caught me stealing the keys. She warned me that if I didn't leave Tansy that she would make certain Tansy paid for it." His voice lowered. "She sent a message to the suppliers, and she told them where Tansy was hidden. She told them I was with her, even though I wasn't. She knew I wasn't. I had to work because the doctor had to have the money up front for the baby, and the larger she grew with our child, the weaker Tansy seemed to get. I couldn't afford to hide."

Emily was silent as he finished speaking. He seemed to stare off into the distance for a long moment.

"I didn't have to hide," he finally said softly. "I knew something was wrong when I eased the boat into the bank that evening. I knew she was dead. The gators were churning in the water, even they could smell her blood. My baby's blood. And they were hungry." His gaze seemed to chill then, became icy, hard. "They ate that night, Emily," he snarled then. "I fed them the bodies of those fucking animals that killed my family."

Emily felt the tears that slid from her eyes and fought to hold back her sobs. Kell wasn't crying. He was stone hard, cold, icy.

"The woman who gave birth to me, who swore for seventeen years of my life that I was the light in her heart, betrayed my family. She signed her grandchild's death warrant without so much as a flicker of regret. And when it was over, when I was standing over my goddamned wife's grave, her fucking lawyer stepped up to me and informed me that if I wished, I would be reinstated within the family." His laughter was mocking. "As though their deaths meant no more to them than a mild inconvenience. As though the six months I had spent scraping together the money to pay a doctor and to feed my wife wasn't even a blip in their little world."

"Oh God. Kell." She reached out to him, seeing the remembered horror of that time on his face.

She expected him to reject her, to push her away, but she needed to touch him. She needed to warm that icy rage in his eyes.

She stepped to him, laid her head on his chest, and pushed her arms beneath his to wrap around his back. He stiffened, his hands clasping her shoulders, before a hard shudder shook his body and he wrapped himself around her instead.

He rocked her. His lips pressed against her neck as he breathed in raggedly.

"I wasn't stupid when I married Tansy," he said softly. "She loved me, but I knew the lure of the drugs would have taken her back. But the baby. That was my baby, Emily. My child."

And he would have died for it. He had killed for it. And he had turned his back on the family whose betrayal had changed his life forever.

"I know," she whispered tearfully.

His chest cushioned her tears as she heard the weary acceptance finally overshadow the rage and pain in his voice.

Then his hands were gripping her head, pulling it back, his gaze blazing into hers, filled with such possessiveness, such heat, it took her breath.

"I won't lose you," he vowed hoarsely then. "Do you

understand me, Emily? Something broke inside me when I lost my family, but if I lose you, I couldn't survive the rage. Do you hear me?"

"Kell—" she whispered in startled surprise at his declaration.

"You can walk away if it's not what you want, but you'll have my soul wrapped around you forever. No matter where you go, what you do, or who you love, Emily. You'll always be a part of me."

Her lips parted as a weight that filled her soul seemed to lift from it.

"The boy that I was loved Tansy," he whispered then. "The man I am is bound to you, Emily. The thought of losing you has me tied into so many knots I left a meeting downstairs with your father to make certain you were safe. To see for myself. To touch you. God help me, to just touch you."

His hands slid around to cup her face, to hold her in place as his lips lowered to breathe a kiss over hers.

"I remember the sight of those stockings beneath that dress," he growled. "Weapons strapped to your thighs, and I thought I was going to come in my dress uniform. My cock has only gotten harder tonight, Emily. I've only grown hungrier."

Her hands covered his, her gaze searching his as erotic pleasure began to tingle through her bloodstream. He lowered his forehead to hers and stared back at her with that damned sexy quirk to his lips.

"I should be downstairs. I should be plotting and planning. Instead, I'm torturing myself with the scent of you, the remembered taste of you."

"Don't leave me," she whispered. "Stay."

"Leave you?" His thumbs smoothed over her cheekbones. "Emily, it's all I can do to think when I'm around you. Leaving you would tear the soul from my body."

Before she could find the words to speak, to make sense of the emotions suddenly flooding through her, his arm lowered, slid around her hips then jerked her close, angling her body so his cock pressed against the aching mound of her pussy.

Her lips parted. A hard breath tore from her lungs at the heat and anticipation that rioted through her.

"I need you. Now." His voice was a sexy rumble of erotic heat.

Emily could feel the desperation in him, the steel core of determination as he lifted her closer, drawing her off her feet, and turning her, only to back her into the wall.

His lips covered hers, his tongue sliding past them to devour the need that rose inside her. It shouldn't be so good. She was angry with him. She was mesmerized by him. The taste of his kiss was as wild as the wind, his hands a force of nature as the skirt of her gown suddenly cleared her thighs.

She had disposed of the weapons, but she still wore the stockings. Stockings that slid over his thighs as he drew her up and her legs wrapped around his hips.

"Yeah. Like that." He groaned, his hand making short work of the snap and zipper of his pants, pushing them to his thighs as the engorged length of his cock slid free.

He was hard. Thick. Hot.

The sound of a foil pack tearing barely caught her attention; the knowledge that he was sheathing the heavy erection with a condom brought an edge of regret. But it lasted for only a second.

Silk covering iron and suddenly plunging forcefully inside her as his lips caught her scream of incredible, ecstatic pleasure.

She could feel the heavy wedge of flesh stretching her pussy, the fiery ache of the penetration blending with the sensitivity of suddenly exposed nerve endings and clenching tissue.

"Sweet God, you're tight," he snarled. "I could die happy fucking you, Emily. Buried inside you. Just like this."

His hips jerked, drawing another desperate cry from her lips, as the zipper at her back suddenly loosened and he drew her breasts free of the silk covering them.

"Perfect nipples." His tongue stroked over one then the

other as a heavy thrust inside her had her fighting for purchase, both physically and emotionally.

"Sweet tight nipples. A perfect innocent pink and hard as ripe, sun-drenched berries." His lips covered a peak, drew it inside then began to suck with deep, heavy draws as his hips set a hard, driving rhythm between her thighs.

"Sweet Emily." The accent was back. "Ah chère, hold me tight. Just so, bébé."

She whimpered as her legs tightened around his waist, feeling his hands palm her rear, fingers clenching in the mounds as he shoved inside her, hard and deep.

She was so wet her thighs were growing damp. So close to climax she could feel it peaking, swelling her clit, burning in her womb, only to have him ease. His thrusts grew gentler as she writhed against him.

"Don't tease," she cried out, her hands gripping his shoulders, her nails pressing into his flesh.

"No tease," he gritted out. "Sweet chère. Let me feel you. So tight and sweet on my dick. Sucking so sweetly at me."

Her breath caught as the air became saturated with the scent and the sound of sex, of pleasure. His erotic, explicit words shocked and titillated. They pulled at the eroticism rising inside her and fed the hunger that only he could sate.

If he would let her orgasm. If he would just stroke a little harder, a little faster.

"Ah bébé, tha' sweet pussy likes it slow and easy, eh?"

She shook her head. It was as though the dark, predatory male inside him had suddenly been loosed, had been given freedom.

His gaze was sharper, hotter. His lips were hungrier. His cock teased and cajoled and shafted inside her with irregular thrusts that had her trying to scream his name with the burning need. Trying, because she didn't have the energy to do more than reach for orgasm, to withstand the unbearable pleasure tearing through her.

"Kell. Please." She arched in his arms as she felt sudden space at her back, felt him moving her.

She expected the bed. She didn't expect the floor. He sank to the carpet, coming over her, his erection still buried inside her as he stripped off first his pants, then her dress.

The material was jerked over her head, taffeta and silk rustling as he tossed it aside, leaving her clad in nothing but the black stockings and high heels she had worn with the dress.

"Fuck. Yes." Satisfaction thrummed through his voice as he leaned back on his knees, drawing her legs over his thighs before his hands clenched at her hips.

Hard. Her hips jerked as he plunged inside her hard. Deep. Once.

"Oh God, you'll kill me, Kell," she whimpered, her hands reaching for his wrists as he held her hips in place.

"I'll love you, chère." His expression was erotic, filled with a heavy sensuality and male pleasure that pierced her womb.

"Will you love me?" she gasped breathlessly, staring back at him, feeling not just the need for the steadily rising pleasure, the heavy thrusts of his cock, or the touch of his hands. But the touch of something far less defined. The touch of his heart.

"Ah chère." He came in closer, bending over her then, his hands gripping her hands to anchor them to the floor as his lips touched hers. His tongue stroked over them. "Don' you know? You own my soul, how could I help but love you?"

Three hard, furious thrusts of his hips followed his words, splintering the pleasure inside her as she began to chant his name, to fly, to fracture with ecstasy.

And still he was hard inside her. Brutally hard. His cock throbbed inside her as her inner muscles clenched around him with a force that had her straining back from the bruising pressure.

"Hold still, sweet sugar," he groaned, rearing back once again, holding her hips in place as he pierced her to the hilt.

She whimpered. Pleading, desperate sounds as tremors raked over her nerve endings, pleasure tearing her apart as the orgasm seemed never-ending.

If he would just hold still long enough. If he would stop those slow, gentle pushes against her, stroking her internally, building her pleasure again even as the final pulses of her orgasm eased.

She was rising again. She cried out, her voice trembling at the feel of the pleasure rising inside her.

"There, chère. Let it have you." His large hand settled on her stomach, fingers outstretched, pressing against the flexing muscles as her head thrashed on the floor, her nails digging into the carpet, clawing at it as she fought to anchor herself amid the sensations beginning to tear through her once again.

Let it have her? It was destroying her. She could feel the fire whipping through her body again, tightening her muscles as he began to move again.

This time, there was rhythm to his thrusts. A hard pounding as he buried his cock inside her with each desperate lunge. His expression intent, his eyes darkening, muscles tightening.

Emily arched beneath him again, pleasure overtaking her, throwing her into another brutal orgasm as a hard male groan echoed around her, and the feel of his cock pulsing violently inside her as his release swept over him had his name gasping from her lips.

She was clenched so tight around him that she could feel the flex of his cock. The jerk of his balls against her rear, the throb of his erection inside her, and the sound of her name pulled from his lips.

"Chère. Sweet, sweet Emily . . ."

Eighteen

EMILY WAS DRAPED OVER HIS chest hours later, exhaustion making her a limp damp weight as his arms surrounded her. The dark flames of her hair cascaded over his chest as her soft breaths tickled the hair on his chest.

He glanced at the clock beside the bed and winced. Two hours. Two hours filled with the tight grip of her pussy and the soft cries that tore from her lips each time he touched her.

But there were things to complete this evening. Plans to be made before they headed back to Georgia. The team would separate again in the morning and Kell wanted to make certain he had all the information involved before he left.

As he lay there, the memory of his grandparents wavered through his memory. His Mamère, so slight and frail now. She had once ruled the Beaulaine mansion with a steel hand. Or she had thought she had. Until his maman had married the Krieger heir and systematically begun to pull that power around herself.

And Papère. He breathed out heavily at the thought of him. He had been closest to his Papère. They had gone fishing and hunting. He had tried to teach Kell the art of catching a vixen and laughed in affection with each failure.

So many memories. He had fought them for so long, and now they came tumbling down around him like a Bayou downpour. Hard, fast, drenching his emotions in sadness.

He had lost his parents not long after Tansy's death. Kell had grieved for his father, and for the mother he had believed existed, rather than the one who had betrayed him.

Unlike his parents, who hadn't come to Tansy's funeral, Kell had shown up at theirs. He had stood carefully out of sight, watched the sealing of the crypt with a heavy heart, and reminded himself that he couldn't go back. He couldn't bring Tansy and their child back, and he couldn't return to the memories of the mother he had cherished.

His love for Tansy had, as he told Emily, been a boy's love. He had been determined to save her, filled with passion for the exotic, beautiful young girl, and certain of his ability to protect her. He was a Beaulaine-Krieger. He was invincible. Wasn't that what his mother had taught him?

Instead, he had learned how very powerless he truly was, and his child had paid the price.

His child. Innocence. Blood of his blood. A defenseless being who would have looked to Kell as he had looked to his own father for nearly eighteen years.

Some nights, he dreamed of that child. Dreamed it had survived that night. That he laughed up at him with green eyes and a vibrant smile. And sometimes he dreamed that the boy watched him with tear-filled eyes as he tried to reach him, tried to save him.

Shaking his head he eased Emily from his chest, almost smiling at her grumpy little sigh before she settled against her pillow and slipped back into slumber.

He brushed her hair back from her face and leaned closer, breathing in the scent of her before kissing her forehead gently.

His eyes closed as his lips lingered.

God help him. She was becoming more important to him than anything else had ever been in his life. She wasn't just invading his soul, she was becoming his soul.

He had to force himself to draw back from her, to leave the bed before pulling his dress slacks back on, gathering the rest of his clothes, and slipping back into his own room for a shower.

He needed to talk to Reno and the team before morning. Returning to Georgia wasn't something he wanted Emily to do. She was too vulnerable there. Her assassins too certain where to find her. As he had been shown earlier in the night, bullets could get past him.

The thought had his guts tightening in rage. God help the Fuentes assassin if Kell managed to get his hands on him.

Getting out of the shower, he dressed quickly, pulled on his lace-up steel-toe boots and secured them, then clipped his holstered weapon to his side and went into his bedroom to meet with his visitor.

He'd heard Ian come in minutes before, alone. The other man was slouched in the easy chair that sat in a corner by a reading lamp and small table. His long legs were stretched out in front of him and his dark blond brows were lowered heavily as he watched Kell come in from the bathroom.

"I could have been someone else." Ian's voice was low and brooding, almost angry, as Kell took a seat on the side of the bed, watching him curiously.

"Then you would have been dead." Kell shrugged.

Ian didn't snicker at that as he usually did. Instead, his expression seemed to grow darker.

"What's doin'?" The Creole flavor of his accent was getting harder to disguise, harder to hold back.

Ian's lips quirked at the sound.

"She relaxes you," Ian remarked. "That's a good thing, bro." He sighed heavily then leaned forward in his chair. "Reno and the team just left with the senator. He has an early meeting in the morning to clear the way for that bill that the Fuentes spy so obviously doesn't want to pass. With the new information Macey received while we were at the party, I thought I'd update you before we head to bed."

"He received something else from Judas? That boy sure is taking an interest in this." Kell snorted.

Ian's gaze flashed dangerously. "Macey managed to trace the transmission from inside the mansion. Whoever Judas is, he was there."

An image flashed in Kell's mind. Kira Porter. There had been something he had seen in her face, her eyes, for a second across the dance floor, that had reminded him of someone.

"Porter?" he asked.

Ian shook his head, a smile tipping his lips as humor lit his odd hazel-blue eyes.

"Our delectable Miss Porter is Homeland Security," he drawled. "She's also the daughter of one of the senator's best friends from his SEAL days."

It clicked into place then. He had seen her twice, once in Russia where she had been a blond sex kitten working a cocktail party for the American ambassador, and then a few years later in South America where she had carried a lethal automatic rifle as easily as other women carried a purse. Her hair had been nut brown then, her eyes a matching color and a razor-thin scar had marred her downy cheek.

"They call her the Chameleon," Ian mused. "She has a different look for every job. The scar in Bolivia was real, by the way. Homeland Security paid to have it put in place and they paid to have it repaired after the mission. She's low-key, normally in watch position only, but the file the senator showed us on her is scary, dude. Real scary."

Ian's tone wasn't in the least intimidated. It was— anticipatory.

"Any suspicions which guest at the party was Judas?"

Ian stared at the wall across the room, his gaze thoughtful. "The message he sent says the spy was there. Macey is working through the guest list looking for our friendly mole. He'll tackle Judas later, I suspect."

Ian crossed his feet slowly. "We head back to Atlanta in the morning, as per the senator's orders. With the Porter girl in place, me on the other side, and you in the condo with Emily, he believes she'll be safe enough at home. I think he's a fool, but that's just between the two of us."

"The only way to eliminate the threat is to run with her," Kell said thoughtfully.

"Reno pointed that out." Ian nodded. "But, as Macey said, that will alert the Fuentes mole that we're closing in on him. And Macey is closing in. That boy is a whiz on the computer."

Ian's ruined voice, dark, serrated, was filled with mockery.

Rage beat at Kell's head before he forced it back. He forced himself to think logically. If he ran with her, they would always be running. Fuentes saw it as a sign of weakness, as cutting out of the game, and it would be sure to enrage him. At this point, they had no choice but to use the hand dealt to them and make certain he didn't win.

"If we catch his spy, then the threat against your woman is gone." Ian shrugged. "That's all that matters."

"I want things in place so I can run if I have to," Kell gritted out. "Fuentes isn't touching Emily, Ian. I won't let this happen."

Ian nodded slowly as he rose to his feet. "Get some sleep, dude. We're taking a Navy flight back to Georgia and a secured SUV back to the condo. Her last party is in three days' time and Judas's message reported that all players will be in place there as well. If we find him, we save your woman, and we find Nathan."

God, Nathan. He hadn't thought about that. The information none of them could believe, but it had come with a picture, with proof. Nathan Malone, the SEAL believed killed during Emily's rescue, was alive. Alive but near death and under the control of the spy known as Mr. White.

"Arrange a meeting with Kira when we get back to Atlanta," Kell ordered. "I want her information and I want to know her backup plans."

Ian nodded before pausing. "I saw you talking to your grandparents," he said then.

Kell froze. "I have no grandparents."

"Whispers were sweeping around the party. Interesting little rumors about the New Orleans Beaulaines and their missing grandson. An heir to two of the largest fortunes in the nation. That would be a hell of a position for a SEAL to be in. We live a dangerous life."

"Drop it."

"Blood is thicker than water, my friend," Ian murmured. "Sometimes, a man has to own up to the past and everyone's mistakes within it. Some things, you don't just throw away."

Kell stared back at him silently, coldly.

Ian lifted his shoulder dismissively. "Just thought I'd mention it. Catch you at daylight, bro."

Kell rose from his seat on the mattress and headed for the closet as Ian left the bedroom. He finished hanging his dress uniform neatly in its protective covering, leaving it for now. From the floor he pulled free the duffel bag he had carried to Atlanta with him and checked it quickly.

Everything he needed was there. Cash, alternate identifications, a change of clothes, weapons, and ammo. Always prepared. He was always prepared. Until he met Emily.

He hadn't been prepared for what she would do to him. How she would make him feel.

She made him feel things he had never believed he could feel, even after Tansy. The love he felt for Emily went so deep, was tangled so tight around his heart and soul that he wondered if he would survive if anything happened to her.

It was damned scary. The time spent with her had been so short. And yet she had a hold on him that he couldn't have expected.

His Papère Beaulaine had warned him once that Beaulaine men, they loved fast, loved hard, and they loved forever. That when a Beaulaine male found his woman, he knew instantly she would change his life forever.

And Kell had scoffed. He had been young. He had been too arrogant. Too certain that no woman would ever fill that much of a man. And his grand-père had smiled. That quiet, knowing smile of his that Kell saw as an elder's acknowl-edgment that young men will be young men. That they'd al-ways scoff at the wisdom of their elders.

God, he had missed that old bastard. As hard as the be-trayal of his parents' disowning him had been, his grandpar-ents' refusal to take his side, to help him, had hurt even more. His papère had been his hero. His grand-mère an angel.

The Kriegers had always been more distant, so their de-fection hadn't been a surprise. But the Beaulaines, they al-ways stuck together, the old man had once told him, because blood was thicker than water. And blood mattered.

As he sighed, a light knock sounded at the door, soft, hes-itant. Emily.

He tossed the duffel bag back into the closet as the door opened and she stepped inside, clad in nothing but a silken robe that couldn't compete with the feel of her skin.

She tucked a strand of dark auburn hair behind her ear as she stood in the doorway, her expression pensive when she saw he was dressed.

He held back his smile. He could see the emotions riding inside her gaze. Hesitancy, arousal, the need to feel him wrapped around her.

She was still new to this intimacy, to having a man capable of controlling her sensuality, and yet allowing it freedom.

"I was going to catch Reno for an update," he said softly as he sat on the bed and removed his boots once again. "It seems he's already left though."

"I saw Ian going downstairs." She played with the belt of her robe, her slender fingers tense.

"He was giving me an update." He set the boots and socks aside. "I would have been back to bed in a few minutes."

She nodded jerkily. "Is everything okay? With the mis-sion, I mean?"

"Everything's fine."

She licked her lips nervously as he rose to his feet and padded toward her.

"It should be over soon?" she asked.

"Soon," he promised, then ignoring her gasp, he lifted her into his arms, watching as the robe parted over her legs and fell to the side. "Let's go back to bed. You need your rest."

Her arms wrapped around his shoulders, though her blue eyes darkened in worry as she stared back at him.

"We need to talk," she reminded him.

"There's going to be plenty of time to talk later, chère." He didn't bother to try to tame his accent now. He was too busy trying to tame the lust rising inside him. "For now, I need to touch you again. To feel you against me."

He entered her bedroom, kicking the door closed behind him before locking it. A second later he was laying her back on her bed, staring down at the white robe as her hard little nipples pressed against it, the shadow of the dusky pink color surrounding them barely discernible beneath the material.

He jerked his shirt over his head before his hands went to his jeans, and he discarded those just as quickly.

He was so hard he was hurting. So filled with hunger he felt as though he had never come in his life. His cock was straining out from his body, furious with Kell's delay in taking her.

A wicked smile curled Emily's lips as her slender fingers pulled at the belt of her robe, releasing the tie and allowing the panels to fall apart as she rolled to her knees and shed the garment.

Kell felt the breath jerk from his body. Blood pooled hot and thick in his cock and drew his balls tight. She was like Venus rising. Like every sexual dream any man had ever conjured up in the dark lonely hours of the night.

And she belonged to him.

"Come here, chère." His hands framed her face as she knelt on the bed before they slid into the rich, silken depths of her fiery hair.

Emily stared up at him, drowning in the emerald depths of his gaze, feeling the air thicken with sensuality, with the hunger that rose between them.

She hadn't expected this. She had never had trouble

pushing away her previous bodyguards. They were her father's goons. She had enough trouble with her protective father; she hadn't been in a hurry to create more by accepting one of his handpicked son-in-law candidates.

But Kell was different.

For one thing, he was harder. Her hands pressed against his chest, smoothed over the flexing muscles as his lips covered hers. He was stronger, more forceful; the very aura of confidence and competence that surrounded him drew her. His air of dominance and sexuality was in harmony with her own sensual desires, which threatened to burn her each time he touched her.

As he was doing now. His lips moving over hers, parting them to dip his tongue in playfully before pulling back and drawing her lower lip between his and sucking lightly, sexually.

His hands moved up her back, then down. Gripped her hips and pulled her closer, cushioning his erection against her belly.

"Are you sore?" he whispered as he pulled back, one hand sliding from her hip and moving confidently between her thighs. She gasped at the feel of his palm cupping her, his fingers sliding over the damp flesh of her pussy.

His fingers rubbed against the folds, shifting between them to circle the sensitive opening.

Emily felt her head fall back on her shoulders. And Kell was there to take advantage. His lips moved along her jaw, down her neck.

"Never too sore," she whimpered. "That feels too good, Kell."

"Never too good, sweetheart." His voice deepened, becoming a sexy murmur along her collarbone as his finger slipped inside the snug entrance.

"Oh. Yes. Too good." Spreading her thighs wider she fought for a deeper penetration, opening herself for him, desperate to experience more of the incredible pleasure his touch brought her.

"You're soft as silk. As hot as fire," he whispered against the curve of her breast before giving her a gentle, erotic bite with strong teeth.

Emily shuddered at the caress. The combination of primal hunger in the bite, the wicked titillation of his finger stroking inside her, teasing her.

"And you're hard," she moaned, her head lifting, her lips finding the hard column of his neck.

Kell let her have her way as he felt her teeth at his neck. Sharp little sensations moved along his flesh before tightening his cock and balls from the feel of her teeth.

Her hands were like satin gliding over his flesh and the gentle cushion of her tummy rubbed against his cock, causing his teeth to grit at the primal arousal growing inside him.

He wanted to throw her to the bed and ride her to ecstasy.

Instead, he held himself before her and let her explore. Like the vixen he had dreamed of catching as a boy, she was curious, inquisitive. Her nails scraped along his chest to his abdomen, making his teeth grind as he fought for patience.

Her lips skimmed over his neck to his chest. She bit. She licked. She had electricity pouring into his body, tightening his nerve endings and cascading along each cell with a pleasure he wasn't certain he could withstand.

She was like whiskey. Potent. Fiery. Burning clear to his soul with her feminine demand, sharp little bites, and satiny licks.

"Ah sugar. Keep this up and I'm going to lose my head," he said, his hands in her hair, sifting his fingers through the strands as she nipped at his lower chest.

She was going lower. Drawing close to his cock, her hungry lips and tongue tightening his muscles into a mass of anticipation.

"I want to feel you," she whispered as her lips went lower, licking inches from the head of his dick. "In my mouth. Against my tongue. I want to feel you like I can't feel you inside me. Without a condom. With nothing but your flesh against me."

Shit. Hell. Fuck. He was going to come before she ever touched him. If he didn't get a hold on her—

She got a hold on him instead. Her tongue slid over the head of his cock, her mouth surrounded it, and Kell knew he was lost. His hands tightened further in her hair for long seconds as he fought the need to control it, to keep her from bringing him to release too soon.

Her mouth surrounded the throbbing head, drew it deep, and began to suckle with such innocent pleasure he swore he felt his eyes water.

He had never been tasted, taken with such pleasure. He had never had another woman worship his body, his cock, as his sweet Emily was worshipping him.

"Chère. Sugar. Sweet, sweet Emily," he groaned, thrusting against her hips with a short jerk of his hips he couldn't control. "You're gonna get in trouble with that wicked mouth."

She shuddered at the sensual threat, then another, harder tremor washed over her as his hand moved from her hair, trailed down her spine then clenched on the rounded curve of her rear.

"Like that, little fox?" he whispered.

The vibration of her approving moan against the flesh of his cock had the hard flesh spasming in warning release.

His fingers clenched again, his lips curving in a tight smile as her suckling faltered. But her moan was just as dangerously exciting.

Slender fingers cupped his balls now as the fingers of her other hand gripped the shaft. And stroked.

Kell drew in a hard breath.

"Let's see if you like this, eh?" He landed a light slap against her rear. Watched her jerk. Felt her moan.

Not hard. Emily wouldn't like a hard caress. She was delicate yet strong. But her flesh was sensitive, easily bruised and easily stung.

He wanted to deliver the lightest touch. Just enough to make her feel the flames, to tempt her, to see how much more she could stand before he went further.

She wiggled her pert little rear and mouthed the head of his cock with enough hunger to send flames racing up his spine. Damn. She would kill him before she finished tonight.

He landed another tap to her rear, grimacing as she tightened, then allowed his fingers to trail along the shallow cleft as she stilled. Like a little fox, waiting, cautious, wary.

He drew back, watching the shudder that raced through her then feeling her mouth draw on his cock again. She was sucking him like a dream. Like a hungry goddess, licking and mouthing his dick as her playful fingers played on his balls and his shaft.

He tapped her rear with his fingers again, just a bit harder, and before she could process the added burn, moved his fingers down her cleft, curved beneath her thighs, and filled her tight, hot pussy with two fingers in a sudden, stretching thrust.

Enough of this playful teasing. He pumped inside the clenching tunnel with the fingers of one hand while the others gripped her hair, held her to him and pumped her mouth with slow, steady strokes.

"Enough teasing, sugar," he growled. "You'll take me now, eh? Now, before we both die from the need."

Nineteen

KELL PULLED AT EMILY'S HAIR and her mouth sank deeper on his dick, her expression transforming in her pleasure as the pressure on her scalp became a delicate pain.

Hell. Damn it to hell. He loved a woman that liked her hair pulled.

He pulled again, felt her moan, watched her lashes flutter against her cheek as her suckling grew harder. Deeper. The stroking motions of her fingers over his shaft became firmer, stronger, as the fingers cupping his balls twitched and flexed until he felt the sweet bite of her nails against the tender flesh.

He pulled again, one hand moving to cover hers on his erection as his hips began to move. To thrust into her mouth, to gain control before it was too late to control.

Force of will, he told himself desperately. That was all it took. Pulling from the heated suckling of her mouth nearly destroyed him.

The edge was so close. The hunger rising so sharply inside him that he took time only to push her around on the bed, lift her hips, and begin penetrating her.

Emily stared across the bed in shock, her gaze locked with her own in the mirror across from her before she lifted it to Kell.

Did he know his expression was tortured? Tormented? Nearly as much as hers. He was pushing inside her by slow degrees, making her feel every bite of the impalement, every inch that stroked across every nerve ending.

He had one hand locked in her hair, the other clamped on her hip, and behind her, his face was a mask of lust and need. But his eyes. His eyes were filled with something. Something hot, possessive, challenging.

She bucked in his grip, pulling away and smiling in triumph as he slipped from her. She watched his lips firm, watched the determination that crossed his expression before he stilled her movements and began pushing inside her again.

Oh God, it was too good. It was delicious. It was burning and tingling and sending wicked, wicked fingers of sensation to race around her already swollen clit.

"Come 'ere, chère." His voice was hoarse as she pulled forward again, almost dislodging him. "Sweet little fox. My own little fox." He surged forward, burying another inch as her back arched.

Emily saw the frank triumph in his expression then. The dark shimmer of male satisfaction on his piratical face. The days' growth of beard and emerald eyes made him look wicked enough. But that lust and triumph in his expression only made it more so.

"Kell!" Her thoughts were scattered as he burrowed in deeper, his fingers pulling and releasing at her hair, his possession filling her, stretching her.

"Tell me what you like, eh love," he groaned, retreating, penetrating, never filling her enough, never hard enough or deep enough.

As his fingers eased in her hair she jerked forward again, dislodging him once more. A frown edged at his brow. Both hands clamped on her hips, and before she could draw a breath and prepare for it, he was plunging inside her.

"Ah God!" He stilled, trembling nearly as hard as she was shaking. "Fuck. Emily. No condom," he panted, a rivulet of sweat running down the side of his face to disappear into his beard.

No condom.

She stilled, trying to breathe, trying not to clench around the brutally hard flesh inside her. She saw his face then. Saw the struggle in his expression, the need, the force of emotion. And suddenly, she didn't care. She had no intentions of letting him go. Ever. Super Glue would have nothing on Emily Stanton when it came to Kell.

"I don't care," she whispered. "I don't care, Kell."

He was staring at where their bodies were interlocked, sweat now beading his face as he swallowed convulsively. His fingers clenched on her hips. The muscles in his thighs tightened and he began to withdraw. Slowly, so slowly.

Emily dragged in a whimpering breath, both at the retreat as well as the sensations. She wouldn't push it. She wouldn't demand. Having Kell's baby would be more joy than she could imagine, but—

A ragged, tortured groan left his throat. A second later, he was buried inside her once more and he didn't stop. His hips moved quickly, hard. Each thrust built in pleasure, the feel of his flesh bare inside hers, the stretching heat, the need building and building as she kept her gaze locked on him.

She had to. If she didn't center herself she would fly away. She would explode into fragments that might never find form again.

She arched in front of him, her fingers digging into the blankets as the thrusts increased. Her ragged cries, his male groans. They blended, forming an erotic, sexual tune that whipped around them in ever-increasing force.

The pleasure rose. It burned. It had her crying out his name, desperate for ease even as she fought to keep her gaze on the mirror, fought to watch his face. His lips.

Lips that were parting as she began to come apart. His teeth were clenched as she began to convulse around him, pleasure fragmenting inside her a second before she saw his expression twist. Agony and ecstasy. Her name on his lips, and then more.

I love you, Emily. He mouthed the words as his eyes closed and he began to jerk, the feel of his release spurting inside her dragging her from the last mooring that held her to earth.

I love you.

There was no sound to the words. Only his lips moving. Only his eyes closed, his expression absorbed, tight with emotion and a male pleasure too sexy to endure.

Emily heard herself scream his name. She felt the shudders shaking her body as she tried to twist out of his grip to escape the sensations that suddenly built upon themselves. Pleasure upon pleasure, explosion upon explosion, until she collapsed to the bed, exhausted. Drained. And holding her secret close to her heart.

Kell loved her. As surely as she knew she loved him, he loved her. And for some reason, he didn't want her to know. He didn't want to give the words voice, and instead kept them silent as his expression twisted with an inner agony. As he lowered himself beside her, still buried in her, still holding her close, he clasped her in his arms as though he feared she would be torn from them.

"I'm sorry," he whispered at her ear. "I shouldn't have done that."

Emily felt her heart drop to her stomach. That was regret in his voice. Not fear. Heavy, remorseless regret.

"No harm done," she whispered. "It's the wrong time of the month anyway."

What the hell was she supposed to say? Okay, it wasn't a foolproof method, but it was true nonetheless. The time of the month couldn't be safer, and yet the ache in her heart couldn't have gone deeper. Having his baby wouldn't have been a hardship for her. Holding him to her wouldn't have bothered her either.

She felt his hand move over her hair, felt the heavy sigh at her back before he slowly eased from her body.

Then he was tucking her beneath the sheets and settling in beside her; the light beside the bed flipped off before his arms were around her again.

And Emily was staring into the dark, blinking back her tears and wondering what the hell had happened.

EMILY WAS SURPRISED WHEN HER father arrived at the house just as they had finished breakfast and were preparing to leave the house.

Ian stepped into the dining room and announced his arrival then stood in the marble foyer as the senator entered surrounded by Reno, Clint, and Macey. His expression was heavy, and the SEALs surrounding him looked—violent.

"What's happened?" She moved toward him, reacting to the fury in his gaze before he caught her in his arms and surrounded her in a hug that reeked of fear.

"Reno?" She heard Kell's voice behind her, dark, brooding, and prepared.

Emily stared at the SEAL behind her father. Macey. With his ragged haircut, the earring in his ear, faded denim shirt with the arms ripped out, and ragged jeans, he looked more like a biker than a computer expert. He had hams for hands and his broad-shouldered physique, like that of the others, didn't possess an ounce of fat.

A heavy frown creased his face now, rather than the flirty twinkle his eyes usually held. And a frown marred his brow. Something had happened and it wasn't good.

"Dad, what's wrong?" she asked as he finally released her, moving back to breathe out roughly, to stare at her as though he wasn't certain she was really there.

"Get ready to roll," Reno ordered Kell. "You'll proceed to the safe house we've set up for Ms. Stanton and stay in place until further orders."

Emily stared at the hard-eyed SEALs, then at her father.

"Daddy, what's happened?"

"Fuentes's assassin, a man named Rudolph Delgado,

arrived via Dulles this morning. Two hours later Macey was contacted by one of his sources that Delgado is here for you. I want you out of here."

He wanted her hiding, he wanted to pull her away, no matter the risks, and force her into hiding for the rest of her life if that was what it took.

"We knew this was coming." She shook her head fiercely. "We've already agreed that I can't run."

"Ms. Stanton, Delgado is the best Fuentes has," Reno argued then. "He arrived within hours of the attempted hit last night. We can't take this chance with your life."

"And I can't run forever." Her heart was chugging in her breasts. "I've listened to Daddy rant about Fuentes. If I run, then I forfeit whatever game he's playing. He won't keep the rules he's laying in place then. Will he?"

Her father's lips flattened as his eyes flashed in rage. "I won't take this chance with your life."

"It's too late." She moved farther away from him, her hand slashing through the air as she fought to think. "Delgado. What does he do? How does he kill?"

Six pairs of male eyes watched her warily.

"His expertise is with a knife," Kell answered when it was obvious no one else intended to.

She could feel her breathing becoming heavier, her heart racing to keep up with the fear and adrenaline tearing through her.

"Why come to D.C.?" She swallowed tightly. "My plans were to return home today. Everyone knew that. Why come here?"

"He'll expect you to stay in the general area when we try to stash you," Kell answered again. "It would be logical, to keep the team close together rather than separating our strength."

"Was that your plan?"

"Not in this lifetime," her father answered. "And our plans aren't changing."

"Yes. They are," she informed him sharply. "I'm not hiding. I'm not running from this."

"Miss Stanton—", Reno began to argue.

"She'll go or I'll carry her," Kell interceded then, causing her to swing toward him, betrayal filling her.

"Why?" she questioned him angrily. "You know yourself this is what they want. Fuentes sent in a knife. He has to face us with a knife. If we run, he'll send guns, and you know it."

"He has to get a bead on you first," Kell said grimly. "And I promise you, he won't."

Emily licked her lips nervously. He was different this morning, quieter, more brooding. Grim, just as his voice was now. She had felt it in him as she lay in his arms the night before, and now she could see it. The rules had changed for him when he spilled his release into her unprotected body. The gloves were coming off, and now she was glimpsing the incredible force he kept so closely hidden.

"I'm not going. And if you weren't letting other things cloud your judgment, you would admit I'm right," she snapped. "Don't start babying me now, Kell. I won't stand for it."

She met his gaze, refusing to back down, refusing to allow him to see her fears. When staring into cold green ice, a woman had to do more than quell her fears of other forces. She had to quell the instinct to instantly submit.

She had been submitting for too many years. She wasn't going to return to that. Not with Kell.

"Emily, stop this stubbornness," her father snarled. "This is your life we're talking about."

"Kell." She whispered his name, not beseechingly, but as a plea for him to understand. "Don't take me out of the game like this. You had a plan, remember? They want to kidnap me, not kill me. If you hide me, they'll go for the jugular."

"What do you think a knife does, Emily?" he asked with chilling politeness.

"A knife gives you a chance to fight," she whispered back. "But even if it were bullets, we wouldn't have any other choice."

"Emily, you're not just risking your own life here." Her

father's voice was calm, indulgent. As it had been when she was a child and she tried to have her own adventures, without him. "You're risking Kell's life. Are you comfortable doing that?"

Emily flinched.

Her gaze went to the men around her. They were watching her, not with condemnation, but thoughtfully, as though curious as to how she would handle this new argument.

"You trained me to be careful when I was a teenager," she said then. "You taught me how to fight. How to make rational decisions, then overnight you decided to take all that away from me."

"This isn't the time for that argument," he snapped.

She continued to stare at Kell. "I'm right, and you know I am."

"You're asking a man to die for you, Emily," Her father's voice filled with anger now. "A damned good man."

"No," she whispered, shaking her head. "I'm asking him to live with me. I can't live in a bubble anymore. I won't hide like this. We have three nights until the next party. A party where Fuentes's spy and his kidnapper are supposed to be in place. Why would he bring in an assassin at this date? Fuentes wants me as insurance. He doesn't want me dead."

"But that spy does, Emily." Her father's voice rose. "You're acting like a child now. Don't you see what's going on here? You're being caught between Fuentes and that son of a bitch he works with. There's no winning here. You don't have a choice."

She didn't take her eyes off Kell.

"Can you protect me outside the safe house?" she asked then. "Without getting yourself killed."

His gaze flicked to Reno.

"She's an adult," Reno answered neutrally. "I can't force her into the safe house."

"With help." He nodded, glancing at Ian.

"We'll have to pull in the senator's agent in Atlanta," Ian answered. "But we can do it. It's just three days."

"And give Fuentes a chance to kill her?" her father yelled. "I forbid it. I won't allow it."

"You don't have a choice, Daddy." She didn't feel triumph, because Kell's expression hadn't changed. If anything, it had grown colder, more distant.

"Kell—" he began.

"She's right." His fists were curled at his sides. "If she hides now, the game is over before we find the spy. The only way to finish this is to play it out. We'll play it out. But you'll play by my rules," he informed her. Without expression. Without emotion. "Or I'll tie you up, gag you, and stuff you in the nearest safe house. Are we clear?"

She nodded sharply. "We're clear."

"What do you need, Kell?" Reno asked then.

"He needs a fucking brain," her father snapped. "Because he's lost his goddamned mind with her just like every other man does."

Emily felt her face flame in embarrassment. Her father was enraged, and if the flicker of response in Kell's gaze was anything to go by, then the cold inner fury he was keeping banked would more than meet it.

"Senator, this isn't your operation," Reno reminded him. "You're the target, not the commander."

"I outrank you."

"Not in this instance." Reno never raised his voice, but it firmed, grew harder. "Stand down, sir."

"Emily, this is foolish." He buried his hands in his hair and grimaced tightly. "Just go to the damned safe house."

"If I go to that safe house then I may as well resign myself to living in it for the rest of my life," she told him wearily. "Because whether you catch Fuentes or not won't matter. None of us will ever know if I have the ability to face life myself. And that matters to me, Dad. It matters more to me than you know."

"You're not trained," he snapped back.

"Because I loved you too much to sign up for the training I wanted. And through the years, I've loved you too much to fight the hurtful words you throw at me when I've tried to stand against you. I'm doing more than standing against you now, Dad. I'm taking what's mine. And my freedom means more to me than you will ever know. More than either of you will ever know." She shot Kell a look as icy as the one he was giving her. "It's easy to mouth platitudes when it suits you," she told him. "Now, let's see if you can put your money where your mouth is."

His eyes flicked over her before pausing at her stomach then rose to meet hers once again. "I've already done that, Emily. Now let's see if you can learn how to follow orders."

She almost snorted at that. "Follow orders? Kell, I've done nothing else for nearly twenty-five years. Following them has never bothered me. Being restrained by them is another thing."

And she was talking about much more than this mission and he knew it.

Start as you mean to go on, she told herself. Never let them see you sweat, and never back down when you're right. She was right. She couldn't risk having Kell see her as anything less than a woman who could aid in her own protection and that of her child, if there was a child.

And that, she guessed, was the whole reason for his distance now. There was the risk now, that she was carrying his baby. That she was walking into danger, refusing protection, and risking not just herself but his child.

Another child after he had already lost the first.

"Let's get Macey's intel and discuss how to proceed," Reno suggested then. "And I would suggest that we do it in more comfortable settings than this foyer."

"I'm going to need a drink," her father growled, glowering at her as they turned and headed for the senator's office.

"It's too early in the morning for a drink, Dad."

His brows lifted almost to his hairline. "Little girl, you're not big enough to tell me when I can drink."

"No, but I am big enough to tell you to remember your ulcer and your blood pressure. It's going to take enough of a beating in the next few years, so you might want to baby it a bit right now."

"And why is that?" he snapped.

Emily paused. "Because I'm not a little girl anymore. And I'm not going to pretend I am, for you or anyone else. I have a feeling that's not something you're going to deal with very well."

She ignored Macey's mocking, "He's not the only one." They stepped into the office and seated themselves.

Emily took a chair, directly across from her father. Kell flashed her a disgruntled expression before sitting on the side of the couch nearest her, with Ian taking the other side. Across from them, Reno and Macey took the other two chairs, with Clint pulling an extra chair in slightly behind her father.

"We can do this civilly?" Reno asked them all.

Her father glowered. Kell stared back with what Emily was beginning to suspect was icy fury.

A smile tugged at Reno's lips. "Good then. I'm glad we all agree. Now, let's see what we can do to throw a monkey wrench in Fuentes's and his spy's little game. It's time to bring them down."

Twenty

ELATION SURGED THROUGH DIEGO. IT was more exhilarating than any drug, pumping hard and fast through his bloodstream and nearly leaving him weak as he stared at the message on his PDA.

I agree.

Two little words. Such a simple phrase and yet it brought tears to his eyes, causing him to blink furiously to hold back his emotions.

He had given his son only the barest help in the past weeks, only enough to keep the girl alive but never enough to lead him to the bastard currently pinching at Diego's nerves.

It was the perfect plan. The perfect weapon to eliminate the man who would see everything Diego had worked for destroyed.

He wasn't a terrorist. He ran drugs and weapons, prostitutes and black market items. Terrorism wasn't good for such commerce. It broke the financial backs of the very people he depended upon for his livelihood. His spy, and the terrorist Sorrell, would use generations of groundwork to destroy not just the Fuentes cartel, but the freedom the Americans enjoyed to buy his drugs, his weapons, and his women.

I agree.

Diego stared at the message for long moments before sending his own. He had to play this carefully. He couldn't seem too eager, too excited. That would be a sign of weakness.

Your brother in arms secure. Proceed to Andover party. Delgado to be advised.

Diego had placed Delgado, his most trusted man, in D.C. to watch his son's back. It would all come together soon. Sorrell had demanded the death of not just the senator, but this SEAL team as well. This team that included Diego's only surviving son. The bastard's demands were insolent, arrogant.

He had demanded it as though Diego were one of his underlings. As though he had the right to demand such things from him.

Snarling in silent fury, Diego turned to the monitor set up in the office he used. There, in the hidden cell, lay the friend his son was willing to sell his soul for.

What would it be like, he wondered then, to command such loyalty? To have such a friend that he would turn his back even on his beliefs to save him?

Diego had never known such loyalty. But that man in the cell, naked, shuddering in the throes of Diego's latest attempt to break him with the last remaining doses of the date rape drug, that man knew a loyalty of which Diego only dreamed.

"You will dress our friend." He nodded to the monitor as he spoke to Saul. "Feed him. Strengthen him enough to aid the boy if it is needed when they come for him. Delgado will kidnap the girl and bring her here. We will have Sorrell and our Mr. White in one place for our SEALs to collect."

"Will you tell him that the girl will be kidnapped?" Saul asked. "Without his cooperation, it may not be possible to take her."

Diego shook his head slowly. "This part I do not control. And there will be no way he and his friends can stop it. This man, our spy, the girl trusts too well. Our friend Mr. White will bring her here, unharmed, as he has been ordered, for this Sorrell to collect. When they arrive, our captive will not be drugged, and he will remember the torture Mr. White has inflicted upon him. There will be no escape for White once he has been rescued. Be sure to place the girl in his cell when she arrives. She may need the additional protection." Diego ran his finger thoughtfully over his lips. "The moment the girl is taken, you will send the coordinates of this place to my son. He will then take care of the rest."

"Can you trust him, Diego?" Saul's voice whispered what was his innermost fear.

Diego stared back at his friend and most trusted advisor.

"I can do nothing but take the chance," he said with a heavy sigh. "It is too late to start over, to train another son, to worry for his safety and give him the freedom he will need to grow confident. We shall see, Saul. But we shall also protect our own backs. My son tries to make it appear as though he has no weakness, but all men know weakness, I have only to find his."

"Should I contact Delgado?" Saul asked then.

Diego shook his head slowly. "I will contact him. He will know his orders have come directly from me and that he is to follow them implicitly. From here on out, Saul, this game is in earnest. There is no room for error, and there are no second chances. We can allow no mistakes from this point forward."

Saul nodded in agreement, but his gaze was worried. Just as Diego was worried, despite the façade he presented. Worried that others could have learned about his son; perhaps this was even why Sorrell was targeting this team. To flush out Diego's weakness. To have something to hold against him in the negotiations he was attempting to undertake for control of the cartel's networks. A control Diego must not allow.

A control his son *would not* allow.

Twenty-one

EMILY WAS CERTAIN SHE SHOULDN'T have been surprised to find Kira waiting for them, in Emily's apartment no less.

She was sprawled on the couch, a bag of Emily's favorite cookies in her lap and the television turned to one of the foreign-language channels she loved so much.

Her long black hair was pulled high into a ponytail that allowed heavy curls to tumble well past her shoulders. Her face was makeup free and she still looked like a million bucks. She wore faded, ripped jeans and a wrinkled camisole top and still managed to appear fashionable. But the gun at her side ruined the image of the lazy, discontented socialite.

"About time you two showed up." Her voice was pitched low as Kell closed and locked the door behind them. "Where's that tall, buff, and completely antisocial hunk who lives on the other side?"

Ian?

"Why is my best friend and next-door neighbor sitting on my couch, eating my cookies, and watching my TV? And why is she doing it with a gun?"

As though she wasn't damned good at guessing. The guess was getting ready to piss her off. She had just endured more time than she considered excusable with a silent, uncommunicative SEAL. The other, Ian, had been vaguely amused but not so much that he was willing to break the silence.

Emily hadn't gotten to sit in the copilot's seat this time, and she hadn't been able to flirt with the pilot or Kell. And she sure as hell hadn't been able to relieve the frustrating pain of this suddenly cold attitude she was receiving from the man who had been her lover.

Had been. Because it was going to be—oh, at least a good couple of hours before she tried to jump *his* bones again. She shot him a silent glare before turning back to Kira.

"Explanations, if you please," she suggested to Kira wearily, shaking her head as she trudged toward the bedroom. "And you can make them without grouch-ass there glowering at both of us."

Kira rose to her feet, winked at Kell, gave him a perky little wave of her fingers then followed Emily into the bedroom.

"Well. I have to say. You have totally outlived my expectations of your ability to handle that piece of man flesh," Kira drawled as she closed the door behind her.

Emily was certain Kell heard every word.

She snorted. "Yeah. Right. I'm handling him really well. He hasn't spoken to me in hours and he's so damned cold he's about to give me frostbite."

"Cold?" Kira paused in front of the door, her hand waving in front of her face in a brief gesture of heat. "Baby. Those eyes are burning and those jeans are bulging. Trust me, that man is ready to rock and roll in the hardest of ways."

Emily sniffed with offended pride. "Then he can rock and roll by himself." For a few hours anyway.

Turning her back on Kira she threw her small bag to the bed, then sat down on the mattress and breathed out heavily.

"Now why the hell are you in my house?"

"Eating your cookies, watching your television, and ogling your man?" Kira suggested helpfully.

"With a gun?"

"Oh yeah. There is that gun." Slender shoulders shrugged. "I flew home last night on a Homeland Security flight and camped out on your couch, just to see if anyone got curious or whatever while you were gone."

Emily fell back on the bed, stared up at the ceiling, and tried not to feel betrayed. She didn't succeed. She did feel betrayed. She had known Kira for two years now and had never suspected that she was an agent for Homeland, or that Emily was an assignment rather than a friendship.

"You're an agent for HS." It wasn't a question. "How did Dad manage to pull that one off? To get you here on such an extended mission?"

"Because he's on the National Security Committee as well as the Drug Enforcement Committee and several oversight committees. Besides, I live in Atlanta anyway and I've been on leave recuperating from a wound for the last eighteen months, so it all worked out."

Staring at the ceiling wasn't a bad thing. Emily traced the small butterfly effect of the design above her with her eyes and reminded herself that she wasn't young enough to be able to excuse a temper tantrum.

But she wanted to throw one. She wanted to scream and rage and demand that every damned one of her father's minions get the hell out of her life. She'd had enough of them. Was sick to her back teeth of them.

She had that pesky friendship thing to deal with where Kira was concerned though. And that damned sex thing with Kell. She couldn't exactly tell them to piss off, now could she?

"You've lived here for two years," she pointed out to Kira.

"Yep. I have." Kira's weight settled on the other side of the bed before she laid back as well, her head settling against the mattress several inches from Emily's. "Your dad suggested the condo when he found out I was looking to move from my dark little apartment in town. The rest was added extras."

"I knew there was a reason I shouldn't like you." Emily

wanted to pout, but she hadn't really pouted in years, and the effort to remember how just seemed too draining right now.

"Yeah, you gave it a good fight." Kira chuckled. "But I'm persistent. Besides, we are friends, Emily. I'm a good friend to have too. I know how to use a gun."

"So do I."

Silence met her statement.

"Cool." It was obvious by Kira's tone that she didn't believe her.

"Mac Tackett's indoor shooting range and proficiency challenge," Emily stated.

She felt Kira's head turn, felt her eyes watching her.

"Senator didn't tell me about that," Kira mused.

"The senator doesn't know. His lackeys did. But it's amazing how Mac can convince those big guys that they would heartily dislike losing a member."

"Uh-huh. I know Mac." Kira turned her head back. "Well, I was watching your back then."

"You were following orders."

Kira was quiet for long moments. "I was your friend as well, Emily."

Friendship. Relationships. There was a twist to all of hers that she was finding unacceptable. Everyone loved her as long as she was agreeable. Everyone but herself. And now that she wasn't agreeable anymore? What now?

"Don't ever come into my home like this again," Emily told her, feeling the resolve that began to harden inside her. "Not without my permission or my knowledge."

Kira sighed heavily. "Unless ordered to?"

"If ordered, you better inform Dad you're going to need hazard pay. Because next time, I'll make you wish you had waited on the front steps."

She should get up. She should shower. She should see about fixing lunch, because she was hungry. But she lay there instead, stared at the ceiling and tried not to think about guns, bullets, and knives coming out of the dark.

"I bet I could take you," Kira decided suddenly. The feel of her head turning had Emily restraining her smile.

"It would be interesting to find out." Emily nodded. "I might look like a marshmallow, but I've been taking some self-defense lessons."

"Research huh?" Kira was laughing.

"Gator Jack's Roundhouse." She loved Gator Jack, mud wrestling, and gutter fighting. She'd learned quite a bit over the last few years while sneaking in there between body-guards.

Okay, she might not be able to take a Homeland agent in a face-to-face fight, but there was a chance she could break a hold, and she knew how to run really fast.

"You're scary," Kira murmured. "Your father has no idea how scary you are."

"Neither does Kell." Emily smiled in satisfaction. "He got turned on by the holstered gun and knife garters though."

Satisfaction edged through her at the memory of that one.

"Speaking of your hard body," Kira drawled. "Why's he mad?"

"He forgot to use a condom last night." Emily frowned up at the ceiling. That had to be the problem.

"Did you remind him?"

"He reminded me. And I didn't care." She frowned at that. "Maybe I was supposed to care?"

She turned her head and stared into Kira's surprised expression.

"Krieger did it without protection?" she fairly whispered. "That's damned surprising. I've read his file and I did some light investigating when I heard Durango Team would be on this op. He's a fanatic about protection. Paranoid about it."

"Uh-huh," Emily murmured, with a sharp sigh of agreement as she turned back to her perusal of the ceiling.

"Wow." Kira shifted on the bed, still watching her. "So, we're still friends, huh?"

"No." Emily shook her head. "I hate skinny bitches. I keep telling you that."

A snort of laughter left the other woman. "And I hate curvy little pocket Venuses, but I put up with your rounded ass."

"Bite me."

"Not even on a dare. You might enjoy it."

They were giggling like teenagers when the bedroom door opened and Kell stood framed in the doorway, staring at them both with a heavy frown.

"If you two can tear yourselves off the bed, Ian's here. We need to go over plans for the next three days and get ready for the Andover party."

"See?" Emily muttered. "Frostbite."

Kira sighed in commiseration. "I had hopes for ya, girl-friend."

"So did I. So did I."

HE WAS FURIOUS WITH HIMSELF. Furious with Emily, and fighting back the need to do a little private hunting. The type of hunting that found a SEAL with a sniper rifle and Diego Fuentes's forehead in his sights. Fuentes and his unknown fucking spy. God help the bastard if Macey ever figured out who he was, because Kell swore he was going to gut him himself.

He enforced his self-control, restrained the need to shift, to stretch the muscles that seemed to itch for action beneath his flesh, and to use the erection torturing him.

Use it on one stubborn, independent, willful little red-headed fox who was close to driving him insane.

God, he felt sorry for the bodyguards who came before him. Those men must have spent untold hours packing heat and fighting to keep up with Emily all at once. It just wasn't possible.

She was like the wind. Wild. Free. Her presence caressed his flesh even when she wasn't touching him and that was damned dangerous. Especially now.

His glance slid along her body, touched on her rounded little belly, and his heart did that melting thing in his chest again. Where it got hot. Where it raced. Where it clenched with emotions he suddenly found himself unable to deal with. Emotions that had torn through his soul the minute he had pumped his seed inside her.

She was unprotected. The chances of getting her pregnant would only grow if he continued with that madness. He couldn't allow it to happen again. He couldn't take the chance. God help him if the pregnancy test he intended to get for her before that damned party came back positive. Because he didn't know if he could go through with it. If he could let her risk her life and their child's life, no matter the situation.

Now, he watched her as she moved back into the living room with Kira. The sight of her lying back on that bed, giggling with the other woman, had filled his guts with irrational jealousy.

He wanted to be lying there with her. He wanted to hear her laughter, feel the warmth that was so much a part of her, that heated the icy reaches of his spirit that had so long been alone.

And yet, it was his own fault he hadn't been there beside her. The need to defend against what could happen was ripping his insides apart. He had to push it back. He had to control it or he would forever destroy whatever fragile feelings she was developing for him now.

He needed her love. He was certain he had been winning it until this morning. Until he forced back the emotions pushing at his soul in order to do the job he knew he had to do.

He had to let his woman aid in her own defense. The very thing he had been so certain he needed in a woman. Her ability to face adversity. To help him protect her. To be strong enough to stay alive if he wasn't with her. Because there would be times he wasn't with her. Times when he would be doing his job. She would have to do hers. Protect herself and their children.

God, what the hell had he been thinking?

His fists clenched at his side at the insanity of having a

woman as frighteningly independent as this one. She was never going to stand behind him. She would always stand beside him as he fought to keep her from stepping in front of him.

"Ian," Kira drawled when neither he nor Ian spoke.

The other man lounged against the bar separating the living room from the kitchen. His elbows were braced on the bar behind him, his tall, leanly muscled body appearing relaxed. But like Kell, he had been anything but relaxed once Kira stepped into the room.

"Kira." Ian nodded, his expression faintly mocking. "I like the black hair. It suits you better than the other colors I've seen you wearing."

She grimaced and rolled her eyes as Emily watched with interest.

"So, what do you two big strong boys have planned?" Kira asked as she stepped past Ian into the kitchen and moved to the refrigerator.

She pulled a bottle of beer from inside, twisted off the cap, and brought it to her lips as Ian turned to watch her.

"A steel cage, whips, and velvet restraints," Ian drawled, surprising Kell with the fact that Ian was dead-stone serious.

"For us, I imagine." Kira smirked. "Keep wishing, sailor, and you might get as close as a dream."

Ian snorted.

Emily shook her head as she moved to the couch and curled into the corner.

She was tired. He could see it in her face, the shadows beneath her eyes, the paleness of her skin. He had kept her up long into the night. Though he had forgotten the condom only once, he had been by no means sated.

He still wasn't sated.

"The Andover party takes place in less than three days," Kell reminded them all. "We're all together and we know who is who and what is what." He looked between Kira and Emily. "We can't leave anything to chance. This is Emily's last party of the season and it's a big one. Our contact says

Fuentes won't wait any longer. It's a definite that the man he sent to do the kidnapping will be there."

He watched as Emily's face seemed to pale further, but she lifted her chin defiantly as her gaze glittered back in anger.

"Jansen Clay and his wife, Elaine, will be there. Their daughter was one of the girls kidnapped the last time as well. Has Dad let him know what's going on?"

Jansen was one of her father's friends from his SEAL days and once a part of the elite covert operations team the senator had led.

"We're not informing anyone." Kell shook his head firmly. "The only thing anyone knows outside the team, your father, and the admiral, is that you're going to be at the party. Period."

Emily nodded. It had been years since she had seen Jansen. He was several years younger than her father, and very influential within D.C. and the Pentagon. His work with the CIA and Homeland Security also made him a very good friend to have. He would be hurt when he learned her father was conducting an operation without him. But then again, so would the rest of her father's team who were still alive.

She watched Kell, letting her gaze be caught by his as he continued to stare at her. He hadn't taken his eyes off her since she had returned to the living room.

"Ian, return Miss Porter to her condo and bring her up to speed on where we are now. Get your information together and we'll meet back here tomorrow evening to figure this out. Emily's too tired for this."

Too tired, her rear. He was horny, that was why he was sending Ian and Kira away. He obviously thought she cared about that steel-and-iron rod he was carrying around in his jeans.

"Gotcha, Kell." Ian's smile was knowing, while Kira just shook her head and winked back at Emily with heavy suggestiveness before she followed Ian to the door.

"Girlfriend, good luck." Kira waggled her brows

suggestively. "And remember, man candy is hard to come by. Enjoy it while it's willing."

Enjoy it while it's willing. Emily snorted at the thought as she flashed Kell an irritated glance. It would be okay if the willing candy was just a tad bit easier to get along with when he got his own shorts in a wad. It wasn't like she had forgotten the rubber.

As Ian and Kira passed through the door, Kell caught it with his hand and closed it with a bang. Emily's brows arched as he turned his back to her, set the alarm, then faced her once again.

He crossed his arms over his chest and a dark brooding frown creased his brow. Oh yeah, willing man candy. How could she have missed that one?

"You know, you could save yourself all this ill temper quite easily," she told him mockingly.

His nostrils flared and his frown deepened. "And how would you I suggest I do that?"

She lifted her shoulders in a dismissing shrug. "Don't forget the rubbers next time; then you won't have to worry about all your powerful little soldiers roaming around untended."

Emily didn't think his expression could have darkened more. But it did.

"You think I'm upset because I forgot to wear a rubber?" he grated out.

"What else would I think?" She uncurled her legs and rose to her feet. "You've been like an ill-tempered bear all day. To my knowledge the only thing I could have done to piss you off was my inability to say no while you were buried inside me."

His gaze flared. Darkened.

"I'm not angry over the condom." A muscle flicked in his jaw. "Not that I'm pleased with my own lack of self-control."

She nodded as though in understanding. "Yeah. I can see where that would bother you."

"I'm in love with you, Emily."

"Control would impor—" She stopped. Blinked. "What did you say?"

"I'm guessing I've been in love with you for years." He gave his head a hard, furious shake. "You think your father spied on you over the years? You should have seen me skulking around your apartment and then this condo. Following you to the library and to school and back and telling myself it was just because I didn't have anything better to do. And knowing all along that I was lying to myself."

Emily suddenly felt off balance, as though she had stepped into a reality that made no sense to her. This was the same Kell she had known for so long. The one she had lusted for, ached for, fantasized about. The one she had fallen in love with, and suddenly he was the man she had dreamed of.

"I don't understand." She shook her head jerkily. "Why didn't you tell me?"

"I couldn't tell myself, Emily." He pushed his fingers through his hair as he kept a careful distance between them. "I couldn't admit to myself that I was so desperate for you that I was worse than any stalker could have been. Because I was so damned scared of losing you. Then Fuentes took you." A grimace contorted his face as his fists clenched at his sides for long seconds. "When he took you I went insane. When I crashed inside that dirty little shack and saw you, pumped on that damned Whore's Dust and trying so hard to keep the other girls calm, a part of me knew I couldn't run any longer."

She didn't remember it. Over the past months, there had been vague memories, shifts in the darkness of her mind about that time, but never anything solid.

"I knew when the limo was forced off the road that you would come for me," she told him then. "I remember that much. Something inside me said that you would save me."

"I saved you." His eyes were so dark they were like gems glittering in his face as he came to her then, his hands framing her face, his thumbs smoothing over her lips. "But you were fighting to save yourself as well. You didn't cower, and when I saw that, you stole the rest of my heart, Emily. My little fox, you made me burn for you until I thought I'd turn to ash."

Emily felt her lips tremble, felt the emotion surging through her soul at his revelations.

"Then why are you so angry?"

"I'm not angry, chère," he whispered. "I have to protect you. Soon it will all be over. I have to keep my head clear. I have to keep enough distance to make certain there are no mistakes made. I survived Tansy's death and the death of the child she carried. But Emily, if I lost you, I don't know if I could survive."

She saw that in his eyes now. Saw it in his earlier actions. He had been distancing himself from his emotions, not from her. Always watching. Tense. Ready.

Dear God, what she had done in forcing him to return here, in refusing to hide?

"I'll hide," she cried brokenly. "We'll go to the safe house." She could feel her lips trembling, feel the fear for him suddenly overwhelming her. "Whatever you want to do."

There was no ice in those green eyes now. They were darker, somber, filled with hunger and torment.

He shook his head as his arm closed around her hips and tightened, jerking her up to him, while the fingers of the other slid into her hair and gripped the strands with sensual force.

"No fear," he growled, his head lowering until his lips were nearly, almost but not quite, touching hers. "Show no fear, Emily. I'll get us through this."

"Don't." She shook her head at the dark confidence she saw in him now. "You don't have to go to the Andover mansion. We'll go to the safe house. I'll hide. I promise, Kell." Her nails dug into his shoulders in desperation. "I'll hide."

For him. She would do anything, even forget her own freedom, to protect him.

He didn't answer her. His lips touched hers, his gaze held

hers. Like rough velvet stroking over her lips, he caressed and tormented, refusing to deepen the contact despite the parting of her lips.

"I'll protect you, Emily." A hint of Cajun spice entered his voice. "There's no hiding. We both know that."

Because he had tried to hide his wife years ago, she knew. He had tried and his enemies had found her.

"Tell me what to do." Her breath hitched brokenly. "Tell me how to keep you safe."

He froze, staring down at her as his pupils dilated and something akin to shock entered his gaze.

"Little fox." His fingers slid from her hair to cup her cheek, his thumb brushing over her lips. "Just be you. Stubborn. Wild. Alive. I'll do the rest."

She tried to shake her head again, tried to deny that it would take so little to protect him.

"Come, chère." His lips touched hers again, embraced the lower curve before moving to the top one. "Be wild with me for now. Later. Later is for taking care, eh?"

Before she could do more than whimper he was gripping her hair again, pulling her head back, and his lips were taking what he needed as he lifted her into his arms and carried her to the bedroom.

Taking and giving. Passion, hunger, heat, and need. And love. She could feel the love, hot and desperate, binding them now, though unspoken and guarded.

It filled each touch. It drew her muscles tight with pleasure and sensitized each cell of flesh covering her body. Like whipping lashes of sensation the pleasure snaked around her, through her, sinking past her clothing and her skin to her very soul.

She twisted against him, her fingers sliding into his hair, gripping it, trying to pull him closer as their lips and tongues interlocked, tangled.

Desperate moans filled the room as clothing was shed. His boots, her shoes. Her jeans and panties in one smooth stroke of his hands. His jeans and underwear, her movements jerky and desperate.

He tore her shirt from her shoulders. He was going to have to start replacing her clothes soon. In turn, she ripped the buttons from his shirt and pushed it over his powerful shoulders.

Flesh to flesh now. She cried out into his kiss, nipped at his lips as her nipples raked over his chest. Sizzling sensation tore across her nerve endings. Burned them. She twisted closer, desperate for more as she pushed him toward the bed.

"Mine," she moaned ruthlessly as they fell to the mattress and she fought to roll from beneath him. "My turn."

She rose above him, panting for air, straddling his hard thighs as her head lowered for more of his drugging kisses. To taste his lust and his need.

Her pussy was wet. So wet she could feel the damp warmth coating the folds as it rubbed against his cock head. The thick crest was velvety soft, steel hard, throbbing. Hot. It slid through the slit of her pussy, caressed her clit, and had her gasping for breath as she knelt above him.

She thought she had things well in hand, so to speak. She thought she could control the need spiraling inside her. She was convinced she could. Until he filled his hands with her breasts, lifted his head, and captured one hard, straining nipple.

Emily's back arched, her head falling back on her shoulders as her hips rolled, and in a single hard thrust, she impaled herself on the straining length of his cock.

A frantic mewling cry left her throat as bursts of pleasure and fire stretched her inner muscles to their limit and exposed the ultrasensitive nerve endings to the fierce heat of his erection.

"Prends-le. Take it," he snarled, his head pushing back into the pillow as he ground his hips upward, stroking her clit, pushing deeper inside her. "Is this what you want?"

He pulled back then plunged deep, impaling her with a

ferocity that had her shaking on the edge of orgasm. "Take it, chère, take all of me."

"Yes. Yes. I want that." She twisted in his grip, writhed above him as she pressed her hands into his chest for purchase and rolled her hips against him.

He held her still, pulled back, and slammed inside her again before retreating completely.

"Oh God. Kell. No." Her nails dug into his chest as he fumbled for the condom he had laid on the bedside table and quickly sheathed his raging erection.

"Easy there, chère," he groaned hoarsely. "Hold for me, jolie, eh. I'll give us both more, bébé."

He fit the wide crest against the entrance to her pussy, paused, then began to push inside her with a slow, agonizingly rapturous thrust. He impaled her by degrees, ignoring her cries, ignoring his own violent need.

His expression was consumed with lust. Emily forced herself to watch him, forced her eyes open. She didn't want to forget a moment of it. She wanted the memory with her forever.

This was the part of Kell he kept so carefully hidden. His large body flexing, his thrusts driving deep inside her, his eyes gazing back at her in a surfeit of emotion and hunger. His eyes glittered, deep, dark, an emerald green so intense they glowed within his sun-darkened face and the midnight shadow of a beard.

As she gazed down at him, her breathing came sharp and irregular from the pleasure of the thrusts inside her. The burning pleasure, the building tension in her womb, the rake of his pelvis against the tight knot of her clit. The sensations inflamed her, consumed her.

"So silky and hot," he whispered, staring up at her, his voice guttural. "I can feel your pussy stroking me, Emily. Tightening on me. So tight and liquid hot I could burn inside you."

His rough tone had her womb clenching.

"You like this, eh?" he asked her with a tight smile. "Hearing what you do to me. Knowing you can burn my soul to ashes."

His voice. Oh God, his voice destroyed her even as the hard thrusts inside her stroked her closer to orgasm.

"Feel this, Emily." He surged inside her, paused, held still as his cock throbbed within the clenching heat of her pussy. "Feel what you do to me, bébé. Even sheathed in a condom I feel your sweet heat, chère. The clench of your pussy—" He groaned then, jerked and thrust deeper inside her. "Sweet heaven. Save me."

Before she could stop him he rolled her to her back, his arms coming beneath her shoulders as he held her to him, his hard body surrounding her, securing her before he began pounding inside her. Desperately. Working his cock in quick, hard strokes as she felt the explosions begin to tear through her.

She was taken. Overwhelmed. She was lost within the inferno of his possession and within seconds arching against his thrusts as her orgasm unraveled inside her.

Radiant heat poured through her veins as she screamed his name, her arms wrapped around his back, her thighs clasping his as he stiffened above her and began to shudder with his own release.

"Love you, Emily." The declaration was no more than a breath amid her wails of ecstasy, whispered at her ear, tearing into her soul.

They were dragged from him unbidden, pushing from within his soul, and all the more precious for the fact that she could feel his control weakening even as she felt his cock jerking in release inside her.

He wasn't ready to give her his emotions freely. Not yet. As she held him to her, feeling his sweat-slick flesh rippling beneath the tension in his shoulders, she knew he wasn't ready to face the emotions.

He was so strong. So sure. Always so certain, but she was learning that Kell didn't deal well with a perceived weakness. And he perceived his emotions for her as a weakness. A risk.

"I love you, Kell," she whispered tearfully against his

chest, knowing he owned not just her heart but her soul. He filled her. He completed her. "I love you so much."

Emily tried to catch her breath as her legs slid from Kell's thighs and her arms loosened their death grip. Her heart was racing out of control, her own emotions in chaos, as he slowly eased from her and rolled to her side.

"You're going to kill me," he growled as he fought to catch his own breath. But his arm still came around her as she moved to drape herself across his chest. And that took effort, because her muscles were still mush.

Instantly, his warmth, his vitality, wrapped around her. Strength. Determination. He was such a powerful force that she wondered how he managed to maintain the control over himself that he did.

Or perhaps it was his control, the very essence of who he was, that created that vitality. Some men were naturally re-strained. Strong, arrogant, determined men. Men who knew their strength and understood their own limits.

Kell had known the horrifying realization that he wasn't Superman. That sometimes the odds were against him, and he had learned at a very young age the fatal results of being on the wrong side of the odds.

The odds had to be with them, she prayed as he pulled her against his chest and surrounded her with the warmth and strength of his body. They had to be, because God help her if she lost him.

Twenty-two

IT WAS LATE WHEN KELL and Emily left the bed to head to the kitchen for a late dinner. As Emily turned on the low living room lights and moved into the kitchen, AC/DC's "Hells Bells" sounded from Kell's cell phone, drawing a smile from her lips.

She should have guessed the dark, hard lyrics and music of that particular group would appeal to Kell. Though she knew his music tastes were eclectic, simply because of the CDs he carried in the Bronco parked in the driveway.

"Come on over then. Use the patio entrance and try not to create a damned traffic jam," she heard Kell mutter. "This is insane."

She turned as he disconnected and stared back at her with offended male irritation.

"Who's creating the traffic jam?" she asked as she glanced down at the clothes she wore. Loose cotton pants and Kell's T-shirt—because she wanted to keep his scent wrapped around her.

"Your father." His voice simmered with frustration. "Admiral Holloran and Captain Malone."

"Captain Malone?" She frowned as she pulled the deli-wrapped sandwich meat from the refrigerator before reaching in for the rest of the sandwich fixings. "That's Nathan

Malone's uncle. He was with Dad and Uncle Sam before he left the SEALs."

The three men had been part of an elite strike force, along with two others. One had died several years back, but Jansen Clay, one of her father's best friends, and the father of one of the girls kidnapped with Emily, was still close to him as well.

As she laid out the sandwich ingredients a frown flitted between her brows at the thought of the men. Why would Jordan Malone be with her father and the admiral?

She dreaded seeing him. She still felt vaguely responsible for the SEAL who had died rescuing her. When she had learned that SEAL was Nathan Malone, her grief had been nearly unbearable.

He was Kell's age, but she had known him all her life, just as she had known Risa Clay all her life. Risa was still in the hospital, her young mind damaged by the effects of the Whore's Dust she had been given during her kidnapping.

Jansen hadn't contacted her since the rescue, and she hadn't seen him or Risa. The doctors were allowing only supervised visits by family members.

". . . reports that Nathan's alive."

Her head jerked up at the sound of his voice.

"What did you say?" She had been so involved with her memories of Risa that she hadn't caught his last sentence.

He stared back at her, his gaze somber.

"We received a report that Nathan's still alive and being held by Fuentes's spy. Pictures were sent to Macey, and it's definitely Nathan."

She stilled, the lettuce she had been tearing apart forgotten as shock resounded through her.

"It's been almost two years," she whispered.

"Nineteen months, and from the looks of those pictures, Nathan has suffered every day of it." Fury flashed in Kell's eyes, and Emily knew that if he ever managed to get his hands on whoever was spying for Fuentes, the man would die. Painfully.

"How could a spy hold Nathan that long?" She shook her head in confusion. Nathan wasn't a weak man. He was one of the strongest she knew. "And where?"

"Where, we don't know." He pushed his fingers restlessly through his long hair as a tight, feral grimace twisted his features. "We'll find him though."

Her lips parted in surprise at the violence that gleamed in his eyes before her head jerked to the patio doors and the soft knock on the outside glass.

Kell turned out the living room lights before checking outside then opening the panel wide enough for the men to slip through.

Her father was first, followed by the admiral, Captain Malone, and then the rest of the SEAL team Kell was working with.

They all looked at the bar where Emily was laying out the food.

"Help yourselves to sandwiches." She waved her hand at the mounds of lunch meat and vegetables before setting out two loaves of bread from the cabinet and pulling a gallon of sweet tea from the inside of the refrigerator. It was a good thing she'd gone grocery shopping before heading to D.C.

She hadn't seen Jordan Malone in years. He was several years younger than her father; he would be forty-five or so. He had just signed on to her father's team the year her father had been wounded and forced into a training position.

His hair was still mostly black, though there was more gray than she had noticed last time. He stood a little over six feet, with dark grayish-blue eyes and a hawklike expression. Texas born and raised, he had a rough-and-ready demeanor, even now.

He was a childless widower and she knew he had loved his nephew as though he were his own child. The report of Nathan's death had hit him hard.

As Emily set out the paper plates and large plastic cups she kept for the rare instances that she had company, she watched the men who filled her living room, along with Kira. They were hard, dangerous men, but they were men whose expressions were also tempered with compassion and friendship.

Helping themselves to sandwiches and sweet tea, they pulled the available kitchen chairs into the living room, arranged them around the living room, and sat down to go over the details of the information they had on Fuentes, his spy, and the missing SEAL they had all grieved for.

The pictures Macey's contact had sent were horrifying. It was Nathan, but if wasn't the Nathan Emily had once known. His large powerful body was rangy and thin now, his ribs standing out beneath the flesh of his abdomen. His face was swollen, bruised. Fresh wounds were cut into his legs, arms, and chest. His face was barely recognizable, and his eyes, deep, deep sapphire-blue eyes, were glazed and bright with violence.

"We've received a little more information from Judas," Macey muttered as the pictures were spread over the coffee table. "The last transmission was several hours ago. We tracked it here, to Atlanta, but that's as far as I've managed to get. He's been pumped up with Whore's Dust during his captivity. The spy, who we've only been able to identify as Mr. White, is determined to break him. He thinks if he can make Nathan break his marriage vows by screwing another woman, even under the influence of drugs, then Nathan will break and give him the information he wants."

"And what does he want?" Jordan's voice was lethal, rasping with fury.

"Information." Macey sighed as he wiped his hand over his harsh, weary face. "Nathan was one of the elite, as you know, Jordan. He had information very few men have. So far, he hasn't broken, but our Mr. White thinks it's only a matter of time."

Emily flinched as she sat on the floor beside Kell's chair. That name, Mr. White. She frowned, feeling the dark areas of her mind shifting, shadows within shadows and a haunting cry. Who was crying?

"Okay?" Kell's hand settled on her shoulder as she nodded quickly.

The doctors had been confident that those memories were never going to return. They were locked in forever by the effects of that drug.

She lifted her gaze, meeting her father's eyes as he sat in the chair across from them. His expression was somber, and filled with grief for Nathan, she knew. He had helped train Nathan, had loved him as he had loved all the men he had fought with and trained.

"Our Mr. White gets around," Jordan spat out with loathing. "He's managed to betray the identities of several SEALs on mission as well as DEA and Homeland Security agents over the past year alone. He's feeding Fuentes, but my sources say he's feeding the terrorist Sorrell as well, and betraying Fuentes with each turn of the knife."

"He's also taken out several OHS Agents," Kira confirmed from where she sat at the bar.

Printouts were laid out on the table from several files. Transmissions and agency reports that had been gathered over several months.

"Fuentes doesn't deal in terrorism," Ian muttered then, his ruined voice gravelly and harsh. "The information we've gathered says he's fighting the merger Sorrell is attempting to make."

"Because it's not a merger, it's an overthrow, with Fuentes standing as cover for the terrorist. It takes Fuentes's power and his control and leaves him vulnerable against the law enforcement agencies searching for him," Jordan mused, while the others went through the papers, took in the information, then placed them back in the folders.

"So we have Fuentes, his spy Mr. White, and Sorrell all with their little fingers involved in our operation now," Kell bit out. "Fuentes has definitely sent out a kidnapper. Are there any other threats?"

Emily watched her father flinch before he answered.

"There's information that Sorrell has asked to take possession of Emily once she's been kidnapped."

Emily reached up, gripping Kell's leg where it tensed beside her. She had heard of Sorrell. The unidentified terrorist traded regularly in human flesh. Kidnapped young women whom he kept drugged and used as sex toys within his organization.

"Without Fuentes's network and his contacts, Sorrell can't achieve the foothold he wants here in the U.S.," Macey broke in at that point. "And without Fuentes, Mr. White can't eliminate the threat the senator is posing."

"Have we gained any information on what that threat is?" Kell asked.

"Whoever Mr. White is, he's a known associate of mine," her father answered, his jaw clenching in anger. "I've figured out that much. And he has to be one of the senators or private members of the committees I'm on. The bill I'm trying to get through Congress at the moment focuses on a stronger checks-and-balance system for assuring that those committees aren't infiltrated by men like Mr. White. The bill has an investigative plan attached to it. If it's passed by the Senate, then Mr. White won't be able to hide any longer."

"Bingo," Kell muttered. "Then it doesn't have anything to do with the destruction of the Fuentes compound during the rescue, or the new laws you're trying to put through against the drug suppliers and dealers that are arrested?"

Richard Stanton shook his head wearily. "I suspected that was it, until the last transmission Macey received. Mr. White agreed with Sorrell's demands that he hold Emily in exchange for my *good behavior,*" he snarled, his tone cutting. "If it were retaliation, they would have killed her outright by now and that bill is the only thing that could interest Sorrell, Mr. White, and Fuentes all at once."

Which meant the stakes were much higher than any of them had realized. If Fuentes's kidnapper actually managed to take her, then she may as well consider her life over.

Kell tightened his hand at Emily's shoulder briefly as he stared back at the senator, meeting the other man's gaze directly.

He had to fight to keep from pulling her out now, to steal away to that safe house he knew was available. He would keep her there, protect her himself, shadow her every move. But for how long? Without her, the kidnapper would fade away, and Fuentes would make certain the next strike was one they couldn't guard against.

As with all his games, he was playing by a predetermined set of rules right now. Keep the queen on the board, and the game would progress. Remove the prize and he would strike immediately.

"Judas is certain the attempt is going to be made at the Andover ball," Ian said then. "Sorrell and Fuentes's spy, Mr. White, will be in attendance. There will be over six hundred guests at that party. There's no way in hell to narrow down who is who in the amount of time we have, even if we did have the information to do it."

"So we're walking in blind," Emily said faintly then, looking at each of the men, as Kell fought to hold back the fury he could feel rising in his gut.

"Durango Team will be at the party," Reno said then. "All of us will be there before you arrive and our priority is making certain you aren't taken. Kira Porter has also been assigned to the mission. White won't have the chance to take you, though he and his cohorts will feel confident enough to make the attempt. Then we'll have him. And our sources say he will know who White is."

White. The name clashed inside her head, sending an ache of tension to center behind her eyes. Why the hell did that name keep affecting her?

"Emily?" her father asked then.

She shook her head. "Mr. White." She worried the name through her mind. "Every time you mention him I swear I get cold chills and a headache." She rubbed at her brow.

"Whore's Dust will do that." Her father grimaced. "You likely heard the name while you were there, sweetheart. It's a code name Fuentes gave his spy. And Fuentes likes to brag to his victims. That's probably where you heard it."

It was a reasonable explanation. She had been in the Fuentes compound nearly forty-eight hours before her rescue; he could have done a lot of bragging in that time.

"The party is in two nights," Kell stated behind her, his voice dark, the shadow of his Cajun accept barely coloring his words—but the fact that it was there was telling. "There are some things I need. I'll make a list and give it to Ian tonight."

"You'll have everything you need, Kell." The admiral spoke up at that point. "Myself and Captain Malone have also been invited to the party. We'll provide what backup we can."

"What about Jansen Clay?" Emily asked. "He'll want to help, because of Risa."

Her father and the admiral shook their heads at once. "This information is need to know only, Emily," her father said. "As highly as I think of Jansen, I can't trust his temper. Risa's in bad shape, from what I hear. He's as likely to go vigilante as he is to follow orders."

Daddy! Help me! Emily jerked violently at the cry that tore through her head and the sense of terror that had her coming to her feet, nearly stumbling before Kell rose and caught her in his arms.

"Emily?" he questioned her roughly. "What's wrong?"

She swallowed tightly, fighting back the burning bile that rose in her throat.

"I'm sorry." She shook her head fiercely as she fought the revulsion building inside her. "I didn't meant to do that." She felt like tearing her hair out in an attempt to tear out the memories.

"It's the discussion. Talking about it pulls at fractured memories that make no sense." The admiral's voice was a vicious growl. "That bastard Fuentes has a lot to answer for."

Emily nodded jerkily. The doctors and phychologists had

pages of information they had given her, enough for a book, on the side effects of the synthetic drug Fuentes's genius scientist had created. The mad bastard had at least been paranoid enough to keep the secret of how to make it hidden from Fuentes. With his death, the secret had died with him, making the remaining Whore's Dust a lost commodity on the drug market.

"I'll be okay." She pulled back from Kell slowly, avoiding his gaze, feeling weak, ineffective in her own defense now.

"Yes, you will." His hands tightened on her shoulders before one lifted and moved to her jaw, forcing her to look up at him. "It's not your fault, Emily."

She was aware of the other men in the room and the fact that they, along with her father, were witnessing her weakness. And she hated that. It only proved to her father that she wasn't as strong or as brave as she thought she was.

"I know that." Her smile was tight as she pulled back. "If you'll excuse me, I think I need to go wash my face."

She needed to escape. She needed to regain her composure before she talked any more about Fuentes.

K ELL WATCHED HER LEAVE, HIS jaw bunching with the effort it took not to follow her, not to comfort her. His head swung around to encompass the men staring back at him thoughtfully before he pushed his fingers through his hair and started after her.

"Kell. Give her a minute," the senator said, his voice rough. "Just a few minutes."

Kell jerked around. "Why?"

The other man shook his head. "She's feeling weak. If you go in there and comfort her, you'll make her feel weaker, and she'll hate that."

"This coming from the man who tries to chain her to any and every controlling asshole he can find?" Kell snapped back furiously. "How would you know what makes her weak or strong?"

Rather than becoming angry, the senator's lips twitched with an edge of humor.

"Between me and you, son, I knew those controlling assholes didn't have a chance. Just as I knew that eventually you'd get tired of watching me send them to her and take the job yourself. Just as you've done."

Kell's eyes narrowed as Richard leaned back in his chair and regarded him with a slight smile.

"She can outshoot most men I know." He ticked off a finger. "She goes to Gator Jack's to learn how to fight. She's nearly talked her shooting instructor into letting her into an open practice range normally reserved for law enforcement and military, and the woman can maneuver through rush-hour traffic like a defensive-driving instructor." He continued to count off fingers. "She thinks that damned research will help her write a book, when the book is just an excuse to research crap guaranteed to piss me off and make her bodyguards crazy. On top of this, you've been following her for the better part of five years whenever you're home on leave, and you have an annoying habit of threatening her bodyguards whenever you catch them looking at her with anything other than polite interest."

Kell felt like squirming.

"I may not be in action anymore, son, but I'm not a SEAL for nothing. My daughter is damned strong, but she doesn't take orders worth a damn. And when it comes to women, neither do you. You two needed a solid kick in your asses years ago. I just gave you one."

"You couldn't have predicted this," Kell snapped, referring to Fuentes's attempts on Emily.

"No, I didn't." The senator breathed out wearily as he shook his head then. "But I didn't have to. I knew it was just a matter of time before you stepped in anyway."

Kell stared at the men around him, their efforts to hold back their amusement bringing a snarl to his lips.

"Sit down, Kell." The admiral waved his hand toward the

chair. "Richard's right. Give the girl a chance to find her composure before you go to her. She's a woman; better learn now when to comfort her tears and when not to."

Was she crying? His gaze snapped to the closed door. God help him if she was in there crying alone.

"I can make that an order, Lieutenant," the admiral reminded him. "Give us ten more minutes, then you can go to her. We still have a few things to discuss here."

Clenching his fists, Kell sat back down slowly, determined that if he heard so much as a whimper from the bathroom then orders be damned, there wasn't a chance in hell that he would stay put.

As he breathed out a frustrated sigh, his gaze lifted, locking with Ian's where he stood behind the senator, leaning casually against the wall. For a moment, just a moment, he could have sworn he saw grief reflected in the other man's eyes. Not that it would have been the first time he caught that flash of emotion. Just as before it was gone as quickly as it had come, and the ever-present mocking amusement took its place.

"Securing the Andover mansion is going to be a bitch," Reno said, interrupting Kell's thoughts, drawing his gaze back to the group and a plan of the house and grounds that Reno was laying on the table. "It's an old plantation mansion with several wings and additions. There's no sign of hidden entrances or tunnels, so we're lucky there." A Southern plantation home with no hidden tunnels or entrances. Hell, someone had been confident when they built that house.

"What we do have"—Macey sat forward to point to the grounds—"are unfenced grounds, thick woods, and so many damned guests we're going to want to start taking potshots. Look alive, boys, and I'll show you what I've done." He rubbed his hands together gleefully then as he glanced at Kell. "I've procured a handy little flesh-toned transmitter to attach to Emily. And getting those bad boys wasn't easy, let me tell you. If—and I stress the if—she's taken, then we'll at least have a chance to get her coordinates. It's called hedging our bets. I've also tapped into the Andovers' security cameras and the Secret Service boys working with us will have monitor duty. We can go over the recordings after the party and see who we can see. We're going to catch this son of a bitch, and when we do, he's going to tell us where Nathan is. God help him then, because there won't be nothin' of Mr. White left once we get finished with him."

Violence simmered in the air, flashed in the gazes of each man there. Mr. White, whoever the hell he was, had tortured Nathan to the point that there wasn't a chance he would ever be the same again.

The laughing Irishman, they had once called him. His mother had come from Ireland with her parents, and Nathan's grandfather's accent had influenced Nathan's speech as a child. With his bright blue eyes and broad, amused smile, he had charmed the women and talked his way out of more trouble than any man had a right to be able to.

His luck had run out when Fuentes captured him though. There was no amusement in the eyes of the man in the photos Macey had printed out. There was madness, rage—death. There was nothing of the man Kell had known and often called a brother.

There would be even less of Emily left if Sorrell managed to get his hands on her. The tales of his tortures, of the lives his women led, were the stuff of nightmares. Fuentes was playing sandbox games compared to Sorrell.

"Judas's last contact promised backup if she is taken," Macey stated. "Whether we can trust him or not, I'm not saying. I know in the last two years, he's not screwed us over yet."

"She won't be taken," Kell informed them all, the guttural tone of his voice almost shocking him. "We cover her and she won't be taken. Then we'll watch the security recordings Macey takes and we'll find the bastard there. Emily is not to be left undefended."

"We'll protect Emily and we'll find Nathan," Ian said then. "No matter the cost."

"No matter the cost," they repeated.

But the edge in Ian's voice had Kell's gaze returning to him once again. Nathan had been Ian's closest friend, even as a teenager, and Kell knew Ian had grieved harder than the rest of them when they lost the other man.

Ian would die for any of his brothers, but for Nathan, he would have sold his own soul. A chill raced up Kell's spine at the thought. If Ian got to Mr. White or Sorrell before the rest of the team managed to pull him off them, God only knew what would happen.

Twenty-three

NIGHTMARES TWISTED THROUGH EMILY'S DREAMS that night, making her sleep restless despite Kell's best attempts to help her rest. When she awoke the next morning she was tired and cranky, and the nervous panic filling her stomach made her feel weaker than ever.

She hated this feeling. She had never known true fear until Fuentes kidnapped her, and since then, she had sworn she would never feel it again. Now, the closer the Andover party came, the more the nerves twisted in her stomach and the more upset her nightmares left her.

Because she couldn't remember them. They were right there at the edge of her memory as she awoke, but they never slid from the shadows enough for her to grasp them.

And they had never left her fighting with the sick feeling of panic that rose within her this morning.

Tomorrow night, they would arrive at the Andover ball, and she had a feeling that whatever happened there, nothing would ever be the same again.

Shaking her head at the thought, Emily finished her shower before quickly drying her hair and dressing in a pair of soft cotton shorts and a matching camisole top. The light material was cool and comfortable, clothes she normally wore when she was arranging research notes on her computer and plotting her books.

She glanced at the laptop as she left her bedroom, and breathed out a sigh of regret. It would have to wait just a little bit longer. The book she had almost finished and that her agent was so excited about seemed part of another world right now, a world she couldn't go back to until after tomorrow night. Everything hinged on tomorrow night.

The scent of coffee greeted her as she entered the living room, and the sight of Kell, shirtless and in bare feet, moving around the kitchen brought an ache to her chest.

He had tried to comfort her each time she awoke from the nightmares last night, but she had felt his anger simmering through the room. Silent. Deadly. Each time his rough voice had dragged her from whatever nightmares tormented her, it seemed his anger had only grown.

"I had Ian go out and get you some fresh cinnamon rolls," he announced as he poured her a cup of coffee. Then, as though he had done it every day of their lives together, he sugared and creamed her coffee before setting the cup on the kitchen table.

"So that's how you get the cinnamon rolls without leaving the house," she said. "I should have known."

A quick grin flashed across his face before his head lowered to steal a kiss. "I have a sweet tooth."

"No kidding." She sat down, picked up the cup of coffee, and gave a sigh of delight before taking her first sip.

He made a perfect cup of coffee.

"Kira stopped by while you were in the shower," he told her as he moved to the other side of the table with his own cup. "She's offered to pick up your dress for the party and bring it to you. I think you should let her."

She met his gaze warily. "The final alterations have been finished." She finally shrugged. "She'll have to pick up the accessories for me though. I hadn't gotten around to that yet."

"I'm sure she could manage it," he said.

Emily nodded before lowering her head and staring at the cinnamon roll that sat in the little saucer by her coffee.

"Em. Everything's going to be okay," he told her again.

"I know that." She flashed him a confident smile. "I know you'll take care of me, Kell."

He was so fierce, so determined. She could see it in his eyes, in the hard set of his expression.

"What were the nightmares about then?" He sipped at his coffee, watching her over the rim of the cup.

"I don't know." She could feel the suffocating sense of fear rising inside her again. "I couldn't remember them after I awoke."

"Do you have them often?" The question was posed casually, but Emily saw the sharp scrutiny in his gaze.

"After the kidnapping I did." She rubbed her hands over her face before shaking her head wearily. "For months afterward I couldn't sleep at night at all. The darkness was terrifying."

"You were probably blindfolded when you were kidnapped," he said gently. "Fuentes is known for that. When he kidnaps one of his victims he keeps them blindfolded for hours. It throws your senses off balance and makes the fear sharper."

"So the psychologist said." She grimaced. "It took days before I could make sense of what was going on around me after the rescue. I don't remember a lot of that week and I remember nothing of the kidnapping itself after the limo was run off the road and we were taken."

She and the other two girls had been on their way home from a party in D.C. Two senators' daughters and Jansen Clay's daughter, Risa. Emily's father and Senator Bridgeport, Carrie Bridgeport's father, had been instrumental in pushing through several bills that had given drug enforcement agents critical freedoms in uncovering the transporters and suppliers of the drugs coming into the United States.

Carrie Bridgeport had died from the dose of Whore's Dust she had been given, and Risa Clay was currently in a private institution due to the mental damage the drug had inflicted on her.

God, those girls were so young. Carrie had been sixteen, Risa barely eighteen.

Her gaze dropped back to the coffee, the steam from the creamy brew rising, thickening, and before Emily could stop it a horrified scream tore through her mind.

Daddy, help me!

"Emily!" Kell's voice shattered the sudden memory that was there, then gone.

Wildly, she stared around the kitchen, realizing she was no longer in her chair. The coffee dripped from the table where the cup had overturned and Kell's arms were around her, dragging her back from the hot liquid, holding her to him as she tried to fight him.

"What is it?" He turned her to face him, his expression fierce, his gaze demanding as he stared down at her, forcing her to look at him. "What did you see, Emily?"

His voice was loud, battering through her mind, hoarse and commanding, as she fought to keep from being dragged back into the darkness awaiting her within her own memories.

"Screams." She shook her head, jerking away from him to put distance between herself and the sheltering warmth she needed so much.

She couldn't let him hold her. She shook her head, shaking as whispers fractured her mind.

"Will he come for you?" A sneer, a voice that filled her with terror. *"Tell me. Tell me how to contact him."*

She shook her head furiously as she gazed back at Kell. "How did you know I'd been kidnapped?" The question wheezed from her lips. Had she betrayed him?

Kell frowned. "I'd just come off a previous assignment in the Gulf. I was entering debriefing when my CO for that mission told me about the kidnapping. I requested an immediate flight to the transport off Colombia's waters where the rescue teams were being flown. Once there, I pretty much demanded to be a part of the rescue. Why?"

She shook her head. It didn't make sense.

"Why, Emily?" he snapped.

"I remember whispers," she gasped. "Screams. I don't know whose they were. Mine or the other girls'. A scream for daddy. Someone whispering questions. Asking if someone will come. How to contact them. And it's so dark . . ." She shuddered as he pulled her into his arms again.

"The stress works against you." His hand covered her head, holding her to him. "The Whore's Dust is destructive. Nothing the victims have remembered in the past has had anything to do with the night they were drugged. Everything's fractured in your head from the time you're given the drug until the time it's completely out of your system. Days for some. Weeks for others. Some never recover, Emily."

Like Risa Clay. She hadn't recovered. Not yet.

"You have every right to be frightened," he told her then. "You know what Fuentes can do. Your subconscious knows how terrified you were when you were taken the first time. That subconscious can be more destructive than the reality. It creates demons and nightmares and whispers of memories that you can't be certain are true or false."

She breathed in roughly. "I haven't had nightmares since those first weeks."

"And once this is over, they'll disappear again," he promised her, pulling back enough to watch her with eyes so deep, so dark, they were like endless pools of emotion.

How could she have ever thought he was cold? That there was no emotion, nothing gentle, to back up the extreme sexiness that was so much a part of him?

"It's just fear," she said then, swallowing tightly, trying to convince herself of that.

"Just fear," he agreed, though she swore she saw suspicion flashing in his eyes. The same suspicion that filled her.

"But you want to know if I remember any more whispers," she guessed.

His lips tightened. "Just in case."

Emily inhaled deeply. "No other victim has ever remembered anything?"

He shook his head as his hand cupped her cheek. "But you're not everyone else," he told her then. "If you remember any whispers, a voice, a face, anything, I want to know."

"I'll let you know."

"And tomorrow night, you'll stay close to me," he ordered. "You'll follow orders. Promise me."

"I promise," she answered with a shaky smile. "And I will, Kell, because I have no desire to ever lose your arms around me. I won't risk allowing harm to either of us."

His jaw clenched tight, the muscle working in it furiously before a tight grimace crossed his face and his arms tightened around her.

"Emily, do you know what you do to me?"

She could feel his erection against her stomach, his arms tight around her, flexing to hold back his strength, to hold back the need to pull her so close that they melted into each other.

"I know what you do to me." Her hands wrapped around his back, smoothed up it, feeling the powerful ripple of muscles beneath her palms. "I know I've dreamed of you for years. Fantasized and ached. And I know I love you more than I thought I could love anyone. I've loved you all along, Kell, I just didn't want to admit it."

"You didn't want to give your father what you thought he wanted," he accused her softly, a sad curve tugging at his lips.

"How did you know that?" She hadn't even admitted it fully to herself.

"Because it's the reason I stayed away from you, chère. Had I taken what I wanted, then I would have been giving the Kriegers and the Beaulaines what they dreamed of. A woman they approved of, and eventually the grandchildren they dreamed of to carry on their bloodline. It took Fuentes to show me what I was throwing away and this new threat to make me move my ass and claim you. And I'll never let you go, Emily. Remember that. Wherever you go in life, I'll be behind you. As well as in death."

He had lost so much, so young. And that loss had scarred him, made him harder, made him bitter for so long. Now, she saw the man he was inside in the heated warmth of the emerald eyes staring back at her.

He was a warrior. Fierce. Determined and strong. And he was her lover.

As his lips caught hers in a kiss of gentle wonder, Emily felt the breath hitch in her throat. She needed him. In ways she had never known she would need a man, she needed Kell.

He needed her.

As he lifted Emily into his arms and carried her back to her bed, he admitted to himself what his heart and soul had known for years. She was the other half of him. Courageous, brave, defiant, and winsome. She was every dream that had sparked in his mind for as long as he had lived.

His Papère Beaulaine had said that once Beaulaine men found the other half of themselves, then they knew it. There was no doubt. There had been no doubt in his mind for years who his woman was. The doubt had been in himself, in his own stubbornness and his inability to reach out for what he wanted without the past interfering.

As he laid her back on the bed and undressed her then himself, he knew the past had nothing to do with this. Emily was his future.

"I'm going to love you to exhaustion today," he told her. "When night falls, you'll have no choice but to sleep."

He gripped the stalk of his cock, his fingers curling around it as her gaze dropped, her hot little tongue swiping over her swollen lips. Her blue eyes were darkening, heating as she shifted on the mattress, her thighs parting.

And Kell's gaze was drawn lower. Over tight hard nipples to paradise. To soft creamy flesh glistening with the sweet juices that drew his tongue like a magnet and a hard little clit peeking from the folds with shy hunger.

"It might be hard to exhaust me," she whispered then. "I've been waiting for you a long time, Kell."

"Ah chère, no longer than I've dreamed of this." He stroked his cock, letting the anticipation rise, feeling the heat of her gaze on the hard flesh as it tightened further, a drop of creamy precum beading at the tip.

He watched as her gaze narrowed on the little pearl of liquid before she rose to her knees, moving with such grace and sensual intent that she stole his breath.

What little oxygen was left in his lungs whooshed out as her tongue curled over the head of his cock, drawing the silky fluid into her before her mouth covered the swollen head.

"Bébé," he groaned, his voice harsh. "Hell yes, suck it deep."

She was drawing him along her tongue, filling her mouth with his flesh as the head of his cock throbbed in eager anticipation.

He loosened his fingers, sliding them deep into the cascade of auburn waves that framed her face, pulling it back and watching her lips as they stretched around his flesh and sucked him into the pleasure-rich depths of her mouth.

"Emily, sweet." He let his senses go, let them fill with the sight and feel of her as she brought him more pleasure than he had ever known.

His balls drew tight along the base of his shaft, the pleasure of it washing up his spine and sizzling through his scalp with never-ending pulses of hot, electric sensation.

She did this to him every time she touched him. Weakened his knees with a pleasure that he never knew he could experience. She filled his head with thoughts of a future and his body with a lust that nearly brought him to his knees.

Tightening his fingers in her hair he pulled her back, grimacing in pleasure at the drag of her lips over his flesh and the sheen of moisture from her mouth that now coated his cock.

He pulled the swollen crest free, his jaw tightening at the

exquisite pleasure of her tongue licking over it and her moan of denial vibrating around it.

Holding her head back, he stared into the velvety depths of eyes so blue they mesmerized him. Gripping his erection, he placed it at her lips once again, sank in, then pulled free as he tensed against the need to fuck her mouth until he'd spilled every drop of semen torturing his balls into the heated depths.

"You're playing with me," she moaned as her fingers slid over his thighs then moved in to wrap around the base of the heavy shaft. "That's not nice, Kell."

"Fucking your mouth should be done slow and easy," he drawled, holding her head back with the thick strands of her hair. "It should be savored, chère. Such sweet pleasure should never be rushed."

He watched her eyes dilate and darken at the thick Cajun accent he couldn't hide when he was with her. It rumbled from his chest, as much a part of him as his upbringing had been.

"I shouldn't be teased either." She was breathing harder as he tucked his cock at her lips once more, watching her eyes flutter closed, feeling her hands tighten at the base as he pressed forward once again.

Slowly. He eased inside the wet heat of her mouth, feeling her tongue lick and stroke against the sensitive underside, feeling one slender palm cup his balls as the other hand began to stroke the shaft as he moved his own fingers.

He gave her her head, watching in ecstasy as she began to suckle his dick with sweet abandon. His hands caressed her head rather than pulling it back, sifting through the silk of her hair, touching her cheek, the shell of her ears, desperate to touch her in any way as she gave him a pleasure that he could never describe. A pleasure he would kill to preserve.

"Ah, sweet Emily," he whispered. "Such a hot, sweet mouth. A wicked little tongue." The wicked tongue in question was lashing at his cock head with each slow move of her mouth. It curled beneath the throbbing crest and undulated against the underside with a ripple of fiery pleasure.

If he wasn't careful, he would spill himself between her lips, and that wasn't what he wanted, for either of them. He needed to be inside her when his release came. To feel the hot pulse of his semen as her pussy contracted around him.

He would have preferred to feel her without the protection of the condom, but it wasn't a risk he could take again. Not yet. God help him, he couldn't take her to that party with the risk that she could have conceived his child.

"Enough, Emily," he groaned as he felt the cum bubbling in his balls. The sac was so tight, drawn so close to his body that he was in agony.

Pulling back, he eased from her grip, his back teeth hurting with the need to fuck. To take her. Possess her. To mark as his forever.

Instead, his lips caught hers as he moved over her, pressing her to the bed and filling his senses with the scent of feminine arousal and the sound of muted whimpers echoing in her throat.

His sweet little fox.

His hands caressed her arms, gripping her wrists to pull them above her head as he plundered her lips with a hunger that would have shocked him at any other time.

He wasn't taking her gently, but he needed to. He wanted to. The hunger was rising inside him like a storm gone wild, pummeling at his control as he fought to touch and to taste as much of her as possible.

"Kell—" The soft, needy cry that fell from her lips as he moved to taste the sensitive flesh of her neck had a shudder racing through him.

She was slightly damp with the heat raging inside her, and he could taste the sweet perfection of her in the curve of her neck, over her collarbone.

Sweet, swollen breasts rose sharply, her nipples tight and flushed with the need to be touched. To be tasted.

With a hungry groan he filled his mouth with one tight bud, his tongue curling around it as he cupped the flushed mound with his hand.

Each lash of his tongue had her jerking against him, pushing her nipple deeper into his mouth as she arched against him. Her thigh rubbed against his swollen cock, pulling a groan from his chest as he moved from one nipple to the next. Her response to his hungry suckling whipped through him.

If he didn't touch more of her, taste more of her, then he was going to go insane from the need. Control? He scoffed at the thought of it as his lips moved down her torso with hungry kisses and quick flicks of his tongue. Each caress whipped through her, jerking her against him, assuring him of her pleasure.

"I need to taste." He nipped at the smooth skin of her hip. "To bury my mouth in your pussy and grow drunk from the taste. You're like the smoothest whiskey, sweet and hot and so damned potent you steal my mind."

He spread her thighs, moving quickly between them as he gazed up at her, filled his senses with the sight of her, arms outstretched on the bed, her fingers clenching into the blankets as her head tipped back in pleasure.

He ran his fingers through the wet slit and she moaned and arched. He opened the fragile folds slowly, the soft inner flesh glistening with its layer of syrup, and a ragged plea tore from her throat.

When his head lowered and he drew in the first taste of her, Kell let the hunger have him. He licked around her clit as his hands wrapped beneath her thighs and lifted them, pushing them close to her chest and tilting the flushed, soaked flesh closer to his mouth. Holding her thighs steady he parted them further, his gaze held by the folds opening, revealing the delicate entrance to the mysterious flesh beyond.

It was a mystery his tongue was determined to solve. The first thrust had her taste exploding through his senses. Sweet, stormy, tinted with the taste of honey and fire, and as intoxicating as any moonshine he had ever consumed as a young man.

She drugged his senses. She rocked his mind. And she owned his soul.

He fucked her with his tongue, feeling the tight grip of her pussy as she tried to arch closer, the feel of her fingers plunging into his hair as he thrust his tongue deep inside her.

Rapid, furious thrusts had her body writhing beneath his hold and her juices flowing to his tongue with an abundance that had him groaning in sheer ecstasy.

Delicate tissue clenched around his tongue with a ferocity that had his dick jerking, demanding ease. Sweat poured from his body, dampened hers, and filled the air with steamy hunger as he quickly lifted his head and moved over her.

He had pushed as far as he dared. Reaching out to the bedside table, he jerked a condom from the drawer, quickly sheathed the raging flesh of his cock, and in one smooth stroke buried himself inside her.

Heat. God, so hot and tight. His balls flexed as they pressed against her wet flesh and his cock flexed in primal warning as the tight grip of her pussy sent his senses into sensory overload.

He couldn't hold back. Straining with the effort to bring her to release before he found his own, Kell began to move with tempered speed. Easy strokes. Containing the agonizing need to give in to the release straining through his body.

Beneath him, Emily was jerking, arching, fighting the hold he had on her thighs as her hands moved to his shoulders, the little nails biting into his flesh as he pumped his cock inside her.

She was tightening on him. Her voice filled with consuming lust as he felt her flesh ripple around him, clenching, spasming, before a keening cry left her lips and she exploded around him.

"Fuck, yes. Come for me," he groaned. "So tight. So hot. Sweet baby, I'm going to fuck you until we're both dying from it."

Her release shredded the last of his control. His hips hammered into hers, thrusting his cock inside her with rapid, jackhammer strokes that parted the spasming flesh that fought to hold him inside her.

He gritted his teeth. His head shook in desperate denial, but holding back his own release was impossible.

He didn't know what he said, words were spilling from his lips as he pumped inside her, feeling his cock erupt and his cum spurt heavily from his body.

All he knew was the heat and the hunger, the release and the desperation.

"Je t'aime. *I love you.* Bébé. My sweet—so sweet."

He came over her, still buried inside her, fighting to breathe as his arms surrounded her and his lips were buried in her neck.

"My precious. My life," he groaned at her neck, hearing her voice at his ear, gasping cries of love.

". . . mine." The keening cry of possession that fell from her lips was accompanied by her sharp little teeth biting into his shoulder and sending another flare of heat tearing through his body.

"We're not finished," he groaned at her neck, stringing sharp little kisses beneath her ear.

"Chère, by no means are we finished." He was still hard, still hungry.

He pulled free, resheathed his still hard cock before pulling her to him and lifting her into his arms as he sat on his knees, impaling her once again on his thick cock.

Her eyes widened, then turned slumberous again as her arms wrapped around him, and she leaned back just enough to give herself leverage before she began riding him.

"Fuck, yes," he growled. "Fuck me, ma bien-aimée." He whispered an endearment he had never used, had never allowed to slip past his lips. His sweet. His darling. "Ça c'est bon, so good. Ride me hard." He gripped her hips, urging her on, feeling the tight clasp of her pussy and the heat surrounding him as he lost himself in possessing her once again.

He watched her as she rode him, her legs clasped around his hips, her torso arched, pushing her breasts to him, sweet hard nipple drawing his mouth as he held her, fucked her, lost himself in her.

"Ma bien-aimée—my beloved."

They exploded together, his harsh exclamation mixing with her cries as they fell to the bed amid tangled limbs and sweat-soaked flesh.

"Give me a minute," he groaned, boneless, barely able to breathe. "We'll go again, eh amoureuse?" His sweetheart. She was his soul.

The soft, defiant snort drew a grin to his lips.

"Touch me, die," she muttered, her pussy flexing around his cock as she held him inside her.

"Die if I don't," he muttered, barely able to withdraw and collapse to his side before drawing her against him. "Might need some food first."

Her murmur, neither encouraging nor denying had a grin tugging at his lips. "You're cooking, right?"

"You're dreaming," she mumbled.

Yes, he was. Of her. Always of her.

He drew her closer, letting her drape over his chest with a sigh of contentment and closed his eyes for a quick nap. Just a little one, before he fixed them both something with enough protein to see them through the day. Tonight, she would sleep. Sexual exhaustion could do wonders for the nightmares, he knew. And he would see that no nightmares came calling. That tonight she would sleep, because tomorrow they would both need all their senses rested. Tomorrow, they would face her demons.

JUDAS STARED AT THE SECURED cell phone in his hand and the message that he had only to click a single button to send. Just one movement of his thumb, and it would be over.

He had made his choice two years before; he didn't know why he was second-guessing it now. After years of ignoring the truth, the knowledge that this day would come, he had accepted there was no chance of fighting it any longer.

But still, he hesitated.

He had accepted his father's demand days ago. He would take his place within the cartel in exchange for Mr. White, Emily's safety, and most especially in exchange for Nathan.

He wiped his hand over his face at the thought of Nathan. The one man who had known the truth about him and had never told it, never judged him for it.

The message waited. He had already agreed, there was no reason to hold back now. All was laid in place and his father was giving him Mr. White on a silver platter. All he had to do was this one last thing. Just send this final message. The message that would lead Macey to him within a matter of days. But it would also finish this final battle between the men of Durango Team and Mr. White. White would be history.

He pushed send, closed the phone, and sat back to stare into the darkness of the room surrounding him. He hoped it was worth it. That the choice he'd made would eventually reap the rewards he dreamed of. And oh, how he dreamed. But lately, he had begun dreaming of more as well. Of gray eyes and long black hair. A hidden smile and a woman's whisper of desire. He was throwing that away and he knew it.

Judas. The betrayer. That's how he would be seen, and he could deal with it. He just had to remember that the rewards were worth it. He had to keep the rewards in sight. Otherwise, the secrets would kill him.

Twenty-four

T HE ANDOVER BALL WAS IN full swing when the limo passed through the heavy gates of the Alabama plantation. Ivy-draped trees lined the drive that circled around the front of the house and heavy shadows flickered among the landscaping lights positioned around the grounds.

The house itself was brightly lit, with guests lingering outside as well as around the grounds. The band positioned in the gardens behind the house could be heard from the front; the subtle jazz-influenced tunes were at once soothing and darkly sensual as they filtered through the night.

Many of the guests stood on the wide front landing where the double doors were thrown open; subtle shaded lighting cast a golden glow on the front lawn, giving the milling guests an ethereal look.

Ball gowns mingled with sheaths and ultrashort designer dresses. The men wore tuxedos, and many were in uniform, though Kell and Ian had opted to wear dress suits instead. It was easier to hide the hardware, Kell had told her.

Beneath her bronze silk dress and stiff petticoat, Emily wore her thigh holster and weapon, though she had opted to leave the dagger in her drawer because the petticoats kept snagging on the wood handle.

Nerves fluttered in her stomach as the limo came to a smooth stop and she inhaled roughly to draw in courage.

Macey had received another message from Judas late the night before, informing him that all parties would definitely be in place and the attempt to kidnap her was proceeding as planned.

"Stay close, love," Kell muttered as the Secret Service chauffeur came around the limo to open her door. "We have you covered."

Emily nodded jerkily.

"Remember to stay close to me. I want you covered at all times. If you have to go to the ladies' room, Kira will go with you. Ian and I will stay close to the doors in that event. Reno and the others are close by and will stay in close proximity to us."

Emily gripped her small purse as she stared back at him, drawing strength from him. "We're just going to enjoy the party." He kept his voice calm, the steady timbre easing her nerves. "Ready?"

She nodded quickly.

Below her dress, low on her back, was a small circular piece of skin-toned tape that he called a skin tag. Just in case they were separated, he told her. He had taken every precaution to protect her, yet an awareness of the danger enfolding her did nothing to comfort her.

Emily inhaled deeply as the limo door opened. Kell stepped out first, then extended his hand inside to her.

Emily moved from the limo, keeping her head up as heads turned and she recognized more of the faces than not. She knew these people. She had gone over the guest list with Kell and Ian, and realized that most of the names listed, she had known most of her life. She couldn't believe that one of them could be a killer or a spy, or God forbid, an international terrorist. No, the elusive Mr. White and his terrorist counterpart Sorrell had to be crashing the party. Which would be too easy to do with this crowd.

Gripping Kell's arm, she followed him up the wide steps

to the landing and entered the spacious marble foyer. Chandeliers glowed with brilliant light overhead, crystal prisms storing and reflecting the glow back tenfold, increasing her feeling of vulnerability. Anyone, everyone could see her.

"Miss Emily Stanton and Mr. Kellian Krieger," the doorman announced loudly as they entered and Kell handed him their invitation.

Great. No way to sneak in here.

"Emily. Kell." Their host and hostess, Markwell and Catherine Andover, were in their forties. Markwell was nearly six feet, with calm brown eyes and thinning brown hair. His wife, Catherine, stood a few inches shorter in her heels and had short red hair and cool light blue eyes. Emily had never cared much for Catherine, but the Andovers had contributed heavily to her father's election fund and they were influential within the political and financial circles her father frequented.

"Markwell." Emily accepted his kiss on her cheek as she held back an instinctive dislike of him. He was a shark, and took every opportunity to touch where he shouldn't.

This time, though, he kept his hands at her shoulders before moving back and shaking Kell's hand.

"Catherine." No problems here. The other woman air-kissed her cheek with enough distance to assure Emily that the other woman thought as much of her as she thought of Catherine.

"It's so nice to see you, Emily," Catherine drawled. "You missed our last few parties. We worried the kidnapping had adversely affected you."

And how the hell was it supposed to affect her?

Emily smiled coolly. "I've just been busy, Catherine," she assured her.

"Ah yes, school is out and you dabble in writing, don't you, dear?"

Emily kept her smile pasted on her face. "Or something," she agreed.

"And Kellian Krieger." Catherine turned to Kell, her catlike smile grating on Emily's nerves then as her gaze flickered over Kell's chest and thighs. The witch. She was coming on to him and Emily didn't like it in the least.

"Mrs. Andover." Kell accepted her hand before lifting it and brushing a gentlemanly kiss across her knuckles. "It's a pleasure."

"It's been too long since we've seen you, Kell." She sighed. "You don't attend enough of the little events we're invited to."

"I've been busy." Kell's voice was cool.

"Ah yes." Catherine's smile curled with a hint of maliciousness. "The Krieger heir risking his neck as a SEAL. It's a shame."

"If you'll excuse us, Catherine." Emily curled her fingers around Kell's arm. "I see some friends I'd like to talk to."

She drew Kell away from their host and hostess, aware of the tension in his body.

"You know them?" she asked, keeping her voice low.

"Friends of the Beaulaines and Kriegers." His voice was cold, scathing. She had a feeling that wasn't a compliment where he was concerned.

"So you come to the parties often?" she asked as they moved into the large ballroom.

"Sometimes." He was in SEAL mode. Tense, prepared.

"Are you this relaxed at all of them?"

He dipped his head closer to hers. "No, I'm usually holding up the wall and cussing Reno for making me accept the invitation."

"Hmm, yes, I should have made a point to attend more parties." She nodded as she let a smile pull at her lips. "I would have shown you how it's done."

"And how's it done?" There was no accent now, but his voice still had the power to make her stomach clench in warning arousal.

"You don't hold up the walls, you hold up the trees in the gardens." She snickered. "They're easier to hide within."

His hand tightened at her hip, but as she glanced up, she saw the smile that tugged at his lips.

"I could have helped you hold up the trees," he murmured as they began to make their way through the crowd. "Though, to be honest, had we been caught, we could have been arrested."

"I doubt it," Emily whispered in reply. "I watched a lot of shadowy freak shows in those gardens, Kell. No one ever got caught."

He rubbed his hand along the back of his neck as he stared at her in surprise. "God, you terrify me. You're not supposed to watch."

At that, Emily stopped and stared up at him with an expression of such false innocence that he only shook his head.

"Remind me to spank you."

Emily sighed. "I keep being bad and you never take the hint. Do I need to take out an advertisement?"

She loved the way his eyes darkened at that, the way they roved over her face, her breasts, then moved back to meet hers with wicked intent.

"I won't forget again."

"Kell Krieger!" Disbelief filled the feminine squeal that came from Kell's right. Emily felt him stiffen again, watched his gaze turned cold just before he turned to greet one of the few people Emily actually detested.

Tabby Deaton.

"Kell. Oh, my God, it's been too long."

Emily stared at the designer original evening gown slit nearly to the top of Tabby's thighs and riding low on her obviously fake breasts. Emily heard Tabby had gotten a boob job, she just hadn't believed it.

Tabby's dark hair flowed around her shoulders and framed her pale face and glistening red lips. Plump red lips. Damn. Tabby had had her lips done too.

"Tabby." Kell nodded coolly.

Tabby glanced at Emily. "Why, Emily, I didn't see you there." She gazed down her perfectly straight, aristocratic nose at Emily. "How cute that Kell brought you. He does so enjoy doing your father these little favors."

Emily felt one of her molars threaten to crack as she grit-ted her teeth. "Tabby, you're as sweetly endearing and charmingly polite as ever," she stated.

Tabby's eyes narrowed. "Of course I am, dear. It's the mark of a lady." She sniffed, causing her boobs to wiggle alarmingly, as she turned back to Kell and extended her hands to him. "No greetings for a friend, Kell?"

He inclined his head politely. "Hello, Tabby."

No love was lost here, Emily thought with pleased satis-faction.

Tabby affected an attempt at a pout; the pouched look appeared a little ridiculous on her though. Tabby, despite the boob job and lip enhancement, was amazingly well put together, so much so that Emily felt out of place every time she stood next to her. The strapless dress should have been lying around the other woman's ankles, but it stayed in place. The slit up the thigh never moved farther than it should, and her artfully arranged dark hair framed her face gracefully.

And she was staring at Kell as though she knew more about his body than she should.

Tabby sighed morosely. "You just disappeared from At-lanta last year as though you had never been there. I went by your apartment several times, you know."

"I was out of town."

Emily felt Kell's fingers at her hip, the tips rubbing against the silk of her gown restlessly.

Tabby pouted again before flashing Emily a look of dis-like from beneath her lashes.

"I heard you had moved from your place to Emily's," she drawled then. "We were all terribly surprised by that, you know."

Ah, D.C. gossip, one had to love it. Or in Emily's case, hate it.

"Why?" Kell's question was sharp, intent.

Whew, Emily could feel the tension rising now. Not in

Kell—he was calm, alert, dangerous—but in Tabby. Her fingers tightened on the little black purse she carried as her scarlet lips thinned marginally.

"We were just surprised," Tabby murmured then. "Emily's always so quiet." It was obvious *quiet* wasn't exactly the word she wanted to use.

"She's refreshing," Kell said softly. "Unlike other people. Now, if you'll excuse us."

"Don't run off, Kell," Tabby pleaded softly then, her hand landing on his arm, her fingers curling against the silk of the material. "I believe several of Emily's friends are here tonight as well. We could all visit."

Emily knew she should have expected this. Tabby was a regular at these parties, and she wasn't the only one.

"I believe I might actually know most everyone who is here," Emily stated with a smile. "Considering the crowd, that's not surprising, Tabby."

Satisfaction gleamed in Tabby's eyes.

"Deuter Meyers seemed quite surprised that you and Kell were living together," Tabby said with a self-satisfied smile. "He flew out from D.C. this morning just for the party after nearly deciding not to come. But when I mentioned you would be here, why he felt he just had to show up."

Emily's arms ached. She could feel the chill racing over them, the echo of the deep bruises that had marred them for weeks after she had left another party that Deuter Meyers had attended.

"Deuter Meyers?" There was an edge of suspicion as Kell glanced down at her.

"I knew him in college." Emily shrugged, careful to control her reactions now.

"Quite well, from what I understand." Tabby's smile was pure spite. "Very well."

At this point, Emily wanted to roll her eyes. She leaned forward instead. "Unlike some of us, when Kell came to my bed he knew exactly who he'd shared me with and who he hadn't. You're barking up the wrong tree." Bitch.

Tabby's eyes narrowed as she glanced at Kell. "Oh please, tell me you didn't fall for the virgin ploy."

"I think Kell's smarter than that, Tabby," Emily pointed out. "He rarely falls for anything, as we both know."

Just as he evidently hadn't fallen for the other woman or her carefully practiced sexuality.

Tabby flashed her a hostile look then slid her hand over Kell's opposite arm. "You should dance with me. It's been a very long time since we've danced."

Oh geez, give her a break.

"Tabby, I think you know that's not going to happen." Kell's voice was a hell of a lot nicer than the other woman deserved. Of course, Emily knew the enmity between her and Tabby might have something to do with her feelings on the matter.

Fury flashed in the other woman's eyes then. "Poor Kell." She sighed. "It's obvious you're still drawn to the poor little creatures outside your own social class. My parents were so certain you would grow out of that habit."

The little bitch.

"Excuse us, Tabby." Kell's voice was ice now. "But I think Emily needs some fresh air. Good night."

Kell drew her quickly away from the other woman, but not before Emily turned back, her gaze connecting with Tabby's in a look of promised retaliation. She may not attend the parties often, but she had her own friends. Friends who could make certain portions of Tabby's life uncomfortable.

"Bet me that Drage Masters rescinds her membership in his clubs for the rest of the year," she muttered, remembering the times she had seen the other woman at the clubs when she had gone to them for research into the BDSM fringe societies.

Kell drew her quickly along the wall, glancing down at her in shock. "How do you know Drage?"

"Drage likes me." She shrugged. "When I wanted to use

his clubs for research I made an appointment with him and Jayne Doe first thing rather than just barging in. He thought I was very polite. He even offered to let me downstairs if I was willing to pretend to be his sub."

He muttered something. Something along the lines of *death, dismemberment,* and *Drage* in the same sentence.

"He's charming." She shrugged.

"He's an alleycat," he argued back.

"They are the most charming of all," she assured him with a smile. "They appreciate the attention."

And the byplay was doing nothing to help her forget the fact that Tabby and Deuter were here. Together.

Damn Tabby and Deuter Meyers. She didn't need this. She still hadn't gotten over the nightmares that little event had produced before Fuentes had kidnapped her. She didn't need to meet that bastard again, especially not while Kell was anywhere around.

"Want to tell me about Meyers?" he asked as they once again began to move and headed through the open French doors into the candlelit gardens beyond.

"There's nothing to tell," she assured him before sipping at her wine again and wishing she had thought to get a refill.

"You know, Em, I've known you a long time," he drawled. "I could tell when you were lying even as a kid. That hasn't changed."

"Then maybe it's just none of your business." She had managed to keep that little event quiet for the most part. Few people knew about it, and even her father hadn't so much as heard a muttered rumor.

"I might have accepted that if it weren't for the fact that I could almost smell the hatred and anger rising off you," he growled. "You hid it damned well while Tabby was there, but I know you a hell of a lot better than she does. Should I ask Deuter about it?"

God forbid.

"You know, Kell, I don't go around questioning your ex-lovers," she pointed out. "Why should you question men that you should have enough sense to know aren't my ex-lovers?"

He was silent for long moments, drawing her through the crowds as she stared at faces and tried to place names to them.

"Because they frighten you," he finally said. "I want to know why."

"Maybe he was just weird."

"And maybe I know weird doesn't frighten you," he snapped. "It takes a hell of a lot more than weird to even faze you and I know it. So what the fuck happened?"

Emily flinched. He was working himself into a seriously pissed mood. Not that she really cared if Kell got pissed; there wasn't a chance he would hurt her. But if they came face-to-face with Deuter, she couldn't exactly predict what he might do.

"Nothing happened," she snapped back. "He wanted it, I said no, end of story. And you shouldn't worry so damned much about a past that is none of your business."

Before she could predict movement, Kell pulled her between the tall flowering shrubs that bordered the walkway, then pushed her against the stone column that hid there.

His body flattened against hers, his hands grabbing both wrists and anchoring them over her head with one broad hand.

"Now. I would like to ask you again. What happened with Deuter Meyers?"

Twenty-five

"HAS IT EVER BEEN POINTED out to you that you are just a shade arrogant?" Emily asked conversationally as she melted against his body.

He was hard. Her body noticed that the instant he pressed against her. His cock pressed against her stomach insistently, reminding her that she hadn't had her daily dose of Kell yet.

"You've mentioned it often," he bit out. "Now tell me about Deuter."

"Look, it was nothing. He was at a party and he freaked me out a little bit. Deuter likes to think he's a ladies' man, end of story."

"How did he freak you out?"

He wasn't buying it and he wasn't bothering to hide it. Dammit, why did Tabby have to be such an interfering bitch? She had managed to keep Deuter alive by the simple fact that she had never allowed her father to know what had happened. His life would be extinguished even faster if Kell found out.

In one single, stupid moment, the other woman had ignored all Emily's careful discretion. Not that she cared if Deuter died; she just cared if her father or Kell spent time in prison for his death.

Emily licked her lips nervously. She really didn't want to lie to Kell. Besides, he always seemed to know when she was lying.

"He was a little rough." She shrugged it away. "That's all. He'd had a little too much to drink and—"

"Don't excuse anything he fucking did," Kell snarled. "Just tell me what the fuck happened."

Deuter had happened. He had been determined to rape her and thought he could hold her still by nearly breaking her arms. If it hadn't been for the training her father had given her when she was a teenager he would have managed it.

"He just scared me a little." Her lips trembled. He had terrified her. "That's all."

Kell had suffered an attack on one woman who had been important to him already. A wife who had died—as well as their unborn child. If she told him what Deuter had done, he would kill the other man. His voice had been tortured, guttural with pain, when he described what he had done to Tansy's killers that night.

"Are you going to make me ask him what happened, Emily?" he asked her softly. "I should warn you, I'm trained to get the answers I want. I know Deuter, it won't take long to break him."

Emily shuddered. No, breaking him would be easy, but Kell would make certain that killing him took a while. And it would be painful. Very painful.

"For God's sake, Kell," she snapped. "Let it go. Don't you think I would have told you if I wanted you to know?"

"No, I don't," he snarled. "Because you know I'd probably kill the little son of a bitch."

"And he's not worth it," she stated fiercely. "Now stop manhandling me before I get really pissed off. It's sexy as hell when you use it for sex, but using it to make me give you answers that should be my choice to give you, it's just wrong."

He frowned at her statement, loosening his grip. "Is that what you think I'm doing?"

"What else could it be? You don't control me so stop trying to convince me that you do."

"I don't want to control you." His lips quirked. "Though I'm beginning to see the merits in it where you're concerned. And don't think for one minute that I won't find out what you're hiding."

"Fine, why don't I just go poking into your past?"

"It's like sex, Emily. If you want to know, just ask. Anything from the day I met you, till now, I don't care to answer. Just as anything that happened from the day I met you is definitely my business."

"Which means most of my life." She pouted as he released her hands, watching as she began to rub her arms.

She stilled the movement. He hadn't touched her arms. And he was too damned smart when it came to picking up clues to stuff.

"Is he the reason you're always rubbing at your arms as though you're trying to wipe away something dirty?"

Damn, damn, damn. She glared back at him. "I get cold easily, and sometimes you make me nervous."

His lips thinned. "Don't lie to me, Emily. I don't like it."

He would dislike the truth even more.

Emily sighed. "I dropped my wine. And aren't we here for a reason?"

"A reason that I'm beginning to believe is fucking stupid," he snapped. "No one can make a move in this crowd, and definitely no one intent on a kidnapping."

"We could find a tree to prop up," she suggested, fighting the nerves building within her.

"You're making me crazy." He sighed then, lowering his forehead to hers as his hands slid over her hips, his fingers gripping them firmly, holding her against him.

"No, that's the people here," she whispered, trying to inject just a little humor into the situation. "All those pesky women wanting a piece of you. I've heard it makes a man a little tense."

"One of these days, I really am going to paddle your ass for being so stubborn," he whispered.

Her rear clenched at the thought of the pleasure that could bring.

"So you keep saying," she whispered back, a real smile tugging at her lips. "I think you're too scared I'll like it."

"I know you'll like it." His lips lowered to her neck. "A lot."

Emily inhaled roughly as his lips slid over her neck, his tongue licking, stroking.

"Kell." She was breathing heavily now. "Umm, maybe we should mingle some more."

If one was going to protest, then she really shouldn't tilt her neck to the side to give him greater access to sensitive flesh. But that was what she did, her lashes fluttering as she struggled to keep them open against the pleasure suddenly rising inside her.

She loved it when he touched her, reveled in it, craved it. It was the culmination of every dream, every fantasy, she had ever known.

"Maybe," he growled into her neck a second before sharp teeth nipped with erotic heat. "In a minute."

He licked the little sting as she flowed against him, her body softening, moving against him, feeling the desire rising hot and fast inside her.

Between her thighs, she could feel her flesh heating, preparing her for him. Just that fast and easy. And now, if the world would just work with her a little here, and give her just a few minutes to enjoy this.

But it seemed the world working against her had other ideas.

Kell stiffened, his head rising dangerously as he turned protectively, glaring as the brush rustled and a feminine figure slipped inside their hiding place.

"Problems," Kira whispered, grimacing as she glanced at Emily. "Reno and the guys outside just busted the cutest little South American assassin. All scars and nasty threats.

He says Mr. White isn't here. I think Judas might have duped us."

Emily tensed, pressing her head against Kell's back as Kira gave the report.

"Let's get the hell out of here," Kell snarled, wrapping his arm around Emily's back and pulling her closer to his side. "Where's Ian?"

"On the other side." She jerked her head toward the brush. "He wasn't about to interrupt you."

Kell reached into his pocket, pulling free the small radio and ear clip. Putting it in place, he turned it on.

"Macey, are you there? We're heading out, bring the limo around."

Disconnecting the ear clip, he pocketed the radio once again and headed back into the garden before turning and advancing toward the house. Kira walked ahead of them, with Ian pulling in behind Kell.

They made an odd group. Emily dressed in her bronze silk gown, the flared skirt rustling over the petticoat she wore beneath it. Kira in snug black satin, and Kell and Ian in their dress suits. And she realized she was focusing on clothes when her stomach was knotting with tension.

Her gown was slit from her feet to her knees in the front, with the gathered skirt showing the darker petticoat and slip beneath.

Strapless, snug from her breasts to her thighs, it was more revealing than the gown she had worn to the previous party. Still, her gown was one of the least revealing, except for the matrons who still covered themselves from wrists to ankles. Not that there were many of those left.

"Let's move," Kell urged her.

"I can only go so fast in heels," she informed him, her voice shaking.

"Then take the damned things off." He pulled her to a stop, knelt, and pulled the shoes from her feet before stuffing them in his jacket pocket and rushing her to the open

French doors. "We go straight to the limo, no stopping in between."

"Fine." She was in no hurry to stay.

They entered the ballroom, cutting a direct path through the center of the dance floor to the open doors on the other side.

He kept her moving through the crowd, ignoring the few guests who tried to stop them and chat. With Kira ahead of them and Ian behind them, it was easy to keep the quick pace without appearing to be in a rush.

"Kell." A voice stopped them just inside the foyer. "Drage said you were here."

Emily stopped, causing Kell to curse behind her. She turned and stared into the gentle, pale blue eyes of the man watching them, his arm thrown around his wife's shoulders.

"Jansen, we were just leaving," Kell announced as Emily stared back at her father's boyhood friend.

His face was so kind. Crow's-feet wrinkled the corners of his eyes and his lips held a fatherly smile.

"I understand." He nodded. "I was just taking Elaine to the powder room to freshen up; she wasn't feeling well." Jansen Clay glanced at Elaine's bent head. "We just received some distressing news about Risa."

Emily felt her mouth go dry. Elaine was pale, her eyes damp with tears.

"Is Risa okay?" she asked, fearing the worse.

"She's alive." Jansen's expression tightened as Emily blinked back at him. His expression seemed to flash with something, fear perhaps.

"She's taken a setback?" Emily reached out to Elaine, her hand touching her shoulder. Elaine was Risa's stepmother, but she had practically raised her after Risa's mother's death.

Elaine broke off a sob as she pushed from Jansen and wrapped her arms around Emily's shoulders. "It's been so hard," she sobbed. "Oh God. I have to find the powder room. Emily, please go with me."

Emily glanced back at Kell, seeing the tight grimace that pulled at his expression.

"Kira, could you help me?" Emily wrapped one arm around Elaine's waist as they headed for the ladies' room.

"I'll find Markwell and let him know we'll be leaving soon, sweetheart." Jansen kissed his wife's head as he glanced at Emily again.

For a moment, his eyes seemed cold, hard.

Emily shook the vision away. Jansen was anything but cold and hard. He had always been filled with laughter, always chiding her father for the bodyguards and his protectiveness.

"Hurry," Kell urged, following behind her. "I'll be waiting outside the ladies' room. Kira, go in with them."

Emily led Elaine through the foyer as the older woman sniffed and wiped at her eyes.

"Risa is such a sweet little girl," Elaine whispered. "It nearly destroyed Jansen to put her in that institution."

Daddy, help me! Risa's frightened pleas echoed through Emily's head as she and Kira helped the other woman into the ladies' room.

They were Risa's screams, not her own. Filled with horror and pain, and realization—

The ladies' room was empty. Silent.

Daddy, why . . .

Emily stumbled as the memory of Risa's frightened cries seemed to wrap around her.

Why, Daddy?

A sudden groan jerked her from the memory.

Emily's head snapped up just in time to hear the soft pop of a silenced pistol and to watch Kira slide to the floor.

"Kira," she cried out, rushing toward the fallen woman, watching in horror as blood bloomed across her chest.

"Stay the hell where you are, you little bitch," Elaine snapped, pressing the gun to Emily's head, her expression creased with malevolent anger as Emily stared back at her.

"It's really too bad." Elaine was no longer crying. She

was staring back at Emily with cold hatred as she backed away slowly, keeping the gun leveled on her.

"You'll never get past Kell," she told the other woman. "He'll stop you."

"That gutter rat." she said, sneering. "He'll never know what happened. Neither will anyone else. These old houses are full of hidden passageways." One such passageway opened up to reveal Jansen.

Emily opened her mouth to scream when he rushed forward, only to have the sound cut off by the nasty-smelling handkerchief he pressed over her mouth and nose.

"There you go, pretty girl," he crooned. It was the voice from her nightmares. "Just go to sleep."

Darkness washed over her as screams and memories echoed in her head.

Jansen Clay. It had been Jansen all along and she had remembered too late.

Twenty-six

Kell paced the hallway, checking his watch, as Ian watched the door with eagle eyes. It wasn't like they could hear anything if there were any problems in the bathroom. The music and chatter from the party was so damned loud in the hallway that guns could have been blasting and it would have blended in.

"A ladies' room is a vortex into another fucking dimension," Ian growled. "They disappear in there and it takes them damned hours to come back out."

Kell stared back at him in surprise. Ian wasn't a big talker. His rough voice, nearly ruined from an assailant's garrote years before, always seemed to make him uncomfortable.

Kell checked his watch again.

Ten minutes. It was ten minutes too long.

"I should have never let her step in there," he told Ian fiercely. "She knows we need to get the hell out of here."

He stalked to the door as Jansen came in from the foyer and stared at him with a frown.

"They've been in there too long," Kell explained as he went to push the door open.

Jansen shook his head as a somber smile tugged at his lips.

"You don't know women," he said, chuckling. "I've seen Elaine disappear into the ladies' room for more than half an hour simply to repair her makeup. Give her a few minutes, Kell. The news about Risa has really shaken her up."

Kell stepped back, his jaw tensing as he glared at the door.

"She's different, isn't she?" Jansen said then, resting against the wall beside him.

Kell snapped his gaze back to the older man.

"Emily," Jansen explained. "She's different for you. I told Richard years ago he would have to watch her closely. I could tell you had a thing for her."

Kell stared back at him with a frown. "Meaning?"

"Well, son, no offense, but without your family's backing, you're not exactly in her social sphere," he said kindly. But something in his gaze reflected back, hard, dangerous.

"Kell!" Ian's voice snapped his head around. "Look at your feet."

Kell glanced down and felt cold murderous rage shake his soul. Blood was inching past the bottom of the door.

Pushing away from Clay, he gripped the doorknob, tugged at it, then threw his shoulder into the door. It cracked open to reveal Kira reaching out, her eyes dazed as blood spilled from her chest.

"Ambulance," he yelled out as Ian hurried to Kira's side, trying to stop the blood from oozing from the wound. Kell jerked the radio from his inner pocket and rushed to Elaine's fallen form.

"Elaine!" Jansen's fear-filled voice echoed through the room.

"Macey. Ambulance. Reno, converge. Emily's missing and Kira's down."

His gaze went around the small room desperately. There had to be a hidden entrance into it. So much for the fucking reports that there were no secret tunnels through this old house.

Jansen was barking orders to a servant as Ian worked to save Kira, and Markwell was shouting orders from the doorway to his security personnel.

"Markwell, where's the hidden door?" Kell turned, fury

burning in his chest as the other man stepped to the doorway. "Where's the hidden fucking door?"

"In the back closet," the other man snapped.

"Goddammit, why don't you bastards tell me about your fucking bolt-holes," he snarled, jerking the door open and rushing into the closet to check the wall.

There it was. The mahogany paneling was just a bit out of joint. As he pulled on it, the door slid into the wall, revealing a small tunnel.

"Where's the exit?" he snapped, pulling the radio free once again to report the coordinates to Reno and the men outside.

"The drain about half a mile down the road. The tunnel opens inside the culvert and leads to the wash," Markwell explained quickly. "But the gates leading to it were welded shut years ago."

Kell radioed the information to Reno. "I'm heading through the drain now, meet me at the exit. Whoever took her has a hell of a head start on us."

"Ian?" Kell glanced around the door as he quickly slid the ear clip over his ear and tucked the radio into his sleeve.

"She's alive. I'll keep her that way," Ian snapped. "Find Emily."

"You'll need light." Markwell pushed a flashlight into his hand. "Let's go."

Kell glanced at Markwell's hand. "I don't need you here."

"Fuck you!" The other man's lip lifted in a snarling sneer. "This is my home they decided to take her from and by God I'll help take them down. Now you're wasting time."

They slid into the tunnel, the flashlight picking out the tracks in the soft sandy floor dirt as well as Emily's thigh holster and pistol. There were two sets of footprints, both male, one boots, the other soft soled.

"Two assailants." He lifted his wrist to snap into the radio. "Emily's not walking."

Kell could feel the fear in his gut now. She had to be unconscious, he assured himself. If they had killed her they would have left her body with Kira's and Elaine's; they wouldn't bother to kidnap her.

"We're heading for the drain," Reno barked into the receiver. "How much head of a start?"

"More than ten minutes and we're half a mile from the exit."

"We're pushing it," Reno stated coldly. "We'll meet you there."

"Let's go." Kell glanced over his shoulder at the anger in Markwell's expression. For all his social pomp and arrogance, the man was known for his quick thinking and honesty.

"Was anyone in the ladies' room when you entered?" Markwell barked as they raced through the tunnel.

"Kira indicated no before she closed the door," Kell stated, remembering Kira's nod that all was clear before she closed the door.

"How did you know there was trouble?"

"Kira's fucking blood running from beneath the door," Kell snapped.

Kira would be lucky to pull out of this. The shot was too damned close to her heart. Someone had aimed to kill, not wound.

"No one knew about this tunnel," Markwell informed him as they rounded another bend. "I hadn't even told Catherine about it when I found it. I just had the gates welded closed and forgot about it."

"Shut up, I can't hear anything."

It was an excuse. He could hear too damned well, and the problem was, there was nothing to hear. Not a whimper or conversation or the sound of orders. In this tunnel sound would travel far.

"Is there another exit?"

"Nothing," Markwell answered quickly.

The women had been in the ladies' room for close to fifteen minutes. The kidnappers would have a vehicle waiting. Goddammit, he wasn't going to get to her time. Once again, he wasn't going to be able to save the woman he loved.

He would kill Fuentes himself, Kell swore. If Emily sustained so much as a damned bruise then he would go hunting when all this was over. When it was over and he had Emily in his arms, in his bed. When she was safe.

He couldn't consider anything less. God help him, if he lost her, he would never survive it. He couldn't live with the knowledge that he had let her down, that he hadn't protected her well enough.

Visions of Tansy raced through his head then. Her fragile body twisted on the old mattress where he had tried to hide her.

Had she screamed his name? He knew she had. Sometimes he heard her voice in his nightmares, screaming for him, begging him to save her. He couldn't add Emily's voice to those demonic dreams.

He couldn't let it happen. She was his life. She was every dream he hadn't dared to allow himself and couldn't keep from reaching for.

Glancing at the sandy dirt of the tunnel, his brows drew into a frown. Sand. When he had stared down at Kira's body he had seen sand on Jansen Clay's shoes. Not a lot, so little that his gaze had at first passed over it. But it had been there. And beside Kira's body and beside Elaine's he had seen the same sand.

Jansen Clay would have known of every move Kell and his team were making. Even if Richard and the admiral hadn't informed him about the exact nature of what was going on, he would have been smart enough to figure it out. An ex-Navy SEAL, and one of the best, Jansen could have accessed via his position at the Pentagon on Homeland Defense whatever he hadn't figured out himself.

"Macey." He lifted his wrist to his mouth and activated the radio.

"Copy," Macey snapped into the receiver.

"Where's Clay?"

"His limo just left. Mrs. Clay finally came around and he was taking her to their private doctor."

"Where are you?"

There was a heavy silence.

"Macey?"

"I'm at the wash, Kell. There are no vehicles, no bodies, but evidence that both were here. They're gone."

Kell snarled. "It's Clay."

"Are you fucking crazy?" Markwell muttered behind him.

"Got your laptop?" Kell asked Macey.

"It's in the limo, heading back there now. Do we turn on the tracker?"

"Negative," Ian snapped on the line. "Do not activate the skin-tag. Not yet."

"Kell?" Macey questioned him.

"Tap into radar," Kell ordered him. "Hack Defense. I want to know if anything lifts off from a private airfield anywhere in the vicinity."

"Got it."

The scent of fresh air grew stronger as Kell practically ran through the tunnel. He came into the wash minutes later through the thick stand of brush covering it as Reno and the rest of the team materialized from the surrounding woods, followed by the Secret Service agents assigned to back them.

"How did you overlook the wash?" Kell snarled to the agent in charge. "It was your job to contain the perimeter."

"No excuse, sir," the agent growled. "We missed it."

"He was meant to miss it," Markwell argued. "Hell, Kell, it's well hidden."

"No excuse, sir," the agent repeated.

"Macey's on the laptop. Jansen Clay is our Mr. White," Kell snapped.

Stunned silence met his words as Reno's head snapped around and his gaze pinned on Kell.

"You're certain?"

"There's a sandy soil in the tunnel. These grounds are

heavily vegetated. Clay had that sand on his shoes, I saw it myself when he was standing over Kira. Is there a report on her?"

"Ambulance is loading her now," Reno reported. "She's alive but in bad shape."

"Conscious?"

"Negative," Reno stated as they rushed up the incline to the limo.

"Ian," Kell snapped into the radio. "Get her loaded then steal one of Markwell's vehicles and follow behind."

"Got it!"

"At least I have insurance." Markwell sighed.

"Kell, Jansen's daughter was raped during that kidnapping," Reno snarled. "You have to be wrong about this."

"I'm not wrong about this."

Kell was aware of the implication. Jansen Clay had caused the death of the daughter of one of his friends, Carrie Bridgeport. But Risa was his own daughter.

"The bastard's dead," Reno snarled. "Fucking dead."

"Kell, I have a lock on radar," Macey called from inside the limo. "There are three private airfields close by; one was shut down last year when the owners left the property."

"That's the one we want, load up."

The limo wasn't the quickest way to get to where they needed to go, but it was their only choice. The six men loaded in, their expressions savagely intent, weapons held ready.

"Where's the bastard Reno caught with the gun?" Kell asked as the limo burned rubber pulling out.

"Gator bait," Reno answered. "He's trussed up about four feet off the ground and waiting on the admiral to collect him. Shouldn't we call the admiral?"

"Called," Macey informed them. "I called his secured cell as I was pulling in. He's arranging things on his end in case we don't catch them before they lift off."

"Not an option," Kell bit out. "They do not lift off."

He was aware of the looks he was receiving from the other men. Jansen had delayed him too long outside the bathroom; the kidnappers had a head start on them, as did Clay. The airfield was in the opposite direction of the wash and they were playing catch-up in a vehicle not meant to catch up.

"We have a Gulfstream lifting off," Macey reported, his voice heavy with regret and resignation as the limo slid onto the side road just in time to see the private jet lifting into the air.

"It's changing call signs. Son of a bitch, Homeland Security has just designated it as a passenger liner."

"Tag it," Kell snapped.

The limo slammed to a stop.

"Get us back to the senator's house," Kell commanded. "Macey, keep that plane in sight, do you understand me?"

"Understanding, Kell," he answered shortly.

Jerking his cell phone from the clip on his slacks, Kell keyed in the senator's number quickly.

"Meet at the house. Do you still have your supplies?" Guns, ammo, everything a SEAL would need to defend himself.

"That and more," the senator snapped, his voice husky. "We're hauling everything out now and waiting for you."

"Clear our way, we're heading back at top speed and I don't have time to deal with the cops in this state."

"Taken care of," the senator snapped. "I have your six, just get said six here pronto. Out."

"Put it to the floor, Macey," Kell demanded, forcing himself to relax back against his seat. "The senator's arming us, expect the admiral to have air gear in place by the time we arrive. Macey, keep him updated on the Gulfstream's tags. I want to know where and when that bastard lands the second he puts down."

"Tagging in progress, chief, but he has help. Homeland Security is changing his call signs like they're free. Let's hope this program works."

"Hope?" Kell growled.

"It'll work. It'll work," Macey promised desperately. "Hell yes, or I'll shoot it."

Kell dragged his fingers through his hair and blew out an unsteady breath as his gaze met Reno's.

"We'll find her, Kell." Reno stared back at him with savage determination. "We'll get to her in time."

They had to find her. For the first time in fifteen years, Kell began to pray.

Twenty-seven

EMILY KNEW EXACTLY WHAT HAD happened when she awoke. The knowledge was just there, certain, painful. Her eyes fluttered open and she took a deep, fortifying breath. She had obviously been out for quite a long time because she wasn't in a car or a plane, she was lying on a cot in a dark room that smelled of wet soil and desperation.

It was too similar to the first kidnapping, but this time Jansen wasn't standing over her, his smile compassionate, his eyes hard. She remembered it now, clearly. How he had entered that shack just after she had been shoved inside it with the other girls. He had shaken his head at her and told her that her father should have chosen his friends more wisely.

And his daughter, his own daughter, Risa had stared back at him, dazed, in shock, because he had allowed one of those bastards to touch her. To rape her.

Tears filled her eyes now at the memory. How Risa had screamed for his help, begged him to make her rapist stop hurting her.

Please, Daddy. Please, she had screamed. But Jansen hadn't made them stop. He had been silent, aloof, allowing the men to rape both Risa and Carrie, while ordering them away from Emily. Declaring that he would take care of her personally.

He had betrayed his own child.

He had helped Fuentes's men hold them down after that while another shoved the syringe in each girl's arm.

She whimpered at the memory. Why hadn't she remembered it? How could she have so completely forgotten the monster he was? How could she have ever forgotten the monster who had allowed other men to rape his own child while saving Emily's virginity for himself.

By time I finish with you, you'll belong to me. You'll beg for my cock. Beg for my touch. The perfect pet for myself and Elaine. She will so enjoy tasting every sweet inch of your body before I take you.

Emily nearly threw up at the memory. She could still see Risa's eyes, the burning rage in the pale blue depths, the murderous hatred and shocked horror.

No wonder Clay had been forced to have her institutionalized. Risa must have somehow remembered. Carrie had died, she hadn't been a threat, but Risa, Risa had never forgotten. The complete horrifying betrayal her father had dealt her had been too much for even that drug to erase.

Easing up from the cot she lay on, Emily whimpered as her stomach spasmed and nausea thickened in her throat.

"Don't move too fast. That drug will pop in your head like a bullet if you do," a dark, male voice warned her.

It was too late. Her head jerked to the side as blinding pain shot across her skull. And she should have known better. She should have been prepared for the pain, because it wasn't the first time it had happened.

"Easy, girl." The voice was weary, strained. "I can't help you. Just ease up. They left some water on the little table beside you. It will help."

Holding her head, Emily rose up again on the thin mattress, reaching shakily for the glass that sat beside a crude pitcher. The water was stale, but clean, and though it did nothing for the pain, it eased the horrible dryness in her mouth.

She had to think now, she reminded herself. She had to

find a way out of this. Kell couldn't save her this time. This time, Jansen would make certain he couldn't find her. Somehow, they had found the weapon she had strapped to her thigh, because it was gone. But the skin-tag was still on her back. She could feel it. It was her only hope.

"It's hard to believe Kell let you out of his sight long enough for you to be kidnapped." A heavy sigh followed the words. "Hell, I thought he'd have figured out who Mr. White was by now and come racing to *my* rescue."

She lifted her head, peering through the dim light to the man crouched in the corner of the room, his brilliant blue eyes blazing through the darkness with an almost demonic brightness.

She knew those eyes. She had attended his memorial service when the DNA results of a recovered body had come through weeks after her release from the hospital.

"Nathan?" she whispered. "Are you Kell's friend? Nathan Malone? Captain Malone's nephew?"

A crazed smile tilted his lips.

"Yeah. That's me." A soft lilt accompanied the mocking reflection. "What's left of me. And I assume you're Emily. It's been a while and the light isn't at its best in here."

Emily glanced around the room. There was a sliver of moonlight shining in from a barred hole above the bed and a whiff of a sea-laden breeze.

"Where are we?" It wasn't where she had been before. Then, she could smell the rotting vegetation of the jungle and hear the call of exotic birds. None of that was present now.

"Not sure." There was a shrug in his words. "Near the ocean. I'm guessing California from some of the slang I've heard from the guards, but I have no idea what part."

Emily massaged her forehead slowly, fighting the dizziness that threatened to overcome her and the sick heaving of her stomach.

"They've been checking on you every little bit," he informed her. "They're about due back. Jansen seems pretty concerned that you hadn't woken yet."

Jansen. Emily clenched her teeth against the sickness threatening to choke her. She had trusted him. Her father trusted him. His daughter had trusted him.

God, why hadn't she remembered? Except for the nightmares, she realized. Until Kell had come, she had suffered the nightmares each time she met with Jansen. And now she knew why.

"Bastard," she muttered.

A snort came from the corner. "Kell told me once that you don't cuss."

"Well, Kell was wrong," she muttered. "I just see no need to insert four-letter words into every other sentence I speak."

She inhaled slowly as the pain in her head began to subside marginally.

She remembered Jansen and Fuentes arguing that night, outside the shack. Jansen had wanted to have her moved immediately, to fly her to Switzerland where he could hide her. Then the other girls, Carrie and his daughter Risa, were to be given to Sorrell.

Oh God. Jansen had been making plans to have Carrie and his daughter turned over to that terrorist. Into a harem where they would never be seen or heard from again. To do it before Richard Stanton and Admiral Holloran could launch a rescue attempt.

Fuentes had been furious. They had argued over it, with Jansen accusing the drug lord of sucking up to a son.

"You think that little bastard is ever going to care what you do?" Jansen hissed. *"He's a SEAL, you stupid bastard!"*

"And you are little more than a terrorist's rutting lackey," Fuentes said. *"I told you, I have not yet decided if my cartel will deal with those vipers. Do not push me."*

"It's too late to back out, Diego."

"I did not make this deal with Sorrell, my friend," Diego snapped. *"Until I decide it is in my best interest, Sorrell can suck my dick. The girls stay. They will make me millions on the black market. The videos of their willing rapes will benefit the cartel. Giving them to a terrorist only benefits your pockets."*

"You're pretty." Nathan sighed then. "Prettier than the other girls they've brought here to torture me with."

"What?" Emily stared back at him in confusion, seeing the glazed madness in his too-lean features, the agonizing pain in his eyes.

"Is Kell coming for you, do you think?" There was a strange vein of wistfulness in his voice as he asked the question.

Emily breathed out roughly. "If he can find me."

"Clay tricked him. Clay tricks everyone, lass." Irish. That was the accent she heard. It was faint, just a soft flavor of a tone.

"Yes, Clay tricked us all." She leaned her head against the wall behind her, her breath hitching at the knowledge that Jansen could have very well won this time. The skin-tag on her back had limited range, Kell had warned her. How limited she wasn't certain.

"Don't discount him." Thin shoulders shrugged wearily. "He's a murderous son of a bitch, our Kell. He'll find you. He'll find me. He'll gut Jansen like he gutted those bastards that killed his wife."

"He'll rescue us. He'll leave Clay to justice. Father and Admiral Hollaran will make certain of it." She had to believe that. Her father and the admiral and Captain Malone would be with them, there wasn't a doubt in her mind.

"Don't fool yourself, lass," A flash of teeth in a mocking smile. "My uncle will hand him the knife. Jordan Malone is nothing if not bloodthirsty as hell. Trust me, Clay won't make it out of here alive."

And he was right. She knew he was right. Kell would cut a swath of death through this place.

"Why has Fuentes kept you like this?" she finally asked him. "The scientist was killed more than a month ago."

"And there, darlin', is the million-dollar question," he grunted. "Welcome to my hell. Meet Nathan 'Irish' Malone, current guinea pig to Diego bastard Fuentes and Jansen son of a bitch Clay. I'm their Whore's Dust experiment, darlin'.

See how much it takes before the SEAL breaks. Have I broken yet?"

Bitterness and rage were reflected in the hoarse voice as he pondered that question. His eyes glittered in the semidarkness, filled with icy, brutal resolve.

"I don't understand," she whispered.

"Join the club." His head tilted back, and as it did, Emily noticed he was naked. He sat on the dirt floor, his legs drawn to his chest, his arms wrapped around them to hide his nakedness.

Pulling at the thin blanket that had covered her when she awoke, she tossed it to him. His head snapped up, a partial snarl curling his lips before he realized what had touched him.

His hand reached out, pulling the narrow blanket over his legs as his fingers seemed to caress it.

"Won't get to keep it long," he said before staring back at her. "They'll be back soon."

There was an air of predatory awareness about him, a wildness contained that was frightening. Several of his words slurred, but she couldn't tell if it was the accent or something else causing it. She was terribly afraid there was something else causing it. Something like that drug, if what he said was true.

"Kell will be here," she whispered. She remembered whispering it before. When she had held Carrie against her, absorbing the other girl's shudders when they had been locked in the shack alone, awaiting Diego Fuentes's decision.

Kell will be here, Emily thought. *He'll save us. Hang on, Risa, just a little while. He'll save us, I swear it. He'll make sure Jansen can never hurt you again.*

She had broken her promise. Emily forced back her tears, her sobs. For nineteen months Risa had been gone. Had Jansen given her to Sorrell after all? Was the institution merely a cover story?

Kell would kill Jansen and for once Emily couldn't even feel regret for it. She wanted to kill him. If she could shove a knife in his heart and twist, it wouldn't cause her to lose a second of sleep. Monsters needed to be destroyed, and Jansen Clay was a monster.

"He'll come for you," Nathan told her softly. "Kell will cut a path of blood through this place that no one will soon forget. I hope they're ready for the beast they've just unleashed."

So did she. She prayed Kell found her. How much of a head start did Clay have on him? It couldn't be much.

"Was Ian on the team?" Nathan suddenly asked, blinking back at her, and for a moment, just a moment, sanity seemed to glitter in his eyes.

"Ian Richards?" She nodded. "He was there."

Nathan hummed as he nodded his head. Then he settled his forehead against his knees and seemed to be rocking himself.

"I see beauty, I see pleasure. I see the dragon's maiden," he whispered then. "Ah, lass, bring me sanity."

A dry chuckle filled the shack as Emily watched the man with compassion. Whatever Fuentes had done to him, it had driven him insane.

Emily laid her head back against the wall, staring at the strip of moonlight that gleamed through the bars on the opposite wall. She could see the stars, but she didn't know enough about them to tell where they were located.

She should have paid more attention in those science classes instead of goofing off, she thought with a small sigh as she rubbed at her bare arms.

"You look like my wife when you sit like that. Please don't do that again."

Her head snapped forward at the tormented sound of Nathan's voice, her eyes widening as she glimpsed the wildness in his eyes.

"I'm sorry," she whispered. "Are you okay?"

"I'll never be okay," he said then, distantly, his voice almost guttural as he watched her. "I see her sometimes in the women they bring to me. I hear her voice. I hear her crying. Is she crying, do you think?"

Emily swallowed tightly. "They drugged you."

A bitter laugh left his throat. "Constantly, girl. I'm a hard-on packin' fool. How long have I been here anyway? They don't tell me these things."

"Nineteen months." She curled closer to the wall. She could distantly remember the effects of those drugs, and they had been hell.

"Nineteen months," he said absently. "That's a long time, isn't it? Longer than I thought."

She watched as he tapped his heel against the dirt. A steady beat, almost unconscious, tapping and grinding his foot against the floor as though searching for something.

"When they come back, they'll bring the needles again." His voice hardened. "When they do, they'll tie you down, close to me. Don't try to talk to me. Don't cry. Play dead, you hear me? No matter what happens, you play dead. You got that, girl?"

Her breath hitched on a sob. Oh God, what were they doing to this man?

"Do you hear me?" Animalistic, grating, his voice demanded an answer.

Emily nodded frantically. "I understand. Play dead."

"I don't want to touch you. God. I don't want this anymore." His heel ground harder into the dirt. "Motherfuckers, they took the damned boots. Where the hell are my fucking boots?"

Emily wrapped her arms around her stomach, watching the anger building in Nathan as the minutes ticked by. She didn't try to speak to him, or to question the madness that seemed to grip him.

She began to pray instead.

Twenty-eight

ELL MANEUVERED THE BLACK HAWK with precise, gentle motions. They were moving fast, below radar, the powerful helicopter eating up the distance as they maneuvered over the mountains and headed toward San Diego. At his side sat Clint McIntyre, behind him Macey worked his wizardry on the laptop, using the satellite link the copter utilized.

So far, they had bypassed any undue notice. Beside Macey, Reno Chavez checked weapons while Senator Stanton's buddy retired Master Chief Strepton checked com links.

Admiral Holloran and Captain Malone and Senator Stanton talked in low voices, checking their weapons and equipment. Kell hated having them here. His attention would be distracted between keeping Emily's father and Nathan's uncle alive.

Kell just hoped like hell they could get through this without more lives lost. Except Clay's and Fuentes's. Those two he wanted for himself. He wanted to feel their blood washing over his hands, watch the life dim in their eyes.

"ETA twenty minutes," Clint reported as he checked navigation and repeated Kell's heading. "Go in as low as you can. The military keeps a close watch here and Clay could be utilizing the spotters."

The mission was so damned clandestine that only Admiral Holloran's office was aware of it. The knowledge that Jansen Clay had involved himself with Fuentes was a bitter pill to swallow, but it made sense. He had the connections to help Fuentes in his arms deals, as well as the drug business. But what was in it for Clay? The man had more money than he could spend in three lifetimes. What would make a man so depraved that he would betray his country, as well as his only child, with such evil?

Macey had detected where and how Clay had hidden his Gulfstream in the commercial air traffic, which suggested Clay had help somewhere in Homeland Security. The net was slowly materializing, but perhaps too late. The skin-tag Emily had worn had been activated after a message from Judas came through reporting Jansen had secured his hostage for the time being.

Three seconds. Macey had three seconds to pinpoint the location before they lost it forever. And he had done it. The son of a bitch was a fucking miracle worker.

Dawn was beginning to streak behind them, moving in closer as Kell flew the military helicopter at top speed, racing to land in their designated area before daylight appeared.

"The boys are in place," Macey said softly through the helicopter mic. "Weapons and vehicles are awaiting us."

The things that boy could do with a computer could make chills race up a man's spine. If he allowed it. Kell had firmly pushed back the man he wanted to be and allowed the killer free. Cajun. That was his call name. That was the man going to war. The Cajun gator. Cold. A killing machine. Today, Jansen Clay and Diego Fuentes were going to die. It was that simple.

"We'll hit the house just after daybreak if we stay on schedule," Macey reported. "SEAL team two has a lock on the security and is awaiting our arrival. They won't know what's hit them."

Macey's boys. SEAL team two was in San Diego on a training exercise. Blood was the perfect teacher.

Emily.

"Town house is still quiet," Macey reported. "Kira is out of danger but still in serious condition. We're covered, locked and loaded."

"I'll take the house," Ian announced from his position next to the doors. "Diego will have an escape plan. I'll move on that and Clay as well if he's following behind."

"Team two, we're moving into position, do you have us?" Kell spoke into the communications link Macey had established with the team as he neared their landing point.

"Team two ready and waiting," Commander Charles reported.

Kell maneuvered the Black Hawk between the ridges several miles from Jansen Clay's seaside mansion and set it down without a bump. He was throwing his safety harness and cutting the power as the doors slid open.

"Commander Charles." Kell affected a hasty salute as he jumped to the ground, taking the gear one of the other black-clad SEALs handed him. "Is your man on point?"

"In place." Commander Charles's dark head nodded. "The mansion is quiet with only a few guards on the perimeter and one dog. They aren't expecting you, Lieutenant. We've located the shed the hostages are being held in and we have one of our snipers in place. Clay and Fuentes are on location and currently heading for the holding cells on the property."

Clay. Kell could feel his blood boiling at the thought of the other man.

"We want the cell empty of unfriendlies before we go in," Commander Charles stated as Kell geared up alongside Reno, Clint, and the senator. Macey and Ian jumped into a jeep, where Macey continued to hammer away on his laptop.

"We'll move into position and await Clay's exit," Kell snapped. "But I want him, Commander. And I want him alive."

"And Fuentes?" Charles asked, his eyes narrowing.

"However you can get him, dead or alive." Unless Kell got to him first.

"Let's load up." Charles nodded. "We have a fifteen-minute

drive ahead of us and dawn is heading this way. Let's get this done."

They raced for the jeeps, loading in with the rest of team two before speeding along the narrow track that led to Clay's property.

No wonder they couldn't find Fuentes. He hadn't needed to buy his own property when Jansen was putting the drug lord up in his mansion. The three-story hacienda-style home sat on a cliff overlooking the ocean, surrounded by high ridges and accessible to normal traffic by only one road.

Normal traffic.

Fifteen minutes later the jeeps were parked a short distance from the cliffs on the sandy beach and SEALs were rappelling up the cliff face toward the mansion.

The mansion's walls only extended to the cliff rather than completely surrounding the mansion. Even a mountain goat would have had problems scaling the cliff's stone face. But SEALs were better than mountain goats. And the Cajun gator was in the lead, his knives ready, his mind clear, and ice for blood.

It was time for payback.

EMILY TRIED TO HUG THE wall, hell, she tried to become the wall as the sound of a key turning in the lock sent chills racing up her spine.

Nathan growled from the corner. The sound of a cornered wolf, terrifying for the subtle softness of it.

Emily scooted back on the cot, pressing herself into the corner as the door opened and Jansen and Diego Fuentes stepped into the room, followed by one of the guards.

A small bulb lit up in the ceiling then. It wasn't a lot of light, but it was enough to clearly see Jansen's handsome face. Even now, she didn't want to believe he could be so evil. His expression was sympathetic, his eyes showing true regret as he watched her. It made her want to kill. To strip away the deceitful veil he wore so easily.

"I see you've survived Diego's heavy-handed guards once again," he said as he tucked his hands in the pockets of his slacks and watched her closely. "Your cheek is going to bruise. Did you try to fight them when you woke on the plane?"

Emily lifted her hand to her cheek, only then realizing it was sore. She had fought them. Now she remembered waking up for a short time, just before they had loaded her onto the plane, and she had fought like a demented animal. If she wasn't mistaken, one of the guards was wearing her claw marks on his face. She didn't answer Jansen though, she merely glared back silently.

His lips quirked as he glanced around the rough cell.

"Your accommodations are better this time. I made certain of it." His gaze fell on Nathan in the corner. "We even made certain you had some company."

The sound that came from Nathan's throat was a frightening one. A low rumble, a promise of retribution. Jansen grimaced, turning back to Emily.

"I'm truly sorry about this, Emily," he said. "If only your father had cooperated a bit more. But it wouldn't have mattered, would it? I think you were already remembering. Your inquiries about Risa's health were always worded very carefully. Diego's drug isn't as powerful as he assumed it was." He threw the South American a gloating glance. "He's made several mistakes over the past two years, wouldn't you say?"

Nathan snarled in fury as Emily clenched her fists to keep from screaming in outrage and horror.

"What are you doing to him?" He was like an animal, his eyes burning in the dim light, his face waxen.

Jansen smiled as he turned back to her. "Did you hear of the great and abiding love Nathan Malone had for his wife?" he asked her. "Some said there was a bond between them that could not be broken. Let's say we're breaking it. He's been a puzzle, our Nathan has been. But before he died, the scientist who developed the Whore's Dust managed to perfect its design. Once Nathan is given the new drug, he won't even remember his wife. All he'll know is the need to fuck. And here you will be, unwilling perhaps, but definitely created to fuck."

"You can't do this." Her gaze flew to the chained SEAL in horror before shifting back to Jansen. "Kell will kill you for this, Jansen."

"He'll never know I was involved." He shrugged carelessly. "Do you think I did anything more than place the chloroform over your mouth and nose? There were others waiting inside the tunnel to spirit you away. Kell has no idea I was involved."

"He is quite good, is he not?" Diego said mockingly as he stared back at her. "We have been associates for years, but his contacts here have made him invaluable. Not indispensable." He shot Jansen a smarmy smile. "But invaluable."

Jansen's expression tightened in irritation.

"Kell will kill you both," she informed them softly. "Neither of you will make it out of here alive."

"He'll gut you." Nathan's raspy voice sounded like a primal hiss. "He'll take his knife and open you up like a fish. And he'll smile. He'll smile because it will be good. Oh, it will be so good. Blood flowing, warm and rich, the dragon feeds on the slayers' flesh."

Emily shivered at the death that sounded in the other man's voice. Nathan was truly insane. What still held him grounded she wasn't certain, but what she was certain of, was that this man, if not in life then in death, would ensure Jansen's and Fuentes's deaths.

"I do believe the drugs have affected his mind," Jansen said. "We've overused him, Fuentes."

Fuentes shrugged. "That sin lies at your feet, my friend. It does not affect me. I only demanded the chance to recoup my losses before you spirited the delectable little Miss Stanton away to your very good friend Sorrell. I am absolved of this."

Jansen grunted as he shook his head then turned his gaze back to Emily. "I'll make certain you're taken care of," he told her then. "As soon as Diego and I hammer out a few details you'll be flown to that little chateau in Switzerland I told you about before. Elaine is already heading there, sweetheart. She's getting ready for you. Eagerly anticipating your arrival. Once we've sampled your no doubt used charms, Sorrell will then collect you."

A sob tore at her chest as her hand covered her mouth, denial raging inside her. "Elaine knows?" Her voice was raw with pain.

Jansen smiled softly, compassionately. "It was Elaine's idea, darling."

He turned to Fuentes. "Have your men inject him. Let's get this over with so we can leave."

Fuentes chuckled. "You have a soft spot for this one, Jansen," he commented as he flicked an amused glance at Emily. "Perhaps before you leave with her, I would like a taste of her as well. Why should our mad SEAL have her alone?"

Jansen stilled. "That wasn't the deal. Get him drugged and get the fucking cameras up. Get it over with so we can leave."

Fuentes sighed with mocking regret. "Perhaps you are right. I hear Krieger has become quite besotted with her. Perhaps after a taste of her, I would not wish to release her, hmmm?"

"Don't make me kill you, Diego."

The sound of Diego's men's weapons snapping in preparation as Jansen moved forward Diego had Nathan's head jerking up again.

"Kill him, Diego." The fanatical glee in Nathan's voice was terrifying. "Do it. You'll gain points. Don't you want to gain points?"

Diego chuckled, much like an overindulgent parent.

"Ahh, if only I could give you your wish, my sad little friend. Unfortunately, he does still have his uses." He turned to his guards. "Prepare them. Let us get this done quickly. Do not drug the woman though."

"That wasn't the deal," Jansen snapped.

Diego shrugged once again. "Her willingness to be raped by you gains me nothing. Do not push your luck, my friend, I believe there are other matters you need my agreement on as well."

Emily felt the icy terror as it began to spread through her body. They were actually going through with this. Jansen was going to destroy them all without a twinge of regret.

"Kell will kill you, Jansen," she whispered hoarsely. "You know him. You know he will."

"He'll never find you, Emily." He smiled gently. "I truly covered my tracks this time, my dear. There's no way he even suspects where you are."

"He won't stop looking." Raw grief overwhelmed her, swamping her emotions, her soul. God, to lose him like this. To know that when he did find her, she would likely be so damaged that it wouldn't matter. As Nathan had proved, a mind could bear only so much horror.

"He may never stop looking, but his search will be in vain." His voice was gentle, his expression almost tender. God, he was so sick. There was something so twisted about him that he went beyond evil.

"Diego, you can inject our reluctant SEAL now. Let's see if your new dosage is actually accurate."

"No!" Emily jumped from the cot as Jansen turned to leave the room. "You can't do this, Jansen."

Rage was beating through her brain, whipping through her bloodstream, as her fist collided with his head. She hadn't meant to hit him. She had meant to plead. To beg.

"You little bitch."

Pain resounded through her head as his fist collided with it, throwing her back as she heard a roar from the corner of the room. Emily bounced against the wall before slumping to the floor.

"You will not do that again, Emily." Hard hands gripped her arms, lifting her from the floor and throwing her back to the cot as lights danced around her and an eerie buzzing filled her head. "The next time, I'll rape you myself."

Fury filled Jansen's voice as Emily fought to right herself, to force her eyes to focus on his enraged face.

"I'd rather die," she snarled, her voice rough, trembling from the dizzying sway of her senses. "I would kill myself first."

"Whore's Dust will change your mind," he snapped. "I saw the tapes of your detox, Emily. I saw how you screamed, how you begged to be fucked. They had to tie you down."

She tasted blood in her mouth and felt the numbness at the side of her face as she finally focused fully on him.

"And I'll scream Kell's name," she whispered raggedly, gloatingly. "Just as I did then. Imagine that one, Jansen. Jack off to it if you have to. You might force me to accept you, but it will always be Kell's name on my lips."

He snapped back from her, breathing roughly, his handsome face flushed with anger.

"Double that bastard's dose." He flicked his fingers toward Nathan. "I want him to hurt her. I want Kell Krieger to see his best friend tearing her up." He shot her a triumphant smile. "Scream Kell's name now, Emily, while his brother in arms fucks you silly."

He swept from the cell as the soldiers converged on Nathan, syringe in hand, and held him down. He wasn't screaming, he was growling, snarling. Enraged animalistic sounds tore from his throat as they jabbed the needle into his arm and sent the diabolical drug into his body.

Emily collapsed on the cot as the cell door slammed shut and the key turned in the lock again.

"Well. Thanks there, Emily," Nathan said. "I believe they may have indeed given me a double dose."

Emily opened her eyes to stare back at him. "How long do we have, do you think?"

She had seen the videos as well, and knew the horrible, enraged lust she had experienced. How much worse would it be for him?

"Hell if I know." He fell back against the wall behind him. One second he was crouched on the floor, the next he was pushing himself closer to the wall. "Sometimes a few hours, sometimes a few minutes. They've been playing with the dosage and the strength. Maybe this one will kill me."

If possible, his eyes were brighter, glowing, eerie in the dim light of the room as his hands scraped at the side of the wall.

"I'm sorry," she whispered tearfully. "I'm so sorry."

"Kell won't get here in time." He grimaced. "There's no way he will get here in time. Ah God. I can't do this."

He pressed his head into the wall behind him as he stared up at the ceiling.

"Have you seen my wife?" he asked desperately. "Did you meet her?"

"No." She could see him tensing, feel him fighting the drugs tearing through him.

"Ahh, she's a wee lit'l thing. Soft as down, her flesh is." The accent thickened. "Her smile like sunshine. Her eyes the prettiest shade of gray. Like a dove."

"She sounds beautiful." Emily's breath released on a sob as his back arched, the chords in his neck standing out in sharp relief as a horrible groan left his chest.

"My beautiful lit'l lass. Will she remember I loved her?"

His head lifted, his arms dropping to his sides, and a second later a crude knife appeared in his hands. It was no more than a thin strip of metal, but the wicked edge that gleamed beneath the light had Emily swallowing tightly.

"Nathan?" Emily sat up straighter in the cot.

"I'd rather die than betray her," he whispered hoarsely, handling the knife confidently, running it over his fingers. "I've had this for a while now, contemplating, planning. You know, she'd rather I fuck than die. If it were her, I'd never hold it against her, would I, now? I'd love her until death took my last breath."

"Hold on, Nathan," Emily sobbed. "Please. Please hold on."

Emily stared back at him dry-eyed, her gaze caught by that knife. She knew what he was going to do. He was going to honor his vows to the woman he loved the only way he knew how. He would end up killing either himself or her.

"I love my wee lass," he whispered, his gaze caught by the knife. "Do ya know suicide is a sin, Emily?"

"Yes." Tears slid down her cheeks. "She wouldn't want you to commit a sin, Nathan."

"So is fornication," he whispered, turning that mad gaze back on her. "Betraying the vows I made to her. Rape is a sin. It's takin' what belongs to another. Which is the lesser sin? Takin' my own life or yours? Or committin' adultery and rape, lass? Where is the greatest pain?"

Rage, pain, and madness were reflected in his eyes. He had survived this long because he hadn't broken those vows to his wife. Nineteen months he had been in this hell, and he hadn't broken.

"Nathan, just a little longer," she whispered. "Kell will be here. He'll take us both out of here and it won't hurt anymore."

"Everything hurts," he said roughly, dragging the blanket closer to his nude body.

"Will she know I loved her?" he asked as he huddled against the wall.

Emily felt her lips tremble. "She knows."

He paused, his eyes closing briefly before focusing on her once more. "I'm sorry," he said then. "It's the drug. It's hard to find her when the drug is like this. I search and search for her. I can hear her. But I can't find her."

For a moment wry humor entered his eyes before the madness took his gaze once again.

A scream echoed through the cell then. Emily's head swung toward the door, hearing the rat-a-tat of gunfire and voices suddenly raised in alarm. Her eyes flew back to Nathan.

"Kell." She moved carefully to the side of the cot. "Kell's here, Nathan. Do you hear that?"

He held the knife easily, tracking her every move.

"Listen, Nathan." The gunfire was closer. "He's here. You can't give up." Tears fell from her eyes then, fear and pain, rage and joy surging inside her all at once as Nathan stepped closer.

In his eyes she saw his death. The drug had stolen what little sanity Nathan Malone possessed and all that was left was the animal the SEALs had created. The drug could rule the body, but the man had been trained, honed, and molded into a creature of death. And rather than betray all he loved, he would die.

The man was stripped away now, and all that was left was the creature.

"Oh God, Nathan, please. He's here. Kell is here," she whispered beseechingly. "Don't let them take this from you. God, please, don't let them steal your rescue."

She had to make him see reason, had to make him listen. What had he said earlier? A certain position reminded him of his wife.

She laid her head back against the wall, revealing only her profile to him, fighting to breathe, certain this was her last chance. If he didn't see reason now, then she was going to be a bloody mess when Kell arrived.

"Kell is here," she said again, softer this time. She had no idea what his wife sounded like, but she was giving it her best shot. "He's come to rescue you, Nathan."

He blinked back in confusion.

"Don't you want to go home?"

His hand shook.

"I want to go home, Nathan. I just want to go home." She wanted to lie in Kell's arms, she wanted to hear him whisper to her again. "Let's go home, Nathan."

"Home is gone." His hand gripped the knife tighter. "Home is gone. Goodbye."

"STOP THAT FUCKING COPTER. STOP it now, goddammit." Kell sprayed a round of gunfire at the copter as it lifted off, wavering for a second before banking and heading out to sea and taking Fuentes with it.

He was escaping again.

"Son of a bitch." Throwing the assault weapon over his

shoulder, Kell sprinted the few feet to the cell where Emily was being held.

Kell jerked the Beretta from the holster on his hip, shot the lock free and burst into the room. Into hell.

"Fuck!"

Naked, aroused, a homemade knife held in his hand, Nathan jerked Emily from the cot and pushed her behind him.

Irish blue eyes stared back at him in madness as Emily's dark eyes, wide with terror, watched him hopefully.

"He's drugged," she gasped. "The Whore's Dust. A lot of it."

"Shut up," Nathan yelled, the knife wavering in his hand. "Stay away from her. Let her alone."

Not his fault. She mouthed the words silently; tears tracking down her cheeks as Nathan dragged her closer to him.

That was his little fox. Always fighting for someone else.

"Nate." Kell kept his voice low despite the desperation clawing inside him. "Let's go, Nate. It's time to evac."

Nathan blinked back at him. "Evac?"

"The chopper is outside, Nate. Time to get the girl out of here and go home. Your wife is waiting for you, Nate. You gonna disappoint her?"

For a second, Kell swore he saw a hint of sanity in Nathan's eyes.

"They found the tracker," Nathan growled. "The heel won't work."

God! They would have cut that damned tracker out of the heel of his foot. Son of a bitch.

"We don't need it, Nate," he said softly. "Come on, man, let's go home."

"I won't let you hurt her," Nathan growled. "They left her here to hurt her. So you could hurt her. I could hurt her. Someone was going to hurt her."

"Not anymore, Nathan. We have Fuentes and Clay," he lied, his eyes locked on that knife. "Let's go home, man."

"Home?" The knife wavered as he seemed to stumble.

And then Emily moved. How she did it, how she knew

to do it, Kell had no idea. Before he could jump for her, her elbow slammed into Nathan's undefended belly as her other hand locked beneath his wrist and pushed at it just enough to give Kell the chance to jump for Nathan and pull her free.

Free. He shoved her behind him, staring at Nathan carefully as rage flickered in his eyes a second before he slumped back to the wall.

"And here I thought he would have the nerve to kill if he found the chance."

Kell swung around, pushing Emily behind him again to stare down the wrong end of the pistol Jansen Clay was holding on them.

"Son of a bitch!" Kell cursed. "I'm just about getting sick of having you in my fucking face, Jansen. There are two teams of SEALs out there. Do you really think you're going to get away this time?"

"Only the three of you know about me." Jansen shrugged. "I kill you and it's over with."

"Wrong." Kell took great satisfaction in watching Jansen's eyes narrow almost fearfully. "We knew who had her. We tracked your wife to that chateau in Switzerland. She's being picked up by American agents even as we speak."

He felt Emily behind him, her slender fingers gripping the Beretta he had tucked into the back of his pants. Fear slammed into his gut.

"It doesn't matter," Jansen stated quietly. "Without witnesses, it will be very hard to prove. You can watch your friend die, then die yourself as I take Emily."

The gun turned on Nathan as Jansen's finger tightened on the trigger, and the little fox that Kell would have sworn would never hurt a fly fired the weapon from his side.

Point-blank at the center of Jansen Clay's chest.

The gun dropped from Jansen's fingers, his hand covering the wound as he turned his surprised gaze back to Emily.

"I didn't hurt you," he whispered in shock. "I was going to save you . . ." He lifted his hand and stared at the blood staining it before his gaze returned to Emily. "I was coming for you—"

He collapsed to the floor as Captain Malone and Commander Charles rushed into the room.

"Em." Kell jerked around, prepared to snatch the gun from her nerveless fingers, prepared for the horror in her eyes. What he saw instead sent a surge of heat rushing through his veins. Her gaze was clear; only a glimmer of remorse touched the blue depths as she deftly turned her wrist, holding the gun, barrel pointing down, out to him.

"Monsters don't deserve to live," she said calmly. "I won't lose any sleep over killing him."

He took the gun carefully, tucked it in the band of his pants again then jerked her into his arms, holding her close, feeling his throat tighten with the emotion that suddenly filled it.

"God, I love you," he whispered.

Kissing her brow, Kell sighed deeply before releasing her just enough to turn and watch the men swarming into the room. The medics had come prepared for Nathan, but Kell wondered if anything could put the man together again.

He was slumped against the wall, naked, his eyes filled with madness as he glared at Jansen's dead body. His muscles twitched spasmodically, his once-strong body nearly emaciated.

"Nathan?" The captain moved slowly into the room, staring at his nephew as tears filled his light blue eyes. "Boy, you're slacking off. Did I give you permission to rest?" Malone's tone snapped with strength.

Nathan jerked, dragging the blanket closer as he tried to struggle to his feet.

"Do you walk out of here or do we carry you?" the captain barked.

"Make him stop." Emily flinched at the tone. "Please, Kell."

"No, Emily. If he doesn't walk out of here, he'll never have a chance of surviving." He held her close, watching as a glimmer of sanity returned to Nathan's eyes as he struggled to come to attention.

"Boy. I said do we carry you out?" the captain yelled.

"No, sir." Nathan shook his head. "No, sir."

"On your feet."

Nathan struggled to his feet, securing the blanket around his hips.

"Sir." He weaved. "On my feet."

"You will walk to that helicopter outside. You will submit yourself to the medic standing by. Are we clear, Lieutenant Malone?"

Nathan shuddered, shivered, but his head tilted before wobbling on his shoulders.

"Sir. Understood." His voice was weak as he moved. One foot in front of the other. A harsh frown creasing his brow.

The captain's eyes gleamed with dampness as his nephew neared him.

"Sir." Nathan paused beside him.

"Yes, Lieutenant." The captain firmed his shaking lips.

"Sir. I could use a crutch." His knees gave way, but the captain was there, his arms going around the taller man's bony body, holding him to him as he shook with silent sobs.

"I have you, son," he whispered. "I'll be your crutch."

Kell watched as they moved through the doorway, nephew and uncle.

His arms tightened around Emily as his gaze was drawn once again to Jansen's dead body.

"Those gun lessons came in handy," he murmured.

"Yeah, they did." Her voice was shaky now, but hell, he was shaky, Kell thought. "And I won't lose a moment's sleep over it."

He met her eyes and saw an understanding there he hadn't expected. One he wouldn't have asked for, because the warrior inside him wouldn't be denied. But she understood. For the first time, he thought, she understood why he and her father had gone off to war, why they had risked their lives and the happiness of those they left behind.

To give innocence a chance.

"You two ready to go home?" the senator asked from the doorway. "We're going to be doing a lot of explaining."

"Home sounds damned good." Emily sighed. "Real damned good."

"Have they picked up Elaine?" Kell asked the senator.

"They took her into custody a while ago." Richard grimaced. "We sent agents to the hospital Risa was admitted to and had her forcibly removed and taken to Bethesda. She was in bad shape."

Kell felt the shaky breath Emily drew in.

"Jansen let the guards rape her on the plane the first time we were kidnapped," she whispered, tears choking her voice. "She'll need help."

Richard nodded. "And she'll get it. Come on, children, let's load up. I'm just getting too damned old for this shit."

He wasn't the only one. Kell swung Emily into his arms, holding her close to his chest as she buried her face against him and let her tears fall free.

She had been strong. So damned strong. She hadn't even hesitated to take Clay out. The single shot had pierced the other man's heart and exploded from his back. At close range, cold as ice and madder than hell, his kitten had taken her vengeance despite his wishes to the contrary.

"Okay?" He cradled her in his arms as the helicopter lifted from Clay's seaside home.

She nodded. "Tired though. Very tired."

"Sleep, baby." He kissed her forehead. "Just sleep and I'll take care of everything else. I promise. I'll take care of it all."

Twenty-nine

SHE DIDN'T HAVE NIGHTMARES. IT was twelve hours before she collapsed into a bed only barely aware of Kell
moving onto the mattress beside her and pulling her into
his arms. There were no nightmares. She slept deep and
undisturbed until a kiss feathered across her lips.

Emily felt the blankets easing slowly from her body as
Kell kissed her with an aching hunger she had never known
from him. Gentle kisses, soft nips at her lips, the lick of his
tongue over the rounded curves as he pulled her closer to
him.

"Emily." He breathed her name into the kiss. "Wake up
for me, baby."

His hands moved over her body, sliding over her skin and
setting off flares of pleasure that overwhelmed her awaken-
ing mind.

She had to touch him. To lean into his kiss, to soak up the
heat and power that was so much a part of him. She needed
him. Here and now, before he had time to remember the
world outside and to walk away from her.

Struggling in his hold, she pushed him to his back, aware
he was lying against the pillow now only because he wanted
to. Whatever the reason, she rose over him, her eyes opening
in drowsy heat to stare into the brilliance of his.

So green. His sun-darkened expression was different. Stronger. More intent than she had ever seen before.

"No condom," she moaned. "I want to feel you. All of you."

"We'll make babies, Emily," he whispered back. "Beautiful little babies."

Emily froze, her hands splayed against his shoulders.

She could feel herself shaking then, a fine tremor beginning in her heart and spreading through her body.

"Babies mean forever," she whispered as he lifted her above him, parting her thighs until she straddled his hips.

"So does love," he said, guiding his hard cock to nudge against the damp folds between her thighs. "Love is forever, Emily. And I love you. Forever."

He eased inside her. The thick crest parted her vagina, fiery warmth began to invade her body.

His lips caught hers as his cock impaled her, easing in to the hilt as the breath caught in her throat and she swore her eyes crossed at the pleasure.

"You ran me to ground." He smiled against her lips as he turned her onto her back before his lips moved to her neck, her shoulder. "I'm yours, Emily. I've always been yours."

His lips moved to her breast, covering a nipple, sipping at it with greedy hunger as his hips began to move, sliding his cock through the slick portal he possessed, sending sensation and exquisite pleasure to build and consume.

Lifting to him, Emily's arms went around his shoulders, her lips to his neck, tasting him, feeling him.

Heat poured from his body, from hers. It was like this each time they touched, as though no part of her body had ever been cold. The fires of need carefully banked whenever he was away, always flared to life once she saw him again.

But the flares were building. Like fingers of wicked, white-hot pleasure they rushed through her, snapping and zapping over tender nerve endings, sensitizing her, building the pleasure until she was crying out for him, begging for more.

"Ah, chère," he groaned in her ear. "You move like silk against me."

Her legs tightened around his thrusting hips as he fucked her harder, deeper. The way she liked it, with desperate demand, without control.

His hips churned above her, thrust and impaled, driving his cock into the tightening muscles of her pussy as she fought to hold back, to milk every particle of sensation, every microsecond of hunger swirling around them.

"I love you, chère," he whispered at her ear, his voice gasping, thick, rough. "With a soul I didn't believe I possessed, I love you. Always, Emily."

"I love you." Her eyes opened as his head lifted from her breast and his eyes snared her. "I love you—Kell—love you."

She was screaming as sensation overtook her now. The orgasm ripped through her, tore through nerve endings, spasmed in her womb, and as she felt his sperm flooding her pussy, she went higher.

Past and future disintegrated. Her mind disintegrated. It melted beneath the heat and the power of release. Her release, his release. The completion of it seared her soul even as he whispered his love again. Vowed it, swore it. Kell collapsed over her, catching his weight on his elbows as his chest heaved with the need for oxygen and something inside his soul seemed to tear free. As though facing what he felt for her, facing her with it, had somehow torn free the shadows that had held him for so many years.

With his dick still semihard inside her, the first wave of hunger sated, he lifted his head from the pillow beside her and found his gaze snared by hers.

Sweet, soft sapphire. Her gaze was filled with emotion, with love. It was soft with gentleness, filled with satiation.

"Say it again," she whispered, her fingers trembling as they lifted to his lips, touching them, like heated silk.

"I love you." He spoke the words against the pads of her fingers, watching the tears well and overflow her eyes, the glistening moisture tracking down her flushed cheeks.

"You love me." Her lips trembled.

"I love you, Emily."

"No more condom fetish?"

"No more condom fetish, Emily." He nipped at the pads of her fingers. "Just the two of us."

He was fully erect once more, his sensitive cock surrounded by the milking heat of her pussy as he began to move again.

"Babies?" she whispered.

"When you're ready." His throat tightened with fear as he leaned his forehead against hers. "Be patient with me, sweetheart. A step at a time."

"A step at a time." Her breath caught as her eyes began to daze. "Oh God, Kell—" She lifted to him, her hips moving beneath him, churning, writhing, as her legs lifted to clasp his back once again.

She surrounded him, held him, warmed him.

"I love you," she cried out.

She loved him.

"I treasure you," he groaned into her neck. "With my life, my heart, my soul. I treasure you, Emily."

As their breathing slowly returned to normal long minutes later, Kell rolled to his back, dragging Emily with him and staring down at her where she rested on his chest.

"So what now?" she asked, her gaze drowsy and replete, despite the questions he could see there.

"What do you mean?" He was almost hesitant to ask.

"It's time to let the past go," she whispered then. "All of it, Kell."

He lifted his gaze from her, staring at the ceiling thoughtfully as he remembered his grandparents. The hope and pain in their eyes, the knowledge that they wouldn't be around much longer. And Emily was right, it was time to let the past go.

"Feel like a trip to Louisiana?" he asked as he stared back down at her, anticipation suddenly filling him, a sense of rightness invading him.

Her smile lit up his heart. "Louisiana sounds wonderful, Kell."

"I have to show Grand-père that I did indeed learn how to catch a fox." He smirked then as he tugged at her hair. "He won't believe me if you aren't with me."

"I'll always be with you," she promised.

And he believed because loving her meant believing. It meant trusting. And it meant life. It meant Kell Krieger was no longer alone.

Epilogue

IAN MOVED THROUGH THE SILENCE of the hospital. It was
close to three in the morning, security was at its weakest
now, and it was easy for him to slip into her room.

She was sleeping. He was grateful she wasn't awake.
Saying goodbye sucked. Hell, he had barely gotten to know
her.

He moved to the bed, brushing the strands of black hair
back from her pale face.

"I wanted to say goodbye," he whispered as he stared
down at her, his lips quirking at the faint frown that marred
her brow. Hell, did she ever really rest? He was certain she
didn't.

"I wanted to tell you that I could have—" He winced. "I
could have cared for you."

She couldn't hear him, and it was better that way. It made
it easier to say the words rather than to just feel them.

"I didn't want to leave without saying goodbye," he said
softly. "Without seeing you one more time."

A frown flitted across her brow, her fingers moved restlessly beneath his.

"Goodbye, Agent Kira Porter."

The Chameleon. She was one of Homeland Security's
best agents.

He leaned forward, his lips touching her brow in the faintest caress before he straightened and left the room. He moved quickly down the hall. He had wasted enough time, he had a meeting to keep.

As the elevator doors opened, he came face-to-face with Macey.

The other man was leaning against the back wall, his brown gaze brooding as Ian stepped into the elevator.

"You getting out?" He held the elevator doors open, praying Macey was there to check on Kira.

"Naw. I came to see you." Macey crossed his arms over his chest and stared back at him.

Shit. He let the doors close.

"I traced that last message," Macey said. "It took a while. Almost two years, but I finally found you. You're Judas."

Ian stared at the elevator doors.

"Tell me what the fuck is going on, Ian. We're buddies, man. Help me out here."

Ian shoved his hands into his pockets. "Let it go, Macey."

"I can't let it go. Judas is one of Fuentes's men. We know that. I just traced his fucking e-mails back to you. Tell me it was a mistake. Tell me something, goddammit."

"It wasn't a mistake."

Diego Fuentes's plane was waiting for him at the airport. A private plane sent to fly him to his *father*. Hell, it wasn't supposed to end like this. Fuentes wasn't supposed to ever learn he had a son. It was a promise Diego's father had made to Ian's mother when she left. That Diego would never know she was pregnant. For some unfathomable reason the old man had wanted to save her from Diego.

"Did you betray us too, Ian?" Macey asked then.

Ian grimaced. Hell no. He had never betrayed his country. He would never betray his friends.

"Lieutenant Richards, I asked you a fucking question," Macey snarled.

Ian turned and faced him slowly. "Fuentes."

"What?"

"Ian Richard Fuentes. He's my father."

Ian took advantage of the elevator doors opening and stepped free, his gaze locked on Maccy's face. On the betrayal in his friend's eyes, the fury building in his face.

He had just made an enemy. The first of many.

Read on for an excerpt
from the next book by Lora Leigh

Killer Secrets

Coming soon from St. Martin's Paperbacks

Killer Secrets

H E WAS THERE. She knew he was.

The moment Kira stepped out of the elevator she knew Ian was waiting in her room. Her nipples peaked against the thin leather covering them.

It wasn't any particular premonition. It was the bodyguard leaning casually against the wall several feet from her door.

Deke Santiago. Age thirty-six, married once, widower. He had been deep cover since his dishonorable discharge from the Rangers ten years before. Dishonorable because he had nearly killed his commanding officer for screwing his then-wife.

The court martial had earned him a year in Leavenworth because he couldn't prove the adultery. There, he had met up with one of Diego Fuentes' lieutenants; four years later he had flown into Columbia and begun his apparent life of crime.

There might be four people in the world who knew that he was no more than a deep cover operative. Kira was one of those people.

She paused as the elevator doors closed behind her, flicked a long swath of black hair over her shoulder, and sighed with an edge of irritation, aware of the security cameras trained on her.

She moved along the hall, ignoring him. That was what she did with bodyguards, she pretended to ignore them. Her own, Daniel Calloway, was proof of that.

"I won't need you to check the room tonight, Daniel," she informed him as they neared his connecting room. "You can go on to bed."

"Are you sure, Ms. Porter?" His voice was colored with suspicion as Deke's lips quirked mockingly.

"I'm positive. I'm certain the room is secure."

Daniel wasn't a stupid man. He entered his own room and closed the door behind him as Kira pulled her key card from the tailored lining on the inside of her boot.

"Is he upset over his poor little Rover?" She twirled the card in her fingers as she stared back at Deke, allowing a small grin to curl the edges of her lips.

Deke glanced at her door. "Ask him yourself and see."

As she turned back to the door, it swung open. A hard hand gripped her wrist and jerked her inside before the door slammed closed behind her.

She was pushed against it, her breath whooshing from her lips as her hands were gripped in one of his, held high above her head, and every inch of her body molded to the hard length of his.

Her juices pooled between the lips of her sex, then eased into the silk of the thongs she wore beneath the leather pants. Her nipples spiked impossibly harder, and she swore she could feel a bead of sweat tickling between her breasts.

No one had ever felt like Ian. Hard, in control, commanding. Every touch, every action gauged for pleasure. Or for pain.

The hand holding her wrists tightened as the fingers of the other threaded through her hair and pulled her head back to stare into the blazing heat of his tobacco-brown eyes. Eyes almost as rich as brandy, fired with dark little hints of red and filled with fury.

Dark blond hair fell over his forehead, the rich mix of colors, sun-lightened and thick, lying long along his nape and falling over his brow, made her long to bury her fingers in it again.

He turned her on in ways she had never been turned on before. She dreamed about sex with Ian. Lusted for it. Had lied to join this mission for it.

"What the fucking hell are you doing here?" he snarled down at her as his head lowered.

His lips buried in her shoulder, opening to allow his teeth to grip the flesh there, his tongue to lap over it with quick heated strokes as she jerked against him.

"Working." Her head lowered as well.

The strong column of his neck was there for her enjoyment. Her teeth raked it, her tongue licked, and the taste of male lust exploded against her taste buds.

God, he tasted good. She sucked at the flesh, a little moan escaping her throat as he picked her up, turned her, and in the next second, bore her to the bed.

"Ian." She gasped his name, feeling the hard length of his body covering hers, his thighs spreading her, his cock pressing hard and demandingly into the butter-soft leather covering her pussy.

Her hands were still stretched above her head, her breasts perilously close to spilling from the cups of the leather bustier she wore.

"You have no business here." His lips drew back from his teeth as his free hand tugged at the ties that secured the front of the bustier. "No business here. No business close to here."

The top loosened, spread apart, and with a flick of his fingers, the cups covering her breasts were released. Her breasts spilled free, nipples hard and pointed, flushed red and aching for his touch.

"You're here." It was a statement and a moan as his head lowered and his lips covered a tight, sensitive nipple.

He wasn't easy on her, and she didn't want easy. His teeth gripped and tugged, his tongue lashed with wicked wet heat. Her eyeballs were going to roll back in her head it was so damned good. He sucked on her like a starving man and her breast was the main course.

Long moments later his head lifted, thick dark blond lashes fanning his cheeks as he stared down at his handiwork.

Her nipple was tighter, if that was possible, gleaming wet and ruby red. The same color of his damned Range Rover.

"You wore too many clothes," he growled. His voice, rough on a good day, was grating now.

"I didn't want to appear too easy," she gasped as his lips moved to the opposite breast and began their less than tender ministrations.

God, this was what she had loved about the first and only time he had touched her. He didn't treat her like spun glass. He didn't touch her like she would break. He touched her like a woman well able to satisfy the dark, hungry sex drive she knew he possessed. Knew he possessed and craved to experience.

"Not easy enough." He nipped the side of her breast, his free hand moving to her hip, tugging at the laces on her pants now as his lips moved back to hers.